HANNAH ALEXANDER

THE HEALING TOUCH ✚ BOOK ONE

Second Opinion

BETHANYHOUSE

MINNEAPOLIS, MINNESOTA

Published by Bethany House Publishers
11400 Hampshire Avenue South
Bloomington, Minnesota 55438
www.bethanyhouse.com

Bethany House Publishers is a Division of
Baker Book House Company, Grand Rapids, Michigan.

Printed in the United States of America

Library of Congress Cataloging-in-Publication Data

Alexander, Hannah.
   Second opinion / by Hannah Alexander.
      p. cm. — (The healing touch ; bk. 1)
   ISBN 0-7642-2528-6 (pbk.)
   1. Emergency physicians—Fiction. 2. Medical personnel—Fiction. I. Title.
PS3551.L35558 S43 2001
813'.54—dc21

                                            2001005681

"I am the true vine, and my Father is the gardener.
He cuts off every branch in me that bears no fruit,
while every branch that does bear fruit he prunes
so that it will be even more fruitful."
JOHN 15:1–2

In memory of our beloved pastor

Ronald Moseley

October 31, 1941 — August 30, 1995
whose fruits continue to multiply on this earth.

"Brother Ron" was our tireless matchmaker, encourager,
and friend, who took time from his busy ministry to
befriend a lonely new man in town and to reassure a
hurting, frightened woman with a broken past that God
is never finished with us and He will hold all our
tomorrows—if we will let Him. As Ron would say,
"What an awesome God we serve!"

Books by
Hannah Alexander
FROM BETHANY HOUSE PUBLISHERS

Sacred Trust

Solemn Oath

Silent Pledge

THE HEALING TOUCH

Second Opinion

Necessary Measures

Urgent Care

Web site for Hannah Alexander:
www.hannahalexander.com

HANNAH ALEXANDER is the pen name for the writing collaboration of Cheryl and Melvin Hodde. They have six previous books to their credit and currently make their home in Missouri, where Melvin practices emergency medicine.

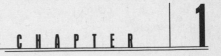

CHAPTER 1

Gina Drake awoke with a violence so frightening that she cried out. The voice she heard was that of a stranger, and she winced at the sudden onslaught of light from a window that looked ragged around the edges. Sudden tears blurred her vision. The sound of her pitiful gasps punctuated the roar in her ears, and she leaped to her feet in a panic. She was lost.

Past the unfocused edges of furniture, she saw a door and stumbled toward it . . . had to get out of this place . . . had to get to air. She was suffocating, couldn't get enough oxygen, couldn't fight her way past the attack of piercing light.

A garbled cry, soft and plaintive, reached her through the haze and the pounding of her heartbeat and checked her escape for just a moment. But she couldn't see past the tearing in her eyes. The cry didn't come again before the threatening roar returned to envelop her in terror. She grabbed the doorknob and forced her way outside. Had to find her children. Had to protect them! She tripped and nearly fell, and that strange, soft cry reached her once more, this time from behind. She turned and saw nothing except blurred shapes and gray splotches. She had to escape! There was danger here! She ran, and kept on running.

Evan Webster stared at his father across the dinner table, thinking about the pills. Shouldn't he be feeling better by now? He glanced at the large clock on the wall. Twenty minutes, and nothing had changed. Kent had told him the pills would give him more energy, make him feel more alive, be more coordinated. Ha! Coordinated. That *would* be an improvement.

A sudden hard thump of his heart startled him, and he caught his breath.

"Evan?" Dad said. "Are you okay?"

Evan nodded. Maybe the pills *were* working. He took a deep breath and once again felt the thumping pressure of his heartbeat pound through his system. He even felt the jolt of its force for a couple of seconds.

"How's the goulash?" Dad's voice came in sharp spurts of sound, lashing across the table like bullets.

Evan blinked. Weird. "Good, Dad." He straightened in his chair and forced himself to eat, trying hard to concentrate on what he was doing. Dad didn't need to know about the stuff that was going on right now.

"You're not eating much," Dad said.

Evan took a bite and chewed automatically. He usually loved Dad's special family recipe, and Dad knew it. He cooked it almost every visitation weekend. Tonight, though, it tasted like dirt. So did the homemade rolls and the butter, even the milk.

Norville Webster laid his fork at the side of his plate, picked up his napkin, and patted around his mouth in his precise way, then swallowed and cleared his throat. "So, how's life treating you these days, Evan? Is it good to be out of school for the summer?"

Evan shook his head. "Not really. I like school." He wouldn't admit that to a lot of people, but Dad expected it.

Evan missed his friends already, even though he'd only been out of classes for two days. He looked forward to seeing them tonight, though. He glanced at the clock. Ten minutes before he had to leave for the theater, and he hadn't broken the news yet. He reached for his milk glass, and his arm jerked involuntarily. He nearly knocked over the glass, and his hand continued to jerk. He placed it in his lap, hoping Dad wouldn't notice.

"Did you get a summer job down at the mill?"

"Unh-uh." Evan swallowed. "I told you, Dad, they won't hire me until I'm sixteen." Five months before he could get a driver's license. Five whole months. How was he going to last that long? Every one of his friends had a license.

"The school grades were okay, then? Your mother didn't send me a copy of them this semester." Dad was just staring at the table. His voice had that casual tone he used when he wanted to disguise his disapproval of his ex-wife.

An alien rush of anger caught Evan unaware. "Why didn't you complain to *her* about it?" he snapped. "You could have called her, you know. You don't have to use me as your messenger—" His voice skidded to a stop as Dad blinked at him in shocked surprise.

It surprised Evan, too. He seldom got mad at his father, and when he did, he never said anything about it. *What is happening to me?* Evan grimaced. He knew how his dad would react to that outburst.

"I'm sorry," Dad said. Some of the color drained from his face. "You're right."

"Oh no, hey, Dad, listen, I didn't mean—"

Dad held his hand up. "I know better, I just forget sometimes. I guess the grades were as good as always."

Evan slumped in his seat, feeling worse than ever. He knew Dad was bitter because Mom had won custody. And Mom would rather be with her stupid boyfriend than with her own son. Why did she fight so hard for custody when she didn't want it? She was the one who'd wanted the divorce in the first place, not Dad.

It was getting easier and easier to hate life.

"Evan?"

"Yeah?" Evan looked up again to find those serious eyes studying him a little too closely.

"Is everything okay? The grades *were* as good as always?"

"Oh, sorry. I meant to tell you—I'm on the honor roll again. And I got this award in English. My teacher says I should think about being a writer." His heart thumped loudly a couple more times, and he flexed his neck muscles to push away some of the tension that made him want to squirm in his chair. "They want me to help on the school paper next year."

Some of the lines of terminal sadness lifted from Dad's expression for a few seconds, and his pale lips raised in the closest thing to a smile Evan had seen tonight. "That's great. I'm proud of you."

Evan hunched his shoulders forward, then he straightened and leaned closer to the table. At least he was good for something. He stared at his skinny arms and hands. He'd never been good in sports, and everything at school seemed to revolve around football or basketball or something else that demanded coordination. The jocks didn't need anything between their ears to be popular; they just needed the right moves. Evan didn't have those.

"Evan? Are you okay?"

"Huh? Yeah, I'm fine."

"I said I'm proud of you. I always have been."

"Thanks, Dad." The good thing was, Dad meant what he said. He always meant what he said. Not like Mom, who'd promised to come to the debate last month, then canceled at the last minute because her boyfriend had come into town unexpectedly. Dad had been there, though. And he'd made it embarrassingly obvious to everyone in the audience who his son was and how proud he was of him. Dad had never been the kind of guy to hide his feelings about anything.

Evan figured that's why this divorce thing had been so hard on Dad—Dad blamed Mom for the breakup, and Evan could tell Dad had to work hard not to say bad things about her to him. Too much pain hovered in this house. Dad was like a black hole. He didn't know how to have fun, didn't know how to laugh, and he took everything way too seriously. Evan never told him anything important anymore. And Mom wasn't just impatient, she was spastic—always nagging him to pick up his things and do his laundry and put the toilet seat—

"Evan," Dad said.

Evan blinked and looked at him.

"Are you sure you're okay?"

"Oh, sorry, Dad. Yeah. I feel . . ." He didn't feel that good right now. His head was starting to hurt. "Fine." He placed a final forkful of Dad's homemade Hungarian goulash into his mouth and washed it down with the milk that tasted like dirt. He could feel Dad still watching him. It made him nervous. The pills. Yeah, that's what he was feeling, and it wasn't good. All he'd wanted was to stop feeling so bad all the time . . .

so-sad-so-mad-so-bad-so . . . so bad.

Dad cleared his throat again. "So is she still seeing . . . uh . . . Mr. Tygart?"

"Yeah." *Swallow food. Get out of the chair. Make the excuses. Apologize. Got to do it. Get out of here. Meet Kent. Ask him exactly what was in those pills.* Evan felt as if he were a rock being skipped across a pond. He pushed back from the table and stood. Time to get out while he could. "I'm supposed to meet . . . some of the guys at the theater for a movie, Dad. I'd better leave now if I'm going to get there in time." His voice caught, held, vibrated, but Dad didn't act like he noticed. He just acted disappointed. He'd probably rented a movie for tonight. He was always trying to do stuff like that. Then he would sit and watch Evan instead of the show. Mom said that was one reason she divorced him—because he suffocated her.

"Do you need a ride downtown?"

Evan shrugged. "It's only four blocks."

Dad slumped in his chair. "Well, then. I'll see you when you get home. Hurry back after the movie, okay?"

"Sure, I will." As Evan grabbed his jacket and pushed his way out the front door, he felt a tingle spread down his back and into his legs, slowly, like cold pancake syrup. He did not like these pills.

———————

It was starting to get dark, so six-year-old Levi Drake had turned on every light in the house. And now he sat next to his little brother, Cody, on the couch in the front room, waiting. They hadn't turned on the television, because the rules were no TV when Mom couldn't sit and watch it with them.

"Mommy's not home yet," Cody said, scooting closer to Levi and pressing his head against Levi's arm. "We go find her."

"It'll be okay. She told us never to leave the house by ourselves. She'll come back soon." Levi hoped Cody wouldn't start crying. Cody was only four, and he threw tantrums when he didn't get his way, especially when Mom was gone.

"Does Mommy have fur now?"

Levi looked down at his silly little brother. "Fur?"

Cody nodded. "She runned away, like the werewolf."

"What werewolf? Mommy isn't a werewolf."

Cody nodded again, and his eyes got big. "Uh-huh. Cartoon werewolf."

"Oh." That Saturday morning werewolf cartoon was Cody's favorite show. Levi liked it, too. He was a nice werewolf who ran away when he started to grow fur so nobody would see him and bashed the bad guys and saved the children. "I don't know, Cody. Maybe she is."

"I'm hungry."

"We can eat when Mom gets back." She would come back any time. Levi knew it. He turned to look out the window and saw that the cars driving along the street had their headlights on. He hoped she would be able to find her way home in the dark. Would she get lost?

Levi had tried to stop being afraid when Mom left them alone, but this time she'd looked so scared, and she was breathing funny. Cody was right. She did sort of look like that werewolf did on cartoons just before his face grew hair. When Levi had asked her if she was sick, she hadn't even looked at him, just jerked open the front door and ran outside. She hadn't heard him when he'd called her. Maybe she really was the werewolf. Maybe she was out there right now, saving other little children from the bad guys.

When she had left before, she had always come back later and said she was sorry, and cried, and told them she thought she was just having bad dreams that scared her when she woke up. She never told them what the dreams were about. She always said everything would be okay. But if she really thought that, why did she cry?

Cody patted Levi's leg. "Can I have soup?"

"I'll get you some crackers, and then when Mom comes, we can have soup." Levi squeezed Cody's arm and slid from the couch.

Cody climbed down, too, and followed right behind him. "You cook soup, Levi."

"No, Mom doesn't want us to turn on the stove when she isn't here. I'll get some cheese. You like that, Cody. Cheese and crackers." Levi got some slices of American cheese out of the fridge and used a step stool to reach the crackers in the cupboard. But when he opened the cupboard door, he knew Cody was going to yell. There were all the cans of soup stacked on top of each other, right next to the HiHo crackers.

Cody caught his breath, getting ready for a long squall. "Soup! I want soup, Levi! You cook soup!" His voice grew so loud Levi wanted to cover his ears with his hands.

"Cody, I can't—"

"Soup, soup, soup! I want soup! I want—"

"Shut up, Cody!" Levi turned around and almost fell off the step stool. "Shut up! Shut—Be quiet!" Cody knew Mom would get mad if she heard him say "shut up."

Cody shouted louder. "I want soup! I'm hungry!" He banged his fist against the cabinet door below the sink and stomped his foot.

Levi couldn't take the screaming anymore. "Okay! I'll get you some soup! Just be quiet!"

Cody kept banging and stomping, but he stopped shouting. Levi was hungry, too. Where was Mom? Why didn't she come back? If she were here Cody wouldn't be this way.

Levi grabbed a can with the noodles on the front picture and set it carefully on the counter. Then he pulled the box of crackers out and set that beside the can. He had to do everything just right. Mom always made him be real careful when he worked with her in the kitchen. He climbed down from the stool and opened the cabinet door where Mom kept the pots. He pulled out the one she always used to cook the soup and closed the door.

Cody stopped the banging and ran across the kitchen. "I can help!"

Levi jerked the pot away and said in his meanest voice, "No, Cody! If you touch anything, I won't feed you!"

Cody looked at him in surprise for a moment. Then his lower lip stuck out and big tears filled his eyes. A long moan grew in his throat and burst into a loud cry that went through the kitchen like a car horn. Levi tried to ignore the wail as he reached into a drawer to get the can opener and opened the can. It was hard to concentrate with Cody screaming behind him, but he kept trying.

The lid came off and Levi poured the soup into the pot, only splashing a few drops out onto the floor. He reached up and turned the knob on the stove to the place where Mom always turned it. He heard a *click, click, click* sound, but nothing else happened. He turned it off again, told Cody to be quiet, and then turned the knob back on.

Click, click, click, but no fire. And Cody kept screaming. Levi climbed onto the first step of the stool and turned the knob a little farther... just a little bit, and then once again ... and a big whoosh of flames licked out at him. He stumbled backward and fell from the stool.

"Mama!" he shouted as he landed with a hard thump on the floor. It knocked the air out of him, and he couldn't catch his breath.

Cody stopped crying.

Click, click, click.

Levi couldn't see the flames around the bottom of the pot, because he couldn't see the bottom of the pot, but he knew there was fire—he'd seen it. Mom said when that happened he had to turn the knob some more to stop the clicking, because it might not be safe. But he wasn't sure if he could get up.

"Levi?"

Click, click, click.

A shadow covered Levi, and he looked up to find his little brother bending over him, eyes wide and scared. And the clicking kept on. Levi's head hurt where he'd bumped it. What if he was hurt bad? What if he'd broken something and he shouldn't get up?

A chubby hand patted his cheek. "Levi?" Cody sounded scared.

Levi knew he had to be a big boy for his little brother. Mom wasn't back yet. He raised his head, then pushed himself up and sat for a minute while Cody watched with wide eyes.

Click, click, click.

Levi shook his head and pushed himself to his feet. He had to get to that knob. He could hear the soup sizzling on the sides of the pot, but Mom said it had to sizzle like that for a while for it to do any good. He reached the knob and turned it, and the clicking stopped. He pulled a spoon out of the drawer and stuck it into the soup. It looked easier when Mom did it, because Mom was taller, and she could see what she was doing. There were too many things to remember, and he couldn't think very well with Cody patting his leg to make sure he was okay.

He turned to Cody. "It's okay, I'm getting soup. You go sit down in your chair."

"Are you hurt?"

"No, Cody. Go to your chair." Levi put his hands on his hips like Mom did when Cody was being bad. "I mean it, Cody. Sit down!"

Cody started to cry again, but he went to his chair. Levi stepped up onto the stool again. He reached for the spoon he'd put in the pot. The spoon was hot, and his arm jerked backward, knocking against the handle of the pot and tipping the pot over to the side.

Hot soup splashed out onto Levi's shoulder. He screamed with pain, and Cody's cries mingled with his.

———

Evan had never felt this horrible before. His hands shook, and his stomach was upset. Before he reached the theater, he knew he couldn't go in. His heart felt like it was beating faster, but he couldn't be sure because of the roaring in his ears.

"Hey!" A voice came from the street so suddenly it scared him, and he jerked violently around to see his friend Kent in a pickup truck. "Come on, get in. Dad let me use his truck. We'll go cruising. The movie's no good tonight."

Evan rushed over to the truck and pulled the door open. "I thought you said those pills you gave me were supposed to make me feel better. Where'd you get them?"

"A friend. Don't worry, you'll be okay. Get in. Haven't you ever done speed before?"

The words didn't sink in for a few seconds. *Speed!* "Speed?"

"Hey, relax, it'll give you go power. You're always so droopy lately."

Evan jumped into the truck and slammed the door. He felt a rush of anger so powerful he wanted to strangle Kent. "It's making me sick, man! Why didn't you tell me what it was? Where did you get the stuff?"

"Peregrine gave me some last week." Kent sounded suddenly defensive.

"Who's that?"

"Come on, Evan, don't you know anything? He hangs out with the guys sometimes."

"Peregrine? You mean like a falcon?" *What a stupid name.* "Is he a pusher or something?"

"Pusher? No way. He gave me the pills. Don't worry, he's okay. He's in his twenties, and the guys like him 'cause he'll buy booze for them on weekends."

Evan buried his face in his hands. This was crazy! He was taking illegal drugs from some loser who thought he was a bird of prey. Why hang out with Kent, anyway? It wasn't as if he had any brains.

"Evan? You okay?"

"No, I'm not okay! How could you do this to me?"

"Hey, you didn't have to take it, you know. Don't blame me."

The tingling in Evan's arms and hands accelerated. It felt as if ants had burst into his veins and arteries and were crawling up his neck. "Do something! This feels awful."

"What am I supposed to do?"

Evan felt another powerful spurt of anger. His heart beat louder and louder in his ears, faster and faster, like it could explode. He grabbed Kent by the arm. "Get me help!"

CHAPTER 2

D r. Grant Sheldon knew better than to believe in love at first sight. Forty years of living had taught him not to get carried away by surface attraction, but he had lost his heart after one glimpse of Dogwood Springs, Missouri, sparkling in a morning blanket of late spring dew, when he first came down to interview for a new job.

The Ozark hillside village had a bustling, homey, five-block-long downtown, with brick streets and streetlights that looked like century-old gaslights. The town's modest population of seven thousand gave welcome relief from the teeming millions of St. Louis. Settled deep in the southern Missouri hills, thirty minutes from Branson, Dogwood Springs offered Grant the convenience of taking off for a weekend with his kids without having to drive miles from home.

He had also been wonderfully surprised when he walked into his prospective place of employment for the first time a month ago and saw the state-of-the-art facilities. Mr. Butler, the sixty-year-old administrator of Dogwood Springs Hospital, had announced with pride that they'd completed the final touches to this ten-bed emergency department about six weeks ago. Staffing at the hospital was great. Not only did they have two registered nurses on duty for the Friday night shift, but they also had two techs, cheerful, well-trained lab and radiology department personnel, and another nurse they could call from the floor if they got too busy.

Tonight, only thirty minutes into his second shift, Grant already felt as if he'd come home for good. They hadn't seen a gunshot wound here in months, according to Mr. Butler, and the last one had been a flesh wound from a hunting accident. No more knife and gun gang emergency work for Grant Sheldon. He couldn't believe his good fortune. What a great town for raising a family!

The ER secretary, Becky, turned and waved to get his attention. "Dr. Sheldon, I have a call from a man who's on his way here with his son. He suspects a drug overdose."

Grant stopped walking. Okay, he hadn't expected that one quite so soon. "Did he say what drug?"

"Speed."

His shoulders slumped. Ouch. That could be bad. "Thanks, Becky. Let me know when he comes in." He glanced at the chart holders on the far wall. Each plastic slot represented an exam room, and six of them contained clipboards. An eleven-year-old boy was in radiology being x-rayed for a possible broken wrist from a bike wreck. He also needed sutures on his leg. His mother had already fainted twice at the sight of his blood. Now she was a patient herself. Her husband had asked for their pastor to be called, and one of the nurses, Lauren McCaffrey, had done so just a few minutes ago. The pastor just happened to be the on-call clergy for Friday night.

Three patients—all with similar intestinal flu symptoms—were stable. It was a little late in the year for an epidemic, but since he'd seen two patients last night with the same symptoms, he couldn't rule out some kind of community-acquired virus. His top priority right now was a lady with chest pain. He pulled out her chart and studied it as he walked toward exam room three.

He stepped into the room, where Lauren hovered over eighty-eight-year-old Mrs. Cecile Piedmont and jotted down vitals from readings on the monitor above the bed on the wall.

"Hello, Mrs. Piedmont, I'm Dr. Grant Sheldon. I understand you're having chest pain."

The sharp-eyed lady sat up in the bed and gave him an appraising glance. Her white hair was only slightly ruffled from the nasal cannula oxygen tubing hooked over her ears, and though she appeared pale to him, he had no way of knowing if that was her normal coloring.

After a few seconds of silent study, she nodded her head. "Hello, Dr. Sheldon. I'm not really having any pain right now." Her voice was deep for a woman, and it didn't waver. "I hope I'm not wasting your time. Sounds to me like you have other patients who need you."

He smiled at her and felt himself relax. He enjoyed working with elderly patients. "Don't worry about wasting my time. I just want to find out what brought you here so I can help." He pulled a stool over and sat down next to her bed. "Why don't you tell me about your pain?"

"I'm only here because my children ganged up on me. They're always doing that."

"When did the pain start?"

Again, that thoughtful pause. "I felt a couple of twinges this afternoon, but I didn't think much about it." Her dark eyes studied him while she spoke. "You're new in town, aren't you?"

"Yes, I am. I just worked my first shift here last night. Mrs. Piedmont, do you remember what you were doing when you first felt the pain?"

She nodded. "I was out picking up some tree limbs in the front yard. You know that storm we had last night? When I stepped out the front door this morning I could have sworn half my trees had dropped their branches. I didn't want to wait for somebody else to get in the mood to clean it up." She leaned forward and lowered her voice. "Don't tell my son that. He's been after me for months to hire someone to do my yard work for me."

"Is he the one who brought you here?"

"Yes, but I shooed him out to the waiting room. He makes me nervous with all his fussing. Family is wonderful, Dr. Sheldon, but if I let all five of my kids smother me like an old woman, I'd never get anything done. I just hope the rest of the tribe doesn't come racing here before you release me." She frowned at him. "You *are* going to release me, aren't you?"

"We'll see." Grant gently directed the conversation back to the subject at hand. "So you were exerting yourself when you felt the twinges? Were you lifting extra-large limbs?"

"Yes, and that was what made me think I'd just pulled a muscle or two, but then I started to worry when the pain got a little worse. Several years ago my regular doc, Alan Roetto, told me I had that brittle bone disease." She glanced over at Lauren, who hovered nearby, keeping watch over the monitor and making notations on her chart. "Lauren, dear, did you tell him about my broken hip?"

Lauren turned to her, obviously surprised. "Broken hip? When did you have a broken hip, Mrs. Piedmont?"

"Oh, blast it, where's my brain? Sorry, I must have forgotten to mention that. I'm so forgetful anymore. I fell down the front porch steps a while back. I guess it must have been a couple or three years ago now." Her frown deepened. "Or was that four years? Let's see, I was eighty-five . . . that would've been three years ago." Satisfied with her conclusion, she nodded. "That's it."

Grant wrote the information down as extra notes on his T-sheet and noted the time Mrs. Piedmont had presented to the ER. "Lauren, have you ordered the EKG?"

"Yes, Dr. Sheldon, the tech will be here any moment."

Mrs. Piedmont shook her head. "EKG? Isn't that where they stick all those wires on your skin and hook you up to a machine? I think you're making too much of—"

A loud commotion outside their door stopped her words.

"Help me!" came a man's strained voice. "Somebody help us—my son's overdosed!"

Grant excused himself briefly and opened the door to make sure Muriel, the other night nurse, was close at hand. A balding middle-aged man rushed up to the central desk with his arm around the shoulders of a skinny teenager with limp brown hair. The boy had his arms wrapped across his chest, as if he thought his body might fly apart if he didn't do something to hold it together, but his movements did not betray any weakness. His frightened gaze darted about the room and bounced from Becky to the desk to Grant and back to Becky. Fear and anger mingled together in his expression, heightening the color in his face and causing his chin to jut forward.

As Grant expected, Muriel Stark and a tech, Lester Burton, rushed toward the father and son, reassured the boy, and helped them both into an exam room. Muriel's voice carried well as she explained that she was dressing him in a hospital gown and connecting him to a monitor. Grant would check on him as soon as he made sure Mrs. Piedmont wasn't in immediate danger of cardiac arrest.

"Doctor, you go ahead and see about those people," the lady called from behind him. "That's a real emergency."

He turned back to her and smiled. "Trying to get rid of me?" He checked her chest with his stethoscope. "Have you had any other broken bones since your hip?"

"Nothing at all. My regular doctor put me on some medicine to help strengthen my bones." She studied Grant as he worked, and a wealth of warmth suddenly glowed from the creases around her eyes. "Do you have a family, Dr. Sheldon?"

Grant suppressed a chuckle. She obviously wasn't as worried about her health as her children were. Still, he needed to stay on course. "Yes, I have sixteen-year-old twins, a boy and a girl. They're at home getting settled in, and I'm not sure I've convinced them yet that we're doing the right thing by moving out of the city."

The door opened, and the EKG tech came in pushing her portable machine.

"Mrs. Piedmont, here's the person we were waiting for," Grant said. "Just like you said, she's going to place more electrodes around your chest and get a detailed reading of your heart activity. While she's doing that, I'll step out for a few moments to give you some privacy. After you're finished with the test, I'll come back and check the results." He gently squeezed her arm and left her in capable care.

The sound of beeps suddenly burst into the air from across the ER, where Muriel had connected the overdosed teenager to the monitor. That rhythm was too fast. Grant stepped into exam room eight to find the fifteen-year-old boy lying in the bed, attached by electrodes to the machine that relayed his elevated heart rate with loud beeps. Muriel, a very efficient, motherly nurse in her late fifties, had already managed to dress him in a gown. His respirations were double what they should be, his eyes obviously dilated. The boy's father paced across the room, his extra-high forehead furrowed with concern. Muriel prepped the patient's arm with Betadine swabs and picked up an IV needle. The boy watched her movements with strange intensity. Once again fear and simmering anger lurked in his expression.

Grant cleared his throat, and both father and son turned toward him. "Hello, I'm Dr. Sheldon. I understand we have a possible overdose problem."

"Thank goodness!" the man exclaimed and rushed to Grant's side. "I'm Norville Webster, and this is Evan, my—"

"Ow! That hurts!" the boy cried out and jerked back as Muriel stuck him.

"Now just relax. The pain won't last long." She braced her arm against his and threaded the plastic IV catheter over the introducer needle. "Dr. Sheldon, his blood pressure is 190 over 100, heart rate of 130."

"My head's killing me," Evan complained. He reached up and massaged his forehead, his skinny fingers shaking.

Grant stepped up to the bed. "Evan, what kind of drug did you take?"

"It's speed," the teenager said. His words were quick, choppy, irritable, and his voice grew louder with each word. "I took some pills. That *jerk* gave me some pills. Told me they would make me feel better, give me go power, whatever. But all it did was make my heart race. I feel like I'm going to crawl out of my skin." His movements became more agitated, and he nearly pulled the IV from his arm before Muriel could secure the catheter. "Do something!"

"He just came running into the house, crying and shaking and rubbing his arms," his father said.

Grant nodded. "Muriel, I need a stat EKG, CBC, chemistry panel. Put him on a liter of saline over an hour." Their first priority was to flush the kidneys of any toxins to prevent kidney failure and clear the toxin from the rest of his system. "I also need a urine, then we'll give him something to calm him down."

"Coming right up, Dr. Sheldon."

Grant turned back to Evan. "Can you tell me how much you had?"

"Two. All I had was two stupid pills! How could this happen? Can't you hurry and stop this? I feel like my heart's going to break through my ribs!"

"Muriel is almost finished, and we'll need a urine sample next. Can you do that for me?"

"Yes, just hurry!"

"How long ago did you take the pills?"

Evan glared at him. "What does it matter?"

"Evan!" Mr. Webster snapped. "Tell the doctor what he needs to know! You got yourself into this mess, and he's trying to help you out of it." Obviously, Mr. Webster was one of those people who disguised their fear as anger. He seemed almost as irritated as his son.

Grant explained to the teenager. "I need to know how long the drug has been in your system so I'll know how to treat it."

Evan glanced around the room in confusion. "About an hour or so. Maybe two. I don't even know what time it is. How am I supposed to tell you anything if I don't know—"

"Dr. Sheldon," Mr. Webster said, glancing at his watch, "he came home wired out of his mind. He was supposed to go to the movies tonight, and it couldn't have been thirty minutes from the time he left the house to the time he came bursting back through the door, shouting that he'd been drugged. He says he took the drug before dinner, and I noticed he was acting a little funny before he left. He was supposed to walk down and meet his friends at the theater." He glared at his son. "Some friends!"

Evan stared down at his own shaking hands. "I told you, I just took two pills."

"I'm sorry, Evan," Grant said, "but illegal drugs are not regulated. We have no way of knowing how much drug was in the dose you took." He wanted to make his point, but he couldn't tell the whole truth until he knew the kid was totally out of danger. Two pills could easily pack enough punch to kill, but the boy's heart was already under enough strain. He didn't need any further agitation.

"Can't you *give* me something? Can't you—"

"Yes, we'll take good care of you." Grant looked at Muriel and nodded. "Try the charcoal."

"Charcoal!" Evan exclaimed. "I saw them do that on TV. You're going to ram a tube down my throat?"

"No," Grant assured him. "If we can convince you to drink it for us, we'll forgo the tube. We don't always do things here the way they do it on television. The charcoal will help neutralize anything that's left in your stomach. Muriel, I'll be in three."

"Yes, Dr. Sheldon."

Grant excused himself and left the room. The respiratory tech should be finished with Mrs. Piedmont's EKG by now, and Grant needed to notify the police about Evan. He shook his head, battling disappointment. An overdose of an illegal drug on his second shift in Dogwood Springs. How many overdosed teenagers had he treated in the past few years in St. Louis? He'd thought this small town would be different. Obviously, it was a foolish expectation. He would like to think Evan Webster was telling the truth, that he really hadn't known what was in those pills, but the episode had smacked Grant in the face with a healthy dose of reality. The only way to keep himself, his own children, and his patients safe was to remain a cynic, even here in Hometown, USA.

He stopped at the central desk. "Becky, I need you to call the police to report some illegal drug activity."

She turned from her computer keyboard and peered up at him over the top of her reading glasses. "Did you know Evan Webster's parents are divorced? His mother has custody, and she and I belong to the library club. Dr. Sheldon, I called her and told her he was here, and she's on her way in. If I call the police on her kid, she's going to bust my head."

"Blame me, then. Catching a pusher is more important right now. I'll be in three."

When Grant entered Mrs. Piedmont's room he greeted her and read the EKG printout. It revealed multi-focal PVCs and a couplet, as well as ST-segment depression over the lateral leads. Not good.

Mrs. Piedmont's face reflected Grant's frown. "Please don't tell me you're going to have to keep me here, Dr. Sheldon."

Grant peered over Lauren's shoulder at the newest numbers she had recorded from the monitor. The vitals were good. Still, the EKG findings concerned him.

He turned back to Mrs. Piedmont. "What I see on the EKG makes me think your chest pain really is heart related, not a pulled muscle. I realize you feel good now, but I want to do more tests. I'd like to know a little more about the pain you experienced today. Would you mind trying to describe it to me?"

"Oh, I just had those twinges, and then kind of a cramp in my chest that didn't want to let up for a while."

"Did you have cramping or pain anywhere else?"

Mrs. Piedmont's gaze remained steady on his face. "My left arm felt like somebody was squeezing it after I picked up that last big old dead branch and piled it up on the stack. It's fine now, though. I didn't hear anyone mention your wife, Dr. Sheldon. I'm on a greeting committee at church—we Baptists like to stick everybody on a committee—and I'd like to call on her with some of my homemade rolls."

Grant was touched. "Thank you for offering. I'd love some home-made rolls, but I want to get you feeling better before you do any more work, in the kitchen or in the yard." He paused. "As for my wife, she's . . . I'm a widower. Tell me, have you had these pains in your chest before today?"

Her smile dimmed. "I'm so sorry. I lost my husband when my children were young, too. How long has your wife been gone?"

"Two years. We were in an automobile accident." Her sincere interest didn't feel intrusive, but again, he needed to refocus the conversation. "Mrs. Piedmont, have you had these pains in your chest before today?"

She considered that. "Not that I can recall. I was hoping it might be indigestion."

"I'm afraid that isn't the case. Did you have any nausea? Shortness of breath?" When she shook her head, he continued to question her about her symptoms. "Did your pain go away when you lay down to rest?"

She blinked at him. "It doesn't bother me now, but I didn't lay down to rest until I got here. I was too busy to take a break today. You know, you'll want to get your children into a church youth group. Our own Lauren, here, helps keep those teenagers occupied. And she has a way with the young ones, too." Mrs. Piedmont beamed at Lauren, whose long blond hair was pulled back in a serviceable ponytail, and whose delicate features held only the barest traces of makeup. "Soon as she joined our church this spring, she pitched right in and started volunteering to help. She's good with the kids, and she teaches Sunday school." She hesitated for less than a second. "She's single, you know."

Lauren looked up from her work again, her green eyes sparkling with laughter. The healthy color of her complexion deepened a shade. "Mrs. Piedmont! Would you please let Dr. Sheldon do his job? How do you think he's going to feel if you keel over before he gets a chance to treat you? All that expensive education gone to waste." She shook her head, and her smile widened. "That'd be a shame."

Grant placed a hand on his patient's arm. "I doubt you'll keel over, but I do feel we need to do some more testing. I'm sorry, Mrs. Piedmont, but there's a possibility you'll have to eat hospital food tonight. Do you take a daily aspirin?"

"No. Why should I?"

"I'll get the baby aspirin, Dr. Sheldon," Lauren said.

"Thank you." He leaned toward his patient. "Aspirin thins the blood and helps reduce mortality when taken during the early stages of a heart attack. In other words, taking an aspirin can help save your life."

Her face quieted with the seriousness of his expression. "I overdid it this time, didn't I?" She laid her head back against the pillow. "My kids are going to tie me to my rocking chair."

CHAPTER 3

G ina Drake came to herself in the heaviness of evening, shivering as a gust of cool wind puckered gooseflesh down her legs. She raised her shaking hands to her face. The sharp teeth of pain bit into her feet, and she realized they were bare. She blinked and stared around her at squares of illumination from nearby homes. In the deepening gray of late twilight she recognized the outline of the elementary school and then looked down at the merry-go-round where she sat. She'd found herself here before. Her memory grew sharper. She'd run here in a panic, unable to control her terror, unable to recognize her surroundings.

And she'd left her children at home.

Gina's breath caught when the truth hit her. "Levi!" she cried. "Cody!"

As she jumped up gravel dug into the flesh of her bare feet. She stumbled to the grass and braced herself, gasping with pain. She had to get to the boys. It was dark—they'd be scared, wondering where she was. She tried to ignore the pain as she limped across the playground. She was still weak and shaky, and she shivered as the dew-soaked grass stung the cuts and bruises of her broken flesh.

"Stupid, stupid," she muttered at herself as frustration and fear shadowed her. How much more afraid must her children be?

"Don't let them be scared," she implored an unknown listener. "Let them be okay." They had to be. They were good boys, and Levi always watched after his little brother. He was so mature for a six-year-old.

But her fear mounted as she reached the sidewalk and crossed through the shadows beneath the overhang of the building. What was happening to her? The terror that had overcome her had also blocked out pieces of time. The terror was more than just a panic attack. Wasn't it?

She thought of Aunt Bridget, and a black feeling of helplessness nearly overwhelmed her. No! It couldn't happen to her! Levi and Cody needed her. She was all they had.

Gina's head ached, and her heart felt as if it were being squeezed into a tiny space. She couldn't keep doing this . . . couldn't leave her own children frightened and alone. The last time she'd done this Levi had been in tears when she returned.

Bad dreams. It had to be nightmares. Something was frightening her, and whatever it was had been so horrible her mind refused to recall it. She remembered in vivid detail the horror all those years ago. . . .

Gina welcomed the pain in her feet and the ache in her head. She deserved the pain. What kind of mother ran out of the house into the darkness and left her children alone?

In spite of her determination not to cry, her throat swelled with tears of frustration and self-condemnation. Trying to ignore her shaking legs, she broke into a stumbling run on the uneven sidewalk. Fresh pain sliced up her legs from her wounded feet. Had to get home . . . had to reach the boys . . . had to comfort them, make sure they were okay, try to explain, one more time, why she'd left . . . if only she knew.

As she caught sight of her house up ahead, with lights shining from every window, Gina felt another tug at her heart. Levi hated the dark. The abundance of lights reproached her. She reached the front sidewalk and saw a square of white against the solid oak darkness of the front door. Large squared letters, quickly scrawled, struck her with accusation: *Levi has been hurt. I'm taking both boys to the emergency room. Agnes.*

———

Lauren McCaffrey felt a slight wave of nausea as she pierced the paper-thin skin of Mrs. Piedmont's right arm with an IV needle. She ignored the distraction and took care not to cause her patient any more pain than necessary.

The lady didn't even flinch, didn't glance at Lauren, but continued her conversation with Dr. Sheldon as if Lauren hadn't touched her. Success!

"I suppose I should have told you this before, Doctor," Mrs. Piedmont said, "but I had a brother who died suddenly of a heart attack when he was forty."

Lauren drew the blood she needed for the test and connected the heplock. Her nausea passed quickly, and she didn't have time to wonder about it.

"You've never had high cholesterol or diabetes or high blood pressure?" Dr. Sheldon asked.

Mrs. Piedmont shook her head. "Nope, nothing."

"You don't smoke?"

"Not since I was twelve. My brother and I tried to smoke one of those roll-your-own cigarettes out in the barn. My brother got sick and upchucked on my good shoes, and I dropped the cigarette into a pile of hay. I nearly caught the barn on fire before we could put the silly thing out. We both got our butts paddled, and that put an end to my cigarette smoking." She leaned toward Lauren. "How about you, Lauren, did you ever smoke?"

"No, ma'am, I never did. I chewed tobacco once, though."

Dr. Sheldon grinned at her. "What happened?"

"I didn't know I was supposed to spit. I got the same results as your brother, Mrs. Piedmont." This topic was not good subject matter in Lauren's present condition, and her stomach reminded her of that fact a little too irritably.

While the patient and doctor chuckled at her expense, Lauren tried to take her mind off the nausea by making a silent, informed guess about her elderly friend's medical problem. It could be stable angina. Fortunately, nobody had to rely on her guesswork. The heart was a complicated piece of equipment, and it often fooled the best of physicians. Lauren was not a physician. Some days she thought of becoming a nurse-practitioner, or even a physician's assistant, but that would take more classes and a lot of aggravation.

She was once more checking the monitor for vitals when someone knocked at the exam room entrance. She glanced up to make sure Mrs. Piedmont was properly covered, then went to the door and pulled it open to find their pastor, Archer Pierce, standing in the hallway. He grinned and stepped forward, his kind eyes, as always, calm and reassuring.

"Hi, Lauren. I saw Calvin Piedmont out in the waiting room, and he's practically chewing the vinyl cushions on the chairs. I promised I'd check on his mother." As he peered past Lauren his grin broadened. "Cecile, what are you doing in bed at this time of night?" Though Archer was a couple of years younger than Lauren, he gave the impression of spiritual maturity that she had often admired and wished she could emulate. His short, slightly ruffled brown hair and quick, friendly smile gave him a boyish look. He stepped into the room and crossed to the bed. He didn't even blink at Mrs. Piedmont's pale features as he leaned down to kiss her on the cheek. "I guess you know your son's mad at you."

A little color touched the lady's face as she reached up to take Archer's hand in both of her own. "Let him be mad. He didn't call you down here just to see me, did he? I told him he'd better not—"

"No, he didn't call me. I'm the chaplain on duty tonight. Lauren called me." He glanced around at Lauren and winked, and she felt her face grow warm. No wonder the number of females in the church youth group was increasing weekly.

As soon as the thought occurred to her, she chided herself. Even if he *was* single and good-looking, with the movements and physique of a star athlete and an incredible sense of humor, he was her pastor. He was also an old friend. Lauren realized she should know better, but she'd never had a great deal of control over whom she found attractive.

Belatedly, she realized she had made no introductions and was staring at Archer like one of the love-struck teenagers in the youth group. The heat beneath her skin increased, and she wondered if she might be coming down with a touch of the virus some of their patients had brought in with them tonight.

"Archer," Mrs. Piedmont finally said, "This is Dr. Sheldon. He's new in town, and he has twins who are sixteen years old. Don't you think we should get them involved in some of the activities you and Lauren have going?"

"Of course." Archer reached out to shake Dr. Sheldon's hand, and the two men assessed each other with the quick, respectful once-over that men use when they are sizing each other up for a game of one-on-one basketball. The smile remained in Archer's eyes, and it was genuine. He had an easygoing grace about him that Lauren knew would help comfort the patients.

Dr. Sheldon returned Archer's smile with equal warmth. "It's great to meet you. Thanks for your assistance." He turned back to his patient. "Mrs. Piedmont, we'll wait for the results of those blood tests—they shouldn't take long—and then I'll contact your family doctor. If you start feeling any more pain, please let us know immediately."

Mrs. Piedmont laid her head back against the pillow and smiled up at him. "I'll do that, Doctor. Do you think I could get word to my son that I'm still alive? I know he's out there fretting."

"Of course. I'll—"

The ER secretary stepped to the threshold of the exam room. "Excuse me, Dr. Sheldon, I just received a call from a woman who is bringing in a burned child."

"Oh?" Dr. Sheldon asked. "Did she say how bad?"

"She said some hot soup splashed onto his shoulder, and he's blistering. I could barely hear her for the screaming in the background."

"What's the ETA?"

"She said it'll take her about ten minutes to get here."

"Okay, Becky, thanks." Dr. Sheldon turned to Lauren. "We'll want to set up for a cool saline soak, and be prepared with Silvadene. We might even need some Demerol if there are no allergies."

Becky cleared her throat. "One more thing, Doctor. The lady is the next-door neighbor, not the mother. She says she doesn't know where the mother is; the boys were at home by themselves."

He frowned. "Boys? More than one?"

"Two little boys, six and four. It's the six-year-old who was burned. They want their mother, and nobody knows where she is. Luckily, the neighbor has watched the kids a couple of times, and she has written permission for treatment with all the information."

"I hope she brings that with her."

"I'll go set up, Dr. Sheldon." Lauren checked the monitor one more time, laid a reassuring hand on Mrs. Piedmont's arm, and excused herself.

Less than ten minutes later the mingled, sobbing shrieks of two frightened children burst through the ER and brought Lauren rushing to the front of the department. She saw Dr. Sheldon carrying a blond-haired little boy in his arms. A woman, who looked to be in her fifties, with graying, short brown hair, entered behind him, carrying a smaller boy.

"I saw her run out of her house about forty-five minutes before I heard the boys' screams." The woman's voice rose in a crescendo of panic. "I didn't think anything about it! I mean, how was I supposed to know there wasn't a baby-sitter?"

The neighbor absently stroked the head of the child in her arms, carrying him as if she was accustomed to holding children. "When I heard the screams, I didn't know what to think. These boys are never loud—their mother makes them mind. They're good boys, especially for children without a father." The little boy in her arms cried out again and reached for his brother. Tears dripped from his scrunched face.

"Did you bring the permission for care, Mrs. . . . ?" Dr. Sheldon asked over his shoulder.

"Walker. Agnes Walker. It's here in my purse. I baby-sat for Gina a couple of times, when she got called in to work suddenly and couldn't get her regular baby-sitter. Please, can't you give Levi something for pain? He screamed all the way here."

"The cool saline will help a lot, and we'll get it applied as quickly as we can. Meanwhile I'll need the information. Does this little guy have any drug allergies, any—"

"He doesn't have any." Mrs. Walker tried to put the younger child down, but he shrieked again and grabbed her around the neck.

"No! No! Levi's crying!" he wailed. "Levi's hurt! I want Mama!"

Dr. Sheldon carried six-year-old Levi into exam room two and settled him onto the bed, where Lauren had already set up for the burn treatment. He turned to the secretary, who stood behind them, waiting to help. "Becky, take Mrs. Walker's information." He removed the little boy's shirt to reveal a softball-sized patch of blistered skin on the right shoulder. "Lauren, start the cool saline on this. Get Lester to help you." His deep, calm voice carried over the screams of the children.

Levi caught his breath for another round of cries, his face contorting in agony. "It hurts, it hurts. Make it stop! Mom! Where's Mama? I want my—" He broke off for another scream as Lauren eased him down onto the bed and prepped for the saline soak.

"It's okay, sweetheart, we're going to take care of you," Lauren murmured with soothing tenderness. "Lie down and let the doctor look at you."

Dr. Sheldon bent over the child and assessed the burn quickly. "It's going to be okay, Levi. Did the soup splash you anywhere but your—"

"Ow! No, don't! That hurts!"

"Yes, I know it does, and we're going to take the burn away." Dr. Sheldon gave Lauren a nod to proceed with the soak. "You'll be feeling a lot better in a few minutes—you'll see."

Lauren grabbed a handful of four-by-four-inch gauze pads and lowered them toward the burn.

Levi jerked away. "What are you doing?"

"Shhh, it's okay, Levi. We're going to put some cool stuff on your shoulder so it won't hurt." She covered the area with the gauze and hurriedly poured cool saline from a plastic bottle onto the pads. Levi tensed when the saline first touched the burn, but then he relaxed. "See?" she said. "Doesn't that feel better? I'll just keep pouring this into the pad, like this, and that'll keep it from burning again." She squeezed the bottle until the saline wept onto the thick layer of towels below.

"There you go," she said. "I burned myself once when I was a little older than you, and my mom put ice on it until it stopped hurting." Lauren kept a continual flow of soft chatter going, which was never a difficult thing for her to do. She had the gift of chatter, like some people had a special touch with a paintbrush. Except for times like this, however, she seldom treasured this "gift."

Tears continued to well in Levi's eyes and drip down the sides of his face, dampening streaks of his hair to dark gold. "Where's my mom? I don't know where Mom is, and Cody's still crying." He sniffed. "Cody was just hungry. It isn't his fault."

"Of course not, sweetheart," Lauren assured him. "Mrs. Walker is with him while our secretary tries to find your mother. Did she say where she was going when she left?"

"No, she just ran out the door. She looked scared, and she didn't have her shoes on. Mom always tells us we have to wear our shoes outside, but *she* didn't wear *hers*."

"Levi," Dr. Sheldon's voice was gentle and soft. "Has your mom ever done anything like that before?"

"Yes, but she always wore her shoes before."

Dr. Sheldon's voice remained calm and casual. "So your mother always wore her shoes the other times she left you at home alone?"

"Yes," Levi replied, then his eyes widened, and he shut his mouth tightly, as if he had picked up some strange tone in Dr. Sheldon's voice.

"Lauren, continue the saline soaks, and I'll see if we need the Demerol." With a smile of assurance for Levi, Dr. Sheldon walked out of the room. Lauren heard him ask Becky about Levi's mother, then give orders to call the child abuse hotline.

"Why did the doctor leave?" Levi asked between sniffles.

"He has another patient." Lauren brushed the strawberry blond tendrils of hair from his forehead and indicated for Lester, the tech, to take over the application of saline while she did her assessment. "Levi, did your mother tell you why she was leaving today?"

"No, but I think it was because she was scared."

"What scared her?"

Tears continued to stream down Levi's cheeks, in spite of his obvious efforts to be brave. "I . . . I think it was one of her bad dreams."

"She has bad dreams?"

"Yeah."

"What's your mother's name?"

"Gina."

Becky's voice rose from the central desk. "Mrs. Walker, did you say the patient's name is Levi Drake?"

Lauren stiffened with surprise. "Levi, your last name is Drake?"

The child nodded, still tearful.

She laid a hand against his soft cheek. "Your mother works here, doesn't she?"

Levi blinked at her and nodded again. "She helps people breathe better."

Oh no. Dr. Sheldon had just left orders for Becky to call the child abuse hotline on one of their best respiratory therapists.

CHAPTER 4

While Grant waited for the test results to come back on Mrs. Piedmont, he slipped into exam room eight to see how Evan Webster was doing. The EKG appeared normal, with the exception of an elevated heart rate. Two large empty Styrofoam cups sat at the bedside with the residue of charcoal clinging in droplets to the inner surfaces. Grant was impressed. Evan had managed to swallow all that nasty, gritty medicine in a short amount of time. Obviously, he wanted the drug out of his system.

The boy's father, Norville, stood watch next to the bed, as if he thought his son might come under physical attack. Grant knew the feeling. He, himself, had hovered just that way beside Beau's hospital bed during those horrible months after Annette's death. The problem was, no matter how close he hovered or how willing he was to place himself between his son and harm, he hadn't been able to prevent Beau's physical and emotional scars.

When Norville saw Grant he straightened and rushed toward him. "Dr. Sheldon," he said, keeping his voice low. "My son doesn't ordinarily do this kind of thing. He's an honor-roll student, a good boy. I don't want you to get the wrong impression of him."

"I'm not here to judge your son, Norville. I think this world has too many judges already. I just want to work with you both to make sure this kind of thing doesn't happen again." Under Evan's quiet observation, Grant read the vitals displayed on the overhead monitor. Muriel had administered Ativan through Evan's IV, and though the heart rate was still elevated, it had slowed, and his blood pressure was dropping.

"How did you like our house beverage tonight, Evan?"

"I kept it down." There was no change in the boy's expression.

"That's good. How are you feeling? Any better?"

"My heart's still beating too fast," Evan said.

"It'll take a while to get back to normal. Does it still feel as if it's going to beat out of your chest?"

Evan considered the question solemnly. "I guess not."

Grant reached for the ophthalmoscope and checked Evan's eyes. They were still dilated, but no worse than before. "Does your head hurt as badly as it did when you came in?"

"No."

Grant checked Evan's breathing with his stethoscope, then listened for a murmur. There was none. Respirations were still a little fast but regular, and breath sounds were clear.

"Evan, it looks as if we might have this under control, but I still need to keep you here two or three more hours."

"Three more *hours*?" Evan exclaimed.

"Two or three. I don't want to take any chances, and I haven't seen the lab results yet." Grant noticed the faint evidence of the charcoal around Evan's mouth and traces of dried tears on his face. "Evan, I have to ask you some questions."

No reaction.

"I need to know why you took the drugs tonight. Were you—"

"I wasn't trying to kill myself, if that's what you mean." Evan scowled at him. "I told you, I just . . . I took the pills to feel better." He looked at his father, then ducked his head. "My friend told me they would give me a lift. You know, he said they would give me some go power."

"Did you know *go* is another name for speed?"

"I'd heard the guys talking about it before, but I didn't think—" He shrugged. "Nobody said anything about speed before I took it. He told me it was fine stuff, that it would be safe, and it would be great, and I'd feel better."

"Better than what?" his father asked. "There was nothing wrong with you before you took the stuff."

Evan sighed and gave the ceiling a long-suffering look. "I don't tell you everything, Dad."

"Obviously not." Norville had clearly been taken by surprise. Was it possible this truly was Evan's first experience with illegal drugs?

The boy shook his head and sighed again. "Dad, if I tell you about something that's bothering me, you automatically blame Mom. And if I tell her something, she blames you."

"Evan," Grant said, "speed does just what it says. It speeds up your system, placing great strain on your heart. And since the drug is illegal, as I told you, there is no quality assurance program where it's manufactured. There are all kinds of potential contaminants."

"But I didn't know it was illegal! I just thought maybe he'd gotten it from his parents."

"Who is *he*?" Norville demanded.

Evan ignored the question and closed his eyes.

"Have you taken this drug before?" Grant asked.

"No!"

Grant wanted to believe him, but an overabundance of experience with this situation in St. Louis made him skeptical. "Have you been drinking alcohol tonight?"

Evan shook his head wearily, as if he knew nobody was going to believe him anyway, so why should he bother to try to convince them otherwise.

"Okay, I need to advise you that the police will be here to talk to you in a few minutes."

Evan's eyes flew open, and he jerked upright in the bed. "What! The police? You called the police on me?"

Norville groaned and leaned back against the exam room wall. "Evan, what have you gotten us into?"

"I'm sorry," Grant said. "I have no choice. If there's drug activity in the area the police need to know about it as soon as possible so they can stop it at the source. Evan, I would advise you to cooperate with them in every way possible."

"Oh sure, so my friends can go to jail!"

"Evan!" Norville snapped. "That's enough. If they were really your friends they wouldn't have tricked you into taking a potentially lethal illegal drug, would they?" He turned to Grant and lowered his voice. "Evan's so young. If this gives him a police record, he'll—"

"Believe me, the police will be looking for information from Evan, not retribution."

Norville bit his lip, and lines of depression settled down around his forehead and eyes, aging him by at least ten years. "I suppose I understand the necessity of reporting this to the police, but do you think it would be possible to keep his mother from finding out about this? She's . . . we're divorced, and she has custody. She'll raise the roof if—"

"I'm sorry, she's already on her way in," Grant said. "The Emergency Department is—"

"Don't tell me," Norville said as he closed his eyes wearily. "I don't want to hear it."

"I know this is difficult for you, Mr. Webster." Grant couldn't help feeling empathy for this man. Parents of teenagers seldom had it easy these days. "Your son is only a year younger than my twins. I can imagine what I would be going through right now." He studied the man more closely. "Would you like to speak with a counselor?"

Norville reached up and rubbed his tired eyes, then he nodded. "Yes, I'd like that."

"Our minister on call tonight is Pastor Archer Pierce. He's already here, in fact, to see a couple of other patients."

"Would he mind coming in here, too? We need some help."

Grant recognized the light, clear sound of Lauren McCaffrey's voice several seconds before he stepped to the threshold of exam room two and saw her perched on the stool beside the bed. Levi Drake listened intently while the energetic nurse concluded an exciting story of David and Goliath with great dramatic emphasis. At just the right time she put the saline bottle down and replayed the slinging of the stone, her hands moving gracefully in the air. As the giant finally fell in a mighty tumble to the earth, Grant could almost feel the earth shake at the impact.

When Lauren raised her head after the death scene, Levi's lips were parted and his eyes were shining.

"More! Tell me more! What happened after that?" He was so engrossed that he didn't see Grant standing in the doorway. "What did David do after that?"

"Exactly what I was going to ask," Grant said, even though he knew the answer. He'd listened to Annette tell their own kids Bible stories when they were little.

Lauren looked over her shoulder at him, and a hint of a flush spread across her cheeks. He'd already learned that she blushed easily. "Oh-oh, I've been caught. Mrs. Piedmont did tell you I teach Sunday school, didn't she?" She picked up the bottle of saline and rewet the gauze on Levi's shoulder. "I've always loved the Bible stories. I still have the book my mother used to read to us when we were kids. I have all those stories memorized, especially the ones about children."

Grant couldn't decide if she was chattering so fast because she was embarrassed or because she was trying to keep Levi's mind off his pain. Probably a combination of both, but for Levi the spell was broken. As soon as Grant stepped to the side of the bed, the child's eyes lost their look of enchantment, and he once more recalled where he was and what he was doing there.

"Sorry I had to leave you for a while, Levi," Grant said. "Sounds like you and Nurse Lauren are having a good story time. How does that shoulder feel now?"

"It hurts sometimes. Are you . . . going to give me a shot?" His voice shook with a tremble of fear.

"Let me check and see." Grant pulled the gauze back from the burn. The patch of angry red was covered with blisters. "What does the pain feel like when it hurts?"

"Like I'm getting stuck by needles."

"Sounds like that really hurts, then," Grant said. "You probably wouldn't mind being stuck once if that would keep you from feeling like you're getting stuck over and over again."

"He's very brave, Dr. Sheldon," Lauren said. "As soon as I apply more cool saline, he says the burn goes away again, and he never complains. He's worried about his little brother, though, so we had Becky go check on him." She reached over and brushed a wisp of hair from Levi's forehead. "We decided if he could just go swimming at his friend's pool until he heals, and if Cody could go with him, everybody would be happy."

"My friend doesn't live in Dogwood Springs, though," Levi said seriously. "He lives in Oregon, where we used to live. Are you going to give me the shot?"

"Not if I can help it," Grant assured him.

The little boy issued an automatic sigh of relief.

"Before we resort to that, we'll put some cream on your burn and see if that helps. Okay?"

"Okay. Did you find my mom yet? What are you going to do now?"

Grant replaced the gauze and sat down beside the bed, eye level with the child. "Some people are looking for your mother, Levi. But while they do that, we've called someone to come in and make sure you and Cody will be okay. Mrs. Walker's in one of the waiting rooms with Cody, helping him color some pictures. Lauren, would you please give us some Silvadene?"

She nodded, but didn't stand up immediately. "Dr. Sheldon, Levi's mom works here at the hospital." She paused, holding his gaze. "Gina's a respiratory therapist."

For a moment, the impact of her words didn't register, and then Grant realized what she meant. Although calling the child abuse hotline was a perfectly logical action for him to take to protect the children, it could easily be perceived as an accusation against Gina Drake. What concerned him more, though, was the fact that someone with her level of expertise and sense of responsibility wouldn't be likely to neglect her own children like this. She could be alone somewhere, ill or injured.

"How many people are searching for her now?" he asked Lauren.

"I'm not sure. Becky's taking care of the calls."

"Tell Becky to call the police for an immediate neighborhood search around their house, in case they haven't already done that."

"Yes, Dr. Sheldon." She handed him the saline bottle. "His shoulder is probably going to start burning again before I get back."

He took it and urged Levi to lie back down.

Levi stared at him with open accusation. "You're calling the police on my mom."

Grant soaked the gauze with fluid and laid a hand on the child's unhurt shoulder. "We don't want to arrest her. We want to make sure she's safe. If she's sick, we want to find her as soon as possible and take care of her."

Levi's lips parted in alarm. "You think she's sick? Why do you think that?"

Grant hesitated and then shook his head. No reason to worry the child yet. "We just want to make sure she's okay."

"Why wouldn't she be okay?" Levi's voice rose with urgency. "I told you, she wasn't *sick,* she was scared."

"Okay, Levi. It's okay." Grant used the soothing voice he once used with his own children when they were younger and something frightened them. "I don't have any way of knowing if your mother is sick. I'm just trying to find out why she left you and Cody, because I don't think she does that a lot, does she?"

Levi studied Grant's face in silence for a moment, and then shook his head.

Grant was relieved when Lauren stepped back into the room and resumed her place beside Levi, with the burn cream in hand.

"Becky is calling the police now, Dr. Sheldon. She said the hospital social worker, Rose, should be here any time."

"But what if Mom's home now?" Levi asked. "Can't I go home?"

Grant felt a familiar ache as he looked into the child's frightened eyes. "If your mother arrives at home, someone will find her and send her here, Levi. Meanwhile, I want to keep you here long enough to make your shoulder stop burning." He watched Lauren apply the cream. Levi barely flinched at her touch.

"There you go," she said with a note of soothing tenderness. "You're so brave and strong. This is special medicine that makes the burn go away fast, but if it doesn't you need to let us know, okay?"

Levi nodded, and Grant knew the child was more worried about his mother than he was about his own pain.

"How long before Cody and I can go home, Dr. Sheldon?" The voice was more insistent this time.

For a moment, Grant didn't answer. Then he sighed and sat down, once more eye to eye with Levi. "I'd love to be able to send you home, Levi, but you need a grown-up with—"

"Mom will be home soon." Levi's eyes spilled fresh tears down his cheeks. "She's never gone this long. She's probably looking all over for us."

There it was again, the hint that Gina had done this kind of thing before. But why? What would cause a mother to leave her young children at home alone? Grant looked at Lauren and saw her watching Levi with a troubled gaze.

"I know you've already answered a lot of questions for us, Levi, but would you answer some more for me?" Grant pulled some tissues from a box on the desk and handed them to Levi.

The little boy studied Grant's face carefully, took the tissues, and nodded.

"Good. When you first came in tonight, you said something about your mother having bad dreams. Can you tell me anything about those dreams? Does she ever describe them to you?"

Levi shook his head and reached up to smear dry the tears with his hands instead of the tissues. "She cries sometimes when she has them, and she runs out of the house. Then later, when she comes back, she's always sorry. But I don't think she's sick. She never throws up."

"How many times has this happened, Levi?"

The child frowned. "It never happened before we came here to live."

"And you don't have any family in this town?"

Levi shook his head. "Mom and Cody are my family. Mom told us that's all we need to be a family."

Grant squeezed Levi's arm as his own heart squeezed inside his chest. Why did it have to be that way so many times? Divorce and death and illness were vicious enemies. He wondered how these children had lost their father.

"Can you tell me exactly how you burned yourself?"

The child nodded. "I *told* you, I spilled soup."

"You were cooking soup for Cody?"

Another nod.

"Do you remember how long your mom was gone?"

Levi shook his head and avoided eye contact. Grant remembered that Mrs. Walker told them she'd seen Gina run out of the house about forty-five minutes before she heard the boys' screams.

Grant turned to speak to Lauren, but her eyes were closed and her face was very pale, with a barely detectable sheen of moisture across her forehead. As he watched, she opened her eyes, caught him looking at her, and looked away quickly, dabbing at her forehead with the back of her hand.

"Levi, would you like me to bring your brother in to see you?" she asked. "That way the two of you can be toge—"

"Yes!" Levi straightened and tried to sit up. "You'll bring Co—" Something in the doorway caught his attention, and his mouth rounded in a big O. "Mom!"

Lauren looked up and gasped. "Gina!"

CHAPTER 5

Lauren was surprised and relieved when Gina, disheveled and flushed, limped into the room. The young mother wore white cut-off shorts and a T-shirt. Smudges of mascara below her eyes looked like bruises. Her short auburn hair fell across her freckled forehead in tangles. Her anguished focus centered on Levi and on the gauze that covered the wound on his shoulder.

Levi sat up and reached his arms toward his mother, sudden joy spreading across his face like sunshine. "Mom, you're back! We were looking for you! Were you scared?"

"Oh, Levi," she whispered, taking him carefully into her arms. "What happened? There was a note on the door at home telling me you were here. Are you okay?"

"Yes, Mom, but don't touch my burned place," he said.

"I won't. I see it. I'm so relieved you're—" She drew back and leaned down to look at his shoulder. "How did it happen? How did you get burned?"

"Soup. Nurse Lauren has been pouring water on it and putting this gunky stuff on it and telling me stories about a boy who killed a big mean giant with a slingshot. I could kill a big mean giant, too. Can I have a slingshot, Mom?"

Gina pulled his head against her chest and pressed her lips to his hair in a tender kiss. Tears streamed in a sudden flood down her cheeks.

"Dr. Sheldon thought you were sick," Levi continued, his bright voice muffled against her T-shirt. "Are you sick? I cooked Cody some soup and it spilled and I didn't know where you were and people are looking for you. Mom, what happened?"

She sniffed and straightened her shoulders as she gave Lauren and Dr. Sheldon a look of appeal. "How bad?"

"He's going to be fine," Dr. Sheldon said. "He's got a second-degree flash burn, but it's only on his shoulder, where you see the gauze. We've already cooled it down with saline, and the burn dressing looks as if it will help a great deal. We'll know soon if he needs additional pain medication, but at this point it doesn't look as if it'll be necessary. Your letter of permission says he has no drug allergies?"

"None, and he isn't taking any other medications." She bent back down to look her son in the eyes. "I'm sorry, Levi."

"It's okay, Mom. Why are you crying? Did you get that dream again?"

She blinked and darted a glance toward Dr. Sheldon. "I-I . . . I'm not . . . I don't remember a dream. I'm okay now. Where's Cody?"

"Cody's fine, Gina," Lauren assured her, noticing with dismay that the nausea she had experienced earlier was returning. What was wrong with her? "He wasn't hurt. He's with Agnes Walker in one of the private waiting rooms." She leaned closer. "Where've you been? We were worried about you."

As Gina took a step backward she stumbled, grimacing with obvious pain. That drew Lauren's attention down, and she saw a flash of vivid red. At first it looked as if Gina had on canvas shoes that were tie-dyed red. But a closer look revealed the splotchy, brown-edged appearance of drying blood.

Dr. Sheldon leaned forward and laid a hand on Gina's shoulder. "Mrs. Drake, I'm Dr. Sheldon. I think I need to check you over and make sure—"

"No." She raised a hand and shrank from his touch. "I'll be okay now that I have my boys." She avoided eye contact with him by bending to study the gauze over her son's wound more closely.

"Mom, what happened?" Levi demanded. "Where did you go? You got up and ran out, and it started getting dark, and you didn't tell us where you were go—" He stopped and caught his breath when he, too, saw her feet. "Mom, your shoes! What did you get on your shoes?" He bent over the side of the bed and studied them closer, then gasped. "Mom!"

Gina moved quickly to divert his attention. "It's okay, don't worry about me. I guess I stumbled on some rocks. I must have stained my shoes when I pulled them on."

"You *guess*?" Dr. Sheldon asked. "You don't remember what happened?"

"You ran away without your shoes this time!" Levi exclaimed. "You're not supposed to do that." He winced, as if the burn had returned to his shoulder.

Lauren drew his squirming body back down on the bed. "Levi, try not to move very much. Your mom's safe now, so you don't have to worry about her. We'll call the police and let them know she's here."

Gina caught her breath and looked up at Lauren, shock and fear streaking across her face. "The police?"

"Gina, I told you, we were worried. We didn't know what had happened to you."

"We needed to find you," Dr. Sheldon explained. "Nobody knew where you were." He hesitated, and his gaze skimmed Levi's face, and then he looked once again into Gina's eyes. "I cannot stress enough how important it is for us to examine you as soon as possible."

She shook her head. "I need to see Cody."

"But Mom, you're bleeding," Levi said. "You've got to make the blood stop. You've got to put some medicine on—"

"Not now, Levi. I'll take care of it when we get home."

"Levi," Dr. Sheldon said, bending down, "I need to take care of your mother's feet, and to do that I have to take her into another exam room. That'll be okay with you, won't it?"

Levi's copper-colored eyes, so much like his mother's, studied Dr. Sheldon's face soberly. "You'll put medicine on them?"

"Yes, I'll take good care of her." He straightened and reached for Gina Drake's shoulder to guide her out.

She stiffened and pulled back. "I said I'm okay. Please, I need to be with my children right now."

"I'm sorry, Gina, but I must insist," Dr. Sheldon said. "If not for you, then for the sake of Levi and Cody. We need to make sure you're capable of caring for them. Levi tells me you don't have family nearby that we can call."

"No family."

"Friends, then?" he asked.

She shook her head. "We've only been here a few months." Her attention switched from Dr. Sheldon to Lauren, and she must have detected something in Lauren's expression that disturbed her. "Why? What's going on? Why do you want to bring—" She froze, and her eyes filled with sudden panic. "Cody. Where's Cody? Is there something you're keeping from me? Is he—"

"Cody's safe in one of the other rooms." Lauren placed an arm around her shoulders.

Gina pulled away. "I want to see him. Please. I've got to—"

"You don't want him to see your feet like this, Gina, it could scare him," Lauren said. "Why don't we bring him in here with Levi so they can be together, then we'll bring you back in here as soon as you're treated, okay? Your feet don't look good right now." She raised her eyebrows in a question to Dr. Sheldon.

He nodded. "I'll have Mrs. Walker bring Cody in here, and we'll let him know his mother's safe."

Lauren got a wheelchair from the front of the ER and pushed it into the room.

"I don't need that," Gina said. "I can walk—"

Lauren took Gina's arm in a firm grip. "You can ride more easily and prevent further damage."

Gina looked again at her son, then relented and allowed Lauren to wheel her out.

Gina was a couple of inches shorter than Lauren's 5'5", with muscular arms and legs that didn't appear to get a lot of sun. In spite of her obvious physical strength and her facade of self-sufficiency, she seemed frightened and vulnerable at the moment. It wasn't a side of Gina that Lauren had ever seen before.

Whenever Gina came into the emergency room to treat a patient she was friendly, with a good bedside manner and a quick wit. According to the patients, she also had a tender touch.

"Something else is going on," Gina said as Lauren wheeled her close to the bed. "What?"

Before Lauren could answer, Dr. Sheldon joined them and closed the door behind him. "Gina, I'm sorry." He pulled a stool over and sat down, hesitated, then leaned forward, resting his elbows on his knees. "You know that as a physician, if I even suspect the possibility of child abuse I'm mandated to report it, just as you are in your position as a respiratory therapist."

Gina's mouth flew open. She caught her breath. Her face lost all color, and she grasped the arms of the wheelchair. "Child abuse!" She looked from him to Lauren with open pain. "You reported me for—"

"We know better than that now," Lauren assured her.

Dr. Sheldon reached across to help Gina out of the wheelchair. "As soon as someone from the Division of Family Services arrives I'll inform them of the change in circumstances."

"They're coming to take Levi and Cody away from me, aren't they?" She covered her face with her hands and doubled over, as if she'd just been kicked in the stomach.

"No, Gina." Dr. Sheldon's voice was gentle and patient. "They're coming to make sure the children are okay. When we called them no one knew where you were."

"This can't be happening," Gina moaned.

Lauren knelt in front of the younger woman and grasped her by the shoulders. "Please, just listen. That's why we need to give you a physical and neurological exam. We have to prove you're physically and mentally capable of caring for them yourself, so that no questions arise. Look at it as a professional. It only makes sense."

Dr. Sheldon stood and pushed the stool out of the way. "Gina, let us help you onto the bed so we can examine and treat you." He reached for her elbow, and she jerked away as if she'd been singed.

Lauren caught a hint of something in Gina's expression. There was something haunted, even terrified, about the way she looked at them.

"Please, Gina." Lauren kept her voice soft and unthreatening. "We didn't even know you were their mother until after the report was called in. No one knew where you were, and Dr. Sheldon wanted to start treatment on Levi quickly. We needed someone to be legally responsible for their care."

Gina's full lips formed a straight, uncompromising line, and she narrowed her smudged eyes. "You said Agnes Walker brought them in. She has letters for permission to treat. Why couldn't you just take her word for it?"

"Because she saw you racing out of the house about forty-five minutes before she heard your sons' screams." Dr. Sheldon's voice was not accusatory. "They were alone in the house all that time, and she didn't know it. Even though you obviously didn't leave them intentionally, Gina, they were still alone long enough to be in danger. And now you've told me that you don't remember how you injured your feet. For your children's sake and your own we need to find out what's going on here. I'll treat your injuries, do a neurologic exam, and take blood and urine tests."

"But you're still going to turn me over to DFS?"

"We aren't going to 'turn you over' to anybody, Gina," he said, leaning closer and making firm eye contact. "What we'll do is ask for their backup support and advice while we try to find out what's wrong with you."

"Those people don't want to help me." The tension in her voice emphasized every word. "They want to take my kids away from me. I know what they'll do. They want my children!"

"No, Gina," Lauren said gently. "I know our staff social worker. Rose will do all she can to help your family through this crisis." She placed an arm around Gina's shoulders once more.

Gina's face puckered, and she covered it with her hands as a sob stole from deep within her. "Maybe this *is* all a nightmare. I wish . . . I should never have come to Missouri."

Finally, Gina allowed Lauren and Dr. Sheldon to help her onto the exam bed, and Lauren removed the blood-soaked canvas shoes and placed them in a biohazard bag.

"Those people can claim I'm mentally incompetent," Gina said.

"They won't," Lauren said.

"But what if they do?" She had her eyes closed, and she lay with her head resting on the pillow, tears running unchecked down the sides of her face and into her hair, darkening it to deep burgundy. "And what if they're right?"

"What makes you think that?" Lauren asked.

Gina shook her head.

Lauren helped Gina turn over onto her stomach and set to work cleaning the blood from her feet as Dr. Sheldon pulled on some sterile gloves and checked for injuries. He found two deep cuts, one with a sliver of glass about the size of half a toothpick in the left instep. No wonder she'd been limping when she came in. Lauren was amazed she could even walk.

Dr. Sheldon requested a suture tray. "Gina, I'm going to try to remove this glass gently, but if it hurts too much let me know and I'll numb you up first. You'll need sutures anyway."

Gina nodded wordlessly. He retrieved the fragment and gently explored both cuts for more glass. She didn't flinch. There was no active bleeding at this point, but it looked as if Dr. Sheldon would be doing several sutures in both feet.

"I don't think there's any more glass, Gina, but we need x-rays to make sure." He removed his gloves. "You're going to be sore for a few days. Lauren, irrigate the wounds while I'm gone. We'll get a urine after I sew her up, and I'll finish examining her later." He walked to the door and opened it. "I'll tell Becky to order us a soft tissue x-ray, bilateral feet, and the appropriate blood work."

Dr. Sheldon was gone for several seconds before Gina gave a heavy sigh and her legs and feet lost some of their tension. "Lauren, I think I'm losing my mind."

Archer was talking quietly with Cecile Piedmont and her son Calvin when Dr. Sheldon returned to the exam room, smiled at Cecile, and stepped over to check her vital signs.

"I notice the family hasn't descended on you yet."

"Only for lack of time," Cecile grumbled. "Most of them live out of state, but Calvin and Archer assure me they're on their way." Her expression cleared, and she leaned closer to Dr. Sheldon and lowered her voice. "We couldn't help overhearing that poor woman and her little boy next door. Is everything going to be okay?"

"I sure hope so." There was a firm quality in his gentle voice. He obviously honored patient confidentiality. He made a notation on the chart and nodded with satisfaction.

"So when do I get to go home?" Cecile asked. "I'm ready *now*."

Dr. Sheldon chuckled. "Why don't you take the rest while you can get it? From what I hear, when your family arrives you'll probably cook up a meal for the whole gang."

"I need to keep active." Cecile said it without a glance at her concerned son.

"Mom, the tests haven't even come back yet," Calvin said gently. There was a special tenderness in his gaze, and Archer knew he was more worried than he allowed his mother to see.

Dr. Sheldon laid a hand on Mrs. Piedmont's shoulder. "It won't be long now, but you do remember what I said, don't you? I may want to keep you overnight, so don't get your hopes too high before we know for sure. Now, do you mind if I borrow your pastor for a few minutes? He's suddenly popular."

"That's fine," the lady assured him. "He's heard all my latest stories, anyway, and I think we're pretty much prayed out. We've even spent some prayers on my next-door neighbors." She gestured in the direction of the exam room to her left, adding softly, "The problems some poor people have . . ."

"I know. Thanks, Mrs. Piedmont. I'll be back in a few minutes." Dr. Sheldon motioned for Archer to follow him. "I've got another job for you, *Doctor* Pierce."

Archer stood up from his bedside seat and shushed Grant with exaggerated movements. "Please, not too loud, Dr. Sheldon, I could be mobbed. I didn't realize what popular people you ER docs are on Friday nights."

Grant chuckled and led the way out into the hall. "Okay, but I wish you'd call me Grant. And don't try to fool me. According to Lauren, you can tame a room full of crazy teenagers. Since I have two of those myself, I have no doubt you can handle an ER full of patients."

Archer easily kept pace with Grant's long-legged stride. "You have twins, according to Cecile."

"Yes, a girl and a boy, Brooke and Beau. And they are about as opposite as twins can be." There were faint lines around Grant's eyes and mouth. They were lines of kindness, which spoke of sleepless nights, long hours of work, and lots of smiles and laughter. Archer guessed him to be somewhere near forty.

"I've made a lot of trips to the hospital with church members over the years, but somehow being a hospital chaplain seems different to me," Archer said.

"Why?" Grant stopped to pick up another chart at the circular central desk.

"I guess you could say the members of my church speak my language. They expect me to pray. They expect me to quote Scripture and give comfort by reminding them of God's provision and love."

"I'd be disappointed if you didn't do that. Wouldn't most people expect the same from you? It's why you're here."

"As long as I don't proselytize, right?"

"Something like that. Give yourself time to get accustomed to the pace. It can be crazy sometimes."

"I've noticed. So fill me in, Grant," Archer said. "What's this next case about?"

Grant checked the chart and turned to lead the way across the room, keeping his voice low. "In exam room eight we have a fifteen-year old, Evan Webster, who suffered an overdose of speed. He claims this is his first offense."

Archer caught the doubt in Grant's voice. "You think he's lying?"

Grant shrugged as he slowed his steps. "I'm from St. Louis. I've seen too many schoolchildren with track marks on their arms and too many virgins with child." He gave Archer a rueful grimace. "Sorry. Just call me Dr. Cynic. Anyway, the boy's father has asked for family counseling, and that's a good sign. I think the shock hit him pretty hard—which is another good sign. It means he probably hasn't had this kind of experience before."

"Meaning it's possible the boy is telling the truth?"

"Could be. To complicate things, the father and mother are divorced, and the mother has custody, so she's been contacted and is on her way in. The police will be here soon to question Evan. You'll probably be just about in the epicenter when everyone arrives. Lauren tells me you teach a class on drug awareness."

"Yes."

"Good. I want my kids to attend."

Archer nodded absently, wondering about his next case. Ordinarily, before a counseling session like this, he would spend a lot of time in prayer. This time he wouldn't get a chance. Even so, he couldn't clear his mind of the young woman with the two little boys. Gina. That was her name. And Levi and Cody. No husband or father?

"What can you tell me about Gina Drake?" he asked.

Grant looked at him. "You know her?"

"Hey, this is Dogwood Springs, my hometown. I know everybody within a fifty-mile radius—at least it seems that way when I try to keep a secret. Why, I've known Lauren since we met at church camp as kids. Her younger brother is my age."

"But how do you know Gina? She's new in town, and—"

"I don't," Archer admitted. "I was eavesdropping. No way could I miss what was going on in that room, even if I'd tried, which I didn't. Mrs. Piedmont is right, these exam room walls are pretty thin, and I learned years ago that eavesdropping was a good way to stay ahead of the game and know what to pray for next. Would you at least ask Gina if I can pray with her? It sounds like she'll need some friends."

Grant slowed to a stop with a smile and a thoughtful shake of his head. "I'll ask. Have I said thanks for coming in tonight? I think the volunteer chaplain program is going to help the staff as much as it helps the patients, especially if all the chaplains show as much concern as you do."

Archer hadn't received a genuine compliment like that in weeks. "Thank you. This place sounds more like a hospital for wounded souls than wounded bodies."

"The two seem to go together." Grant gestured toward an exam room. "Norville Webster and his son, Evan, are in there."

Archer took a sustaining breath as he raised a silent prayer to heaven. "Let me at 'em."

Lauren pressed some tissues into Gina's hand. "As soon as I get your feet cleaned, I'll put some temporary bandages on them and wheel you over to get your x-rays. On the way, we can check on your children."

"Thank you." Gina's voice was muffled against the pillow. She sniffed and mopped her face with the tissues. "I'm sorry about this. I'm not usually such a baby."

"You're not acting like a baby—you're acting like a worried mother with two children and a medical condition she doesn't understand. I wish I knew what to tell you. I don't think I'd be as brave under the circumstances." Lauren quickly revised her words. "Not that the circumstances are hopeless, Gina. My impression is that Dr. Sheldon is knowledgeable and thorough, and if anyone can figure out what's going on, he can." Lauren bit off her babbling as she finished cleaning the wounds and placed Telfa dressings over them.

She wrapped both of Gina's feet with gauze. "You can turn over and sit up."

When Gina did as she was told, Lauren saw that the mascara had spread even farther across her face. Time to try to lighten the mood, if possible. "Honey, you look like you've got a couple of shiners." She pulled her gloves off and reached for a paper towel. "Hold still for a minute." She dampened the towel and went to work on the makeup mess.

"Levi and Cody will think their mother suddenly turned into a raccoon." She grinned to assure Gina she was teasing.

Gina closed her eyes and held still while Lauren dabbed around her eyes. "Thank you."

"For what? You'd tell me if my makeup was smeared, wouldn't you?"

The copper-colored eyes opened again. "Thank you for taking such good care of Levi. He doesn't usually trust strangers so quickly."

"You're welcome, Gina. He's precious. I'd love five just like him, but I need a husband first."

Gina grimaced and looked away. "Why? You can't depend on them. I tried."

"I can't imagine a daddy not wanting to stay around to watch those two angels grow up."

"Their father barely waited until Cody was born before he took off with somebody who didn't have any kids to tie her down." Gina's voice was layered with pain.

Lauren placed a hand on Gina's shoulder. *Oh, Lord, touch her heart. Teach her that real love doesn't fail.* Aloud, she said, "Then he's the one who will lose the most. Your children have a mother who obviously loves them very much."

"I left them alone tonight." Gina's voice wobbled and her chin dimpled in an obvious effort to control another onset of tears. "I can't believe I did that. I made a vow years ago that I would never allow my own children to feel the way—" She stopped and bit her lip, then straightened her shoulders and sniffed. "I'm sorry. This isn't your problem. I'll figure it all out later. Do I still look like a raccoon?"

Lauren wiped the last smudge, then stepped back to admire her handiwork. "Aha! Now I recognize you. You're Gina Drake from Respiratory, the one who's so good with children. No wonder your own kids are so sweet."

Something warmed in Gina's eyes, and Lauren thought she caught a hint of a smile before the worry took root once more.

"Levi was so brave while we treated him, Gina."

"Do you think he'll be okay to come home tonight?"

"We'll be sure and ask Dr. Sheldon when he comes back in." Lauren continued to chatter about how cute both little boys were and how the neighbor had told the staff how obedient the children usually were. She allowed her chatterbox mode to continue instead of stifling it midstream.

At first Gina watched Lauren's face closely, as if she were trying to detect any false note. But soon her expression relaxed. Lauren realized she was probably seeing a side of Gina Drake that few of her coworkers ever saw. Ordinarily, the respiratory therapist was calm and kind, but strictly professional. She kept to herself. She never showed any vulnerability. Some of the less inhibited male members of the hospital staff claimed that Gina was a snob because she turned down all invitations to lunch, dinner, breaks, or breakfast. Lauren always quickly informed them that was simply because Gina had good taste.

"Lauren," Gina said at last, interrupting the quick-paced monologue.

She held Lauren's gaze with her own and worried her full lower lip with her front teeth.

"Yes?" Lauren sat down on the stool so they were eye to eye.

Gina's mouth worked silently for several seconds. Her face flushed, and her eyes watered again. "I'm scared."

"Of course you are, honey. Who wouldn't be?"

"I don't know what's happening to me."

"That's what we're going to try to find out." Lauren leaned closer. "Meanwhile, I want you to know that you do have a friend in town. I haven't been in Dogwood Springs very long, either, and I know how lonely it can get."

"Where are you from?"

"A beautiful place called Knolls. It's about an hour's drive east of here, and sometimes I think I must have been crazy to move. Do you ever feel that way?"

An invisible strain of tension seemed to fill the room. "No. Never. At least not until this happened."

"Good. I'll give you my home phone number before you leave tonight, and you can call me any time."

"*Am* I going to be allowed to leave?" Gina asked. "With my children?"

"We're going to do everything in our power to see that you do. In the meantime, it won't do you or your children any good to worry about it."

Gina studied Lauren's eyes for several seconds, then some of her tension dissipated, as if she had run out of energy to continue.

"How about lunch Monday?" Lauren asked.

There was a flash of surprise and then a nod that seemed to open the gates to a flood of gratitude. Lauren had never before noticed what an expressive face Gina had.

"Can I go see my boys now?" she asked.

"Of course; then we'll get your x-rays. Let me get you back into the wheelchair."

CHAPTER 6

A rcher said a short but intense prayer as he stepped into exam room eight to face Evan Webster. The fifteen-year-old sat upright in the bed, and his longish brown hair tangled into brown eyes that darted back and forth, nervous and suspicious. His pale features were pinched close together on his face, as if the head of a child of ten had been superimposed onto a teenager's body—a skinny teenager.

A middle-aged, balding man with hands rubbing together fretfully occupied a chair against the wall. He stood as Archer crossed the room.

"Are you the minister?"

"Yes, hello, I'm Archer Pierce. I'm the volunteer chaplain tonight."

The man took Archer's hand with both of his own in a firm grip, as if Archer had suddenly announced he was their sure salvation. "Norville Webster. Thank you for coming to see us, Reverend Pierce."

"Please call me Archer."

"Thank you, Archer." A heavy frown fell back over Norville's patrician features as he returned his attention to the teenager in the bed. "Meet Evan, my son." He spoke the words as if he were introducing himself as an alcoholic at an AA meeting.

A reflection of pain crossed the teenager's face but disappeared into a fresh composite of studied indifference.

"Hello, Evan," Archer said gently. "I understand you've had a rough night."

The boy nodded. "It's going to get worse when my mom sees you here."

"She doesn't like chaplains?"

"She hates preachers." There was no animosity behind the words, just a statement of fact.

"Evan, don't be rude," Norville warned.

"I'm not. She's going to freak when—"

"That's enough." Norville turned to Archer. "Sorry. I tried to raise my son with more manners, but lately it seems like he's following in his *mother's* footsteps."

Archer winced inwardly when he saw another glimpse of surprise and raw pain in Evan's face. So there was open animosity between the estranged parents, and they used their son as a weapon.

"Why don't we have a seat, Norville?" Archer took the backless swivel stool that had been pushed beneath a small built-in desk and counter area.

Norville sank into his chair and rested his elbows on his legs. "Somewhere I've failed my son. He never listens to me anymore. He hardly ever talks to me when he stays with me." He looked over at his son as if he expected Evan to contradict that statement.

There was no response. It was as if Evan had mentally retreated from the room.

"Lucy and I are divorced," Norville continued. "She has custody, except for those rare occasions when she can't find an excuse to keep him from coming to my place on visitation weekends." The bitterness was evident in his voice as well as his words. "If he weren't so unhappy living with her—"

"Stop it, Dad," Evan said quietly. "If you'd stop blaming Mom for everything and—"

Norville straightened. "I'm not just blaming her, I'm—"

"Yes, you are." The teenager leaned forward. "Why don't you give it up and get on with life? I mean, it's over." His voice gentled. "She isn't coming back."

"Just because your *mother* decided it was over. What was I supposed to—"

"Hold it." Archer held his hands in a T, calling time out. "Accusations won't do us any good at this point. We need to focus on how to improve this situation for the future."

There was a tense silence for several seconds, and then Evan lay back against the pillows and trained his gaze on the rescue equipment against the wall. "Whatever."

"See what I mean?" Norville asked Archer. "It's my weekend to keep him, and no sooner does he get to my place than he gulps his dinner and darts out of the house like I'm contagious. Then he comes back later, zoned out of his brain on drugs, looking to me for answers." He slumped back into his chair. "And I don't have any."

Archer knew the statistics. He could quote them, and he often did to the youth in his church. There was only one answer to all of the pain he saw and felt in this room, and if these were members of his congregation, he would know exactly what to say. The problem was, he'd been told repeatedly not to proselytize at the hospital. He felt like a tethered mule.

Still, he needed to say something, if for no other reason than to allow them time out from their own battle of words. "The first thing to realize," he said, "is that you're not alone. Drug use among teenagers and young adults is exploding in this country. A lot of people are caught in the same trap, because education about the dangers of particular drugs has been outdistanced by the rate of drug use. Evan, you need to be aware of the dangers, and I think the experience you had tonight might have given you a taste of it."

Evan nodded.

"You and your parents are welcome to attend the class I teach on Tuesday nights. We have some pretty open discussions about drug use and abuse."

"You can forget trying to get Mom into a church for anything but a wedding or a funeral," Evan muttered.

"I'll go with you, Evan," Norville said. "Unlike your—I'll do anything it takes to keep this from happening again."

"Look, Dad, I'm not planning to do it again, okay? Like he says, we shouldn't blame each other—we should decide what to do in the future."

Archer was about to suggest prayer when the exam room door

swung open and a tall, slender woman with short brown hair and angry eyes stormed into the room.

Archer stood automatically. Norville Webster remained seated and glared at her.

The woman gave Archer a quick look of curiosity, then dismissed his presence with a shrug. She shut the door behind her.

"Mom, don't blow your top," Evan said. "The doctor says I need to stay calm and—"

"I know what the doctor says." Her voice was husky and slightly hoarse, her words clipped. "I just finished talking to him." She leveled a chilling glare at her ex-husband. "I should have known you weren't even capable of keeping a fifteen-year-old boy out of trouble for a single night. What have you done to my son?"

Norville returned glare for glare. "Oh, so he's my responsibility now that the pressure's on, Lucy? Did you know the police are coming to talk to him? I bet you'll love having a son with a criminal record."

"Dad, I'm not going to have a criminal—"

"Watch it, Luce," Norville snapped. "If I wanted to I might even take this evidence to court to get custody."

"You don't want custody. It would cramp your style to have a drug addict living in your bachelor "

"Don't try to fool yourself. I'd love custody."

"Mom, I'm not a drug addict," Evan said. "I didn't—"

"So what happened?" Evan's mother crossed her arms in front of her. Archer saw that her hands were shaking as she dug her nails a little too sharply into the flesh of her arms, as if she were using the sting of pain to keep her emotions under control.

He reached a hand toward her in concern. "Ma'am, why don't you have a seat. I can get you a more comfortable chair out in—"

"What did you take?" she demanded, ignoring Archer and stepping to her son's bedside.

Evan rolled his eyes. "A couple of pills, okay? I thought they were probably Valium or something."

"The doctor said you tested positive for methamphetamine."

Evan shrugged. "I didn't know that when I took them."

"Why did you take them if you didn't even know what they were?"

Evan's jaw muscles clenched and unclenched as he stared hard at the wall. "I just wanted to get away from everything for a while."

"Away from *what*? You're out of school, so you don't have any stress. You don't even have a job for the summer. So what do you have to get away from?"

"It isn't easy being a rope in a tug-of-war."

"Oh, no, you're not dumping the blame on us for this little trick," she snapped. "You're the one who chose to do the drug. You're the—"

"Stop it," Norville said. "None of that's going to do any good right now."

"Oh?" Lucy pivoted toward him, and Archer saw from the play of light across her face that her eyes were filling with tears as a flush crept up her neck. "Maybe you should give it a try sometime. It's called discipline. All *you* ever do is try to undermine my authority and win some popularity contest with Evan."

"I don't try to undermine anyone's authority, I just try to give him a little attention when he's with me. That happens seldom enough these days."

"You let him get away with anything, believe every story he tells—"

"You're wrong!" Evan shouted at his mother, and the increasing rhythm of his heartbeat showed up on the monitor above the bed. "You think I'm always out trying to get into trouble. Why should you even care? If I moved in with Dad, you and your *boyfriend* could be together all the time, and I'd be out of your way. You'd love that."

Archer stepped forward. "Mr. and Mrs. Webster, Evan is still experiencing physical difficulties from the drug, and—"

"My name is not Mrs. Webster!" Lucy spun on him. "And who are you? What gives you the right to eavesdrop on a private conversation?"

"I'm sorry I didn't introduce myself sooner. My name is Archer Pierce, and I'm a volunteer—"

"He's a counselor," Norville said quickly. "He's a volunteer counselor for the hospital, and I requested the visit."

"A shrink?" she demanded.

"No, ma'am, I'm acting chaplain tonight." Archer ignored the expression of distress that crossed Norville's face. He wasn't about to lie to this woman. "I know enough about Evan's case to realize he needs to calm—"

"Chaplain? You're a *minister*?" She said the word with contempt.

"That's right. I'm a pastor here in Dogwood Springs." Archer kept his voice gentle but firm, and he watched the monitor with growing concern.

"My son doesn't need a preacher," Lucy said.

"It isn't my wish to interfere, ma'am, I'm just here for moral support and—"

"How old are you?" she asked.

"Thirty-three."

"Do you have any children?"

"No, I don't." This conversation was going downhill, but at least he was taking some of the heat away from Evan. "I've had a lot of experience with the youth of—"

"Are you even *married*?" Lucy placed her hands on her hips, animosity flashing in her eyes.

"No, ma'am, I'm not."

"Then what makes you think you can come in here and try to tell me and my son how to live our lives?"

"I wouldn't dream of doing that, and I don't claim to be an expert. I'm just here to offer support during a trying time, and for Evan this is becoming increasingly difficult. We need to remain calm and let him rest for—"

Lucy spun on Norville. "Trust you to drag someone like him into the middle of this mess!"

Evan raised his hands to his ears. "Stop it."

Norville stepped between her and the bed. "Trust you to start trouble the minute you arrive. No wonder Evan's so confused."

"Stop it!" Evan snapped.

His mother ignored him. "Oh, that's right, it's always my fault. It has to be that way, doesn't it? That's because you're not man enough—"

"Shut up!" Evan shouted even louder. "Everybody get out of here and leave me alone!" His face had reddened, and tears filled his eyes. On the monitor, his rhythm gyrated across the screen. "I can't take any more of this. Doctor! Where's the doctor? I've got to get out of here."

He reached for the IV site and grasped it as if he would pull it out.

Archer and Norville converged on him in tandem, and Norville grabbed his arm. "No, son, don't!"

"Leave me alone!" Evan tried to jerk away.

Norville held steady. "Evan! Stop. I'm sorry. Calm down and lie back, and I'll get the doctor. Please, son, it's going to be okay. I need to control my temper. I promise I'll try harder."

Evan did not look convinced. "All I ever hear is fight, fight, fight. Can't you guys ever say one nice word to each other? What if I *do* become a drug addict? What if I *do* go out and kill myself? You would love it. That would just give you more to fight about!"

"Evan, how can you say that?" Lucy cried.

Evan looked at his mother, and the lines of his face tightened into a cold mask. "Get out of this room and get out of my life."

Archer was halfway across the room to call for assistance when the door swung open and Grant stepped inside, followed by Muriel. The doctor appeared calm and unhurried, his expression serene, even friendly, with no indication that he'd heard anything out of the ordinary through the walls of the exam room.

"Folks, we've had a slight change of plans. The police are here to take Evan's statement." His deep voice remained unperturbed as he indicated Norville and Lucy. "If you would like, feel free to continue your discussion in one of our hospital's private conference rooms." He gave Archer an understanding glance and stepped back to allow Evan's parents to file out of the room.

Norville hesitated. The worry lines of his face continued a silent argument.

Lucy remained standing beside her son's bed. "I'll stay, if you don't mind."

"*I mind*," Evan said, turning his back to her and pulling his arm, at last, from his father's grasp. "I don't want either of you in here."

"If you'll forgive me," Grant said, "our ER has a one-visitor policy. I think it's best for our patient if we abide by that policy. Muriel will stay with him and make sure he's safe." His voice was sympathetic but firm, and Archer felt a wash of relief as the embittered ex-spouses relented and grudgingly filed from the exam room. He also felt a heavy sadness for this broken family as he followed the parents out the door, listening to the low-voiced sniper fire continue between them.

Archer did not attempt to rejoin the conversation. His presence had already caused enough disruption in this wounded family tonight.

"Tell them to stay out of here!" Evan laid his head back and closed his eyes.

Grant stayed long enough to calm Evan and check to make sure his vitals were stable again. As he left Muriel with the boy he reminded himself to never, never, ever do anything like that to his own children. He would rather remain single for the rest of his life than see that expression of frustrated pain and anger cross Brooke's or Beau's face. Of course, Brooke had a very expressive face, and she used it to great advantage.

Grant caught sight of Archer Pierce trudging along the hallway, hands in the pockets of his Dockers slacks, head bent—whether in deep thought, or prayer, or despondency, Grant couldn't tell. He was exactly as Lauren had described him—a friendly, thoughtful young man with an air of maturity that belied his age. Lauren had said he was thirty-three. She had said a lot of things about him. All good. But even if he *was* mature and confident, that headlong attack from Evan's mother couldn't have been comfortable.

"Thanks for stepping in to help, Archer," Grant said as he caught up with the young minister.

"You're welcome, but—"

"I trust you've had an interesting evening so far."

Archer walked with him toward the central station. "I didn't help that situation. I'm sorry."

"Nothing will help until those two adults start behaving like adults."

"Is Evan going to be okay?"

"He'll be fine for now, unless he decides he still hates his life and takes permanent steps to make his parents pay for their behavior."

"I'd never before considered how much spiritual suffering joins forces with physical suffering to attack a patient when he's down."

Grant nodded. "That is exactly why it was such a good idea for you to be here. Do you plan to talk to the Websters again?"

"I'll find Norville later and let him know I'm available if he needs to talk."

"Good. Are you ready to tackle another case?" Grant asked.

Archer looked at him hopefully. "Gina Drake?"

Grant couldn't prevent a wry smile. The man was either very brave or an incredible glutton for punishment. Or maybe he was doing exactly what God had called him to. . . . Did people actually do that anymore? "Lauren convinced her to talk to you."

"She did?"

"Lauren seems to think all you have to do is snap your fingers to make all the evil and pain in the world disappear. Wish I had that talent."

Archer chuckled. It was a relaxing sound. "We're talking about Lauren McCaffrey? The Lauren who beats me in basketball and volleyball, and earlier this spring had to cut a fishhook out of my arm in the middle of a fishing tournament?"

Grant leaned closer and lowered his voice. "The one who thinks you could almost walk on water." He stopped and cleared his throat. Grant had learned quickly that Lauren was a talker and that she often revealed more about herself than she realized. Archer probably had no idea she had a crush on him. Grant had heard other staff members talking about it, though, so Archer was probably the only one who hadn't caught the undercurrent.

"She knows better," Archer said with a fond smile. "She saw me nearly drown at church camp twenty years ago. She and her brothers dragged me out and pumped the lake out of my lungs."

"Oh, really?" Grant was intrigued. "You've known Lauren for twenty years?"

"Actually, for twenty-five. Church camp, rival schools, that kind of thing. Lauren and her brothers and sisters were deacon's kids in a sister church in Knolls, so since my dad was our church pastor, we were thrown together a lot through the years. I was good friends with her younger brothers, and she tolerated me back when I had a huge crush on her."

Grant grinned and shook his head. Small towns. "Anyway," he said, "I can't tell you how much it means for you to be here. I'm sure you're acquainted with the old adage 'They don't care how much you know until they know how much you care.' These people need to know they count with someone, and sometimes we docs get so busy we can't afford to take the time to give them as much reassurance as they need. That's where you come in. Think of it as an interactive sermon."

"Interactive, huh? I like that." He bent down for a quick drink at the water fountain. "I think this really was a first offense with Evan."

"I hope," Grant said. "Forgive my cynicism."

"You don't sound like a cynic to me. You sound like a man with common sense. Have the tests come back on Mrs. Piedmont?"

"Yes, and they don't show anything significant." Grant paused. "Still, I'm concerned that she does have underlying heart pain. I've spoken with her family doc, and he says she can go home as long as she sees him Monday."

"That'll make her happy. I'd volunteer to take her, but I'd have to wrestle her children for the privilege."

"I hear she goes to your church."

"Yes. I've known her all my life. I went to school with her grandchildren, and she's attended Dogwood Springs Baptist since before my father became the pastor there. She's one of my favorite people—always helping someone, always willing to visit the sick." Archer paused and glanced at Grant. "She's good at collecting information, too. She already knows a lot about you. While I was in her room earlier, she told me about your wife's passing. I hated to hear that."

Grant winced involuntarily. It still hurt.

Archer's intense gaze flickered momentarily. "I'm sorry, I shouldn't have—"

"It's okay." Grant nodded to Lester, the tech, who was escorting a patient toward the exit. When they were out of earshot, he continued. "You'd think a man would have recovered from his wife's death after two years."

"Actually, my father always told me to give someone at least three years to grieve the death of a spouse," Archer said. "How do your kids feel about the move to Dogwood Springs?"

"My son doesn't seem to mind. My daughter, on the other hand, is still fighting it."

"It's a big change from St. Louis."

"According to Brooke, we might as well have moved to Jupiter."

"I'd like to try to help you there. We'd love to have your whole family visit our church—oops, I hope that doesn't mean I'm proselytizing." He smiled at Grant.

Grant hesitated, uncomfortable. "I'd like the kids to go."

"We have an active youth group, especially since Lauren arrived. She's great with the kids."

"I think they would like that," Grant said.

"And how about you?"

Grant didn't answer, and he was glad when Archer didn't push the matter. They walked toward the central desk, where two police officers in black uniforms leaned against the waist-high counter, exchanging casual, friendly banter with Becky. The secretary worked the computer keyboard and kept up with their conversation without missing a stroke. The men straightened when Grant and Archer approached.

"Tony, how are you?" Archer stepped forward to shake hands with the senior officer. He turned to Grant. "I graduated from high school with this guy. He was valedictorian."

"Archer Pierce, don't you ever sleep?" Tony asked.

"I do that at my desk at work," Archer joked. "Sometimes it shows in my sermons. Not that you'd notice, since you're hardly ever at services. When are you going to earn enough seniority that you don't have to work every Sunday?"

Tony grinned and shrugged. "When your sermons start sinking in and the crime rate goes down. So far, you're not making much headway. Is our patient ready for questioning?"

"Yes," Grant said, "but be gentle with him. He's already suffered enough."

The two officers nodded and sauntered toward exam room eight. They had obviously been here before and knew the layout.

"I do want to talk with Gina," Archer said. "When can I see her?"

"Don't get your hopes up," Grant warned. "She may not say much, but I think she's particularly afraid of our social worker. I'm not sure what's going on in her mind about this, but whatever it is, she isn't willing to discuss it at this point." He stepped over to the chart rack and pulled out a clipboard. "Rose Pascal went in to speak with her once already and didn't get a very good response. Unfortunately, you're not going to have time to prepare or talk to her before you're thrown into the fray."

"What fray?"

"There's an IIS therapist driving down from Branson. They want to have a wraparound meeting tonight, if—"

"Uh, wait, you've lost me. Apparently my daddy didn't teach me *everything* I needed to know about pastoring. What is an IIS therapist, and what is a wraparound meeting?"

At that moment the door opened to exam room four, and Lauren stepped out and saw Grant and Archer. "Good, you're both free. I've got Gina's feet bandaged, and I'm ready to put her in the wheelchair for a trip to the conference room. Rose Pascal and Natalie Frasier are already in there with Agnes Walker, Gina's next-door neighbor. We have an aide watching the children for us during the meeting. Can you come now?"

"We'll be right in," Grant told her.

She stepped back into the room and closed the door.

"Wraparound meeting?" Archer asked.

"It's a term they use with the Division of Family Services," Grant reached for a pad of paper and pulled an ink pen out of the pocket of his lab coat. "Typically, when a family is in crisis, the social workers assigned to their case like to have a meeting with everyone connected to that family so they can brainstorm the best ways to provide emotional support when help is needed."

"That sounds like a good idea."

"In Gina's case, she claims she doesn't have family except for her children. She's fairly new in town, so she hasn't had time to make friends. And except for the employment physical she had before she came to work here, I'm the only physician who's seen her since she arrived. Lauren has chosen to take an active role. Thanks for your offer to help."

"You're welcome. What is an IIS therapist?"

"IIS stands for Intensive In-Home Service, and the therapist does exactly what her title suggests. She's an employee of the state who goes into the home of the family in crisis to research ways to improve the family relationship. She does exhaustive counseling to help the family learn to cope with their crisis so that they have a better chance of staying together."

Gina's exam room door opened once more, and Lauren guided her out in a wheelchair. Gina's copper-colored eyes were wide with fear, and her hands gripped the arms of the wheelchair so tightly that the veins stood out in stark relief against the whiteness of her skin.

"We're ready," Lauren said. "Are you guys coming?"

"We're right behind you," Grant said.

CHAPTER 7

Lauren was wheeling Gina into the small conference room when nausea suddenly struck again, this time with stomach cramps. As she emitted a soft moan she squeezed the handles of the wheelchair and gritted her teeth to keep from doubling over.

Gina turned to look up at her. "Are you okay?"

At the moment, all Lauren could do was nod, taking a deep breath in through her nose, out through her mouth, using the old trick she often suggested to patients in the emergency room

She couldn't get sick now, had to get through this meeting. Gina needed her support.

Dr. Sheldon stepped up behind her and touched her elbow. "Is something wrong?"

Lauren shook her head, took another practiced breath, and felt a flash of perspiration bead her face. She had to concentrate.

Archer joined them. "Lauren, are you feeling okay?"

She rolled her eyes and nodded. *Talk about your sensitive men.* "I will be." She would *not* forgive herself if she created a spectacle by rushing from the room, leaving poor Gina feeling as if she didn't have an ally. Of course, it probably wouldn't help things if she lost her dinner in the middle of the conference, either.

With a final deep breath, Lauren settled Gina at the conference table, then turned to find Dr. Sheldon pulling a chair out for her. She thanked him and sank down.

He leaned closer until she caught a faint scent of aftershave that smelled like crushed citrus leaves. "Pardon me for being blunt, but you don't look the greatest. Are you sure you'll be okay?"

"No, but I need to get through this meeting."

"Anything I can do to help?"

"Thanks, Dr. Sheldon. I'll let you know."

He nodded and took a seat on the other side of Gina, placing a folder with Gina's chart on the table in front of him.

Rose Pascal entered at her usual brisk pace, carrying an armload of cold sodas from the machine in the ER waiting room. Lauren accepted one gratefully and held it to her face for a moment, ignoring the curious glances she received. Its bracing coolness gave some relief. She popped the top and took several hesitant sips. It stayed down. She leaned back in her chair. Maybe this would just go away.

Along with Dr. Sheldon and Archer Pierce, who both sat to Gina's right side, the meeting participants consisted of Gina's neighbor, Agnes Walker; the hospital social worker, Rose Pascal; and the IIS therapist, whom Rose introduced as Natalie Frasier. The therapist was a tall young woman who was so slender she appeared to be all sharp angles. She was probably in her late twenties or early thirties, with a serious, earnest expression on her long face. Several times Lauren noticed her casting Gina curious, compassionate glances.

There was no evidence of the friendly chatter and jokes that often accompanied conferences in this room, but Lauren had been to a wrap-around meeting before, and it had also been tense.

Rose chatted quietly with Natalie, who was seated at the far end of the table with her note pad and ink pen. Gina stared at the table without acknowledging anybody.

As soon as everyone settled, Rose called the meeting to order, made introductions, and gave a brief overview of Gina's predicament. Rose had short gray-blond hair and gentle gray eyes with laugh lines radiating from them, and her voice had a decided Ozark accent—heavy on the *r*'s.

As the hospital social worker spoke, Gina's tension seemed to radiate across the room. She clasped her hands together on the table, and her fingertips whitened. Lauren stole a quick look at Gina's face and saw that her full lips were drawn into a tight line.

"Gina, I'm not gonna bite," Rose said. "We're havin' this meeting to find out how we can help your family stay together while we keep your children safe."

Gina nodded without looking up.

At Rose's request, Dr. Sheldon quoted Gina's test results. They revealed nothing helpful. Neurologically she was normal. She tested negative for drugs, and her chemical levels were comparable to the normal numbers she'd had on her employment physical.

"What about blood sugar?" Gina asked softly, still staring at her hands clasped at the table.

"Eighty," Grant replied.

There was a soft sigh, and Gina shook her head with bewilderment at the normal level. Lauren empathized. If they'd discovered a blood sugar problem, they would have something with which to work.

"I want to emphasize one thing." Dr. Sheldon closed the folder. "I observed Gina interacting with her children when she was reunited with them tonight. After she assured them she was not badly hurt, they were happy and talkative, with very trusting, loving dispositions. I'm sure you saw for yourself that both children appear well cared for and well behaved."

"They are very sweet children. I visited with them for a little bit." Rose leaned forward. "Gina, don't you remember anything about tonight's episode?"

"I already spoke with Dr. Sheldon about this." Gina's voice was unemotional, as if she was keeping herself under tight control. She still did not look up. "I worked overtime today, and Levi and Cody ate a late-afternoon snack at child care, so they didn't want dinner when we got home. I was tired, and I lay down on the sofa in the living room. That is the last clear recollection I have until when I realized I was sitting on the merry-go-round at Levi's elementary school, several blocks from our house." Her voice wavered.

"It's okay, Gina," Rose said softly. "Take your time."

"My feet were already injured at that time, and I have no recollection of hurting them. All I have is a vague memory of fear as I . . . searched for my children."

"Panic attack, perhaps?" Rose suggested. "I know you're still kind of new here, and perhaps your concern for your children's well-being—"

"I've moved before and never experienced panic attacks." There was a note of defensiveness in Gina's voice.

"But I got the impression from Dr. Sheldon and your boys that this kind of thing's happened before," Rose said.

Gina met her gaze, then looked at Dr. Sheldon. She swallowed hard and nodded.

"Do you remember ever having any kind of warning signs when this happened before?" Dr. Sheldon asked.

"Not that I can recall."

Rose picked up her pen and jotted something in her notes, then laid her pen down again. "Gina, how do you feel about an overnight guest?"

Gina looked up again, obviously startled. "Overnight? You mean—"

"I mean that in order to keep the same thing from happening again, we will need to either request that the court have Levi and Cody temporarily removed from the home on an emergency basis—"

Gina gasped and grabbed the table edge as she came part way out of her chair. "No! You can't—"

"Let me finish." This time there was a hint of steel in Rose's voice as she raised a hand to silence Gina. "Another option is for Natalie to stay with you and your children until we can set up somethin' else." She gestured to the IIS therapist, who had observed the interaction in silence from her end of the table.

The young woman watched Gina with an expression of gentle concern. "I'd be glad to stay with you tonight to make sure the children will be okay if you have another episode." She had a deep voice, husky but soft.

Lauren was watching Gina closely, waiting for her reaction, when the stomach cramps started again. She picked up her soda and took another sip, trying once more to will the nausea away.

"This would also give you some time for your feet to heal," Rose continued. "Ordinarily, we'd try to bring another adult family member into the picture, but you don't have family, right?"

"None." Gina's reply came a little too quickly.

Lauren's nausea grew worse. Her mouth started to water. She

pressed the can against her temples and neck, taking several quick breaths. *Not now.*

"Later we'll try to set up an emergency plan with Mrs. Walker." Natalie gestured to Gina's next-door neighbor, Agnes Walker, who had brought the children in tonight. "She's willing to be on call in case you or the children need her. We will set up appointments with your physician for a complete physical work-up, and we will also require you to have a psychological screening exam."

"A psychological exam? You want me to go to a psychiatrist?"

None of Lauren's attempts to stave off the nausea worked this time. The cramps grew worse, and her stomach heaved. Gina had just turned to her, eyes filling with tears, with one hand reaching out to her, when Lauren had to push back from the table. She covered her mouth with her hand and ran from the room.

"Is Lauren going to be okay?" Rose asked.

"I'll check on her in a minute," Grant assured her. "We've already treated three patients with flu symptoms tonight. That could be the problem." He turned his attention to their patient, whose facade of control had slipped away, leaving her teary-eyed and shaky, especially after Lauren's abrupt departure. "Gina, you need to understand that we are only trying to do what's best for you and your children. Rose and Natalie are attempting to create a support network for you so that—"

"I know what they're *attempting* to do," Gina said. Her voice wobbled, and she swallowed hard and took a breath. Before she spoke she gave Rose a less than friendly look across the table. "What I don't understand is how they could even consider taking my children away from me and sticking them with some stranger. Does she think that won't traumatize—"

"But I told you," Rose interrupted, "we're doing all we can to keep that from hap—"

"So you were just trying to threaten me with the loss of my children so you could force me to do whatever you wanted me to?" Gina's eyes narrowed, and she caught and held Rose's gaze.

Rose matched her stare for a moment, but then her shoulders slumped and she shook her head. "Do you have any other suggestions?"

Gina bit her lower lip and looked back down at the table. "No. I just don't like the idea of some stranger coming into my house and telling me how to take care of my children."

"I understand that," Rose said. "I'm a single mother myself. Would it help you to know that four people have already volunteered to be on call over the next few weeks in case you run into a crisis?"

Gina's lips parted in surprise. She looked around at the others in the room.

"We will arrange a schedule so that there will always be someone available," Natalie said. "Dr. Sheldon has given us his numbers for both office and home, and the same with Archer Pierce." She gestured toward Agnes Walker. "Your neighbor will step in whenever you need her, and Lauren McCaffrey was the first one tonight to ask if she could be a part of the team. I will be available for you twenty-four/seven, and I'll be spending a lot of time with you in these next few weeks. You have some friends who want to be there for you, Gina. You're not nearly as alone as you think you are."

Slowly, Gina met Rose's gaze again, and then she looked at Natalie. She blinked back tears, and her chin trembled. "Okay," she said quietly. "Tell me what I need to do."

———

The ER was peaceful at last, and Grant completed his last chart, placed it on top of the stack, and walked down the short, broad hallway to the exam room where Lauren rested. At her insistence, he had left the door ajar earlier so she could hear what was going on in case they got busy.

He knocked, then at her soft reply he pushed the door open and stuck his head inside. "How are you feeling?"

She started to sit up. "Better. The Compazine shot worked wonders. Do you need—"

"No, stay put. Muriel has everything under control."

She lay back in obvious relief. "Thanks. Whatever this stuff is, it's nasty. I don't understand—I had my annual flu shot."

"Those don't always catch everything, you know." He walked to the sink, dampened some paper towels, then folded them and placed them on her pale forehead.

Her clear green eyes closed, and her face relaxed with obvious relief. "Thanks, Dr. Sheldon. You'd make a good nurse. Has Gina left yet?"

"Yes. Natalie took her and Levi and Cody home about thirty minutes ago. Gina said to tell you thanks."

Lauren gave him a sleepy grimace. "I abandoned her."

"She understood. She was concerned about you." He watched as Lauren's eyes closed once more. "Mrs. Piedmont went home, too," he said softly.

Lauren's face relaxed further, and her lips parted as her breathing deepened. Good. The Compazine had helped her to sleep. Maybe she would feel better when she woke up.

Grant didn't leave immediately, but stood watching her in silence for a moment. With her blond hair loose and splayed out across the pillow and her face relaxed, she could almost pass for a teenager. But she had the heart of a seasoned nurse. He had known last night, the first time he worked with her, that they would make a good team.

It had surprised him how many times she anticipated his orders before he voiced them and how quickly she met the needs of the patients. She did not grow cranky or irritable even when the volume picked up, and he actually appreciated the fact that she seemed to have the gift of gab, especially since she always seemed to say the right thing to put the patients at ease.

He shut the door behind him as he left to check on Evan Webster. Thankfully, Lauren had convinced the teenager's parents to take their argument to a private conference room. Evan probably wished they'd disappear for good. Poor kid.

Grant slipped into exam room eight, managing not to wake its occupant. The monitor continued to beep, its reassuring screen showing a sinus rhythm. The fifteen-year-old lay sleeping peacefully, wisps of brown hair falling across his forehead in damp tendrils, eyelashes fanning above his cheeks. All the lines of fear and tension and pain had dissolved with slumber, allowing the appearance of childhood innocence to return.

There had been so many times when Grant wanted desperately to lift the cares of the world from the shoulders of these young ones. He wanted to bar the doors and protect them from the anger and bitterness of mismanaged parenting and divorce and the seduction of the dark side of life. But what made him think he could help? Without Annette's loving, God-trusting guidance, he didn't even know what to do for Brooke and Beau, how to help them heal.

He did know that the hostility between Evan's parents could push their child ever closer to drug addiction or alcoholism or some other monster that lurked just below the surface of human awareness, waiting for the gullible and needy to search for comfort—for a place to belong—and wander into the wrong places.

In times like this Grant wished he were still a praying man. But God probably didn't even know he existed—or at least He must be trying hard to forget. Grant couldn't blame Him. Men like Archer Pierce would have to carry the prayer load now.

A slight sound from the bed drew Grant's gaze back to Evan's face. The boy's eyes were open and blinking sleepily. He yawned, stretched his arms, and caught sight of Grant.

"I'm sorry," Grant said. "I didn't mean to wake you."

Evan looked around the room cautiously. When he saw no one had accompanied Grant, his relief was obvious. "So, you going to spring me now? Is it time to go?"

Grant stepped over to the bed. "Not yet. Just relax and rest. All your vitals look good, but I don't want to take any chances with you."

The young man looked away.

"I hope you told them where you got the speed."

"I told them." Evan's face distorted downward with lines of tension. "Peregrine. I think it's some stupid street name. He's this guy who cruises the streets with high schoolers on Friday and Saturday nights. I think he's a pusher."

"He's a friend of yours?"

Evan shook his head. "No way."

"I thought you said your friend gave you the pills."

"Peregrine gave them to my friend in the first place. Passed them out free."

"Did you give the police your friend's name?"

"Yes." Evan sighed. "Now my friends won't have anything to do with me. They hardly put up with me as it is."

"Why is that?"

"I'm younger than they are. The school started this accelerated program a few years ago, and I guess I'm pretty good with words and numbers. I'm a grade ahead of all my old classmates." He shrugged. "It gets lonely sometimes. A guy's got to have somebody to hang out with."

Grant's well of compassion suddenly overflowed.

"My parents think I'm a drug addict."

"They aren't thinking logically right now."

"They hate each other."

"Maybe so," Grant said, "but you're not the object of their hatred."

"Tell *them* that."

"I think they know it. But they're going through so much emotional turmoil right now, they can't see how they're hurting you."

Evan closed his eyes, and his lids fluttered as if he was holding back tears. "What am I supposed to do about it? I'm not even old enough to drive, so it isn't like I can get out of the house. When I'm at Mom's, all she can do is whine about my stingy, uptight dad. When I'm at Dad's, he's always pumping me for information about the guy Mom's dating."

"Overdosing on drugs is not a good way to get back at them," Grant said.

Evan opened his eyes to give Grant a resentful glance. "I didn't know those pills were—"

"It doesn't matter, Evan. The problem is, you swallowed them without even knowing *what* they were. You're going to have to learn how to be responsible for your own actions. If you don't, you'll be the one to pay for it, like you did tonight."

Evan sighed. "Haven't I been lectured enough already?"

"I don't know. Has it helped?"

"I already told you I'm not going to do it again."

"But I want to make sure. You say that now to me, and to your parents, but will you change your mind when the adults aren't around? That was what I did."

Evan's gaze focused. "*You?*"

"Illegal drugs existed when I was in high school, too," Grant said dryly.

Evan frowned, as if he was having trouble with the concept, as if he was just now seeing Grant as an ordinary human being with a past. "What happened?" He rose up on his elbows. "Did you get hooked?"

"Yes, I did."

Evan's eyes widened, and he sat up. "Really?"

"Really. It was a hard fight to break the hold drugs had on me. I wouldn't want you to go through that." While Evan was sitting up, Grant checked his vitals, listened to his heart and breathing. He was satisfied with the boy's progress. Another couple of hours and he could go home—wherever that might be tonight. Poor guy. Grant knew how it felt.

When Grant walked out of the room, he was surprised to find Archer waiting for him outside the door, arms crossed over his broad chest, leaning against the wall. They nodded to each other, and Archer pushed away from the wall and fell into step beside Grant. The only sounds they heard were the muffled beeps of Evan's monitor and the click of computer keys down the hallway at the central desk—and Archer's squeaky rubber-soled shoes. It was suddenly surprisingly peaceful for a Friday night.

"I heard what you told Evan," Archer said.

When Grant looked at him in surprise, he explained. "I was just going in to check on Evan myself when I heard you tell him you'd done illegal drugs. That took a lot of guts. You accomplished more in there talking to that kid for a few minutes than I did with the whole family earlier. I'm sorry I didn't do better than I did."

Grant slowed his steps. "Were your parents divorced?"

Archer blinked. "My parents? No. I can't imagine anyone with a happier marriage."

Grant lowered his voice. "Were you ever addicted to drugs?"

"No."

"Then that's why you couldn't relate. Being a drug addict and the product of a broken home isn't anything to be proud of."

"Not until you bare your underbelly and risk your reputation just to help a hurting kid," Archer said. "You care. That changes everything."

Grant shook his head, haunted by old frustrations, still thinking about Evan. "Nothing ever really changes. Kids still allow themselves to be tricked into believing the lie about drugs. But sadly, it isn't only kids, and it isn't only drugs."

"But then God keeps sending people like you, who open their hearts to all those people who've allowed themselves to be tricked."

Grant stopped walking and turned to take a closer look at Archer Pierce, at the direct, blue-eyed gaze filled with a gleam of . . . what? Admiration? "I'm sorry, but you're wrong. God wouldn't—"

Archer raised a hand. "Don't try to tell me God doesn't use you. I saw how patient you were with Cecile Piedmont and how gentle you were with Gina Drake. I saw the way you handled the Websters, without further upsetting Evan." He shook his head. "I wish I knew how you did it. My father has always had a calming presence like that, and I want to emulate him."

Grant frowned at the younger man. Didn't he realize the influence he had? "That's how it works. Heart to heart. One person at a time. You look into their eyes, and then you look deeper. You see their . . . I don't know . . . I guess you'd call it their soul. You see their pain, and you identify. And you listen. That's the big trick." Grant shrugged and looked away. He'd shared more than he had intended. "I worked in a busy ER in St. Louis. It felt like an assembly line. They expected a doctor to listen to his patients for sixty seconds and be able to pinpoint the main symptoms. But I found over the years that I like to give them more than a minute. Listening is important for diagnosis. It took some hard lessons before I learned. You're doing what I'd hoped you would. You're listening."

A slow smile spread across Archer's face. "Ever thought about being a pastor?"

The question startled Grant. "Never. God wouldn't want—" He paused. Enough sharing for one day. "Pastoring's your job."

"I checked on Lauren. She's fast asleep," Archer said.

"I'll just let her stay here tonight. She shouldn't drive home since the drug I gave made her groggy. Why don't you take off, Archer? If we need you we can call you back in. You might as well take your rest while you can get it. There's no predicting what could happen here between now and morning."

CHAPTER 8

A rcher stepped through the front door of the beautifully decorated, but very lonely, parsonage and sat down in the first available chair. Enough light came through the window from the street to give outline to the living room without switching on a lamp, and he wanted to rest in the silence for a moment.

Jessica had decorated this room only a few weeks before she ended their engagement and left on tour with a musical group from Branson. Archer felt the impact of her joyful personality every time he entered his home, and he still missed her.

"Oh, Lord, where from here?" he whispered into the silence. It had been his heart's cry for the past month—ever since Jessica tearfully returned the engagement ring. That was the day all his plans for the future took a new twist. He was still trying to sort his life into some kind of logical order.

At thirty-three, he was young to be the pastor of such a rapidly growing church, especially as a single man. He could take no credit for it. His father had been called to the ministry of Dogwood Springs Baptist Church thirty-four years ago, before Archer was born, and this had always been home. When Dad retired last year, Archer was completing an interim position as a youth pastor in Branson and was falling in love with the most talented singer—and the most beautiful woman—in a town filled with talented musicians. It had seemed a simple choice at the time, to take the position as pastor of the church family he had known all his life and to ask Jessica to marry him and serve with him.

Now he wished he'd been more cautious before committing to either. What had made him think he could compete with the calling God had given Jessica—the calling to glorify Him with her music? How could he have expected her to settle for the life of a small-town pastor's wife when the stage beckoned for the special message she had been chosen to give?

The problem was that the breakup had not only devastated him, but it had also put him in an uncomfortable position. This church—which had always been known for its somewhat legalistic sense of order—had called him as pastor with the implicit understanding that he would soon be a married man and that his wife would serve with him. Many of them wouldn't have agreed even to that arrangement if he hadn't been one of their own.

Archer also knew that some of the older, more traditional members would have preferred someone of a more mature generation. Only a few days after his breakup with Jessica word had spread, and he'd begun to hear complaints. Or maybe he'd just begun to listen to them.

Because of the complaints, Archer was putting in more hours than ever before, trying to attend everything—committee meetings, youth events, ball games at the high school. He tried to be available for the members of his church every day of the week. If God had called him to Dogwood Springs Baptist, then God would show him how he would be used.

To the surprise of many of the older members, the church was growing. Sunday school classes were becoming overcrowded, and during the last Wednesday night business meeting a heated discussion had erupted between the old-timers and the newcomers about whether or not they should begin holding two services on Sunday mornings. If they waited much longer the decision would be taken out of their hands, because the auditorium was often so packed they had to bring in extra chairs from the classrooms.

Sadly, some of the longtime members were even complaining about the growth. Wednesday night Bible study had become so popular they'd moved the meetings from the classroom downstairs to the main auditorium, and some worried about the extra money needed to heat the auditorium comfortably for another service.

Those worriers were the same people—thankfully, few in number—who complained because the personnel committee was presently searching for a part-time youth director to take some of the load from Archer's shoulders. Until they found someone, Archer had to carry the load. But he was getting paid good money for the effort. Couldn't let those devoted people down.

He sighed as he stood from the chair and was making his way through the darkness to bed when the telephone rang. He frowned and turned on the light, then glanced at the shadowed numbers of the clock on the fireplace mantel. Tonight had been so packed with action he couldn't believe it was only eleven. It wasn't until he caught sight of the calendar on the wall beside the phone that he remembered the significance of this day. Jessica should have arrived home from her tour.

His hopes flared. He grabbed the phone. "Hello?"

"Yes, is this Reverend Archer Pierce?" It was a man.

Of course it wouldn't be Jessica. He should have known. Still, the disappointment stung. It took Archer a few seconds to recover and place the voice. "Yes. Norville? Is everything okay? Has Evan—"

"He was fine when I left the hospital." Norville blew a sigh over the telephone. "His mother decided I was a bad influence on him, and she's taking him home with her. The poor kid decided to keep the peace and do what she says, even though this is my weekend to have him." There was a pause. "I . . . I just wanted to apologize again for all that mess tonight."

Archer sat down again. "You don't have to apologize. I wish I could have been more help to you."

"Well . . . maybe you can. I told Dr. Sheldon that I would like counseling. That hasn't changed. I know Evan's mother would never take him." The sharpness of his words shot through the receiver. "But she doesn't control every single minute of his life. Not if I have anything to say about it. I have visitation rights every other weekend. . . ."

The unhappy voice continued to float through the receiver in a wave. Archer leaned back and listened. The poor guy probably just needed to talk.

"... can't see past the hood of your car...!"

"... shouldn't even have a license to drive a tractor..."

Angry words thrust through the darkness until the velocity behind them pounded Lauren from her sleep. She opened her eyes just enough to see a dimly lit room. She shook her head and sat up, and her vision cleared. Light filtered through the crack between door and jamb from a brightly illuminated hallway outside. She was still in the ER.

And still on duty! With a gasp, she swung her legs over the side of the exam bed, then paused to make sure the nausea didn't overwhelm her again.

"None of your family's ever been worth shootin'...."

"... cows and pigs are smarter than ..."

For a moment, Lauren listened more closely to the growling of two angry old farm dogs who were arguing somewhere beyond the door, but then Dr. Sheldon spoke with calm authority, and for a moment they fell silent.

Lauren flipped on the light and turned the water on in the sink. After a quick splash at her face, she grabbed a paper towel and dabbed at her mouth. If she was going to go in there and help with their treatment, she would need a mask to protect the grumpy patients from influenza germs—if it was, indeed, the flu. Though she had her doubts, Lauren grabbed a mask from the supply room next door and tied it over her face as she stepped along the hallway toward the zone of conflict.

Muriel Stark stood with her hands on her hips in a pose of formidable threat at the entrance to exam room two. Lauren suppressed a giggle. The last time she'd seen Muriel bare her teeth like that was when some drunks had stumbled into the ER one Saturday night, one with an obviously broken nose and a glare in his eyes that told everyone within striking distance that he wasn't ready to shut up and go home. Muriel had called the police and then proceeded to convince the drunk that he needed treatment. She convinced him that if he caused any more trouble in her exam room, he'd find his nose sewn to the wrong side of his face.

Muriel could be pretty convincing when she wanted to be—her bark was backed by an underbite and a substantial neck, which gave her a very slight bulldog appearance. But one look into the cozy warmth of her brown eyes had dispelled forever any doubts Lauren might have had about the woman's professional calling.

Lauren caught up with the athletic older nurse at the central station. "Hey, Muriel, what's going on in there?"

Muriel turned and looked at Lauren's mask, and her eyes narrowed. Her fists returned once more to her hips. "What are you doing up? You're sick. Get back to bed. I can handle this."

"In a minute." Lauren waved away the words. "What's happening?"

Muriel rubbed her chin and shook her head. She pointed to exam room two, keeping her voice low. "From what I can make out of it, Old Brisco was following his neighbor, Scroggs"—she pointed to exam room three—"too closely from behind. Scroggs got blinded by the headlights in his rearview mirror and missed a sharp curve out in the hills east of town. Unfortunately, since Brisco was following too close, he joined Scroggs in his plunge off a hillside."

"Hurt badly?"

"Maybe some broken ribs on Brisco, a possible broken arm on Scroggs, and he's got a lot of cuts and bruises. Obviously nothing got their vocal cords. They put two ambulances and two fire trucks out of commission for the hour it took to pull them out of the hollow. Tough old coots are too mean to get hurt too bad."

Lauren went to the sink and washed her hands. "Which one do you want me to take?"

Muriel's hands came back up to her hips, but Lauren grabbed one of the charts. "I'm feeling better, and I'm still on duty." She glanced at the chart. "I'll take Brisco." Before the older nurse could protest, Lauren strode to exam room two and stepped through the open door.

Lester, the tech, was busy picking glass out of Mr. Brisco's thinning gray hair, which was not an easy chore, because Brisco would not hold still. If he had broken ribs, nobody had told *him* about it.

"Man's a thief, to boot!" He grimaced and grabbed the right side of his chest, but he didn't stop shouting. "He's been a thief all his life. His daddy was a thief—"

Lauren stepped forward. "Hello, Mr. Bris—"

A muttered expletive reached them from the next room, then,

"*You're* the only thief in *this* county, Brisco!"

Brisco grabbed the rail on the left side of his bed and raised a gowned leg, as if preparing to climb, then he grunted and fell back. Lester grasped him by the shoulders, and Lauren rushed to his side.

"Now, Mr. Brisco, you could do further—"

"If he'd fix his fences every once in a while, instead of forcing his neighbors to put out all the time and money to keep them fixed, his harebrained bulls wouldn't keep knocking them down all the—"

"See?" came Scroggs's crackly bass from the next room. "I knew it! I knew it was you! Those sixteen new calves in your back pasture are half *mine*!"

"Gentlemen." Dr. Sheldon's voice was deeper and more authoritarian than Lauren had yet heard it. "There is a county courthouse in the next town that can handle paternity suits. Our hospital is strictly for your physical problems. We need to attend to the injuries at hand, and worry about old history when I know you're out of danger."

For the next few moments, while Dr. Sheldon directed treatment and Lauren limited her activities to noninvasive procedures due to continued fuzzy-headedness from the Compazine, the men remained silent. Lauren knew it was too good to last.

"On top of all that," Brisco muttered a few moments later, while Lauren cleaned the cuts on his face, "his pigs stink the whole countryside up."

There came a grunt from the other room. "Stink! My pigs don't stink!"

Brisco gave Lauren a satisfied nod. "It's his pigs, all right. All the neighbors are noticing it. Smells like the stockyards."

"Smells like money, you mean," came the retort. "Ever heard of that stuff? It's green. I guess you ain't got any, or you wouldn't be stealing my fertilizer at night."

Brisco's weathered face reddened in anger, and he jerked away from Lauren's hand. "I'm not stealing your fertilizer, you foul-breathed, lazy—"

"Gentlemen," Dr. Sheldon chided once more, "I don't want to have to get tough with you, but the police station is only—"

"I heard you, I heard you," Brisco grumbled, laying his head back against the pillow and allowing Lauren to complete her clean-up job.

Lauren decided she wasn't feeling that great, after all. After she completed her chore, she went back to bed.

———

" . . . has a right to choose. He's old enough to make his own decision about where he's going to live." Norville's voice wasn't filled with nearly as much anger now as it had been fifteen minutes ago. He was winding down.

"Norville, I'd be glad to speak with Evan if you feel it would help."

There was a short, airless silence, then, "Yes. I think that would be good, if he can convince his mother to ease up on her stranglehold." Another pause, this time longer, and then a sigh that sounded like relief. "I'm sorry for taking up so much of your time tonight, Archer. Maybe you're right. Maybe I need to give it some more thought before I stir up any more trouble with that . . . that *woman*."

"How about a tentative appointment time for you to bring Evan in to see me?"

"I'd better wait on that. I wouldn't be surprised if that . . . if his mother calls for a new hearing to reduce my visitation time."

"If you have a chance to speak with Evan, ask him if he wants to meet with me. Norville, I will keep you in my prayers."

The session ended, and Archer said a gentle good-night and hung up the phone. It was times like this that he wondered if it wasn't better to remain single and not risk the possible grief that came from a difficult marriage. But then he thought of his parents, and he smiled.

Good marriages were possible with the right foundation and proper nurturing. Dad had spent a lot of quality time with his family and had often included them in his ministry. Mom had been a stay-at-home mother who was the epitome of a pastor's wife. But in spite of their busy schedules, they reserved time to spend together every week, without children, without church. Their marriage had always been a priority for them.

Archer jotted a note to call Norville next week to see how he was doing. He wrote another note to call to check on Cecile Piedmont tomorrow, and also on Lauren, and on Gina Drake, and on the Spencers—especially Mrs. Spencer, who had passed out twice while her son, Jeff, was getting his leg sutured after a bike accident. Archer hadn't realized, when he volunteered for the chaplain program, how much time he would be spending on follow-up care or how many more notes he would be accumulating.

He'd discovered years ago that if he wrote everything down in an organized notebook life wouldn't be quite so hectic, and he wouldn't be so likely to forget anything or anybody. Church members hated it when he forgot to visit. Unfortunately, he'd lost that organized notebook months ago, and he'd regressed to an old sloppy habit of placing sticky notes wherever he happened to be standing or sitting at the time. Now he could never find the notes he needed—at least not when he needed them.

Periodically, he got his exercise running madly through the house grabbing up colored notes like a kid on an Easter egg hunt and then struggling to place them in proper order.

It was getting late, so Archer tore off the last handwritten square of paper and stuck it on the coffee table, then wrote one more note to remind himself to catch Lauren when she was feeling better and ask her if she would be interested in organizing a fishing trip specifically for Norville and Evan. They could also invite Grant and his twins. That should be an interesting combination.

Archer liked Grant. The man obviously had some private demons that haunted him, but he also had a solid core of human decency and compassion that became obvious very quickly. That compassionate nature extended past the patients to include staff. He'd been gentle, attentive, and reassuring with Lauren tonight when she was embarrassed about her sickness.

Archer's gaze swept over the room, and again he thought of Jessica. Why not call her? He had a good reason. She was scheduled to sing in a Fourth of July concert at the church, and it wouldn't hurt to touch base and make sure she hadn't changed her mind.

He picked up the telephone receiver again and dialed the number as he allowed his gaze to linger on the rich warmth of a floral design Jessica had painted over the threshold into the living room. He couldn't forget her excitement and passion as she planned the colors she would use in each part of the house. She'd helped him choose special pieces of furniture, joyfully planning for the future. And then one day it was over. The engagement ring had come back with many tears and sweet words of apology. She blamed herself. She wasn't ready to commit.

He had buried the ring in his top dresser drawer under some handkerchiefs his mother had given him for Christmas last year.

The answering machine picked up, and he listened helplessly to the rich tones of Jessica's voice as she instructed him to leave a message after the tone.

"Hi, Jessica, this is Archer. I guess you're not home yet. I'll call back next—"

A click and a screech interrupted Archer's message, and then, "Hello? Archer? Don't hang up, it's me." The soothing rhythm of Jessica's greeting floated over him like a tonic.

"Jessica."

She hesitated briefly, and then Archer thought he heard a soft intake of breath. "Hi." There was a smile in her voice, and he could picture her face perfectly.

He closed his eyes and savored the hesitant-hopeful greeting. "I'm sorry, I didn't realize you might already be asleep."

"I wasn't. Not quite, anyway. We got in at about three this afternoon, and I took a nap as soon as I walked in the door. How's everything going in Dogwood Springs?"

He wanted to tell her how lonely this town was without her. "Growing. I thought I'd better call and check on your schedule." His heart accused him of being a liar even as he said the words. He didn't need to hear about any schedule. "Are you still planning to give us a concert at the Independence Day celebration?"

"Of course." She gave a soft sigh. "Was that . . . all you wanted?"

He hesitated. Was that disappointment he heard?

But she said nothing more. Jessica had always been more comfortable than Archer with the tension of silence in a conversation. She'd told him one time that it was because of some Navajo ancestry in her bloodline. He'd found her ease with silence to be attractive—along with every other quality about her that made her uniquely Jessica Lane.

"I also wanted to know how you were doing," he said at last.

She sighed again with a soft, let-down groan that told of her weariness. "It was a long trip."

"Difficult tour?" He wanted to sound sympathetic. Instead, that nasty little inner voice betrayed itself, hoping she'd been homesick and never wanted to go on tour again.

"As I said, it was long. Heather loved it, though." Jessica's younger sister, Heather, sang with her. "She didn't want to come home. I guess I'm just not into touring the way I used to be. Living out of a suitcase was never my life's dream."

Yes! Archer cleared his throat. "More of a home girl than you thought?"

He sensed a change in her silence, which alerted him to the fact that she'd caught his message. When she answered, however, her voice gave nothing away. "I guess that's probably it. I could be happy in Branson the rest of my life."

How about Dogwood Springs? "Why travel out of town when you live in a music center?"

"Exactly." She sighed again, and he knew she was probably stretching out on the floor, flexing her legs, arching her back to unkink the muscles.

He closed his eyes and pictured the angular planes of her face, the hazel eyes, the shoulder-length light brown hair that never behaved.

He held his breath, and his heart took a couple of extra hard beats as he swallowed his pride. "Jessica, I've missed you." He barely contained the words that wanted to follow—*and I love you, and I haven't been able to get you out of my mind . . .*

"I know." There was a breathless, waiting quality to her voice. "I've missed you, too. Why don't we keep in touch?"

He frowned. Keep in touch? What did she mean by that? "Um, okay, you mean, like, we'll always be friends? That kind of thing?" He wasn't sure he was up to that yet.

"How could we ever have dreamed of anything else without a firm friendship first?"

First? That might not be too bad. In fact, it could be a good idea. "You mean a *firm* friendship? As in . . . a close relationship where we spend time together and share our thoughts and dreams and—"

"Archer." There was a warning in her voice. "When I say friendship, I mean friendship. Buddies, you know? Friends who can be casual with each other, who can be themselves with each other, and who don't have to pass the scrutiny of five hundred church members."

Archer felt a jolt of disappointment at the sharpness of her final words, and it took him a moment to recover.

This time she was the one to break the silence. "I'm sorry, Archer. That came out a little rough."

He thought about Norville's depression earlier and identified with it. No wonder the poor guy could barely function right now. A woman could really pack a wallop when she wanted to.

"Still working thirty-six hours a day for the church?" she asked.

Archer frowned. He was working for *God*. Big difference. "Do I hear sarcasm?"

"Hyperbole, pal. Unfortunately, it's almost true. *You* try carrying on a relationship with someone who has dedicated himself to serving a church instead of a marriage."

Definitely depression. "Ouch." Still, she hadn't said she hated him. She hadn't said she was tired of him.

"I've had a month to think about why I broke it off, and that's still pretty much what I came up with. I've missed you like crazy, and I wish so badly that we could see each other right now. But I also wish we could have a normal relationship, without a bunch of voyeurs eavesdropping on our dates and spreading rumors about us."

"You sound so bitter, Jessica."

"I know, and I'm trying to work through that, but I'm not there yet." She sighed. "I'm sorry."

"It's okay." There was still hope, wasn't there? "I like the idea of the friendship thing. I'm not sure I can be around you for hours at a time without wanting to kiss you, but, hey, I'm a preacher's kid. Well disciplined. I can do it. Probably. Okay, maybe a little kiss here and there, you know, a peck on the cheek, and if you'll hold my hand I can probably get by—"

"Archer." The laughter returned to her voice.

"Yes?"

"Good night."

"I can call you?"

"Or I'll call you."

"I'd rather have the permission to call you. That way I won't have to sit and watch the telephone, waiting for it to ring."

"It'll do you good."

"But—"

"Good night, Archer."

"Good—"

There was a soft click, and then a dial tone. Jessica had said a final good-night.

CHAPTER 9

The savory fragrance of grilled onions and hamburgers mingled with the sounds of footsteps and talk and laughter at lunchtime Monday. The comfortable familiarity blunted the edge of homesickness with which Lauren McCaffrey had struggled since moving to Dogwood Springs late in February. She stood waiting while Gina Drake paid for her own food—she should've known the independent young woman would not allow anyone to pay for her lunch—and then led the way toward a quiet corner of the dining area, where they could talk in relative privacy.

Sliding her tray onto a two-person table, Lauren gazed out the window at the hillside town of Dogwood Springs. It was a pretty community, with winding streets and lush foliage. Sometimes the citizens complained about the inconvenience of those winding streets, but they worked better than speed bumps to control traffic.

After a quiet prayer of thanks, Lauren looked across at Gina, who was already biting into an onion ring, although she had her gaze lowered, as if to respect Lauren's privacy as she prayed.

The golden-red highlights of Gina's hair glowed in the indirect sunlight from the window, and the freckles across the bridge of her nose made her look about ten years old instead of twenty-eight. Her job had brought her into the ER countless times, helping with codes or treating patients with breathing problems. There had never been a patient complaint about her, and as Lauren had mentioned the other night, she was especially good with children.

"Busy morning?" Lauren asked.

"Not bad so far. You?" Gina still didn't look up, almost as if she were still embarrassed about Friday night.

"Hectic. I think we've had about double the usual volume for a Monday. I haven't been this busy since I left Knolls. I'm amazed I could get away to meet you, but I'm glad I did."

"I haven't thanked you for helping me Friday night." Still keeping her gaze to the table, Gina took a bite of her cheeseburger.

"I wish I could have done more, and I was so sorry to run out on you like that. How did the overnighter go with Natalie?"

"She's pushy. What did you think of her when you met her Friday night?"

"I couldn't form an opinion based on the few words I heard her say, and my stomach was getting most of my attention." There were so many things Lauren wanted to ask, but where to start? Gina wasn't exactly the most talkative person. "Are your feet healing?"

Gina nodded. "I'm a fast healer, and I have a high pain tolerance. Are you over the flu?"

Lauren hesitated. She was still having bouts of nausea and weakness, but not as bad. She didn't think it was the flu, but she didn't want to talk about herself right now. "I'm better." She leaned forward. "Gina, I meant what I said the other night, about wanting to be on call if you need me. I know how it feels to be alone in a new place."

Gina took another bite of onion ring, chewed and swallowed, and sipped on her soda. Finally, she looked at Lauren. There was a hesitance in her gaze, and she looked away again quickly. "Thanks. So how do you adjust from night shift to day shift?"

"I don't ordinarily work nights, I was just covering for someone else Friday." Lauren paused. "Gina." She waited until the younger woman met her gaze, and then she grinned to take any sting from her words. "Do you always answer a question with another question?"

A slight flush colored Gina's cheeks, and then she returned Lauren's grin. "Sorry. It's an old habit."

Lauren resisted the urge to ask Gina why she felt the need to use such a defense mechanism.

"Besides, I'm hungry." Gina spread her hands out to her sides to indicate her generous curves. "I'm always hungry. Can't you tell?"

Lauren smiled again. "You're doing it again."

"Sorry."

"Natalie's pushy, huh?"

"She was nice enough," Gina admitted at last. "She helped me get the boys to bed Friday night, and she slept on the sofa because I don't have a guest bedroom. That couldn't have been comfortable as tall as she is. She fixed us breakfast and lunch Saturday morning, then made arrangements for Mrs. Walker to check on us a couple of times a day."

"That was pushy?"

"No, but then she insisted on taking us back to the ER Sunday morning for Levi's wound recheck. And she wanted to take him *herself* so I wouldn't have to walk so much. I just don't feel comfortable with all that attention. I like to take care of things myself. I guess it comes from my Irish ancestry."

Lauren couldn't miss the undertone of suspicion in Gina's voice. "She wants to help you, Gina, just like I do, and Archer, and Dr. Sheldon."

"It's been my experience those people try too hard to play God."

"Experience?"

Gina grimaced. "A lifetime ago. And none of them even *know* me. How can they help me if they don't know what I need?"

"What do you mean when you say 'those people,' Gina?"

"Family Services." She gave Lauren an obviously forced smile, as if she were trying to pass it all off as a joke. "Never trust anyone in the government."

Lauren put her hamburger down. "I don't work for the government, and I want to help."

The statement obviously caught Gina off guard, and then she recovered and smiled—this time the smile seemed genuine. "Okay, after work tonight I'll let you check my feet and change my bandages. Will that satisfy you?"

Before Lauren could answer, an overhead page blared from the speakers in the center of the dining room ceiling. She was being called back to the ER. Stat.

At the same time, Gina's beeper went off, and she checked it. "Oh-oh, sounds like something's up. They need me, too. Think it's a code?"

"Could be. Here, put all your stuff on my tray and I'll shove it into the ER break room on my way by. Maybe we'll get a chance to eat later."

"I wouldn't count on it."

Grant Sheldon stood watching the flashing lights reflect against the glass of the ambulance entrance while the EMT wrenched open the back doors of the van and reached in to pull out a stretcher. On that stretcher was eight-year-old Stacie Kimble, who had been one of Grant's flu patients Friday night. Stacie was unconscious, and according to the last report, her breathing was markedly labored. Her blood sugar was off the scale. Her temperature was normal, as it had been Friday night. Had he missed something then?

Grant had already told Vivian to call Lifeline, the airlift service out of St. John's Hospital in Springfield, and place them on standby. His first thought was, of course, diabetic ketoacidosis, but he wouldn't jump to conclusions without even seeing the patient and without being more familiar with the skill of the ambulance attendants. Learning the protocol and personnel of a new place took time.

Stacie's mother had told the paramedic that Stacie had still been sick last night, so they had allowed her to sleep in this morning. When Mrs. Kimble tried to awaken Stacie for a late breakfast, the child wouldn't wake up.

Grant looked back to make sure everything was set. He'd had Lauren paged minutes ago, so she should be back soon, and the other nurse, Emma, was already setting up for a possible intubation.

Meanwhile Grant worried. As he recalled, Stacie's brothers had also been ill with flu symptoms, but no elevated temperatures. Neither had most of the other patients with flu symptoms.

He had requested a copy of Stacie's chart from Medical Records as soon as he received the first call and would check it when it arrived.

The secretary, sixty-three-year-old Vivian, waved at him from her desk at the circular central station. "Dr. Sheldon, Archer Pierce is driving the parents in. They belong to his church.".

"Good. Thanks, Vivian." He hoped Archer was able to keep the parents calm. The less distraction the staff had from their work right now, the better Stacie's chances.

Christy and Bill, the paramedic and EMT, came rushing through the open doors with Stacie lying on the gurney with a strap over her legs and chest. Emma, the double-coverage nurse, waited in the designated exam room.

"Dr. Sheldon, respirations are dropping, and she's just starting to have apneic periods," Christy said. "I was unable to get a line in—she's really dry."

"Get her to exam room two." Grant turned and led the way, glad he had two experienced RNs on duty.

The child was on a 100 percent nonrebreather mask, and folded two-by-two-inch gauze pads were taped in place on each arm, marking the failed IV attempts. The weak sound of her breathing could barely be heard above the swish of closing doors and the squeak of rushing footsteps. She was wearing down.

Grant motioned to Vivian. "Call Lifeline and launch that chopper."

Just in time, Lauren walked through the employee entrance, followed by Gina Drake.

"Good," Grant said with relief. "Lauren, we have an unresponsive child, probably DKA. I need an IV line, normal saline, 20 cc's per kilo over thirty minutes. Five hundred cc's should do it. I'm getting ready to do an emergency intubation. Draw a stat lab, CBC, chem panel, serum ketones. Gina, I need a blood gas."

Both went to work, and he turned back and directed the EMT to put an ambu-bag on Stacie to help her breathe. Emma connected the monitor, then assisted Grant with the intubation.

Grant was standing at the head of the bed with his laryngoscope blade, with the child in position, when Gina stuck her for the blood gas. There was a soft moan, but the little girl did not attempt to pull away.

The intubation was fast and smooth, and the relief in the room was palpable when the EMT took over the breathing for her with the bag.

Grant reached for the ophthalmoscope hanging on the wall. "Bill, ventilate her at 20 bpm's." When he shined the light into the child's eyes, he noted the pupils were a little sluggish, but equal and not dilated. Further checking showed no evidence of cerebral edema. Not yet.

Grant placed his stethoscope over the patient's chest, listened, nodded. Her heart rate was starting to drop. Good. "Vitals?"

Lauren gave them to him. Blood pressure was still low. He felt for a distal pulse and checked for capillary refill over the nail bed of Stacie's fingers. It was definitely decreased at three to four seconds, but not as bad as he had feared.

The x-ray tech came into the room to take a portable chest film, and the ambulance attendants left on another call. The tech draped a lead apron over Lauren as she took over the ambu-bag to help Stacie breathe. Just as Gina walked back in with the results of the blood gas, Mr. and Mrs. Kimble entered the department with Archer. Grant stepped outside the exam room to speak with them.

Friday night Mrs. Kimble had been calm and unperturbed. Today her face and eyes were red from crying. "How is Stacie? What's happening? What's wrong with her?"

"We had to do an intubation to help her breathe better," Grant explained. "Right now they're taking an x-ray to make sure we have that tube in the right place, and we're waiting on some blood tests to come back so I can make a better diagnosis."

"You mean you don't even know what's wrong with her yet?" Mr. Kimble demanded. Grant could hear the accusation in his voice, and part of him could identify with the father's fear. It was just panic. He'd felt the same way. He'd even asked that same angry question. More would probably follow.

He gently explained what the staff had done so far, the tests they had taken. "I have a probable diagnosis, but I don't want to jump in prematurely. We've called an airlift helicopter to fly her to Springfield."

Mrs. Kimble grasped her husband's arm with both hands. "She's that bad?"

Mr. Kimble put both arms around his wife, still watching Grant. "You're going to *airlift* her?"

"Yes, I want to get her up there as quickly as possible. We don't have the kind of doctor she needs here, or the level of care," Grant explained.

"I'm waiting on a call now from a pediatric intensive care specialist associated with St. John's. Do you have a hospital preference?"

"St. John's," Mr. Kimble said. "We've always gone to St. John's. What is your probable diagnosis?"

"Diabetic coma."

"Diabetes!" Mrs. Kimble's face twisted in pain.

"She's very dehydrated," Grant continued gently, "so what we have to concentrate on now is getting her rehydrated so we can give her insulin and lower the sugar level."

Mrs. Kimble swallowed and dabbed at the tears in her eyes with her fingers. "Let me get this straight, Dr. Sheldon." Her voice wobbled with emotion. "You're telling us our daughter—whom you were supposed to treat Friday night—now has *diabetes*? And you thought it was the flu?" Again, that strong thrust of accusation in her voice and eyes.

A lab tech came walking through at that moment and handed Grant another printout. He checked it quickly. The blood sugar was 527. "What Stacie had Friday could very well have been the flu, Mrs. Kimble," he said. "We seem to have a city-wide epidemic right now, and diabetes can often be brought on by an initial infection of some kind. What we need to concentrate on at the moment is her care from here on."

The x-ray tech came out, pushing her portable machine.

"I want to see her now." Mrs. Kimble pulled from her husband's grasp and moved as if to walk past Grant.

Archer stepped forward and took her by the arm. "Kelly, not yet." His voice was suddenly filled with deep authority, and Grant could see how he must command the respect of his congregation.

"I'll get you in to see her before they fly her out," Grant said gently.

"Come on, my friends," Archer said, placing an arm around each parent. "We have some serious praying to do while we allow this capable staff to do their job."

CHAPTER 10

Does he think we're children?" Kelly stalked across the consultation room, arms crossed over her chest. "Why won't he let us at least *see* our own daughter?" She stopped and turned back, eyes widening in alarm. "Archer, you don't think he's hiding something from—"

"No." Archer kept his voice sympathetic but firm. "Dr. Sheldon will do what he says, and he will be honest with you. Trust me, I know from recent personal experience. Your daughter needs our prayers right now, you two. Do you mind if we—".

"Kelly, come here," Steve said gently. "It's okay. She's in good hands."

Kelly walked over to her husband and stepped into his open arms. "I'm so scared," she whispered.

"I know. I am, too."

Archer placed his hand on Steve's arm. "Let's have a seat and talk to God about it, shall we?"

The shaken couple took the sofa, and Archer took the chair next to them. Together they bowed their heads.

"Lord, we need you," Archer said softly. "Please meet with us here." He paused and waited for their thoughts—and his own—to quiet so they could turn their attention to their prime objective. As he waited he heard Kelly's quiet sobs. Steve sniffed hard.

"Dear Lord, you are the Great Physician," Archer continued. "We praise you for your power and your ability to heal any illness, no matter how serious it looks to us. Thank you for making medical science possible, but help us to remember that we place our total trust in you, not in human flesh. Lord, we need your peace and your comfort, and we need your healing touch on Stacie's body. You know what's happening to her; you know what she needs. Please guide Grant and Lauren and the rest of the staff as they fight in this physical world for Stacie's life and health. You are in control. Please touch them with your divine hand."

He paused as Kelly's sobs grew louder, and reached for the box of tissues beside the sofa. He placed two sheets in her hand while Steve tightened his arms around his wife.

Archer continued the prayer. "Thank you for giving us the Comforter, dear God. Please increase our faith as we depend on you."

There was a knock at the door as he said amen, and Grant Sheldon stepped inside.

"Mr. and Mrs. Kimble, the Lifeline helicopter has radioed us. It will be here in about five minutes. Would you like to come—"

Kelly exhaled a great sweep of air and sprang to her feet before her husband could help her. "Is she awake?"

"No, I'm sorry."

"How is she doing, Doctor?" Steve asked quietly. "Have you started the insulin yet?"

"No." Grant turned and escorted them out of the room ahead of Archer. "We have to treat her dehydration first, and we can't push the fluids too quickly or it will drop the blood sugar too fast, and that could run us into complications."

"What kinds of complications?" Kelly asked, the sharpness back in her voice.

Grant's answer, if anything, became more gentle. "It could cause brain swelling."

"Can't you give her some drug for that?" Kelly asked.

"Yes, we could administer mannitol if that happened, but it's less risky to prevent the swelling in the first place. We want to make sure everything in her body is as balanced as possible, so she can assimilate the fluids we're giving her. Drugs can't do everything, and the human body has an amazing capacity to correct problems if we can just allow it the time to work."

"What about the specialist you called?" Steve asked. The sharpness was returning to his voice, too.

"I haven't received a call back from him yet," Grant said. "As soon as I hear from him, I'll make the modifications he suggests."

Archer stopped in the doorway of the waiting room and let them go on without him for a moment. *Lord, please protect Stacie and her parents. And please, don't let their attitudes and words repel Grant from seeking you.*

Steve and Kelly were new to the congregation, so Archer hadn't grown up with them as he had with many of the other members. Steve worked as a sound technician in two Branson theaters, and he had moved his family here to get them away from the daily tourist traffic and congestion. At times, the Kimbles could be difficult. Some of the other parents with young children in the church had complained about Kelly's sharp, critical tongue and Steve's impatience. They both had a lot of spiritual maturing to do. But wasn't that the case with every Christian?

Archer had often heard his father explain that prickly people in the church had their function, too—they were God's tools to hone the sharp edges from all the other Christians, who also had their weak spots. Aside from their negative points, Kelly was a tireless nursery worker, and Steve often had insights during Bible study on Sunday morning that no one else had considered.

Archer walked to the doorway of the exam room where Stacie still lay unconscious. Lauren stood beside Kelly with an arm around her shoulders, talking quietly with her—probably praying—while Steve stood gazing into his daughter's face. Grant leaned over the desk, jotting notes on a chart. He looked up and caught Archer's eye with a hesitant smile.

"Can we talk for a minute?" Archer asked.

Grant nodded and followed him out of the room.

They found a quiet corner out of the way of foot traffic from patients and staff. "Are you going to drive them to Springfield?" Grant asked.

"Yes, they'll need someone with them for a while. I wish we could assure them she is going to be okay."

"I thought preachers had the innate ability to trust God in all things." Laced through Grant's steady, deep voice was the questioning tone of a seeker, and Archer knew he didn't mean to offend.

"*This* one still struggles," Archer said. "In fact, I don't know very many people who have the ability to trust completely in every situation."

Grant smiled. "It's nice to know that even you have doubts from time to time." He turned and gestured toward the room where the Kimbles waited. "I think she has a good chance. She seemed to rouse a few minutes ago, not to complete consciousness, but enough to encourage us. It didn't last long, but her neurological signs did improve. I'm glad you'll be with them, Archer. Do the Kimbles have family in the area?"

"No, all their family lives in Ohio. I'll contact some church members and see if I can find some folks to make the drive to Springfield and take turns sitting with them." Archer hesitated. "Grant, how dangerous is her condition?"

"The mortality rate in children for diabetic ketoacidosis ranges from 5 to 20 percent."

Archer felt an icy stab of fear. "What's her blood sugar level?"

"Five twenty-seven. However," Grant continued, "the prognosis does not correlate with the sugar level, but rather with the degree of acidosis, which wasn't as bad as I expected. Her blood pH was 7.18."

"I don't suppose you could put that in English, could you?"

Grant nodded. "Sorry. Let's just say her body's chemical balance isn't as dangerous as it could be."

"Good." Archer glanced again toward Stacie's exam room, where Lauren continued to hover near Kelly and Steve. "Grant, I realize the Kimbles aren't handling this thing very well, and they've been short with you. I hope—"

"They're taking it fine," Grant said.

"They're making it sound as if they feel you're to blame for Stacie's illness."

"They care about their child. In a world like ours, where there's so little love to go around, that's a good thing to see. Excuse me—I need to check on a couple more things before the flight team arrives." He walked back to the exam room and spoke to the Kimbles as the *whomp-whomp-whomp* of rotary blades grew louder and echoed through the room.

As Grant entered the room, Lauren stepped out of it and strolled toward Archer. He saw a sheen of wetness against her cheeks and realized how this must be affecting her. Stacie was in her Sunday school class, and Lauren had a soft spot for the children.

"Are you okay?" he asked.

"I'm fine." She turned to gaze back through the open door of Stacie's exam room. "I just hate to see that lively little girl having to struggle with diabetes for the rest of her life. Still, she's strong-willed, like her parents. She's already showing signs of returning to consciousness."

"That's what Grant told me. I'm driving the Kimbles to Springfield," Archer said. "If you weren't on duty I'd ask you to go with us."

She looked up at him in surprise. "You would?"

"Of course." Didn't she know the soothing influence she had on patients? "You could interpret the medicalese."

She gave him a thoughtful half smile. "Thanks for the suggestion, but I still have a lunch date with Gina. When things slow down here a little bit I'm going to see if we can slip away to the break room and resume our talk."

"You're already touching base with Gina? I thought you were sick this weekend."

"I'm better."

He grinned. This woman amazed him. "Lauren McCaffrey, you're one of the most supportive, insightful, and compassionate people I know. I wish we had fifty more just like you in our congregation."

He should have known that would make her blush. Compliments always embarrassed her. "And since you're already making friends with Gina," he added, "could you find it in your heart to go with me to visit her when things slow down a little? Say, next week, after she's had a chance to adjust and heal?"

A smile lit her green eyes. "I'd love to, Archer." She glanced toward the ambulance bay as the flight crew came in wheeling their gurney. "I need to give report. If I don't get another chance to talk to the Kimbles, would you tell them I'll be praying?"

"Of course." Archer watched her rush to meet the entering crew, then turn to walk with them, downloading verbal information to the flight nurse as she went. Stacie would be on her way up in just a few moments. Time to prepare her parents for lift-off.

———

The hamburgers and onion rings were cold by the time Lauren and Gina made it to the staff break room, but Lauren was thankful they could make it at all. Normally, the noon rush hit them hard on Mondays and didn't let up the rest of the day.

Lauren shoved the food into the microwave and reached into the fridge for soda as Gina limped to the window and stared out across the valley below them.

"Looks like your feet are beginning to hurt," Lauren said.

Gina shrugged. "I'll be fine."

Lauren sighed. It would take time to coax Gina out of her shell again. "You could have asked off for the next couple of days to give you time to heal."

Gina turned from the window and pulled a chair out to sit down. "I told you, I'm tough. I'm also too new to take any sick days, and I need the money."

The microwave beeped, and Lauren pulled out the heated, soggy food and sat across from Gina. "Your supervisor probably doesn't even know about your injuries, does she?"

Gina grabbed an onion ring and held it up with a grimace. It drooped, and some of the coating plopped off. "No, and you're not going to tell her, are you?" She didn't give Lauren time to answer, but changed the subject. "So why did you move to Dogwood Springs?"

Lauren chuckled. "One thing about you, Gina Drake, you'll never bore anybody with stories about yourself."

Gina smiled and sipped her soda, and Lauren decided not to fight it. "You want the real reason I moved or the one I gave my parents?"

"Both." Gina pulled a chair to her side of the table and put her feet up, as if settling in for a good story. Lauren couldn't keep from smiling at the childlike curiosity that suddenly filled those pretty eyes. Her expression reminded Lauren of the one on Levi's face during her story about David and Goliath.

"I'm thirty-five and have never been married. Does that tell you anything?" Lauren said.

"So? Why would you want to be?"

Lauren knew she was talking to the wrong person about marriage. "Well, I have two older sisters and two younger brothers, and all of them are happily married and have provided the doting grandparents with nine grandchildren. My mother keeps reminding me I need to start carrying my share of the load. She wants an even ten, at least. You know how parents are."

Gina's smile drifted away like a stray thought. "Not normal ones."

Lauren hid her surprise and repressed her curiosity. *Normal?* "Well, mine have a tendency to meddle."

"And *that's* why you left home?"

Lauren grimaced. *Not exactly.* "Let's just say my prospects in Knolls, Missouri, were recently reduced."

"Why? Did all the men die?"

"No, but the one man worth marrying got engaged to someone else."

"Ouch," Gina said gently.

"And not before I made a fool of myself over him." Lauren still cringed when she remembered the way she had behaved with Dr. Lukas Bower, boldly asking him to go fishing with her, making a point to sit near him in church, going out of her way to engage him in conversation and spend time with him at work. And then he'd proposed to Dr. Mercy Richmond. "So now it seems as if my family's biggest project is to get poor lonely Lauren married off."

"You're kidding, right? You don't look lonely to me."

Lauren hadn't intended to spill her personal problems out as a burden for someone else to bear, especially Gina, who had an overabundance of her own problems. "We all get lonely sometimes."

"You have four brothers and sisters, and they're all happily married?" Gina's voice took a cynical tone. "Nobody's divorced? Nobody's fighting?"

"Oh, sure they fight. My baby brother had a lot of trouble settling down, but his wife is mature enough to handle him."

"You told me the other night you'd love to have kids," Gina said.

"You bet I would. But for that I'd need a husband." Lauren leaned forward. "So, enough whining about my problems. How are things going with you? Do you have an appointment for a physical exam?"

"Tomorrow afternoon." Gina grimaced. "I just hope they find something. Maybe low blood sugar, even though it didn't show up the other night or during my employment physical." She studied Lauren's face for a moment, as if trying to decide if she was trustworthy. "Do you get many patients here in the ER with panic attacks?"

"A few. Do you think that's what you're having?"

"No." Gina shook her head. "I don't think so." She frowned and leaned back in her chair. "I don't think you lose your memory during a panic attack. Friday night I didn't know where I was, but I knew I was terrified."

"Of what?"

"All I remember is the fear. I was looking for my children, but I didn't even know who they were. According to Levi I was looking right at him. He said I ran right past him and out the door, and when he called to me I didn't seem to hear him." Gina took the time to eat another droopy onion ring and swallow several gulps of her soda. "What if we'd lost Stacie?"

Lauren was becoming accustomed to Gina's sudden subject changes. "You mean how would I have felt if she would have died?"

"Yes. I've assisted with a lot of codes, so I've seen a lot of patients die. It's always tough to take. It feels as if I've lost a battle, even though I didn't know them personally. It wasn't as if they were my own patients. But you know Stacie."

"I think being raised on a farm taught me a better understanding of death as a natural part of the life cycle," Lauren said. "I learned not to be so afraid of it. I'll never get used to it, though, especially when we lose a child. But heaven makes it easier."

"Heaven." Gina's deadpan voice gave Lauren a slight hint about her hesitance to talk about this subject.

"When a child dies, I grieve, but I know she's bound for heaven.

When a Christian dies, I know where that soul will be. That keeps me going."

Gina studied Lauren's face, as if trying to decide whether Lauren was serious. "You wouldn't feel that way if it were your own death." It was a gentle challenge.

"If I were to suddenly find out that I have some deadly disease that's going to kill me in a few months, I know I'd do the normal thing and grieve just like anyone else. I don't want to leave my family and friends behind, and I hate the thought of my parents losing a child. But I know where I'm going when I die. I don't control my life or measure my days. God does. It's a comfort to me to know I don't have to worry about it."

Gina shook her head adamantly. "Nobody's ever going to control my life again."

Lauren couldn't help admiring Gina's independent spirit, even as she felt a strong sadness for the difficulties the younger woman faced. "Somebody else already is," she replied softly.

Gina blinked, as if an invisible hand had nudged her, and then she recovered. "If you're talking about the social workers—"

"I'm not talking about humans." Lauren leaned forward. "I truly believe there's good and there's evil, and if we're not under God's control we're helpless pawns of the devil. That's the way my grandma used to put it."

Gina put her burger down. "Your grandmother, too? Everybody in your family is a Christian?"

Lauren smiled. That was one of the blessings of her life. "Yes, most of them."

Gina's expression held disbelief. "I wasn't raised that way."

Lauren tried again. "When I realized I couldn't do everything right in my life, I went to Someone who could. In a way, it's like getting a second opinion when I encounter physical problems that my doctor can't treat."

Gina looked up at her then. "You mean like this . . . stuff that's happening to me right now?"

"Yeah, the out-of-control parts of our lives. So often we try to treat our own spiritual illnesses, but we can't. When we finally realize that and give up on ourselves, we can turn to the Great Physician and ask for help, turn the case over to Him. When I did that, I realized He was just waiting to take my life and make something beautiful out of it. I got a second opinion and then left it all in His hands."

Gina shook her head and looked away again. "Nobody that perfect would want to take me on and ruin a flawless record."

"One of His favorite things to do is take broken lives and fix them, then transform them. It's a wonderful experience."

Gina finished her soda and took her feet out of the chair. "So how do you like the new ER director?" Another abrupt change of subject.

"I like him."

"Did you notice anything . . . you know . . . interesting about him?"

Lauren shrugged. "What?"

"Like he's gorgeous, and kind, and single, and good with patients, and single, and—"

Lauren laughed. "I thought you weren't interested in getting married again."

"*Me?* I never said anything about me. You're the one whose mother wants you married. You're the one who wants to have kids before it's too late. I think he looks like Antonio Banderas—you know, that actor? Except, of course, he doesn't have a Spanish accent or a ponytail."

"And?" Lauren prompted.

Gina leaned back in her chair and smiled. "He's not *my* type."

"What's your type?"

Gina shrugged. "I usually go for irresponsible guys who run as soon as the subject of commitment comes up. How about you?"

"A praying man," Lauren said. "A Christian who is sold out to God. In fact, he must be sold out enough that people who don't share his faith would call him a fanatic." Again, she thought of Lukas Bower. Some people had called him a fanatic. A few had laughed at him behind his back because he was never ashamed to pray for his patients or to witness about his faith. Lauren could only hope they'd laugh at her for the same reason.

"Must not be many of those around," Gina said.

"Why do you say that?"

"As pretty as you are, you should be married with six kids by now," Gina said.

Lauren tried to force a smile, but it probably gravitated to her face in the form of a grimace. Gina couldn't realize how those words hurt or how insignificant they made her feel. A radical Christian would be able to look past the outside package to the spirit inside. So maybe that meant she was lacking in spiritual depth. She'd come to wonder that in the past few years, especially with the repeated questions from Mom and co-workers and well-meaning church members. She'd tried to tell herself that she was just selective, that the right person hadn't come into her life yet. But how long was she supposed to wait?

Gina's copper-colored eyes suddenly widened. She leaned forward. "It's the *reverend*."

Lauren had never been able to suppress a blush. She took a bite of her burger. Gina was right, partially. But emotions didn't die easily, and sometimes Lauren still thought about Lukas.

"You want to be a *preacher's* wife?" Gina made it sound like Lauren had just ordered a plate of slugs for lunch.

Lauren glanced toward the break room door. "Shhh!"

Gina lowered her voice and giggled. "You do!"

For at least the millionth time in her life, Lauren wished she wasn't quite so readable. But she couldn't lie, either. "Don't act so shocked. It isn't as if he's married, but please don't tell anyone else." This was so embarrassing, especially since she had known Archer for so long, and there had never even been a hint of any kind of romantic relationship between them. "I shouldn't even be thinking about him like that. I mean, he's my *pastor*. And he's younger than me."

"How much younger?"

"Two years."

"Don't forget the studies that advise that a husband should be seven years younger than his wife. Has he asked you out yet?"

Lauren lowered her voice. "Of course not."

"Why 'of course'?"

"He's only been officially unattached for a little over a month."

"Your biological clock is ticking," Gina teased.

Lauren grimaced. "Like a time bomb. Maybe I should just ignore it and let it wind down. Not everybody is meant to be married and have a family. There are a lot of things I'm free to do now that I wouldn't be able to do if I had other commitments."

"But you want children," Gina said. "You were so good with Levi the other night."

Lauren nodded thoughtfully. Children. Lately she hadn't been able to ignore the tugging ache in her heart when any patient under the age of ten came into the ER. She couldn't help it. "I'd love a child," she admitted softly.

"And do you think Archer would be a good father?"

"Not just a good father, a good daddy. Almost any man can father a child."

There was a startled gasp from the other side of the partially open door, and Lauren froze. *Someone had heard them.* There was an awkward swish and a squeak of shoes. Lauren jumped up and ran to the hallway in time to see a familiar flowered smock covering the oversized end portion of Fiona Perkins.

"Oh, that's just great."

"Who was it?"

"Only the one person in this hospital who's reputed to have a bigger mouth than mine. I think I'm going to be sick."

Gina laughed. It was a light, tinkling sound that almost made Lauren's humiliation worthwhile. Almost.

As soon as Lauren returned to work, she learned that Stacie Kimble was in stable condition at St. John's in Springfield. She was out of her coma.

CHAPTER 11

By seven o'clock Wednesday evening, the second week in June, traffic in the emergency room had steadily increased until eight of the ten exam beds were occupied. During the week and a half following the heart-stopping scare with eight-year-old Stacie, Grant Sheldon had discovered many interesting things about Dogwood Springs. A sweet sense of community spirit ran deep in this town, and it seemed to be one of curiosity mingled with compassion, especially when word spread about Stacie's fight with diabetes.

To Grant's amusement and dismay that same spirit extended into the ER. Patient confidentiality was not an option when the man with the broken leg in exam room three could call across the department to the teenager in room seven with the flu and inform him, at the top of his lungs, who was in each exam room and what was wrong with them.

At least three people had stopped by the ER while Grant was on duty, not for medical care, but just to meet him, welcome him to town, and find out more about him. He was invited to join the local Kiwanis Club, which met for lunch each Tuesday at the Copper Pot Café. He was given a free month's subscription to *The Dogwood*, the local newspaper, which was filled—charmingly—with local news and only the most basic coverage of national news. Of course, the current issue featured a picture and dramatically written article about Stacie's plight. Grant had spoken with the Kimbles last week, and although the child was better, she had continued to struggle since they brought her back home.

Grant was disturbed and disappointed to discover that alcohol and drug abuse, domestic violence, and Medicaid abuse spread like malignant cancers throughout Dogwood Springs, as they did elsewhere. Obviously, there was no paradise left in the world if this picturesque hillside community could be oppressed by the same problems that attacked the meanest streets of St. Louis.

However, something else equally sinister seemed to be attacking this town. After the episode with Stacie, Grant had kept a closer watch on the flu patients who presented to the ER while he was on duty. He didn't like what he found. The numbers approached epidemic proportions, and the month of June was not a common time of year for such an occurrence.

At the end of a busy Wednesday in the ER, Grant picked up a chart from the circular central desk and turned to give report to his night shift replacement, Dr. Mitchell Caine, a primary care doc who had his own practice in town and moonlighted in the ER.

"What's this I hear about shift reductions?" Dr. Caine was an impressive-looking man, maybe an inch shorter than Grant's 6'2", with silver blond hair and steel blue eyes, which, at the moment, revealed an edge of displeasure.

"You heard correctly. I want to shorten the shifts, and eventually I'd like to add overlapping double coverage for the busier evening hours."

"And when will this take place?" Caine demanded.

"I hope to put some of it into effect for next month's schedule. Business is picking up, and we don't want our staff worn out by twelve-hour shifts." Grant continued with his report, listing patient after patient, all miserable and begging for relief, and for whom he intended to stay a while longer, in spite of his sermon-in-progress to the contrary.

"Perhaps it would be wise for you to learn a little more about Dogwood Springs before you start making decisions that could disrupt a lot of lives," Dr. Caine said after Grant had finished his inventory of sufferers. "I *need* my twelve-hour shifts, and tomorrow is my day off. I can sleep then." He reached up to straighten the crisply starched lab coat that he wore over dress clothes instead of donning the traditional ER scrubs.

"But you worked all day today, right?" Grant asked. "You've probably been up since eight this morning, at the latest, and you probably had hospital rounds before you started seeing patients in your office. By the end of this shift you will have been up twenty-three hours without sleep if you're at all busy tonight, and from the way we've been going since I arrived, believe me, you will be busy. Would you want to be a patient of a doctor on his twenty-third hour?"

Lines of irritability deepened around Caine's eyes and mouth. "We aren't that busy in this town yet. There are usually several hours during the night when we only have a trickle of patients."

"A trickle? Even if there's only one in at a time, the doctor can't sleep through it."

"Do you know how expensive it is to run a family practice these days?" Caine's voice grew deeper, the words more clipped. "Every ER doctor should try it at least once. The experience would do them some good, not to mention the fact that being on call would give them a new appreciation for the difficulties we face when you drag us out in the middle of the night for a sore throat."

The barb was spoken casually, and Grant curbed his irritation. He never used an on-call service unless he felt it was absolutely necessary for the safety of a patient. However, there was often a discrepancy of opinions between physicians as to the severity of a case, and he could empathize with the frustration of being awakened from a sound sleep night after night.

Still, patients had not yet learned how to get sick only at the more convenient times of the day, and Caine's complaint only emphasized more completely the need for a physician to have adequate sleep.

Grant forced a smile. "Studies show that during medical shift work, optimum performance drops—"

"Spare me," Caine said dryly, raising a hand as if to ward off Grant's words. He gave a grimace of a smile, as if he, too, were trying to pass off his irritation with humor. "I'm sure you're right, but you'd be more sympathetic, I think, if you had a wife with a Ferrari."

Grant doubted that, but before he could respond the buzzer sounded at the front window, and he heard a slightly familiar, crusty voice rise above the normal chatter of the bustling ER.

"Would you stand up? I'm not going to carry you. Hey! Listen to me, I've got some cracked ribs, you know."

There was a grunt and a moan, and Grant stepped around the partition that separated the ER proper from the reception area and waiting room. There stood the two feuding farmers who had been brought in nearly two weeks ago after an automobile accident.

Mr. Brisco braced himself against the reception counter and grimaced as he held his previously loudmouthed neighbor by the right arm. Mr. Scroggs was swaying like a drunk, and he had a small blood-encrusted cut over his left eye. The cast on his left arm was stained with dirt and blood.

Grant turned and signaled for a nurse, then walked around to the entry door and into the waiting room. He gently eased Brisco away and took Scroggs. "You shouldn't be lifting any weight yet, Mr. Brisco. Let's get him to the back and lay him down. Did you two get into another tangle?"

"Nope, somebody else walloped him on the head," Brisco muttered as he tagged along behind them. "Right there in his own barn in broad daylight. What's this world coming to?" His voice shook with indignation.

Grant ushered Brisco and Scroggs into one of the two exam rooms that remained empty and gently sat Scroggs on the edge of the bed. The nurse murmured comforting words to the old farmer as she took his shirt off and replaced it with a gown. Grant pressed his stethoscope against the patient's back. The breathing sounded fine.

"I found him lying on his face in the middle of his barn floor," Brisco said as the nurse checked Scroggs's blood pressure.

"Unconscious?" Grant asked.

"I think he was just coming out of it. I'd driven over to complain about the fence being down again." He looked down at his ailing neighbor. "It's your turn to fix it this time, you know. Look what you're doing to get out of it." His voice carried through the ER with nearly as much volume as Friday night, as if Scroggs were hard of hearing.

"Mr. Scroggs," Grant said, checking the cut, "can you talk to me?"

The farmer's eyes opened slightly, and he winced. "What do you want?"

"Can you tell me what happened? How long ago?" Grant pressed his stethoscope to the older man's bony chest. Heart sounded okay, too.

"I heard something out in the barn when I came in from the field this afternoon." He reached up and felt for the cut on his temple, then grunted again when Grant intercepted his hand and guided it away. "Thought it was a possum."

"That's not what you told me when I found you," Brisco interrupted. "You told me you thought I was in there stealing one of your—"

"And I decided to get a jump on him," Scroggs interrupted with a grimace. He laid his head back on the pillow. "Either the possums in these parts are getting bigger, or that rat-faced weirdo who hit me wasn't no possum. I should've laid this here cast to his skull."

"Blood pressure is 130 over 80, Dr. Sheldon," the nurse said. "Respirations are 20."

"So you saw who hit you?" Grant asked.

"I saw him bending over the spigot of my fertilizer tank. I shouted, and he jumped at me with some metal container in his hand. Knocked me out cold till I heard Brisco snooping around."

"Your fertilizer tank?" Brisco said, leaning forward. "He's probably as sick of the stink around your place as the rest of us are. Now all the neighbors will be mad at you because they'll have to buy new locks for their doors when word gets out." He sounded a little too satisfied about that.

"Mr. Brisco," Grant said, "I appreciate what you've done for your neighbor, but—"

"He was already acting all loopy and odd when I found him," Brisco said. "Not that it was too noticeable. He's always loopy and odd."

"Wait a minute, Mr. Scroggs," Grant said as the old farmer's previous statement registered at last. "Could you identify the man who hit you? Could you give a description of him to the police?"

"Guess I could. I saw him, but not for long."

Grant excused himself and stepped out of the exam room. He walked over to the secretary. "Barbara, call the police," he said softly. "We have a crime victim who needs to make a statement."

Lauren joined him at the central desk. "The police? Again? What is it with you, Dr. Sheldon? All the hard cases seem to come out of the woodwork when you're on duty. Maybe you should start parking your car someplace else so they won't know you're here."

Grant looked up at Lauren and smiled at her joke. "Maybe I should." He took a closer look at her, then frowned. Her face looked pale, and there were dark circles beneath her eyes. "I thought your shift was over, Lauren. What are you still doing here?"

"Probably the same thing you are—trying to help our replacements get caught up, but two more patients just checked in, and we've had three calls. Care to guess the most common complaint?"

"Nausea, vomiting, dizziness, headache—"

"You got it. I'll hang around a little longer, or they'll have to call in reinforcements."

"Are you sure? You don't look like you're feeling much better than the patients."

"How kind of you to notice." Lauren's voice held just the right inflection of amused offense, and Grant chuckled at her. Over the past two weeks they had grown comfortable enough with each other to tease, and he'd found that Lauren had an excellent sense of humor. She had learned quickly to anticipate his orders and the questions he would probably ask a patient, and he had learned to trust her judgment. The last time Grant had felt this comfortable with someone he had eventually married her.

The thought disturbed him, and he glanced again at Lauren as she stepped to the automated drug dispenser and punched in her code number on a keypad.

He continued to watch her, telling himself he would show this much concern for any member of his staff. "Has that flu still got a hold on you, too?"

A motor whined, and a drawer popped open. She reached inside for an ampule of Phenergan, an antiemetic he had prescribed for a patient just before Dr. Caine arrived. "It comes and goes," she said. "Do you need some help with your crime victim?"

"No, but I do think you need to go home and get some rest. You're back on duty in the morning, aren't you?"

"Yes, but so are you." Lauren gave him a tired smile. "I don't see you checking out yet."

He picked up an empty clipboard and selected an appropriate blank T-sheet from the cabinet, then turned back toward the exam room. "Don't push yourself too hard, Lauren. You know how many return patients we've had with this stuff."

On his way back to the room Grant realized Lauren was right about the police. He'd been calling them a lot since he arrived. It wasn't a comfortable thought, but maybe things would settle down. Even the quietest towns had their share of trouble. At least he didn't know all the officers by their first names yet, as he had in St. Louis.

To Grant's surprise, he found Dr. Caine at Scroggs's bedside, asking questions, listening to his heart and breathing, issuing orders to the night shift nurse, and asking questions about the attack. Brisco was gone.

"Dr. Caine, I can take care of this gentleman," Grant said. "I've already started with—"

"And I've already taken over." Caine held up his own chart, not even gracing Grant with eye contact. "You're off duty—you can go on home." He waved his hand as if he were brushing away a pesky fly.

"Thanks, but—"

"Who was just lecturing me about optimum performance?" Caine turned and gave Grant a cool smile. "You should practice what you preach before you try to force it on the rest of the medical staff." He pressed the bell of his stethoscope against Scroggs's chest and issued an order for the night shift nurse to prepare a suture tray.

The nurse glanced at Grant and rolled her eyes, shrugging as she went to follow orders. Grant felt himself bristling at Caine's superior attitude and casual disregard for the eight other miserable patients waiting to be seen. The man was right, of course. Grant's shift was over.

But how long would it take one physician to get to the remainder of the patients with the waiting room filling up so quickly? Perhaps tonight would be a good one to test the double-coverage waters, at least for a little while. He'd been on duty for twelve hours, but he could hang around for a little while and leave before he got too tired. As Lauren had said, he was also scheduled to be back on duty in the morning.

At the desk Grant picked up the chart on the next patient to be seen and walked to exam room three, thinking about Caine's Ferrari-driving wife. Annette would have been outraged at the thought of spending that much money on a car. He could almost hear her saying, "Why, honey, just imagine how many homeless people that could feed for a year!" When he closed his eyes all he could see was a hazy outline of her face.

The haziness depressed him. A few months ago he could see his wife so clearly that every tiny laugh line around her eyes radiated her caring spirit. Now he had to open his billfold and look at a picture. And he was dismayed to realize that when he closed his eyes and thought of her it was actually the picture in the photograph he remembered. Maybe it really was time to go home and get some rest.

But when he saw his next patient, an older lady who was miserable with the same flu symptoms that it seemed half the town was enduring, he knew it wasn't time to leave yet. Mrs. Henson looked at Grant with obvious relief when he introduced himself. She'd been waiting more than an hour and a half. She was gracious, but her two younger sisters who waited with her voiced their concern about the long wait.

Grant apologized in spite of the fact that it would have been impossible for him to get to her more quickly. He'd had two patients with chest pain come in by ambulance only a few moments before she arrived. Two auto accident victims had followed. This always seemed to be the time of night when everything hit at once.

Mrs. Henson's fast heart rate and dizziness, with the absence of a fever, combined with several bouts of vomiting, indicated that she was dehydrated, and Grant ordered IV fluids for her. He also ordered a blood draw to check for infection and electrolyte imbalance. After his experience with little Stacie Kimble he didn't want to take any flu complaint lightly.

When the test results returned from the lab, nothing had been flagged for notice, which meant all her numbers were within the normal range. Her potassium level was a little low, but that wasn't surprising, as she hadn't been able to keep anything down all day. Grant gave her an antiemetic, and two hours after he was scheduled to be off work, when he was fighting fatigue and she was feeling better, he discharged her with orders to return if she got worse. He must have treated twenty other patients with the same symptoms and same test results in the last week. This little virus—or bacteria, or whatever—was getting old in a hurry.

Grant wrote his final discharge sheet and was retrieving his medical bag from the call room when he heard the sound of male laughter from one of the exam rooms in back. And then he heard something he'd never heard before—Lauren McCaffrey's voice, suddenly deep and strong with authority.

"Keep your hands off me!"

The fingers of Lauren's right hand tensed into a hard, tight fist, and she felt a tingle race up her arm. She hadn't wanted to punch anybody this badly since she was in fifth grade and Kevin Pulaski picked on her youngest brother and made him cry. After she'd finished with Kevin that day, he'd apologized to her brother and never bothered him again. It didn't matter that the patient to whom she now spoke was twice as big as she was, with the body of an all-star wrestler and the brains, at this moment, of an inebriated microorganism.

She shouldn't have stayed this long, should have gone home when her shift was over. But even if she felt a hundred percent, she would not have been gracious about being manhandled, pinched, or groped. Within the space of five minutes, this bozo had managed to do all three under the guise of drunken awkwardness, and then faked a look of wide-eyed innocence. And then, to make matters worse, she had turned just in time to catch his friend reaching out to accost her in some form or fashion. When she caught him, he chuckled and lowered his arm, sitting back in his chair with a leer that promised that, given the opportunity, he would try again.

"The two of you can keep your hands to yourself, or I can call the police and charge you with assault."

"Sorry."

The brute on the bed didn't sound sorry—he looked annoyed. His face darkened to deep red, and he finally looked into her face—a surprise, since up until now he'd barely lifted his stare above her rib cage. "Can't blame a guy for trying."

His inebriated buddy, who had brought him in and smelled similarly of booze, snickered again from his seat in the only chair in the room.

Lauren wanted to walk out of the room and out of the hospital and leave this guy to wait until one of the male nurses got a chance to come in. But the new female grad would probably get stuck with him, and something similar would happen to her. Any other time Lauren would have been more alert. No matter how modestly she dressed, sometimes this kind of thing happened.

She took a deep breath and reattached the blood pressure cuff, taking care to keep every vulnerable area of her anatomy away from his wandering touch. She hated dealing with the obnoxious drunks, but it was part of the job in the emergency room. She had to remind herself that they, too, needed compassion.

All the automatic blood pressure machines were in use, so she pumped the manual cuff by hand and placed her stethoscope on the man's muscle-bound arm. What she really needed was a thigh cuff to encompass the girth more comfortably. She'd pumped it to maximum and was just getting ready to release the valve for a reading when Dr. Sheldon stepped into the room.

"Lauren? Is everything okay in here?" His presence had never been more welcomed, and she looked around at him gratefully.

"Uh, Nurse," the patient grunted, "are you trying to squeeze my arm off?"

Lauren turned and released the valve, checking the numbers. She wrote the vitals down and removed the cuff, then turned gratefully to Dr. Sheldon. "Mr. Beneker had an accident at work today—fell off his backhoe. He has lower back pain, and a couple of hours ago he began to experience blurred vision." The reek of alcohol suggested a good explanation for the blurred vision, but she would allow the doctor to decide that for himself.

Dr. Sheldon picked up the chart Lauren had filled out and read the assessment. He stepped over to the patient's side. "So, Mr. Beneker, you're a heavy-equipment operator?"

"Yeah."

"You're from Springfield? What are you doing all the way out here in our neck of the woods?" Dr. Sheldon was a big man with a commanding presence, and his voice of authority seemed to sober the men a little. He was professional in every way, yet he seemed to establish control with every movement, every facial expression, every word. Lauren noticed his usual smile was missing.

She moved to the end of the bed, as far away from Beneker and his buddy as she could get without calling too much attention to her actions. She listened as the patient answered the same questions she had asked him earlier. He'd fallen from his backhoe and didn't report it to his foreman at the time. He'd gone back to work, and then later his back started hurting.

"Got a job clearing a dump site a few miles out of town on Highway Z," Beneker said. "They're getting it all cleaned up for this big inspection some company is doing before they buy."

"Oh?" Dr. Sheldon asked as he studied Lauren's written assessment and started one of his own, marking the checklist on his sheet. "What company is that?"

"Beats me, I just run the backhoe. Some investors and their bean counters out of Kansas City lined it up, I think. Wantin' to put in some kind of water-bottling plant."

"A water-bottling plant?" Lauren asked. "Where?" There had been rumors that the mayor of the city was looking for new ways to attract some of the Branson tourism into Dogwood Springs. "You said you're working out on Highway Z?"

Some of the cocky bravado slid back into the man's expression when he noticed Lauren's interest. Once again, his gaze didn't reach her face. "They call it Honey Spring."

She stifled her curiosity with difficulty. Honey Spring was her favorite fishing spot—a favorite of most of the old, serious fishermen around these parts. She hoped a new bottling plant wouldn't disrupt the creek.

Dr. Sheldon took out his penlight and did a neurological test on Beneker. "That must be some cleanup. So tell me about what happened today."

"We got all tangled up in some concrete somebody poured out there. You know how they do it—those concrete trucks can't get rid of all their goop when they get done with a house, and they got to dump it somewhere. Must be a concrete company out there. It's safe landfill, but it's sure a booger to dig out. I hit a hard spot and got stuck, started to climb off the rig to see what was going on, and part of the concrete gave way with me. I lost my footing. Cut my arm a little, but not bad enough to worry about."

Dr. Sheldon studied Lauren's assessment. "It says here you've had a recent tetanus shot."

"Yeah, I got it when I cut my leg with a chain saw a few months ago."

Dr. Sheldon asked the patient a few more questions focusing on his neurologic status, then checked his reflexes and strength, listened to his chest and neck with his stethoscope, and carefully examined his eyes with an ophthalmoscope. "Mr. Beneker, I haven't found any obvious problem, with the exception of some sore back muscles. I'll request an x-ray of your lower back, just to be safe, and we're going to run a few tests, including blood alcohol and drug screen. Did you lose consciousness?"

The patient stiffened. "Hold it. What's this about a blood alcohol and drug screen?"

"That's customary policy for workers' comp claims. Unless—"

"But that's not fair. I've been off work for a while. I've had a couple of beers since quitting time, and the test'll show that."

"I'm sure the board will take that into consideration, Mr. Beneker. It isn't my call. You didn't tell me, did you lose consciousness? Did you pass out when you fell?"

The patient brooded about it for a few seconds, glared at Dr. Sheldon, and then sighed. "Nope."

"No other complaints besides lower back pain and blurred vision?"

"Nope."

"I'll run the orders," Lauren said.

Dr. Sheldon held his hand up and shook his head. "No, we'll let Eugene take care of this one. He's on duty tonight. Mr. Beneker, I don't know what your experience has been at other hospitals, but this hospital doesn't allow its staff to be mistreated, particularly when it comes to sexual misconduct."

"What?" Beneker exclaimed.

Dr. Sheldon continued. "We do not tolerate the sexual harassment of our nurses, our techs, our housekeepers, or any other employee.

What we do is call the police and file charges." His voice was steady and calm, and he established and maintained eye contact with the patient as he spoke.

Lauren could not mask her surprise.

Beneker's gaze gradually darkened with anger. "What d'you mean sexual harassment? She was touching *me* all over the place." His angry gaze flicked to Lauren. "I didn't do—"

"Lauren, would you please go ask Eugene to come in here?" Dr. Sheldon said, cutting off the patient's words as he turned to her. "He'll finish this case."

Lauren suppressed a smile as she walked out the door and heard Beneker threaten to call and complain to the hospital administrator that he was being unfairly treated. Once again, Dr. Sheldon's voice was calm when he replied. Once again, Lauren could have hugged him.

CHAPTER | **12**

At six-forty-five Thursday morning Grant Sheldon couldn't help noticing the magnificent beauty of summer as he maneuvered his car along the curving street toward the hospital at the crest of the steep hill. Flower boxes burgeoned with color, and the gingerbread trim on brightly colored Victorian houses was freshly washed by the rain from last night's storm. Broken, sodden limbs littered the picket-fenced yards.

Grant wondered about eighty-eight-year-old Mrs. Piedmont, who had been clearing her own yard of limbs from the last storm almost two weeks ago when she'd experienced her first symptoms of chest pain. He'd received word from her family physician that she would be fine as long as she took her medication and didn't overstress her heart. That meant no more heavy lifting or strenuous yard work. Poor Mrs. Piedmont. He hoped she didn't pick up the limbs this morning, but he couldn't blame her if she did. Habits were hard to change.

He pulled into the employee parking lot just as an ambulance eased out of the bay, and he felt a familiar tightening in his gut.

Inside, he found two tearful middle-aged women with familiar faces clinging to each other beside the reception window. When one of them spoke, he remembered his flu patient from last night, Mrs. Henson. These were her younger sisters, who had been concerned about the long wait.

Before Grant had a chance to walk over and speak to them, a

haggard Dr. Mitchell Caine came through the doorway that connected the waiting room with the emergency department. His broad shoulders drooped beneath the stained lab coat, and his bloodshot eyes held that familiar, dull look of frustration that every physician experienced when a patient case had not gone well. It was obvious that he had gotten no sleep last night. He looked past Grant as if he didn't see him, and turned his attention to the two women.

"I'm sorry; we did all we could." His voice was rough with fatigue. "She went into cardiac arrest, and we tried to resuscitate her." He shook his head. "We couldn't get her back."

"What . . . does that mean?" the taller sister asked, a quiver in her voice revealing that she knew exactly what he meant, but shock and horror prevented her from accepting the truth.

"She died five minutes ago."

The impact of the words hit Grant with an almost physical force, just as it did the sisters. He had been working in emergency medicine too long to be surprised by this kind of occurrence, but it shouldn't have happened. Last night there were no signs that their sister was experiencing anything more than a simple case of the flu.

Instead of staying to comfort the women through the onslaught of grief that followed the announcement, Dr. Caine turned his attention to Grant and pinned him in place with a stiletto gaze. The facade of compassion dropped away like an unwanted garment and his eyes narrowed, making his assessment of blame obvious.

"I wonder if you understand the significance of this." Caine didn't bother to keep his voice down. He crossed his arms over his chest and took three calculated steps toward Grant, like a hunter stalking his prey. "One of the supposed 'flu' patients you insisted on treating last night after your shift was over has just died. Heart failure."

Grant decided to overlook the man's highly unprofessional conduct in light of his emotional state, but the two women needed assistance right now. Did they have family they needed to call? A minister? If Dr. Caine wasn't going to assist them, he would.

He moved to step around Caine, but the man put a restraining hand on Grant's arm. "You make calls like this, and you're trying to tell me I'm the one who needs my hours cut?"

"I don't think this is the time or the place for a discussion about work schedules." Grant removed his arm from Caine's grip. "We can make an appointment for that later. Why don't we limit our attention to those who are truly grieving at the moment, shall we?"

Caine leaned closer, until Grant felt the heat of his breath. "Then you take care of this one," he hissed. "My shift's over."

Lauren watched in shocked silence from the waiting room door while Dr. Sheldon pushed past Dr. Caine and approached the weeping women. He spoke a few soft words to them, and with gentle hands to guide them, he ushered them into a private alcove. As they went, Lauren heard him offer assistance with calls and arrangements.

Dr. Caine shoved past Lauren on his way through the door into the emergency department. When the telephone rang for him a few moments later she overheard the secretary, Vivian, explain that he had already left for the day. Lauren was relieved.

For many years, Lauren had worked side by side with a varied assortment of physicians both in the emergency room and in private practice. For some of those doctors—some of the very best in the world, in her opinion—she had changed her work schedule in order to cover more shifts with them. Lukas Bower had been one such doctor, as well as Mercy Richmond. Both held their own professional conduct to a high standard and put the quality of their own lives on the line for their patients. They believed in what they did.

A few doctors, however, had the opposite effect on Lauren. She had worked with physicians whose egos had reached a level of arrogance so insufferable and self-centered that they ceased to give good care. In her opinion, Dr. Caine had passed that point. He was good and kind and caring only as long as things went his way.

Let a patient complain, however, or let a staff member show the smallest amount of doubt about one of his orders, and Caine's kindness evaporated like fog in the August sunlight. When Lauren first arrived she had heard about his attitude via the grapevine and dismissed it as rumor. But then she'd witnessed it for herself when she was on duty with him. After that, she'd avoided his shifts whenever possible. With Dr.

Sheldon's new policies about to take effect next month, that would not be so difficult.

An hour later, after the hearse had left with the body of Mrs. Henson, and her sisters had left with other family members, Lauren caught sight of Dr. Sheldon walking toward the physicians' work desk at the rear of the department. She picked up the file she had pulled while he was busy and carried it to him as he sat down.

"I thought you would want this." She laid the file in front of him. It was Mrs. Henson's medical chart from last night, along with some copies of additional pages from this morning's tragedy.

He looked at the chart and then at her. She could read the gratitude in his expression. "You've probably read it, too," he said.

"I didn't find a thing out of place. Nothing last night showed a heart problem." Without waiting for an invitation, she pulled another chair over and sat down. "Of course, you're the doctor, and you might find a lot of things I wouldn't know to look for."

Grant studied the pages for a few moments, then shook his head and leaned back in his chair. "I can't find anything out of place. I would make the same call again. That's what scares me. Is it possible that her flu just suddenly took a turn for the worse during the night? She was feeling much better before I sent her home. And she had no history of heart problems, no chest pain, nothing on the monitor when I saw her. I could have done an EKG, but I saw no reason for it last night."

Lauren knew he wasn't talking for her benefit, but for his own. "Dr. Sheldon, you—"

He held his hand up. "I like to be a little more casual around the office, if it isn't against some kind of company policy I haven't yet read. Would you mind calling me Grant?"

"Of course not." She felt a pang of compassion for this big masculine doctor. He seemed to have everything under control. He had handled an obnoxious, lecherous patient with firmness and grace while getting her out of the line of fire, and yet he felt comfortable enough with her—a nurse who worked under his direction in this department—to express his doubts and bare a part of his soul.

"Grant, stop second-guessing yourself just because of one man who doesn't know what he's talking about. He obviously didn't even look at this chart, because I had to search all over the department for it. He doesn't know what went on between you and your patient last night. He's using this poor woman's death to further his own agenda." She stopped herself from saying anything else, abiding by her belief that if she made any unfounded accusations against another person, she was opening herself up for the same kind of attack. She had only stated the obvious.

"Thank you." He picked up the chart and sorted through the pages once again. Lauren had made copies of everything she could find. "Lauren, how long have you been an ER nurse?"

"Ten years."

"Have you ever seen a flu epidemic in early June such as the one we seem to have here now?"

"Not in June."

"And you've experienced it yourself, even though you had a flu shot."

"Yes, and we've had several patients return with reoccurring bouts with it, though it only began around the end of May, about the time you arrived. The severity is what concerns me."

His face relaxed with the first smile she had seen today. "Are you saying I make people sick?"

With some other doctors, she would begin to tread lightly about now. Many would take offense at the most unintentional slight. She grinned at him. "We'll just have to wait and see, won't we? Do you mind if I offer a suggestion?"

"I'd appreciate it."

"I could call some friends of mine in Knolls and see if they're having the same problem. Dr. Lukas Bower would have picked up on something like this quickly, and he would definitely see it in the ER. Dr. Mercy Richmond has her own clinic. This is her day off, but I could try to catch her at home. Maybe some of the other hospitals in surrounding towns have experienced the same thing."

"Excellent idea. I'll ask our secretaries if they will keep track of our flu patients for the next few days and make some calls to the local physicians. Meanwhile, I'll have Medical Records pull some old files, and I'll make some phone calls myself. The patients might be able to tell me something." He paused and thumped his fingers on Mrs. Henson's chart. "Her sisters are requesting an autopsy."

"Because of what Dr. Caine said this morning?"

"That could have something to do with it," he said dryly. "The coroner doesn't have to agree to it, and if he doesn't they'll have to pay for it themselves. I'm going to call and urge him to abide by their wishes."

Lauren really did like this man. "It could be risky for your career if they find something."

"It could be more risky for the citizens of Dogwood Springs if we don't."

"I hope your attitude spreads out a little in this town. We could use it." Unfortunately, if the pathologist found blocked arteries or other signs of previous heart problems in Mrs. Henson's body, the family could decide to sue for malpractice, even though the records for last night showed nothing amiss. It didn't mean they would win, but this was America, where people sued in search of hidden treasure.

"I find it comforting that there's a doctor willing to dig deeper," she said, "to find out if there really is a problem or if all these cases are just coincidental."

Grant smiled again, and Lauren realized Gina was right, he did look a bit like a more cerebral Antonio Banderas, without the ponytail.

"Have you ever considered changing careers?" he asked.

"Changing?"

"You could be a counselor. You're good with people. You listen."

"You think so?" The man was serious? "I've been told I talk faster than a runaway freight train."

"I never noticed. Much." Grant's smile widened. "What I do notice is how people open up with you. Mrs. Piedmont dotes on you like another grandchild, and Archer obviously thinks you're great."

Archer? Really? "He does?"

"He's mentioned it."

Lauren wanted to ask about other things Archer might have mentioned, but this conversation wasn't about her love life—or lack of it. "Has he mentioned the fact that you are invited to attend our church and bring your kids any time you feel like it?"

Grant's smile froze in place. "He's mentioned it."

She'd hit a nerve with that one. "Of course, you may already attend church somewhere."

"No." His tone couldn't have said more clearly, though gently, "Don't go there."

She nodded. She'd seen that look often enough. "It must be hard raising teenagers alone. Your wife has been gone two years now?" She knew she was getting more and more personal, but he didn't seem to mind. Much.

"It will be two years next month."

"I'm so sorry, Grant. Lately I've been whining because I'm homesick, and you're grieving over something that has changed your life permanently. I've never even been married, and here I am babbling like—"

"You're not babbling." He leaned back in his chair and stretched his long legs out in front of him.

"You must really miss her. I can't imagine how painful that is."

He nodded. "Sometimes it seems as if the suffering will never end."

"Someone once told me that the period of mourning after a death actually serves to honor the memory of the one who passed on."

Grant thought about her words for a moment. "I like that. It fits. Annette deserves to be honored."

"It sounds as if you had a good relationship."

"We did. We were best friends before we even dated." He looked over at her. "I think it's vital to like someone before you love them."

"Is . . . was Annette a . . . Christian?" Lauren always hesitated to ask the question, because if the answer was no, what kind of response could she offer?

"Yes. My greatest comfort comes from that." Grant fell silent and his movements stilled. The chatter of the tech and the secretary, punctuated by hints of laughter, filled the space where words, for a few moments, refused to enter. Then the telephone rang, and the chatter stopped.

"For the record I, too, once called myself a Christian," Grant said softly.

She concealed her surprise. "Once?"

"I'm not sure God would want to claim me now."

"Of course He—"

"He has no reason to. Annette carried the weight of spiritual leadership in our family since the children were little. She was their teacher. She tucked them in at night . . . sometimes it seemed she tucked half the world in at night. She reached out to so many people, and all I did was my job."

"You're a doctor, and from what I've seen you always go beyond the call of duty. How much more caring could you get? It sounds like you two were a good match."

The warmth that deepened in his dark gray eyes revealed more to Lauren about Grant's love for his wife than any words could have. And then the triage bell rang. Lauren got up to check on their first patient of the day, and as she walked away she thought she heard Grant sigh.

"Hello, Archer."

The rich, melodious voice startled Archer so much he nearly dropped the receiver. Then he smiled and leaned forward in his chair, resting his elbows on his desk. "Jessica? Is this possible? Are you actually *calling* me at last?"

There was a soft chuckle. "I know, I deserved that."

"You sure did. If you only knew how many times I've sat at home alone by the telephone, watching it, waiting for it to—"

"And it never did."

"It always did. But it was never you."

Another chuckle. "I'm booked at the theater most nights, remember?"

"You're not only booked, you're booked *up*. Congratulations. Every time I've tried to reserve a ticket for your performance, they've been sold out."

"Why didn't you tell me? I could have gotten you a ticket."

"You told me not to call you."

She didn't answer for a few seconds. "I'm sorry. I was wrong. You can call me."

Thank you, Lord! "So what finally made you break down?" He had so many things he wanted to talk to her about. Archer was suddenly in the best mood he'd been in for weeks.

"Well . . . get this . . . I missed you."

Oh, yeah! It felt good to hear her say that. "It took you long enough."

"No it didn't, I just couldn't bring myself to pick up the telephone and dial the church number, and when I dialed your home number I never got an answer." There was an unspoken question in her voice.

"Business as usual."

"Sounds like it."

"Why didn't you leave a message for me?"

"Because sometimes a recording just doesn't get the job done. So how've you been doing?"

"I've . . . um . . . taken on another little job at the—"

"Oh, Archer, you didn't."

"It didn't seem like much at first, but—"

"That's what you always say. What is it this time? Are you the music director now, too? Let me guess, graded choirs as well as adult choir practice on Wednesday nights, and—"

"Not music. Jerry's doing an excellent job with the music and education."

"Then what? Did your janitor quit?"

"Nope. I had a lot of time on my hands without you, so I volunteered to be an on-call chaplain at Dogwood Springs Hospital."

This time the silence was longer, more thoughtful. Jessica was the one person in the world with whom he could read the silences as well as the spoken words. He had come to know her that well. "Do you enjoy that kind of work?" she asked.

"Enjoy isn't exactly the word I would use. It only started out to be one night of call a week."

"And now?"

"And since that first night I discovered that I can't just let those patients go without another word of comfort. I'm getting more personally involved. I need to do follow-up, even though it isn't required, and that takes a lot more time than I realized. Still, I need to do it."

"Archer," she chided softly, "of course you do. It's your nature to care about people."

He loved the sound of her voice when she talked like that. "To put your mind at ease, the church is searching for a youth minister to take some of my duties, and Lauren is helping out a lot with the kids until we get someone in officially. She's also helping me keep in contact with some of the patients, since she's a nurse there at the ER."

"Lauren. Didn't she just join the church a few months ago?"

Jessica's voice was still soft, thoughtful, but for some reason Archer felt just a touch of tension. "The last part of February. She came from Knolls. Remember? I told you about her. I've known her forever."

"She's a very pretty woman. Single, isn't she?"

"Yes. That's why she has free time to help me."

"If my memory serves me, the kids at the church stuck to her like Velcro."

"That's the one. She's great."

"Was the chaplain position Lauren's idea?"

"Only my participation in it. Surprisingly, our new ER director requested that the program be put into motion while he was still negotiating with the hospital on his contract. As soon as Lauren heard about it she called me. When can we get together?" he asked, changing the subject abruptly.

There was a quiet hesitation. "Friday is still your day off, isn't it?"

"Yes." Oh no, hold it. That wasn't exactly true. He had a couple of appointments tomorrow, but maybe he could fit everything in. "How about lunch?"

"How about making a day of it? I can get you a ticket to our afternoon show at two."

He bit his lip, thinking. Yes, it could be done. "I'd love it. I have a counseling session in the morning, and then Lauren and I are making a visit late tomorrow afternoon to follow up on a patient, but I should be back in time for that."

"Oh. Well . . . I guess I'll see you tomorrow about noon?"

"I'll pick you up. Thanks for calling, Jessica."

There was a long silence. "Sure. Good-bye."

Somehow, when Archer hung up, he didn't feel quite as elated as he would have expected to. It might have had something to do with Jessica's sudden apparent lack of enthusiasm. Maybe she wasn't feeling well. Archer hoped she hadn't caught the flu bug that was going around.

CHAPTER 13

Sergeant Tony Dalton gripped his gun and crept with precise, soundless steps across the concrete front porch of the only unoccupied house on Sycamore Street. With a quick nod of his head he signaled for his younger partner, Henry, to come in close. The station had received a call ten minutes ago about suspicious activity here. The caller described an intruder he saw stealthily enter the home just after dawn. His description sounded uncomfortably familiar. For six weeks they'd been after a man who used the street name "Peregrine." The man befriended the teenagers who cruised on Friday and Saturday nights.

The problem with Peregrine was that he always seemed to be a step ahead of them, as if he had inside information. He knew whom to approach, and he knew how to avoid arrest. Tony had no doubt that the man was a drug peddler, but until two weeks ago no one had been willing to talk.

Thanks to frightened but brave Evan Webster, they now had a little more information to go on. And thanks to old Mr. Scroggs, who had a good memory for detail, they might even have a good case with which to nail this guy. If Peregrine thought he could hide out in this empty house, he'd underestimated the neighborhood watch.

Avoiding the windows, Tony inched toward the front door with calm caution. He figured the two officers going around to the back of the house would be in place by now. He made no noise, cast no giveaway shadow, but before he could reach the knob and test it, he heard a soft thud of footsteps inside the house.

"He's moving," he whispered to Henry. "Get into place."

There was a cry of alarm from the back of the house, and a report of gunfire.

Tony signaled for Henry to stay by the door and quick-stepped to the side of the porch. He turned the corner just in time to see a dark figure retreating into the trees, with two officers in pursuit.

"Door's unlocked," Henry called from behind him. "I'm going in."

Tony swung around. "No! Not—"

His partner pushed the door open as Tony rushed toward him. Tony reached Henry and shoved him out of the doorway just as he heard the sudden telltale sound of a popped cork.

The burning pain of spewing ammonia caught him full in the face, like knives of fire stabbing his eyes.

Reacting with the instinct of recent training, he did not inhale as he stumbled off the porch into ankle-deep grass. Only then did he allow himself to breathe. He gasped and then exhaled with a scream of agony.

———

"All's fine in Knolls, Lauren. The only repeat customer we've had lately has been Cowboy." The strong tones of Lukas Bower's voice over the telephone gave Lauren a feeling of peace she hadn't expected—and for reasons she wouldn't have imagined a few weeks ago. "He's adding camels to his ranch, and when he got his first shipment the bison didn't take too kindly to the newcomers. He had to do some herding and fix a few fences."

"Nothing new, then."

"Nope. Are you really concerned about an epidemic?"

"I think it's a definite possibility at this point," she said. "We lost a patient this morning who presented to the ER last night with simple flu symptoms. Dr. Sheldon has been reviewing the case and can't find anything unusual."

She explained more about the problem and found herself relaxing further as she talked and Lukas replied. He was still the kind, dedicated man she had worked with, but now that she was removed from the situation in Knolls, she realized it was that kindness and dedication she had responded to. He was an attractive man in every way. She simply liked him. Maybe she hadn't made quite the fool of herself she'd always believed she had.

Then again, maybe she had. "Thank you for your help, Lukas."

"I wish there was more I could do. I'll be praying."

"That's what we need most at this point. Give my love to Mercy."

After she hung up, Lauren leaned back in her chair and tried to study the notes she had been taking for the past thirty minutes. Instead, she considered what she'd told Gina last week about the reason she came to Dogwood Springs.

When she was a teenager and in her twenties, she hadn't been terribly interested in dating. Now, all of a sudden, in the space of a year, she had reacted to two attractive men like some of the hormone-driven teenagers she used to run around with in high school. Her biological clock truly was ticking, and her mother's constant reminders about grandchildren didn't help.

But something else was at work here. She was lonely. Everywhere she looked, she saw married couples, engaged couples, families—all spending time together. Sure, a lot of those families had problems, but at least they had someone to come home to. Maybe the married couples who complained about their spouses wouldn't be so critical if they knew how it felt to live alone, if they could imagine not having a confidant to share their thoughts with or a companion who cared more for them than anyone else in the world. Everybody she knew had someone else.

Until recently, Lauren had been able to deal with the single life. But in the past year she'd come to realize that this sense of being alone in the world—in spite of loving parents and brothers and sisters—might be her experience for the rest of her life.

She didn't want to live that way.

And yet, how many more times did she want to express her attraction to a man only to discover he had no interest in her whatsoever?

Grant came back and sat down beside her, and she gave him her report. "Nothing out of the ordinary in Knolls, Branson, West Plains, or Harrison. Whatever this is, it's selective."

"So it's all local." He completed his first stack of files and shoved it aside. "It could be an epidemic, but it doesn't seem to be spreading yet. I'll do some more checking and then talk to our administrator. Right now, though, I doubt if anyone will pay much attention, and I could be jumping to conclusions that are all based on suppositions. I'd like to interview some patients before we take this further. Maybe they're all eating at the same restaurant or something. We might have a new version of Typhoid Mary on our hands. Except this isn't typhoid."

Lauren watched him for a moment as he jotted a few notes. "Grant, do you mind if I ask you one more personal question?"

He laid the pen down and slid the writing pad aside before he turned to make eye contact with her. "Let me guess, you want to know the time and date I accepted Christ as my savior, and what song they were playing during the invitation, and—"

She laughed. "How did you know?"

"Because it's something Annette—" He stopped midsentence and looked away for a few seconds.

Lauren waited.

"Because you're obviously a Christian, and you care," he said softly.

"You don't have to tell me anything. Have I ever warned you I'm nosy? Something that is none of my business—"

"I was seventeen," he said, looking back at her

She smiled her thanks, and he returned the smile.

"Guess who influenced me."

"Annette."

"I was doing speed, and getting drunk when I couldn't get high, and staying away from home on weekends—my parents were going through a nasty divorce, and I didn't want anything to do with them."

Lauren studied his face for a moment to make sure he was serious. He didn't smile. For once, she didn't know what to say. She had discovered, after working only a few shifts with this man, that he was very forthright about himself, both with patients and the staff. If he didn't know something about a patient's case, he admitted it. He was never afraid to ask the opinion of a nurse or a tech, and his honesty inspired confidence. He was willing to share facts about his personal experiences if he thought it would make an impact on one of his patients. But he had never shared this much before.

"Annette was a newcomer to my high school in eleventh grade," he continued. "She was an innocent. A teetotaling Christian. She didn't want anything to do with me—except get me 'saved.' She had these magnificent eyes that seemed to look right through me. She talked with her whole body, with her hands constantly in motion. I couldn't stay away from her. So when she invited me to a youth rally, I went." He shrugged. "Apparently, she thought she saw something worthwhile in me. It was only a matter of time before I was confessing my sins and praying for Christ to take control of my life." There was an edge of sarcasm in Grant's voice, but it sounded more directed toward himself than God.

"And did He?" Lauren asked.

Grant nodded. "I kicked the speed and the alcohol, started going to church, and stopped skipping school so often. My grades improved so dramatically I earned a scholarship the next year. After dating Annette for three years, I married her."

Lauren leaned forward until Grant was forced to look at her. "After all this time, why haven't you forgiven yourself if you know God forgave you?"

"Don't you Baptists still believe there's such a thing as backsliding?"

"It depends on what you mean. You didn't expect to be a perfect Christian after you became a believer, did you?"

"No, but I didn't expect to doubt my faith years later, either."

"God is more than an emotional experience. Doubts are normal, Grant. There's nothing wrong with examining your faith."

"I didn't just examine it, I think I lost it."

"But *God* didn't lose *you*. He didn't break the faith with you."

Grant shook his head. "After the auto accident that killed Annette, my addiction found me again. I sustained a back injury in the crash, and I had to have pain medication. I continued to need it after the damage healed. I was hooked again—after all those years thinking God had healed me for good."

"That happens a lot, Grant. You know it does."

"Brooke and Beau were struggling to come to terms with the loss of their mother—Beau was injured and enduring repeated surgeries—and I couldn't be the father they needed because I was strung out on drugs half the time."

"Legal drugs."

"They were drugs. Don't tempt me to make excuses for myself."

"Are you still addicted?"

"No."

"Not to drugs, anyway, huh? Sounds like you're addicted to an old enemy, though."

He looked up at her.

"Guilt," she said.

Grant pushed away from the desk and stood—a strong signal to Lauren that she was probing a sensitive area a little too deeply. He reached for the folders, stacked them, and turned back to her. "Archer has invited my family to go fishing with your group a week from tomorrow."

She didn't react to the sudden change of subject. "That's great. We'll have fun."

He raised a hand to silence her. "Before you meet Beau, there's something you need to know about him. A piece of metal from the doorframe took a couple of slices out of his face during the accident, and he suffered considerable nerve damage."

Lauren caught her breath. How much pain was one family expected to endure?

"He's had extensive plastic surgery since the accident, but the best surgeons in the state weren't able to repair the damaged nerve," Grant said. "He actually cannot express a smile or laughter with his facial muscles. It's important to me that he isn't made to feel uncomfortable about it."

"Of course it would be. I'm glad you told me."

He slumped back down into the chair and sighed. "I try not to do this. I know I hover too much over my children. It's a habit I've been attempting to break for two years."

"I think it's a loving trait," she said softly, feeling her eyes sting with compassion for this man and his wounded family. "Isn't that what parental love is all about? My parents hover too much. I may feel smothered sometimes, but I always feel loved. Was Brooke injured?"

"She wasn't with us."

"Dr. Sheldon," the secretary called from the front desk. "We just got a call from the police. The ambulance is on its way here with an officer who was caught by an ammonia booby trap of some kind. It got him in the face. The paramedic is requesting medical control."

Grant nodded to Lauren and they rushed toward the front.

Thirty-three-year-old Tony Dalton was guided feet first through the automatic double doors of the ER. His gurney was being pulled by an EMT and pushed by one of the police officers as a paramedic continually irrigated Tony's gauze-covered eyes with saline from a plastic bottle. The police sergeant's body was secured to the gurney by straps and raised rails. His moans of pain were a definite improvement from the loud cries Grant had heard over the ambulance radio a few moments ago.

"Is that morphine easing any of the pain?" Grant asked.

"Yes, it's eased down a lot," the paramedic said. "It's okay, Tony, we're here now."

Two officers dressed in black uniforms surged into the department before the entrance doors closed. They stayed out of the way but announced their presence to their sergeant.

"My wife? Where's Caryn?" Tony asked.

"Henry said he'd call her as soon as we drove off," one of the officers replied.

"I heard. I don't believe him." Tony's voice disintegrated into another moan. "He promised to wait for my order. He didn't . . . didn't do it."

"Our secretary will call your wife, Sergeant Dalton," Grant said as he directed the attendants to the trauma room. "Is there anyone else you need us to contact?"

"Archer. Get Archer. I need all the prayer . . . oh, help me, God. My eyes . . . they're burning so bad . . . did they get the perp?"

"No, Sergeant, he escaped out the back."

Tony moaned again. "I heard a shot. Did someone—"

"He fired at us when he ran out the back door. We couldn't return fire. Too many homes nearby."

"Get back out there and help the others look. Stop wasting your time in here with me. That creep's going to end up killing all our kids if we don't stop him."

Grant helped the attendants transfer his patient to a bed. "Officers, no more questions until we start treatment on his eyes. Lauren, are the Morgan lenses ready? I want one for each eye. And have the litmus paper ready."

"Yes, Dr. Sheldon, I've got it, and here's the tetracaine."

He removed the gauze from Tony's right eye and winced at the damage from the caustic burns. The cornea and sclera were distorted.

Grant took the litmus paper and touched it to the eye, then took the small vial of tetracaine from Lauren, snapped the top off and squeezed four drops into the eye. Meanwhile, the paper turned dark green. Very caustic. If they didn't hurry and do something, this man was going to lose his sight.

The tetracaine worked quickly, and Grant placed a Morgan lens beneath the upper and lower lids of the right eye while Lauren hung the IV fluid from the bedside pole and connected the tubing to the lens to give continuous irrigation. They quickly repeated the process with the left eye.

"Can you tell me exactly what happened?" Grant asked.

"It was a rigged trap, Doctor, as far as we could tell," one of the officers told him. "A container of ammonia was set to spew when the front door opened. Sergeant Dalton caught it in the face when he tried to knock his partner out of the way."

"Do you have any throat irritation? Shortness of breath?" Grant asked Tony.

"Not much. I didn't breathe it."

Grant gave orders to administer additional morphine through the IV the paramedic had established. In spite of the patient's protests to the contrary, Grant noted that his respirations were slightly elevated. That could be the result of pain and anxiety. His blood pressure was within normal limits. Lauren reported her assessment findings as she got them.

Tony's face, neck, and arms were red with blisters.

Grant turned to the other RN on duty. "Emma, have Vivian call Lifeline and make sure that airlift is on its way. Get me the ophthalmologist on call with St. John's, and notify the burn team. Has Archer been called?"

"Yes, Vivian contacted him a moment ago."

"Might as well divert him to Springfield. He'll want to be there for his friend."

Twenty minutes later, when the helicopter made its noisy arrival outside, a repeat litmus test still proved markedly alkaline, and they continued irrigation. Grant had charted a mild chemical pneumonia caused by the ammonia he had inhaled. The prognosis for Tony's eyes, though better than when he first came in, was still discouraging.

At ten-thirty Thursday night Archer drove down a familiar street in Branson and parked in front of a residential complex with an incredible view—in the daytime—of a valley of trees and uninhabited wilderness. Despite a central theme of lights and shows and traffic and congestion, this center of entertainment still held a powerful charm just past the gaudy flicker of neon.

A glow outlined the front window of Jessica's townhouse. Maybe she was home from her show. Archer could have called from the hospital in Springfield, but since he had to pass through Branson to get to Dogwood Springs, he couldn't resist stopping. It had been too long since he'd seen her face, and tomorrow he wouldn't have a chance.

When he rang the doorbell the front porch light came on almost immediately, and he posed for the peephole with a smile and a wave. He heard soft laughter, and the door opened.

Jessica had already removed her stage makeup, and the strong, smiling planes of her expressive face had a translucent glow. She wore faded, baggy jeans and a "Jesus Is Life" T-shirt. Her wavy brown hair—the shade of autumn oak leaves—scattered across her neck and shoulders as she reached for him and drew him into an enthusiastic embrace. He melted against her and held her close. And heaven was better than this? Amazing.

"Oh, Archer, how did you know? I was just praying, telling God how much I wanted to see you again, how much I—" She stopped and drew back to look into his face. "I believe God answers prayers long before we ask them, don't you? And then He holds them for us until the time is right. And He even answers some we forget to ask—some we pray in our hearts but that never touch our lips, and perhaps they shouldn't."

Archer stood in the doorway watching the sparkle in her eyes, knowing it wasn't all for him. It was for God, and he was now basking in the abundance of joy that flowed from her love for God. He knew he was behaving like the biggest dope in a town full of some pretty dopey people, and he suddenly remembered every single reason he loved her so much. The songs she sang were all an overflow of her praise for God.

Jessica took his arm and led him inside, closing the door behind him. Then she sat on the sofa and patted the spot beside her. "So tell me, why did you come tonight instead of tomorrow? And what are you doing out so late on a weeknight?"

"A friend of mine was wounded in the line of duty today," he said as he sank to her side, then told her about Tony and about haunting the hallways at St. John's Hospital in Springfield for most of the day, waiting to hear from the doctors about whether or not Tony's eyes could be saved. He had done a lot of praying, sometimes in the company of one or more members of the Dalton family, sometimes alone.

Before he had said good-night, he had arranged for the Daltons to spend the night at a hospital-owned property so they could be nearby if Tony needed them. When he left the hospital, they didn't know whether Tony would see again.

"Oh, Archer, I'm so sorry." Jessica's voice was a little softer than usual, as it always was after a night of singing. "You look tired."

"I can't get Tony out of my mind. I know it doesn't make any sense, but I almost feel guilty. He was wounded protecting people like me."

"I understand what you mean, but I don't think you need to feel guilty." She leaned closer to him and took his arm. "I know exactly why you came here tonight."

"Why is that?"

"Because you're breaking our date for tomorrow, and coming by to tell me in person was the gentlest way to do it."

"No, I came by for entirely selfish motives. I wanted to see you."

"But you did come to break our date, because you're not going to be available tomorrow. You're taking your day off to go back to Tony's bedside, because that's where you know you need to be, and that's your chosen profession."

Archer watched her face, surprised by the fact that he saw no resentment there. Maybe some disappointment, but in a way that was a good thing.

"And you will slowly give your whole self to your profession, just the way Tony has done. You're taking risks that may not be as dangerous physically, but they take their toll emotionally, and in the long run, they will take just as much out of you."

"That used to upset you. What's changed?"

She gave him a gentle smile. "I told you, I've been praying. God's been showing me a lot of things. How can I find fault in what you do when I do the same thing myself? I work long hours and I don't always get enough sleep. I risk damaging my vocal cords when I don't take the time to practice and stretch my range before I tackle a demanding piece of music." She reached up and touched her throat. "And yet I keep pushing. When someone asks me to sing, I accept, even to the point of overuse. Because I love it, I do it."

"Jessica, does this mean—"

She touched his lips with her fingers. "What it means, Archer Pierce, is that because I care so very much about you, I am going to send you home now so you can get some rest. And so can I."

"But maybe we could—"

"I told you I've been talking a lot to God about this. That doesn't mean He's given me all the answers yet. You know I have a tendency to be impulsive. I don't want to be impulsive about this. It means too much. It affects too many people—and too much of my heart. I want to make the right decision for you and for me, but most of all for God." With a charming display of that impulsive nature Jessica tried so hard to discipline, she gave him a sweet, intoxicating kiss, then stood and held out her hand.

She saw him to the door and out into the night. He drove home with the memory of her kiss enveloping his whole heart.

CHAPTER 14

Archer arrived late for his appointment with Norville and Evan Webster at the church Friday morning—something that rarely happened, even on a day off. In spite of his fatigue last night when he got home, he'd felt compelled to call his parents and let them know about Tony. The Daltons had been friends with the Pierces for many years. After that conversation, several more members of the church family had called to ask about Tony. This was a church emergency.

Archer was tired, but there would be no time to rest today. This session with the Websters would be quickly followed by another trip to Springfield to be with Tony to await the doctor's verdict.

If Dad and Mom weren't spending part of the year with Uncle Virgil in Washington they would be at the hospital right now.

"Good morning, Archer." Mrs. Boucher, the church secretary, looked up from a stack of mail on her desk. "The Websters are already in your office waiting for you."

"Thank you." He took a deep breath and rubbed his neck in an attempt to restore some function to his tired brain.

Today Evan's eyes were clear and his gaze more alert. When Archer greeted him he stood respectfully and shook hands. He had a firm grip, much like his father's.

"I'm glad you could make it today," Archer said. He took a chair across from them instead of sitting behind his desk. "Evan, before I forget it, some of us are planning a little fishing trip next Friday. Would you like to join us?"

Evan's eyes widened in surprise. "Sure. If I can. I mean, I'd have to ask my mom first, but she hasn't grounded me or anything." A fresh smile of eager excitement transformed him. "Yeah, I'd really like that."

"Good. I'll try to pick you up around one-forty-five." Archer looked at Norville, whose expression mirrored his son's. "How about you, Norville? You're welcome to join us."

"I'll be at work, of course, but by all means, take Evan with you. He's never been fishing before."

"Good. We're planning to invite some other teenagers from church. Since Dr. Sheldon just moved to the area with his son and daughter we want to make them all feel welcome in the community, show them around a little."

Evan's expression brightened further. "Dr. Sheldon's going to be there? All right!"

Norville's smile faded into concern. "Does he know Evan will . . . I mean, he may not want his own kids—"

Evan caught his breath, and the pain caused by his father's stumbling words etched across his face like a crack in the ground. "Dad!"

"No, I didn't . . . I mean . . . that isn't what—"

Archer rushed to intercept. "If I know Grant, he'll be happy to see Evan. I think they established a good rapport, don't you, Evan?"

The boy's face reddened, and he slumped in his chair as the earlier transformation reversed itself. "Yeah." He cupped his hands together in his lap.

Before Archer could say anything more, the telephone rang at his desk. He glanced at it, surprised. Mrs. Boucher never sent him calls during counseling sessions.

Except for emergencies.

He reached across the front of the desk and picked up. "Yes?"

"Archer, I wouldn't have disturbed you," Mrs. Boucher told him, "but you need to take this call from Caryn Dalton. She's very upset. It's about Tony. You need to talk to her."

Oh no. This could be their answer, and it didn't sound good. "Yes, of course. Thank you." He mouthed the words *I'm sorry* to Norville and Evan.

There was a click, and Archer heard the soft sound of crying. "Caryn, this is Archer. What's going on? What's happening with Tony?"

For a moment she didn't respond, and while he waited for her reply he saw Evan lean toward his father. "Dad, how could you say something like that? You make it sound like I'm some kind of contagious sicko. I blew it, okay? Do you have to remind me about it for the rest of my life?"

"I'm sorry, son, I didn't mean for it to come out like—"

"Archer?" Caryn's voice came shaky and faint across the line. Archer turned his back to the arguing family and switched gears again.

"Yes, what's happening with Tony? Are you okay?"

"The doctors just told us he's going to be blind. There's too much damage. . . ." Her voice faded in and out with tears, mingling with the quiet discussion that continued behind him.

" . . . what people tend to think when something like this happens. You'll have to rebuild your reputation one act at a time, and it won't be . . ."

" . . . can't do anything to save his eyes. Archer, can you come up? He needs somebody to talk to."

Archer checked his watch. It was eight-thirty. "Yes, I'll be there." He couldn't just dismiss Evan and Norville. They needed reassurance, too, and the drive to Springfield took about an hour and fifteen minutes. "I'll try to make it by ten-thirty. Meanwhile, I'll be praying." It was times like this he wished he could still call Jessica. When they were engaged, there were a couple of times he'd called her to make the drive from Branson to Springfield.

After he said good-bye and had hung up, Archer turned to find father and son still in discussion about the trouble Evan had caused his parents—how he'd let them down and needed to make amends.

"I think Evan is painfully aware of the problems his decision caused," Archer said, trying hard not to be irritated by Norville's tendency to lay the blame for the whole incident onto his son's shoulders. "We need to move past that and help direct him to make the right decision the next time something like this comes up. He needs to be able to—"

"No, the situation needs to stop coming up," Evan said. His voice was firm, deeper than it had been a few moments ago. He sat straighter in his chair, and he made eye contact with his father. "You and Mom need to find some common ground where we can all practice behaving like intelligent human beings. I can't do this alone, Dad. It isn't just *my* problem, it's *our* problem."

Archer and Norville both stared at him in surprise.

Evan held his father's gaze for several seconds before his face reddened and his shoulders slumped. "Anyway, that's what Dr. Sheldon said. He understands. He . . . he's a good doctor."

"You're right, Evan," Archer said. "And I think Dr. Sheldon's right. But it isn't just a family problem—it's a societal problem. It's my problem, because what happens to you affects me, and it affects your friends. Most important, it's God's problem, because He doesn't want you to struggle with it alone. Why don't we pray and bring Him into the equation?"

Norville looked relieved. Evan looked hopeful. Archer was excited. *Lord, wait until they see what you can do.*

———

Grant had never noticed how friendly folks could be in a small town, but as he drove downhill toward City Hall, he counted seven people waving at him. And they weren't the angry waves of overstressed freeway drivers. Four of them were elderly pedestrians in jogging outfits and running shoes. One was a policeman in his cruiser, one was an older lady who was barely tall enough to peer over her steering wheel, and the last one was a gardener pruning blooms in one of a multitude of side gardens dotting the town.

Grant had always admired Thomas Kinkade's paintings of quaint village shops surrounded by flowers, set deep into a craggy hillside, with a stream trickling beneath a rock bridge. In Dogwood Springs he felt as if he were living in the center of one of those pictures, complete with streets constructed of brick. Virginia creeper vines climbed the concrete block walls of City Hall, and a stream half-circled the building like a castle moat. Unfortunately, Grant had begun to realize, lurking beneath the bed of cheerful flowers could be a snake. Maybe more than one. Try as he might, he couldn't stop thinking about the nasty attack on Sergeant Tony Dalton yesterday. That trap had been set to cause serious injury. Someone in Dogwood Springs had a rotten heart.

At City Hall, he pulled open the glass door and stepped into another picturesque scene—this time a Norman Rockwell. A huge, high-ceilinged area the size of an old-fashioned ballroom reverberated with the chatter and laughter of at least fifteen conversations. Clusters of well-dressed people sat at tables around the great hall, eating and drinking, laughing, calling to one another. The smell of food reminded Grant that he hadn't even eaten breakfast yet, and these people were already taking their morning break.

Two elderly men, two suit-clad women, and two children leaned over a table covered with pieces of a puzzle. In the top left corner a square of blue and green had already been put together. One of the women at the table turned her head to the side and coughed. A child across from her sneezed into his hand, then picked up a puzzle piece with that same hand.

Grant cringed at the thought of the germs they must be spreading. Annette used to tease him about what she called his obsession with infection.

He ambled over to the table. "Nice picture." He actually couldn't tell what the setting was supposed to be yet. "Is this a community project?"

One of the men, who looked to be in his eighties, placed a piece and chuckled with satisfaction. "Sure is." He didn't look up, but picked up another piece and continued to study the board. "This table's always busy. Just look over there." He gestured toward the wall to their west, his thick gray eyebrows forming a straight line across his face, lending gravity to the expressive good humor in his eyes.

Grant saw three framed scenes hanging on the wall. He recognized two of them from his forays through Dogwood Springs, and they all had a common theme—streams coursing across a meadow or garden or trickling down a hillside.

"It's the springs." The man straightened and squinted at Grant.

"Springs?"

"Not from around here, huh?"

"No, I'm not."

The man stood, turned from the table, and held out his hand with a slight bow. "Ernest Mourglia. And you might be?"

"Grant Sheldon. I moved down from St. Louis recently with my family. This is obviously a popular place."

Ernest glanced toward the puzzle, as if afraid someone else might take his spot while he was otherwise occupied. "Jade got the bright idea a few months ago to have puzzles made out of pictures of our springs, then sell 'em to the tourists."

"Jade?"

"You really are new here. Jade Myers is the mayor. Bright girl still wet behind the ears, not even thirty-five yet." A smile pressed itself across his craggy, sun-worn face. "My niece. After they started selling the puzzles, Jade decided that wasn't good enough. She decided to make a city-wide effort to put 'em together and display 'em on the walls, kind of make it a showcase to draw some of that Branson traffic our way."

"She sounds like an industrious lady." And one he would speak with as soon as possible about the risk of the community puzzle.

"I didn't like it at first," Ernest continued. "Didn't want the crowds. This used to be a nice peaceful place to come and sit for a few hours and talk to a couple of friends who might wander over for lunch. But now, you wouldn't believe how many old friends I get to see every day." He shook his head. "Always need something to get you out of yourself when you live alone and can't find a fishin' partner."

"How many springs does the city have?"

Mr. Mourglia stepped closer, obviously glad to find a listening ear. "We've got fifteen of 'em inside the city limits, and quite a few more outside, so we've got our work cut out for us, but just you wait—as soon as they get that bottling plant up and runnin', we'll be famous. And that'll be good for the puzzle business. Stores are already carryin' 'em all over town. Sellin', too."

"Bottling plant?"

The old man grimaced. "That was another one of Jade's wild ideas.

But I guess she convinced somebody to listen. They say it won't take too much of our water."

"Ernest!" another man called from across the room.

Ernest turned and squinted, then brightened and turned back to Grant. "You know what? I might've found me a fishin' buddy, after all! And he's my barber, too. Maybe he'll give me a haircut if the fish aren't bitin'. Pleased to meet you, Mr. Sheldon." He reached out to shake hands again, and said good-bye.

Grant felt a weight settle on him as he watched others wander up to the table and pick up where Ernest had left off. A community-wide jigsaw puzzle could feasibly be spreading the pervasive virus, which had already taken one life and threatened another and seemed to be infecting more and more people every day. What was he supposed to do, march into the mayor's office and demand she stop all the fun? Or maybe he should insist they sterilize the puzzle pieces every time someone new came to the table. But even that wouldn't stop it all.

He had run some blood tests—for Giardia and E. coli and a few other infectious diseases—on several of the more serious patients. Nothing. Not influenza, not some weird, community-acquired pneumonia. He had a stack of files on his desk at least two feet high. His comparisons, so far, had turned up no related facts that he considered significant, and several times he'd almost convinced himself he was being paranoid. Almost.

Lives were definitely at stake. When Grant asked directions to the mayor's office, the receptionist told him Jade was out running errands. He decided to wait.

———

By ten-fifteen Archer was walking down a too familiar, wide hallway of St. John's Hospital in Springfield. He'd spent a lot of time here over the years—making visits with his father when he was still in high school, and afterward on his own.

Some pastors dreaded making hospital visits, and Archer could understand their feelings. He had never found hospitals to be the most comforting of places to pass the day, either, but they were certainly one of the best places for a guy to go when he wanted to tell somebody about God. Stuck in a hospital bed, people had to listen—and most often they were eager to do so. Nothing could open the human heart to important matters of the spirit like a threat to life or health.

Today, he wouldn't have to do any proselytizing. Tony Dalton had walked the aisle of the Dogwood Springs Baptist Church to get saved two months before Archer had. Both of them had been ten at the time. Both had been raised in church, attended the same Sunday school classes, and sang in the youth choir. And Tony had always done it better.

Tony got high grades, Tony got the solo tenor parts in choir, Tony excelled in math and sports, and he was valedictorian when they graduated. Probably the only thing that had kept Archer and Tony from being the best of friends was Archer's dad's admiration for Tony. Archer had struggled with jealousy. He'd repented of it years ago.

As he stepped into the private room, Archer saw Tony lying in bed with white bandages covering his eyes. His wife, Caryn, sat at his side with her forehead resting on his pillow, her sparrow brown hair falling across the tanned flesh of his arm.

"Hello, you two." Archer swallowed, fighting to keep his voice steady.

Caryn stiffened and sat up. Her face was pale and her lips were bloodless, as if grief had drained her completely. "Hi, Archer." She got up and walked around the bed to hug him. She felt frail in his arms when he hugged her back. "Talk to him," she whispered.

Tony turned his head toward the sound. "Arch?" He held his hand out, fingers spread in an unconscious gesture of vulnerability.

Archer stepped forward and took it. "Hi, Tony. You look like you're doing a little better than you were last night."

The hand tightened on Archer's with a strength that, for a few seconds, became nearly unbearable, then it relaxed. Tony laid his head back. He licked his lips, pressed them together, and sighed. "Caryn said she told you."

"Yes."

As if he had to review the facts himself in order to continue to make sense of them, Tony repeated what Archer had already heard. "The eyes are too badly damaged." Tony's hand squeezed into a fist, and he pressed it against his chest. "The insurance guys were here already. I'm a great candidate for full disability."

"If they think *that* they don't know you," Archer said.

Tony's voice grew ragged. "They want me to sit on my butt and draw checks for doing nothing the rest of my life."

"But we know—"

"I might as well be—"

"No, Tony." Caryn stepped to the end of the bed and gripped the rail with both hands. "Please don't talk like that, sweetheart." She gave Archer a beseeching look.

"You know better than that," Archer said.

Tony shook his head. "My job is over. I'll never be a policeman again. I'll never be able to drive again. My wife will have to drive me around and watch after me like an invalid."

Archer saw the lance of pain race across Caryn's face, and in response to her continued silence he protested. "Anthony Dalton, I can't believe you would even use that word."

Tony didn't reply.

Archer pressed harder. "Did that chemical reach your brain as well as your eyes?"

Caryn's mouth flew open in shock, but Archer raised a hand to keep her from speaking. "Don't you remember that beautiful speech you gave graduation night?" he asked. "Come on, Tony, it wasn't *that* long ago."

For a moment there was no response, and then Tony gave a barely perceptible nod. "I didn't know any better then. I do now. I was a stupid kid."

"You were obviously smarter then than you are now."

"Archer," Caryn warned.

"Caryn, I bet he never told you about his valedictorian speech, did he?"

She shook her head.

"He received a standing ovation. He talked about the role of the physically challenged in the scheme of life, that they can be the strongest of us all because they're forced to fight harder and build extra muscle. Then he dissected the word *invalid*, explaining that no one was in-valid. Everyone has validity. His inspiration had come from working with disabled children down at the elementary school during his free hour."

Caryn blinked and looked back at her husband, who had not moved.

"I remember the speech really well," Archer added, "because Tony spoke the same passionate words to our congregation that next Sunday, at Dad's request. And Dad reminded me of that speech for the next six months, until I was sick to death of Tony Dalton's name."

At that, a bare hint of a smile touched Tony's lips, and then it was gone. Caryn stood at the end of the bed, still grasping the rail, her eyes suddenly focused on her husband's mouth.

"This accident has done nothing to invalidate who you are," Archer continued. "It doesn't invalidate you in God's eyes, or in Caryn's, or in—"

Tony raised his hand. "Archer, didn't you hear me? They want me to draw disability for the rest of my life."

"So? Since when did you ever take stupid advice?"

"What good is a blind policeman?"

"As good as you're willing to be," Archer said. "What do you want to do? That's usually what you've done."

Tony's jaw muscles flexed. He shook his head. "I don't know what—"

"Of course you know, Tony." Caryn stepped from the foot of the bed to her husband's side. "Sweetheart, you've always told me you want to teach." She looked up at Archer. "His chief told me two weeks ago that Tony knows more about meth production in our county than anyone else on the force."

"I'm also supposed to know more about the traps they set," Tony muttered. "Look where that got me."

"Tony, it isn't as if you can crawl into the minds of these people," Archer protested.

"I'm supposed to try. If I can't, I won't be much good to myself or anyone else."

"But that's crazy," Caryn said.

"No, it's essential." Tony sat forward, and the keenly contained energy that had always been a part of Tony Dalton once more filled the air around him. "It's vital, because the rules are always changing. All a guy has to do is let down his guard one time, and it's over." Tony spread his hands. "You've got to think like a monster. We can't wait around until they change something on us; we've got to beat them at their own game." The energy increased.

Archer and Caryn looked at each other, and Caryn nodded.

"I don't think it's over for you," Archer said to his old friend.

"It's dangerous out there, Archer. I told you the other night—crime is on the rise. I keep trying to warn people that our little town is right in the middle of some nasty drug activity. Nobody wants to listen."

"I'm listening, Tony," Archer said.

"It's like this big black cloud is hovering over Dogwood Springs, and it's silently seeping into every neighborhood. Our officers are always on the prowl for signs of new meth houses springing up. We have our regular routes we follow several times a shift, keeping a lookout for suspicious activity. The problem is, no one who uses their stuff is willing to blow the whistle—and you'd be amazed at the number of people in our community who do meth." Tony turned his face toward Archer, as if he could see him.

"I've been concerned about rising drug use for a long time," Archer said. "I worry about some of the people in our own congregation. That's why I started the classes on Tuesday nights."

"It's bigger than it looks on the surface. You wouldn't believe how many crimes in our own town are direct results of meth production and addiction."

"Then why don't you start by talking to my drug awareness class as soon as they spring you from here," Archer said.

Tony nodded. "They need to know. It's just so hard to keep up with all of it. I've been too busy fighting it to . . . But I guess all that's changed, hasn't it?"

Archer looked across the bed at Caryn. She nodded. Tony's job would never end.

CHAPTER 15

L auren appreciated the changing seasons in the Ozarks, and every
season had its own special mood. At the moment, summer was her
favorite in this town. These people did things a little differently—
with more style, more extravagance, more flowers—than in her
hometown.

On Friday afternoon, as she rode in the passenger's seat of Archer's
two-year-old Kia, she drank in the effusive beauty of the hillside community while she allowed herself to enjoy the fact that Archer had
sought her company for this visit.

"Grant Sheldon impresses me." Archer touched the brake and
turned onto a road that wound between widely spaced homes, most of
them painted in pretty pastel colors, with broad porches that invited
visitors to make themselves comfortable on a porch swing or a wicker
chair. The late afternoon sun highlighted Archer's handsome silhouette
against a backdrop of blue sky.

"The staff likes him," Lauren said. "He knows how to handle people." She thought again about the drunk who had gotten out of hand
Wednesday night. "He's making some good changes in the ER, like
shortening shift hours and overlapping schedules so we have double
physician coverage at peak times. We needed that."

"Shortening hours?" He gave her a quick look. "And that makes him
popular?"

"So far he's managing to do it without ruffling too many feathers."

She thought of Dr. Mitchell Caine. "Some feathers need to be ruffled, and he doesn't mind doing that. You have to respect that kind of leadership."

Archer gave her his customary sideways teasing grin that she always thought made him look like a young Paul Newman. "You wouldn't happen to be slightly biased, would you? He *is* a good-looking, eligible bachelor."

Without thinking, Lauren returned the grin in full measure, and winked at him. "Oh, I don't know, he isn't the only good-looking single guy in town." As soon as the words were out of her mouth she felt the warmth of embarrassment spread across her face. Perhaps she should have asked to ride in the trunk.

At thirty-five, she had long ago despaired of ever learning to control her tongue, whether it be talking too much or saying the wrong thing at the wrong time.

Lauren had known Archer for a lot of years. Until recently she'd never been uncomfortable in his presence. Never before had she thought of him as anything other than a very likeable friend of her younger brothers, with whom she had arm wrestled and played one-on-one basketball, and to whom she'd given Dutch rubs when he and her brothers got out of line and no grown-ups were around.

Lately, however, she'd become increasingly aware of him as a very attractive man, with an inner light that filled his eyes with passion and excitement whenever he spoke about his love for Jesus Christ. To her, that was one of the most appealing things about him. The better she came to understand him as a man, and not just "one of the boys," the more powerful grew that appeal. She thought about her discussion with Gina last week. It had been difficult enough to get accustomed to the idea of Archer Pierce as her pastor when she joined the church. But it felt really weird to be attracted to him as a man, especially one who had been very happily engaged until a few weeks ago.

A stray dog ambled out onto the road, and Archer stomped on the brakes. Characteristically, he didn't honk, didn't complain, didn't even shake his head—he just watched to make sure the animal was off the road completely before moving on.

That was another thing she had always liked about him. He was patient.

"Lauren, did you hear about Tony?" He glanced across to find her watching him.

She looked away. "Yes. I called this afternoon to check on him. How's he handling it?"

"He's already making plans for a career change." There was admiration in his voice.

"I'll give Caryn a call."

"I thought you might." He signaled and turned onto Cascade Circle Drive.

The road wound through an older neighborhood that had recently received a facelift. The address they sought was in a cul-de-sac, set slightly apart from the other more stately homes. Gina's house was an attractive, dove gray color with burgundy gingerbread trim and Victorian lace curtains in the windows, but it seemed enshrouded by an evergreen hedge that threatened to overtake the sidewalk and yard.

When Gina answered the doorbell she was barefoot except for inconspicuous skin-colored bandages. She wore a pair of denim cutoffs frayed above the knees, and curls of golden copper hair tumbled across her wide freckled forehead. She could have passed for a carefree teenager except for the tight lines around her mouth and the flash of anger in her eyes.

"I don't know how much more of this I can take." Instead of inviting them inside, she stepped out onto the porch and allowed the door to shut behind her. She and Lauren had been to lunch a few times, and the comfort of deepening friendship continued to grow between them. "That woman doesn't give me any breaks."

"What woman?" Lauren asked, although she already knew.

"Natalie—who else? She's always following me around the house, asking me personal questions, grilling my kids. She's like a long-legged, long-necked goose who's flown south for the winter, and she thinks my house is her own private lake."

"I'm sorry, Gina," Archer said. "Did we come at a bad time? If she's—"

"No." There was a defensiveness in Gina's tone. "I have a right to receive company in my own home."

"Of course you do," Archer said soothingly. "You have a beautiful home." He stepped over and examined the sculpted gingerbread trim around a window.

"Thanks." Gina shoved her hands into the back pockets of her shorts.

Lauren didn't comment. She knew from several talks with Gina these past two weeks that her reluctance to accept help from Family Services went a lot deeper than just an independent nature. Something else was going on here—something Gina still hesitated to share.

The young respiratory therapist didn't smile much at work lately, and several people on the emergency staff had noticed. Last week, when Gina had her physical exam, none of her tests had shown a problem. She had placed her hope on some evidence of low blood sugar, and when her levels were normal, that hope had been dashed. Her psychological tests had also revealed no problem.

"She's in the dining room with the kids right now," Gina continued at last, her voice softer, but no less resentful. "She's probably trying to find out if I've been abusing them."

"Gina," Lauren said, "you know that isn't fair. Finding blame isn't what all this is about."

Gina shrugged and sighed. "We'll see."

"Want to sit down and talk about it?" Archer asked.

Gina hesitated, and the steady directness of her gaze shifted from him to Lauren.

He corrected quickly. "Better yet, why don't you point me to your hedge trimmers, and I'll have a go at the jungle that's threatening to take over your yard while the two of you talk."

The tightness relaxed from around Gina's mouth, and a hesitant smile spread to her eyes. She told Archer where to find the hedge trimmers in her garage, and he leaped from the porch. As he jogged away from them Lauren couldn't resist an appreciative glance at the way the late afternoon sunlight teased flashes of flame from his short brown hair. Of course, the broad shoulders were also nice . . . the muscular arms . . . the—

"I see what you mean."

Lauren blinked and looked at Gina to find an amused grin on her face. "What do I mean?"

"No wonder you like him so much. He's good-looking, sensitive, and he does yard work. Obviously athletic, too. He has muscles where most men have flab."

"And he loves God."

Gina considered Lauren for a few seconds. "According to you, that's the most important qualification."

"Believe me, it is." Since there was no porch furniture, Lauren led the way to the front steps and sat down. "Come and talk to me, Gina. What's wrong? What's going on between you and Natalie? You're obviously still striking sparks."

Gina sighed and sank down beside her, ruffling her hair with her fingers in a frenzied, frustrated shake. "I just can't get used to her barging into my home and trying to take over my life. She hardly knows me, and yet she bombards me with all these questions, from my eating habits to the medicines we take to the kinds of cookware I use. She even checked out my vitamins. And she snooped into my family background, called it a genogram. I mean, this woman did a family tree on me! Wanted to know what my childhood was like, how my parents raised me . . ." She shivered. "It's creepy."

"She wouldn't do it if she didn't think it was going to help. I hope you gave her the information she asked for."

There was a short, expressive silence. "Only what she needed to know." Gina pressed her lips together as Archer came striding back around to the front of the house, hedge clippers in hand. She lowered her voice. "My past is nobody's business."

Lauren covered her frustration and kept her voice soft. "But since she's an unbiased stranger, she might be able to find some clue about what's going on with you."

"Oh, sure, and she might also find enough evidence against me to go flying into court and convince them to take my kids away from me."

"But why would they *want* to?" Lauren hoped Natalie was a patient person. Gina seemed to have a phobia about losing her children. Of course, what parent wouldn't? Gina was just more sensitive than most because of what happened to her. Natalie could surely understand that.

"Last night she brought up the subject of foster care again. 'Just as a worst-case scenario,' she says." Gina glared at the sidewalk in front of them. "I told her if she didn't change the subject, I'd show *her* a worst-case scenario."

Lauren suppressed a sigh.

"Sorry," Gina said. "I'm venting. Honest, I'm not usually this cranky, but it's been so long since I've had anybody try to tell me how to live my life. She just barges in and plants herself in my home. And that other social worker, the one from the hospital—"

"Rose Pascal?"

"Yes, Rose. You heard what she said at that wraparound meeting. If I don't cooperate with this investigation they can request that the court take my children away."

Lauren knew it would do no good to argue with Gina right now. All Rose wanted to do was ensure the safety of Levi and Cody while they helped Gina work out her problems. What continued to catch Lauren's attention was Gina's resistance to answering any questions about her past.

This young woman desperately needed a friend, but there were places in her life that seemed untouchable.

"What upset me most," Gina continued, "was that last night Levi overheard her talking to me about foster care, and after she left it took me nearly an hour to calm him down."

"Oh, poor Levi. I'm sure he was pretty frightened."

"Wouldn't you have been scared when you were six if someone threatened to take you away from your parents?"

"Terrified."

"Anybody would be." Gina's voice spiked in agitation, and she immediately pressed her lips together and took a deep breath, as if trying to control her emotions. She glanced at Archer and lowered her voice again. "I'm embarrassed about my yard. I was going to trim those hedges last weekend, but then . . . all this happened." She let her hands drop to her lap. "It seems as if I always have something else to do, and I'm not that great with yard work."

"I love yard work. If you want I'll come over and help you later."

"Natalie said she'd help. Speaking of Natalie, she wants to talk to me again after she grills my—excuse me, I mean after she interviews my children."

Archer finished one section and started stacking branches, and for a few moments both Gina and Lauren watched him in silence.

"You remember what we talked about during our first lunch together?" Gina said at last. "You know, about getting that second opinion?"

Lauren looked at her. "Yes—from the Great Physician." Had her words actually made an impact?

Gina continued to watch Archer, though her expression told Lauren she wasn't really seeing him.

"But the way you described it made it sound as if I would have to turn my whole life over to Him."

"He works best when we keep our own hands out of the way," Lauren said.

"I'm not planning to turn my life over to anyone; I'm talking about a consultation. Why would I want to make a change? It sounds to me as if I'd just be taking on a whole new set of rules, and I'd still be in the same mess I'm in now. Physically, it isn't going to change anything. I mean, this Great Physician stuff is really just about the spiritual realm, right?"

Lauren gave Archer a wishful glance. She could use his support in this conversation . . . but then, Gina might feel as if they were ganging up on her.

"It's hard to explain, because everything about your life would be so different with Christ in it."

"In what way?"

"Your whole mind-set changes. There's this overwhelming love that goes with you wherever you go."

"You mean, I'll have all these sappy, good feelings for everyone?"

Lauren chuckled. "It isn't a feeling, and it doesn't come from you. It comes from God. You begin to understand that God loves you more perfectly than any parent could love her child."

Gina shook her head. "I can't imagine that."

"It's impossible for a human being to imagine God, because His power and goodness are so far out of our realm. When you turn to Him, you grow more and more aware of His power in your life, and the more you turn your life over to Him, the more complete it becomes. You learn that living for Him isn't a chore or a burden—it's a gift from Him. It's a privilege."

"So you're saying I'll be this nice little robot for God, and in exchange for all my hard work, I should be thankful that He lets me do it?"

"No, because we discover that the very things God calls us to do are the most fulfilling elements of our lives. We are all created with different gifts, different talents. I believe God gave me the gift of healing, and so I use my healing touch with my nursing skills. I also have a gift for teaching, and so I use that gift teaching children in Sunday school."

"But Lauren," Gina said, her voice suddenly going soft as she gave Archer a cautious glance, "what about children of your own? I know you want that more than just about anything else. Why won't He give you that?"

The question caught Lauren off guard. Trust Gina to find the chink in her armor. "He never said He wouldn't give me children. It isn't as if I'm seventy years—"

"Well, if He's going to do it, He'd better get going."

In spite of Lauren's desire to reach out to Gina, those words cut deeply, and Lauren fell silent.

Gina caught her breath and looked at Lauren. "I'm sorry. That sounded mean, and I didn't intend for it to be." She sighed and shook her head. "Go ahead and tell me about God."

Lauren detected a note of resignation in Gina's voice. Why even bother? Gina wasn't listening. All she wanted to do was argue, and God was just a good subject to debate.

Gina touched Lauren's arm hesitantly, gently. "I mean it, Lauren. I'm sorry. I didn't mean for it to come out that way. But I do have a lot of questions, and I don't know anyone else to ask. I mean . . . it isn't as if I can go straight to God like you can."

"You could, you know."

Gina shook her head. "Not me."

"Yes, you. He would walk beside you and help you with any

changes that needed to be made. He wouldn't just slap a bunch of heavy rules on you—he would gently guide you in a better direction for your life. He would love you unconditionally, like a loving father. He would—"

"My father died when I was ten."

"Oh, Gina, I'm sorry."

She didn't respond for a moment but continued to watch Archer. Lauren didn't know what to say. *Lord, please touch her heart. Let me know how to reach her.*

"He was a good dad," Gina said at last. "He cared enough to teach me important things, even when I was young. I remember he used to give me an allowance, and he always made me save half of it. By the time I was nine, I'd saved enough to buy my own bicycle. Because I learned how to manage my money, I was able to buy this house with very small monthly payments."

"I love my father very much," Lauren told her. "I can't imagine what it would have been like to grow up without him, grumpy and cantankerous as he gets sometimes. But God doesn't get cantankerous, and He's always patient with me." Even when she made a mess of things, like right now.

Gina slumped and looked down at her hands. "Sorry, Lauren. It's kind of hard to compare God to my father." She sighed and spread her hands in the air. "I just don't get it. I've got too much to think about right now. Maybe . . . maybe later."

"Of course. I'll be here for you, Gina. You can talk to me about it anytime."

The younger woman nodded stiffly and pulled herself up. "I think I'll go check on Natalie and see if the kids are finished. If they are, would you mind keeping them occupied for a while out here? That way maybe Levi won't overhear another argument."

"I'd be glad to."

Gina nodded and murmured her thanks as she rushed in the front door.

Lauren sighed.

"You handled that well," Archer said over his shoulder as he continued to clip.

Lauren stood up and walked over to gather some of the branches he'd scattered behind him. "You were eavesdropping again."

"I have ears like an eagle."

"Eagles are famous for their vision, not their sense of hearing."

"Trust me, this eagle was born with 20/20 hearing."

"It's obvious to me you're not medically inclined, because—"

Archer chuckled. "Lauren, did I ever tell you that I have always admired your ability to overanalyze my jokes? You remember the year you made me promise not to lure your brothers into the lake at church camp?"

"You did it anyway."

"I did not lure them, they lured me."

"Aha! So that's why I had to pull you out."

"Your brothers tricked me."

"And you got in over your head and nearly drowned."

"See? There you go overanalyzing me again!" He clipped a couple more big branches, then stood back and admired his uneven handiwork. "Don't tell Gina I've never trimmed a hedge before in my life."

"I won't say a word." She stifled a laugh. "I won't have to."

"Your mother would have loved Dogwood Springs." Grant tapped the brake and slowed to wait for a pedestrian to jaywalk across the red-brick street. Under protest from his daughter, Brooke, he had rolled down the windows, and now he drove slowly so that the wind wouldn't ruffle her hair as she rode in sullen silence in the middle of the backseat.

"I wish we'd moved here sooner," Grant said.

There was a snort from the back, then more silence.

"Mom loved St. Louis, too, Dad," Beau said as they stopped at a traffic signal and watched that same pedestrian rush in front of them in the crosswalk. Beau rested his arm in the passenger seat window and studied the quiet bustle of the downtown area with interest. His firm, square jaw came from the Sheldon side of the family, but the dreamy tenderness of his eyes behind those wire-framed glasses came from Annette's side. The dark gray color was pure Grant, but the kindness and caring evident in them, in Grant's opinion, came from Annette.

"Maybe if we had come here a few years ago she could have learned to relax a little more, to take some time for herself every once in a while," Grant said.

Beau gave his dad a pointed look. "You're dreaming again. She would have volunteered at the hospital and joined the nearest, neediest church and cruised the town in search of someone who didn't have a home or food or—"

"Light's green, Dad," Brooke said. "Come on. I've got things to do and people to see."

Grant waited until another jaywalking pedestrian cleared their path and then pressed his foot on the accelerator. "I guess you're right," he told his son. "She was a natural encourager." He glanced into the rear-view mirror at his daughter. "It's a good habit to get into."

Brooke met his gaze in the mirror. "You'd be surprised what an encourager I would be if I had a car. You know that Meals-on-Wheels thing Mom used to do? I could do that."

Beau snorted. "How long would that last? You'd have to get up before noon."

"Hey, I made it to school on time every morning all year, didn't I? It can be done. For a car, I'd do it."

"Tell you what," Grant said. "If you two get part-time jobs and earn enough this summer to pay half the price of a car, I'll sign for you to get a loan so you can pay off the other half."

There was a gasp from the backseat. "What? You're serious? You'd let us get a car?"

"Yes, but the two of you would have to share it, and you'd have to make payments and share the cost of insur—"

A high-pitched squeal assaulted Grant's ears and earned him a dirty look from his son when Brooke unsnapped her seat belt and grabbed her brother around the neck in a stranglehold of excitement.

Beau fought her off. "Would you stop it? Put your seat belt back on."

"Why? We can't be going more than five miles an hour."

"Brooke," Grant warned.

She did as she was told.

"He's tricking us, Brooke," Beau informed her. "There's no way we'd be able to earn enough money for the kind of car you'd have to have—"

"Oh, shut up." Brooke giggled. "You could use a little of Mom's gift of encouragement yourself, you know. Let's start looking for jobs today."

While his children continued their bantering, Grant once again allowed his thoughts to rest on Annette. It was true that she had been an encourager. Sometimes the job pressures that went with that particular role in life got her into situations she hadn't been able to handle alone. Her caring spirit had seemed to radiate from her eyes, and hurting souls had read that compassion clearly.

Annette had given of herself when too many people only wanted to take and take and keep on taking. Too many abused and injured hearts were starved for the godly love Annette was eager to share. Grant had seen her in tears because she couldn't always meet the pressing emotional, physical, or financial needs of others.

Her natural tendency to encourage attracted people to her like wedding guests to the cake.

Grant had loved her completely. Throughout their romance and marriage no other woman had drawn him. How could they? Annette was the standard by which he viewed all other women. When she gained weight with her pregnancy and later failed to lose much of it, the height-weight tables might just as well have been adjusted upward for the whole world.

Compared to Annette, Grant had found every other woman lacking that divine ingredient that had always attracted him to her. And he wasn't the only one who experienced that attraction.

Now it frightened him that someone else had begun to set a few of her own standards. Now if a woman didn't have a green-eyed smile that illuminated the room with sudden sunshine—and didn't answer to the name of Lauren McCaffrey—she was relegated to the ranks of "Thank you, but not interested."

Grant was aware that some poor nearsighted women occasionally seemed to find him attractive. Sometimes he even picked up on gestures of flirtation—Annette had taught him to watch for the signs.

But Lauren had never implied in any way that she thought him attractive or that she even noticed he was a male member of her species.

"Dad! Where are you going?" Brooke's sudden cry of alarm jerked Grant's attention back to his driving just in time. He had signaled to turn the wrong way onto the only one-way street in Dogwood Springs.

"Oops. Sorry." He switched off the signal, waved into the rearview mirror in apology to the confused driver behind them, and drove another two blocks.

"Dad, maybe we don't need another car," Brooke said. "You need a chaperone."

CHAPTER 16

When Archer was nine years old, he had attempted to help his mom out one day by cutting his younger brother's hair. By the time he finished, his brother was nearly bald, with stray tufts of blond hair sticking up from strange places on his scalp.

Apparently, Archer hadn't learned his lesson, because now, as he stood gazing across his latest effort, he realized that if he continued, poor Gina would be left with privacy *stubs* instead of privacy *shrubs*.

In frustration, he laid the clippers on the sidewalk and started stacking branches, and he continued to practice one of the things he did well—eavesdropping.

"Mama says I'm smart enough to read numbers and call for help on the telephone if she starts acting weird again." Six-year-old Levi sat squeezed next to Lauren so his little brother couldn't fit between them, even though Cody kept trying to do just that.

"Your mother's right." Lauren's voice was soft and gentle. "One of those telephone numbers is for me."

"Yes, and she wrote down some numbers and put them by the telephone so we can call for help, because she says I'm a big boy and I'm so smart she knows I can do the job right." Levi paused and looked up at Lauren. "Do you have any more stories?"

"Werewolf stories?" Cody asked. "Like Mama!"

"Your mother tells werewolf stories?" Lauren asked.

"No, she says there isn't any such thing." Levi huddled closer to

Lauren. "But sometimes we watch cartoons on Saturday morning. Cody likes the werewolf cartoons. It's a good werewolf, though, like Mom. He acts weird and starts to make scary sounds in his throat like Mom."

"But Levi, you know there isn't any such thing as a werewolf," Lauren said gently.

"Not mean ones. But this is a nice werewolf, and he runs away so nobody will see him grow hair and claws. Mom doesn't want us to see her grow hair and claws, and that's why she runs away."

"I know your mother didn't tell you she's a werewolf." There was no shock or surprise in Lauren's voice. She had Archer's absolute admiration.

Levi didn't answer for a moment, and Archer glanced toward him to see his face twisted up in concentration. "No, but that's what she does. What happened to David, the shepherd boy? Will you tell us a story?"

"Tell us a story!" Cody echoed his brother. "A werewolf story!"

Levi turned and put his hand on Cody's arm. "Shh. Mom said to be good." He turned back to Lauren. "I don't like that lady."

"What lady?"

He pointed toward the door.

"You mean Natalie? Why don't you like her?"

"Because she told Mama she's going to take us away, and it made Mama cry. Is she going to take us away? I don't want to go live with somebody else."

"Of course you don't, and your mom will do everything she can to make sure that doesn't happen." Bless Lauren for her soothing voice.

"Mama said if Natalie took us away, she was going with us," Levi said. "Mama says some people hit their kids and hurt them, and the police have to take the kids away, but Mama never does that."

Lauren reached down and wrapped her arms around Levi. "I'll tell you what, honey. Before anybody tries to take you away, you tell your mama to call me, and I'll bring my sleeping bag and come here and stay with you. Okay?"

Levi blinked up at her. "Okay!"

"Okay!" Cody repeated.

"Dad, where *are* we going?" Brooke asked, leaning forward until she was nearly in the front seat with him and Beau.

"Do you have your seat belt on?"

"Yes, but it's loose." In spite of her attempts to behave like the typical, bored teenager, Brooke couldn't conceal her interest in the quaint fixtures of the downtown shops. And she didn't even try to hide her interest when they passed a group of young men working in shirtless glory beside a backhoe on a side street. She straightened and smiled and automatically combed her fingers through her super-short dark hair.

"Your radar's out again," Beau warned.

"In full working order," she replied.

Grant chuckled and glanced at his daughter in the mirror. Her dark gray eyes, peering out from beneath extra-long dark bangs, were, as always, overly coated with dark makeup. Her skin was flawless. Ever since Brooke was twelve, well-meaning people had commented on her beauty. Like her brother, she had inherited the firm Sheldon chin, and though few people knew it, she also had her mother's tender heart—something she attempted to disguise at every opportunity.

"You still haven't told us what we're doing here, Dad," she complained.

"I want you guys to see a little more of Dogwood Springs. Starting with City Hall."

Accompanied by his daughter's groans, Grant described the popularity of the community puzzle and the possibility that the illness they were seeing in the emergency room could be spreading at City Hall.

That got Beau's attention. "Shouldn't somebody do something about it?" he asked. "If it's a dangerous virus, and you've already lost a patient—"

"And if people are coughing and sneezing all over each other and spreading it everywhere, who knows where it could spread to next?" Brooke finished for him.

"Good question. I just hope the mayor listened to me. We'll soon see."

"Who've you called?" Beau asked.

"Every town within an hour's drive, and if there isn't an ER in the town I'm calling the clinics."

"Branson?" Beau asked.

"Yes, Lauren called Branson for me. She called several area hospitals as well as some doctor friends from her hometown of Knolls. All of the towns have had a few cases of flu, but nothing out of the ordinary."

"Good thing," Beau said. "You know Branson gets visitors from all over the world. If this is some horrible plague, it could spread everywhere. It could be famous—known as the Dogwood Springs Killer."

"Oh thanks, Dr. Beau, for *that* encouraging word," Brooke chided.

Beau shrugged. "Just telling the truth." He turned in his seat to look at his sister as Grant parked in the City Hall parking lot. "You know, Brooke, you're going to have to be nice to me if you want me to help you get that car."

There was a long startled silence as Grant turned off the engine. He had just pulled the key from the ignition when there was a sudden rush from behind, and Brooke tackled her brother from the backseat with a smothering hug, raining kisses all over his face.

"Oh, Beau, I love you so much! Do you know that? You really *are* planning to help me earn the money for our car, aren't you?"

Beau tried to pull away, and Brooke only giggled and held him closer. Beau's mouth spread into a grimace—the closest to a smile he could come—and he gave an amused chuckle. "Not if you leave slimy lip gloss on my face."

She gave him a final kiss on his cheek and wiped at his face with her fingers. "There, you're fine."

"And you have to promise not to embarrass Dad or me in City Hall."

"Don't push it," she warned. "This will be your car, too. Do you know they still go cruising around here on Friday and Saturday nights?" she said as the three of them got out of the car and strolled toward the picturesque building with Virginia creeper etched in green across its block walls. "Cruising! Like they did in *American Graffiti*. They actually drive around town with their windows down and yell at each other and play Chinese fire drills and honk when they see somebody they know, and—"

"So they do that instead of dating?" Grant asked her.

"How would I know? Who would ask me out on a date? Nobody knows me here."

"That'll change soon enough," he assured her. "Remember we've been invited to that fishing thing next week. We'll probably meet some kids from Lauren's church."

Brooke groaned again, and the delicate but firm tilt of her chin grew a little firmer. "Fishing. What a thrill. Dad, I don't want to ruin your fun, but really—"

"Try it. You want to meet guys. Besides, you'll really like Lauren."

In the middle of another groan, Brooke's footsteps faltered and her lips parted. Two young men, probably in the upper range of their teens, rode bicycles past them on the street. They were tan. They wore muscle shirts. They noticed her. One nearly collided with a car.

While Grant and his son enjoyed the show, Beau ambled over to walk closer to Grant. "So Dad," he said quietly, "Lauren's a nurse you work with, right?"

"That's right. She helps out with the youth group at the Baptist church. That's where I'd like to see you and Brooke attend. You'll like the pastor, too. He's a good guy." As Brooke lost interest in the clumsy muscle-bound hunks, she rejoined her brother and father.

"They probably don't have cars if they're riding bikes," she said dismissively.

"Brooke, don't be so shallow," Beau said.

"I'm not, I'm being practical. If somebody does ask me out, I'm not riding to the movies with his mother."

"I'll drive you, then." Grant reached for the door and opened it, and they stepped into the bustling, noisy city hall. "Or you and Beau could hurry up and buy that car so you could drive him."

"I'm not driving a guy around on our first date."

They mingled with the crowd. Grant had been wanting to talk to his kids about something for a few days. Now the subject had arisen, and with Brooke, he had learned to take his opportunities when they presented themselves.

"Since we're on the subject of dating, how would you feel if I decided to test the waters again?" Grant felt as if he'd chosen his timing wisely. Brooke was less likely to become upset if her attention was diverted by a busy—

She stopped in her tracks and turned to him. "If you *what*?" The wide-eyed shock in her overly-darkened eyes and the crystal clarity of horror that threaded through her voice gave him a little thrill of fear. "You'd go *out* on *Mom*?" Her voice grew even louder, and it seemed as if, in reaction, the hall grew quieter. Several people glanced their way.

"Brooke, of course I never would have gone out on your mother. You know that." Grant kept his voice low, hoping his irrepressible daughter would do the same. "It isn't as if I have someone specifically in mind, it's just that—"

"I don't know how you could even think about it! I mean, Beau and I aren't testing the waters for a new mother, are we? Why should you want a new wife?" If she had grabbed a microphone and called for the attention of the crowd, she would not have done a better job of attracting it. Silence surrounded them like a hovering presence.

"Brooke," Beau said, stepping to her side and leaning close to her ear. "Shut up, okay? Let's just go check on this puzzle table and get off the stage, if you don't mind." Without waiting for a reaction, he took her by the arm and guided her forward.

Grant led the way through their curious audience toward the spot where he had last seen the puzzle table. And that was where he saw the only people in the building who had their attention diverted elsewhere. Their focus was on a puzzle—on the table.

There was one change, however. A small sign stood beside the table. It read, "At the request of medical personnel, please wash your hands before joining the table."

A delicate snort sounded directly beside Grant. If he was lucky, that snort had come from an angry bull. He looked. No, it had come from his daughter, and it meant trouble. He reached out to take her arm before she could do further damage to his reputation and his career. She lunged forward, out of his reach.

"I don't believe this day! I don't believe this town!" She stomped to the sign and pointed to it. "This is the way our illustrious mayor intends to wipe out the disease that's threatening this town? It's a joke, right?"

Grant and Beau looked at each other. Grant had learned to read the humor in his son's eyes. He saw it now. "Beau, don't you dare make fun of this moment. Do you know what these small towns are like? I'll never live this down if we don't get her out of here."

"Head for the door, Dad. I'll grab her as soon as I get a chance."

"No, we're in this together."

Grant could talk to the mayor over the telephone tonight. Maybe she would listen better than his daughter did. He and Beau took Brooke by the arms and guided her out of City Hall. Just before they reached the doors, she caught sight of a map of the city and grabbed a free copy from the stand, still complaining loudly about the lack of civic responsibility she had witnessed today.

Grant knew much of what she did was for dramatic effect. She had these little embarrassing spurts of outspokenness lately—not embarrassing for her, of course, because she did not embarrass easily. Her theatrics were only embarrassing for innocent family members who happened to be nearby.

If Annette were here, she would know how to react appropriately. It was a woman thing.

"You know, Dad," Beau said softly as Brooke jerked away and marched ahead of them toward the car, "you might want to wait a couple of days before you broach the subject of dating again."

The sun had dropped behind the cloudy horizon in a blaze of fire opal by the time Archer and Lauren left Gina's house, and Lauren couldn't stop watching the constantly changing beauty. But a nagging concern had begun to haunt her thoughts. It was stupid, really, but she couldn't get it out of her mind.

"Archer, do you ever wonder if you'd make a better pastor if you'd been a sinning rebel in your formative years?"

He gave her a quick look. "Why do you ask that?"

"Because I've been wondering lately if I couldn't identify better with people if I'd experienced more of the things other people do. I mean people who weren't raised in church. It's obvious Gina's had a painful past, but I've never even been married, much less divorced, so why would she bother confiding in me? I don't have children. How can I understand her pain?"

"What you do have is a caring heart. And I think that reaches people faster than anything. You don't have anything to worry about. Actually, though, it's funny you should mention it."

"Funny?"

"That same thought occurred to me the first night I took chaplain call at the hospital. I've wondered about it a few other times, too."

"Did you ever draw any conclusions?"

"Only that sin never helped a thing. Maybe I could identify with people better, but then maybe I couldn't identify with God as well. Don't get me wrong—it's not that I'm this pure and obedient Christian who never sins. I just don't think you should be ashamed of your obedience."

"I'm not ashamed," she said, "but sometimes I wonder if I might be a spiritual lightweight. I've never suffered a horrible loss. I don't come from a dysfunctional family . . . well, not *too* dysfunctional." They both knew Lauren's youngest brother had been a handful for her parents for a few years.

"But you're not afraid to get your hands dirty or immerse yourself in someone else's problems," Archer said. "Look how you're helping Gina. You don't have to be a single mother with a mysterious medical problem in order to be there for her. You just have to let her know you care, and I think she knows that."

Archer tapped the brake and waved at a pedestrian in jogging clothes alongside the road. It was one of the older church deacons, Mr. Netz. He slowed his steps when he saw them and gave a halfhearted salute.

"I admire Gina's independent spirit," Lauren said.

He smiled. "Takes one to know one. You're pretty independent yourself."

"But she frustrates me. She won't let down her guard long enough for anyone to help her."

"It sounds like she's willing to let her guard down with you. Just be her friend. I think you're doing a great job."

"Thanks." She wasn't so sure.

"Oh, and Lauren?"

"Yeah?"

"You are definitely *not* a spiritual lightweight." He looked at her and smiled, and she couldn't look away, even when he turned back to concentrate on his driving. It didn't take much attention from Archer Pierce to make her act like one of those giggling teenagers at church.

His expression grew sober as he turned onto her street. "Lauren, I know the drug tests on Gina have all showed negative results."

"That's right. The printout we got on her the first night we saw her didn't show anything except caffeine and benzodiazepine, which is in a sleeping pill she's been taking for insomnia lately."

"Did the test show how much of the drug she had taken?"

She looked at him. "No, the test was just qualitative, but the sample was sent off for further testing, and the lab found nothing outstanding. Archer, what are you saying? You can't think her problem comes from drugs—"

"I'm open to all suggestions right now. I don't want to believe she would hide that from us and risk her children just for the sake of getting high, but after talking to Tony, I feel less trusting of others."

"I think we can trust Gina."

"I'm glad. I feel she and her kids need protection from whatever is happening to her. But I know enough about drugs to realize that the tests can't rule out everything. Do you understand what I'm saying?"

Lauren hesitated. She understood, but she didn't want to. She liked Gina. But it was true that, as a health professional who worked with the children, she was a mandated reporter, and so was Archer, as well as Grant. Their first priority was to protect those children no matter what. She just hated to feel like a traitor to Gina.

"Yes, Archer, I understand. I just hope you're wrong."

"So do I."

CHAPTER 17

S he's here," came the intentionally bored tones of Brooke's voice as she peered out the front window. "Oh, pu-*leeze*, Dad, you didn't tell me she was a hillbilly redneck. Would you look at that? She's driving a truck. Oh, hello, and look at what she's *wearing*. Overalls. And no makeup. No wonder she's middle-aged and still not married. She doesn't even try."

Grant grimaced as he spread chicken liver pâté on a split croissant. They'd lived in Dogwood Springs a little more than three weeks now, and Brooke was still complaining. "She isn't even *close* to middle-aged, and don't you dare say anything to her about what she's wearing. We're going to do fishing, not fashion."

He wrapped the sandwich and wiped his hands on a paper towel, then rushed from the kitchen toward the front door to make a quick interception. The last thing he wanted was for his occasionally overbearing kid to frighten off the nicest nurse he'd worked with in a long while.

"A truck! I don't believe it." Brooke's favorite class in high school so far had been drama, and she excelled in it. As far as Grant could see, that flair for the dramatic was the only thing Brooke and Lauren were going to have in common—that and the fact that they were both females. Pretty females.

The feminine lines of Brooke's face turned down in a good imitation of agony as her thick, dark bangs fell into her overly made-up eyes.

"Please tell me we won't have to all squeeze into that thing. If we do, I'm not going. I don't care how many cute guys—"

"Nobody's forcing you to go," Grant said, "and the only cute guy even close to your age, other than Beau, is only fifteen." He resisted a smile. That would go over like a lead bubble. "Besides," he continued, peering out the curtained window of the front door, "looks like her truck has a backseat. It's one of them-there city-girl trucks." His affected hillbilly accent failed to evoke a response from Brooke, and he gave it up. His daughter was not his biggest fan right now.

Too late, he saw Brooke's eyes narrow with sudden threat. "What do you mean, only one other teenager?" she demanded. "I thought we were supposed to be going with a group from somebody's church."

"All the other kids your age have summer jobs, I guess. The pastor, Archer Pierce, is coming with one other—"

"*Archer?* What kind of a name is—"

"Don't start with me. Lauren has gone out of her way to try to make us feel wel—"

"Want to know what I think?" Brooke's dark gray eyes—beautiful in spite of, not because of, the makeup—tightened into slits of suspicion. *Oh, boy, here it comes.* "Probably not."

"I think she's setting you up. She's going to haul us all out to the middle of the woods and murder Beau and me to get us out of the way, and then she's going to cage you like an animal so you can be her—"

"Brooke, that's enough."

"I was just going to say—"

"I don't want to hear it." And he certainly didn't want Lauren to hear it. He hovered over his daughter menacingly and gave her his most authoritarian glare. "Think of someone else's feelings for once, Brooke, and don't you dare accuse Lauren of manipulating a date with me. She isn't interested. Believe me, I know."

She squared off with him, shoulder to shoulder, undaunted by his size or his authority. "*How* do you know? What ditzy, single, desperate blonde *wouldn't* be interested in snagging a rich doctor with two adorable kids?"

Grant stifled a laugh. "She isn't ditzy, we're not rich, and—"

"Okay, fine, have it your way. But when you wake up tomorrow morning with Beau and me hanging lifeless on hooks outside some log cabin with bars on the windows, and she's—"

Grant grasped her chin and forced her to look into his eyes. "Read my lips. I happen to know whom she's interested in, and it isn't me, so don't you dare embarrass me. How would you like it if I teased you about a guy you liked, and—"

Her eyes widened, and he realized he'd made a fatal slip.

She disengaged her chin from his grip. "You *like* this female John Boy?"

He ignored the question. "If this woman were trying to snag me, don't you think she'd at least have dressed up a little and put on a little makeup?"

As the first touch of doubt entered Brooke's eyes, the doorbell rang.

Grant raised a hand for silence. "Shhh! Zip your lips."

Brooke lowered her voice less than half a decibel. "So that's what you were talking about when you said you were lonely! I thought you said you didn't have anybody in mind to—"

"Brooke!"

"I'm just glad *you* cooked the food. Don't accept anything—"

He placed his hands on her shoulders and shushed her again. She grimaced. He opened the door.

Sure enough, Lauren did not look like her usual professional self, although her smile was still in place. It didn't even waver when Brooke issued a long, heartfelt groan and slumped out of the room, calling to her brother, "Hey, Beau, drag your lazy bod in here! It's time to hunt some fish!"

Lauren's long blond hair was pulled back from her face, as usual, and she wore baggy, comfortable looking bib overalls with a long-sleeved, oversized T-shirt. Oh, yeah, everything about her shouted siren. Where was Brooke's brain?

The annoyed voice of his daughter continued its harangue from half-way down the hall, and Grant cringed.

"Sorry."

Lauren's grin widened. "I take it they're still not happy about the move."

"Beau's doing fine. Brooke's willingness to go on this fishing trip is a testament to the fact that she is bored silly. They've both been looking for jobs the past week, and there's nothing available, which could mean they won't get the car Brooke wants, which would mean the end of life as we know it—not necessarily for Brooke, but for everyone who lives with her."

"They might find something if they keep trying. I think the hospital cafeteria was hiring a couple of weeks ago."

"I'll have them fill out applications on Monday. Speaking of the cafeteria, I've packed food, as promised. Are you ready for me to carry the cooler out?"

"Sure, let's get everything loaded and head to the woods. Archer will meet us there with Evan at about two." She glanced at her watch. "It'll take us about fifteen minutes to get there, and then we'll have fifteen minutes to set up before they arrive. Isn't it great to be off on Friday? We should have the spot all to ourselves for at least a couple of hours, maybe longer."

Ten minutes later, Grant found himself sitting behind the driver's side in the back seat of a gray, three-year-old Chevy Crew Cab pickup.

Grant had hunted down the fishing poles he and Annette had used years ago, and after introducing his teenage twins to Lauren, he had manipulated the seating so that Beau rode in front with Lauren. Grant was confident his son wouldn't cause any trouble—he would just sit with his nose buried in today's reading of choice, one of Grant's texts, *The Merck Manual of Medical Information*. With a stranger in their midst, he had retreated into his customary shell. Judging by the way Brooke was behaving, she was not to be trusted, and Grant felt a need to hover.

"Hicktown, population seven thousand three hundred and seventeen." Brooke's deadpan voice broke the peaceful silence as they drove west out of town. "Does that count the cows?" She grinned at her twin brother in the front seat as she poked him on the shoulder. Her dark eyes darkened further with disappointment when she didn't get a reaction. She pursed her highly glossed lips together and fell silent as Lauren picked up speed along Highway Z.

The city of Dogwood Springs, like many smalls towns of southern Missouri, sat in a patchwork square between checkerboard properties of the Mark Twain National Forest. Grant had visited this area years ago, when he and Annette went on one of their rare vacations. They'd dared to dream that someday, maybe when he retired, they would move here.

"What's Branson like now, Lauren?" he asked. "I haven't been there since before the kids were born."

"It's fun. It can get crowded," Lauren said. "Traffic's moving better than it used to, since they built all those bypasses, but I think they still sell souvenir T-shirts that say, 'I survived Highway 76 traffic.' I go about every month—to a show or just to shop. If you get a chance, try to catch *The Promise*. It's a musical about the life of Christ."

Brooke sat forward, eyes alert. "Do you ever go with . . . you know . . . a *date* or anything?"

Grant tensed and glared.

Lauren rounded a curve, then glanced at Brooke in her rearview mirror, her expression one of mystification. "A date? I usually just go with friends or a church group. Branson has a lot of good shows. And they're not just country anymore. I think you might like Silver Dollar City. We take a group of high schoolers a couple times a year."

"Silver Dollar City?" Brooke challenged, her voice mimicking Lauren's slight Ozark accent. "Isn't that some glorified theme park? St. Louis has Six Flags."

Grant tapped her on the arm. "Be nice."

She rolled her eyes and gave a long-suffering sigh.

He glared at her. The stubborn set of her chin and the tension in her neck told him that his little girl was still resisting the move, resisting Dogwood Springs, and resisting any possibility that he might be able to enjoy the company of another woman.

It was times like this he missed Annette the most. Brooke needed a woman to talk to and to gripe at. He didn't feel up to the challenge of fielding Brooke's sarcasm the rest of the day. He seldom felt ill at ease with people, but when Brooke was feeling irritable, he never knew what to expect.

She was just like he had been when he was younger. Nowadays he tempered his words with some of the wisdom he'd learned the hard way. But Brooke was still learning. Occasionally, she behaved like a brat.

What hurt him the most was that when she acted that way, it gave people the wrong impression of who she was down deep.

He must have gotten through to her, because for the next few minutes she was silent, and peace reigned in the cab of the truck.

"Pastor, don't take it personal, but we've been praying about this, and under the circumstances we feel it would be best if you stepped down from your position." Sixty-eight-year-old Dwight Hahnfeld, who served this year as chairman of the personnel committee, did not sit down on the sofa, as Archer had casually directed him, but instead perched on one of the chairs in front of Archer's desk.

Dwight looked everywhere but at the object of his declaration while his two buddies rustled up their own chairs and pulled them forward to sit beside him. None of them looked Archer in the face.

As Archer sat down at his desk and stared at the committee of three, he felt the numbness of shock travel down his spine—almost the same kind of shock he'd felt when Jessica broke their engagement seven weeks ago.

"What are you talking about?" he finally asked when he could manage to speak without betraying his shock.

"I know this might come as a bit of a surprise," Dwight said, "but our best interests need to be with the corporate integrity of the church."

Archer felt as if he were listening to this man trying to speak a foreign language. Had the church taken a vote behind his back? "Let me make sure I have this straight," he said slowly. "Am I being fired?"

"No, no, nothing like that." Mr. John Netz, the most outspoken and active deacon in the church, waved his hand irritably. "We just think you might want to check out other jobs . . . you know . . . maybe other positions. Now that you're not getting married, we don't think it looks proper for you . . ." He cleared his throat.

"A single man should not be leading a congregation," Hahnfeld declared. "According to Scripture, a pastor is supposed to be the husband of one wife. And he's supposed to be able to keep his children under control. How can you do that if you don't even *have* a wife? And as for children . . ." He shifted uncomfortably. "Well . . . obviously, you need a wife."

Archer said a quick, desperate prayer for God to control his thoughts, his temper, and his tongue, and then he plunged forward without waiting for God to answer. "Have you ever heard of the apostle Paul? Not only wasn't he married, but he was audacious enough to advise against it, warning that having a spouse would draw a person's loyalties from God." He heard the force of his own words, clipped into tight little knots of anger. He hated the sound of it. Archer seldom gave in to anger these days.

"That advice was directed toward those who could keep their bodies under control," Hahnfeld snapped. "Something you don't seem to be—"

"Dwight!" John Netz gave his buddy a quick, hard look.

Hahnfeld fell silent.

Archer studied them for a moment, wondering at the tension that blazed through the room. An unspoken knowledge ran from face to face—some knowledge he did not own. "Am I missing something?"

The three men avoided looking at each other, and they particularly avoided Archer.

He didn't need this today. He shouldn't have even come into the office. This was supposed to be his day off.

Besides that, Evan was waiting for a ride, and Lauren and the Sheldons were probably already at the fishing spot.

But something was going on here. Obviously, the community grapevine had struck Dogwood Springs Baptist once again. Archer knew the signs, because gossip was a nasty little sin that nobody wanted to admit to but was so hard to resist. Like a bag of chocolate chips—what would it hurt to eat just one little chip? And then another? As the three men continued to avert their eyes, the guilt stained their faces.

Archer sat back in his chair and sighed. *I'm sorry, Lord. I should not have spoken in anger.* "At least have the decency to tell me what I've done this time, gentlemen."

Silence screamed through the office.

"Maybe I can help prompt your memory." Archer tried to keep his voice gentle. "Let me see . . . I shouted too loudly at the softball game the other night."

The continued silence and averted eyes said no.

"Okay, then, I forgot to visit someone in the hospital."

Gene Thomas cleared his throat and looked at Hahnfeld and Netz. He was the youngest and newest member of the committee, and judging by his obvious discomfort, Archer guessed he'd been coerced into this.

"Well, he needs to know what's being said," Gene told them.

Netz stared out the window. Hahnfeld shifted in his seat and favored Archer with a brief look of sadness, then he shook his head and averted his eyes once more.

"Well, I'm not saying this is true, Brother Archer," Gene blurted, "but we feel that . . . well, you see . . . a pastor should be living such a pure life that ideas like this wouldn't take root in the first—"

"Ideas like what?"

More silence. Scuffling of feet.

Netz finally straightened and looked Archer in the face, though he still couldn't quite make eye contact. "Brother Archer, I know you didn't do what they're saying, probably. It's just that, when some new pretty woman comes to town and joins the church, and then you start spending all that time with her, and then your engagement gets broken, and then that pretty woman turns up pregnant, people—"

Archer nearly came out of his chair. "What?!"

Netz looked back out the window.

"The only single young woman who has joined our church in the past few months is Lauren McCaffrey," Archer said.

Netz nodded. "That's right."

"Lauren McCaffrey is *not* pregnant! Where did you hear such a lie?"

Gene shrunk farther down in his seat. "They're talking about it over at the hospital."

"Don't you work at the hospital?" Archer asked.

"Yeah, I'm in Medical Records. One of the techs said she overheard Lauren telling somebody about it, and she was sick the other night, and—"

"Well, they lied." Archer would not listen to this any longer. He pushed back from his desk and stood. "If you'll excuse me." He nodded to them, too afraid of his growing anger to say more. He walked out of his office, leaving the committee sitting there like three stone statues.

When Lauren turned from the highway onto a rough, potholed gravel road, Brooke seemed unable to keep her mouth shut any longer. "*Hel-lo!* Where are we going? I thought we were going to a lake or something, you know, where there are, like, people and boats and swimming?" She turned her insistent gaze on Grant, her eyes widened in a very expressive, unspoken plea for him to protest.

Grant laid his arm across the back of the seat and held his hand up for silence. "I guess you also expected a yacht with a pool and a waiter, and maybe a movie screen with the latest releases? It wouldn't hurt you to be flexible for once."

He caught Lauren's quick glance of concern in the rearview mirror and was suddenly chagrined by the sharpness of his own voice. Brooke was making him more nervous than usual. This outing was probably a bad idea, but the kids couldn't just sit at home the whole summer.

"It's a neat place, Brooke, really," Lauren said. "Give it a chance, okay? The creek is fed by Honey Spring. The water is pure and sweet. This spot has the best fishing in the county. It's where all the old fishermen come to catch their limit."

"Limit of what? Ticks and chiggers?"

"Rainbow trout," Lauren replied, apparently not offended by Brooke's continued bratty attitude. "They stock it from the fish hatchery in Knolls County."

"There wouldn't happen to be any cabins out here, would there?" Brooke asked, casting Grant a wide-eyed stare. "You know, with, like, bars on the windows or something?"

Lauren gave her a quick glance in the mirror, then shrugged. "None I know about. But sometimes I find empty beer cans and cigarette butts along the road leading to the creek, so it's obviously a weekend party spot. I avoid it then. Beau, have you ever gone fishing before?"

Beau glanced at Lauren, then quickly turned away. "Yeah." His baritone voice barely reached the backseat, and the rearview mirror reflected Lauren's expression of deepening interest.

"Where'd you go?"

Beau shrugged. "Mississippi River."

"Their mother and I used to take them to the river on my days off when they were out of school," Grant explained. "They enjoyed it then. Archer tells me you're an excellent fisherman, Lauren."

She smiled with pleasure. "He said that?"

"Just a couple of days ago." He glanced sideways at his daughter and was not convinced by her expression of disinterest. In matters of the heart, Brooke was uncomfortably astute. "He told me you're quite an athlete."

"I'm fair, but fishing's my favorite pastime. As soon as I arrived here in February, I started going down to the barbershop where the old guys hang out. They always know where the fishing's the best. The barber got tired of me after a couple of days and finally divulged the location of his favorite spot so I'd leave him alone. I've been coming here ever since."

"So this is, like, what you do for *fun*?" Brooke caught Grant's attention and rolled her eyes. "You know, if you hung out with some *younger* guys, you might get a real date to take you to Silver Podunk City."

"Lauren, it's hard to believe you've only been in Dogwood Springs a few months," Grant interrupted, reaching across to catch his daughter's hand in a very firm grip. "You seem like such a part of the community."

"That's because I come from a small town a lot like it."

"I'm curious why you decided to come here."

"Yeah, why here?" Brooke's voice echoed as she tried to jerk her hand away. He held on.

Something about Lauren caught Grant's attention, something about the way her typically open expression closed in on itself all of a sudden. "It's a pretty town. The emergency department is new, and they made me an offer I couldn't refuse."

"And that would mean, then, that you weren't happy with your former job." Grant couldn't curb his own curiosity.

Yes, there was definitely some resistance in Lauren's attitude. "Knolls is a great town. I grew up there and I know everybody, and the hospital was the best. Last fall we had an explosion that leveled the ER, and while that department of the hospital was out of commission, I covered a few shifts here. Something clicked for me, and . . . when I decided to leave Knolls, this was the first hospital that offered me a contract."

"So?" Brooke prodded. "That still doesn't explain why you decided to leave Knolls in the first place."

"I guess I felt like I was missing something."

"You mean, like a man?" Brooke asked. "And you came *here*?" She lowered her voice to a bare whisper and leaned toward Grant. "Not exactly a rational decision, if you ask me."

Grant knew there were laws against passengers riding in the bed of a pickup truck, but he wondered if the police might make an exception in certain cases.

"So why do you come way out here in the middle of nowhere to go fishing?" Brooke asked. "We're not doing anything, like, illegal, are we?" She gave her dad a teasing wink.

Lauren laughed. "Last time I checked my fishing license it was up to date." She looked at the book Beau held open in his lap. "Medicine, huh? You planning to follow in your father's footsteps and become a doctor?"

Beau didn't look up. He just shrugged and nodded.

"Emergency medicine?" Lauren continued to prompt.

Beau looked at her then. Unlike Brooke, there was no mischief in his expression, just a self-conscious awkwardness. "I'd love to be a doctor."

Grant's heart squeezed tightly in his chest at the sincerity in his son's voice. Beau was truly the child who most took after his mother, quiet and thoughtful, sensitive to the needs of everyone around him.

All of Grant's protective instincts had come out with his son since the accident, and Grant knew that sometimes rankled Beau's masculine pride. Fortunately, Brooke's attitude toward her twin brother had always been one of adoration, and though she teased him mercilessly at times, she made no secret of her love for him. The one thing the accident had not changed was their relationship.

"Looks like you're getting a good start," Lauren told Beau. "Since you just moved here, you may not be aware of the great health services program we have at the high school."

Beau shifted in his seat and gave her more of his attention. "Health services? Here?"

Lauren smiled. "I know Dogwood Springs is the Missouri outback to you, but our school system is ranked with the best in the country, not just the state. If you take a health services course, you'll be able to do some on-site training at the hospital."

Beau's eyes came alive. "How old do I have to be?"

"Sixteen."

Even Brooke lost her bored expression for a moment and leaned forward to hear what they were saying up front. "You mean he'd get to give shots and everything? He'd love that. Mom and Dad got him this doctor set for Christmas one year, and he wanted to put real needles in the syringe. Guess who was always the patient."

"He wouldn't give shots, but he could take vitals," Lauren said. "Most important, he would be in on patient cases and watch how it works in the medical world." Lauren slowed the truck and turned onto an even rougher dirt track. "Of course, I'm sure it won't be as exciting in our ER as it would be in some big St. Louis trauma center."

"Not as dangerous, either," Grant said. "Inside the hospital or outside. And the variety here is better. At the trauma center, it seems as if all I ever saw were life-and-death situations. The stress level was always high. Here I get everything from nosebleeds and sore throats to industrial accidents and heart attacks. I'll take this any day."

Brooke gave an ostentatious yawn and reached out to nudge Grant's arm with her fingers. "You're a born hick, Dad."

"That isn't a bad thing," Lauren said. "There's a lot to be said for small towns. We *do* have a lot of variety in our emergency room, and in a small town everybody knows everybody else, so the patients are better than the local paper for keeping us up with the latest news." Lauren pulled beneath a stand of sycamore trees and parked the truck. "We're here."

Archer was just stepping out of the house with his fishing clothes on—twenty minutes late to pick up Evan—when the telephone rang. He looked at the clock. It was probably Evan or Lauren wondering where he was, and if he didn't answer they would know he was on his way.

But what if it was an emergency?

Before the phone could stop ringing, Archer fumbled with the door, rushed back inside, and grabbed the receiver. Couldn't let those devoted people down . . . even if they did plan to fire him because of some rumor straight from Satan.

"Hello?"

"Yes . . . hello . . . is this Archer Pierce?" The words tumbled through the phone in waves of broken tension. Definitely female.

"That's me." He frowned, recognizing the voice. "Gina?"

"I think . . . is Lauren . . . do you know where she is?"

"Yes. Gina, are you feeling sick? Do you need help?"

"Yes, please help me. They're all around me. They won't shut up, they won't leave me alone. I can't concentrate, can't—" There was a soft gush of air and then a sob.

"Gina, who are you talking about? Who's there? Where are you? I'll be right there. Are you at home?"

"I'm at work. I didn't . . . don't want to tell . . . I've got to get away—"

"No, Gina, wait! Tell somebody! Get to the emergency—"

The line disconnected.

Archer dialed the hospital. By the time he was transferred to Gina's department she had left her desk. He gave a quick account of the problem to the woman on the phone, then hung up and ran out the door. He could call Lauren and Grant from the hospital.

Three weeks ago Gina had cut her bare feet. What would happen to her this time?

CHAPTER 18

My pole's jerking!" Brooke exclaimed less than three minutes after Lauren cast the line and handed her the fishing rod. "What should I do now?"

Lauren looked up from the fishhook she was baiting. Sure enough, Brooke's line was taut. "Tug hard to set the hook, then reel it in, just like I showed you."

Brooke jerked on the pole hard enough to decapitate a trout and stumbled backward over a rock. She caught herself and turned to see if anyone was watching. Everyone was.

Lauren retained her sober expression with difficulty. How was the youth group of Dogwood Springs Baptist Church going to handle Brooke Sheldon?

"Okay, I got it. I think."

"Keep reeling," Lauren said. "Bring it on in to the bank."

"But it's so wiggly, and it—aack! What is that?" Brooke screeched. "*That's* a *fish*? Lauren, you take this thing! This is not—" With another screeching attack on their eardrums, she threw the rod toward the water and scrambled across the rocky shoreline away from the creek. "I can't do this!"

"No, Brooke, wait!" Lauren shoved her own fishing rod into Grant's hands and leaped forward to rescue Brooke's catch. Luckily, it hadn't escaped, and she reeled with precision and speed. It wasn't until the taut line pulled the wriggling body up above the water's surface that she discovered Brooke was right.

It wasn't a fish.

"Snake!" Brooke's scream split the peace of the little fishing hollow and echoed from the cliffside across the creek as she did a skittering dance across the rocks. "I told you! I can't believe this! She's trying to get us killed! Dad!"

Lauren was too busy handling the rod to attempt to stifle her laughter. "Relax, Brooke, it's a plain brown water snake. It isn't going to hurt us."

"Isn't going to *hurt* us!" Brooke shrieked in outrage. "Dad, I'm going back to St. Louis. I'm calling Grandma tonight, and she'll come and get me. If she doesn't, I'll catch a bus or I'll hitchhike. I mean it, Dad! This place is crawling with snakes! And don't forget the spider I saw when we parked. You know I hate those things!"

Lauren laid down the rod and grabbed the line to the entertaining sound of Brooke's outraged chatter. "Hey, Brooke, watch this." She grasped the head of the poor struggling snake just behind the spot where the hook had caught it.

Brooke screamed again, and Lauren winced. Okay, that was a bad idea, but she'd truly wanted to prove the little thing wasn't dangerous.

"Brooke, he's just scared. See? Even if he bit me, he couldn't hurt me. Have you ever had a puppy? They can bite harder than this fellow."

"Puppies do not slither through the water and sneak up on people."

"Still, this guy's harmless. Look, he didn't even swallow the hook— it just pierced his side. As soon as I release him he'll slither back to the creek and head downstream with the current. Grant, give me my tackle box, would you?"

"You *can't* be serious," Brooke said, backing away, appalled.

Without a word, Grant put down Lauren's pole, carried the box over to Lauren, set it down, opened the lid, and reached for a set of wire cutters.

"Are you *crazy*?" Brooke cried. "Just cut the line!"

"We can't," Grant said. "We've got to get the hook out, or the snake could get snagged and suffer a miserable death."

Lauren looked up at Grant with fresh respect and saw from his calm expression that, unlike his daughter, he wasn't the least bit intimidated by the snake.

"Then kill it now so it won't suffer." Brooke's voice lost its edge of panic, and instead was filled with a thick thread of frustration.

"No." This soft reply came from farther down the creek, and they all glanced up to see Beau coming toward them with his first catch. "First do no harm."

"Oh, no, don't you start, too, *Doctor* Beau. And *what* is that *thing* you're carrying—a minnow? I've seen bigger fish than that in Grandma's aquarium."

To Lauren's surprise and relief Brooke was sidetracked. Though her theatrically disgusted voice continued, it was now focused on Beau's measly catch. Lauren and Grant snipped the hook in two and gently removed it from the snake. Then, while Brooke still had her back turned, Lauren took the snake to the creek and released it. Beau kept his sister occupied and entertained throughout the operation.

"Good job," Grant said softly, under cover of Brooke's harangue.

Lauren looked up at him. "Thanks, Doc. You didn't do so badly yourself."

He nodded graciously, with a slow, appreciative smile. Grant Sheldon had dark gray eyes the color of a lake on a cloudy day, with firm, straight brows that often belied a keen appreciation for humor. As Gina had remarked recently, he was an attractive man, and Lauren felt comfortable. It didn't seem to matter to him that her face was scrubbed free of makeup and that her baggy old clothes probably stunk of bait by now and that he'd been witness to even worse in the past weeks when she'd been sick.

"Thanks for putting up with Brooke," he said softly, as his twins—mostly Brooke—continued their friendly insults several yards away. "I should have warned you about her. Down deep inside she has a tender heart, but her irritability hormones have kicked into overdrive the past year or so."

"I work with teenagers at church, remember? I just hope you don't expect me to patronize her."

"I'd be horrified if you did. She's bad enough already." Grant chuckled and glanced at his arguing children, then his attention once more focused on Lauren. "I'm glad you invited us to come with you today. I'm having a good time." The way he said it made Lauren wonder if having a good time was a rare experience for him. "Even more important, believe it or not, I think my kids are enjoying themselves. They love to argue."

"I heard that, Dad," Brooke said suddenly from close behind Lauren. She looked at their bloodstained hands suspiciously. "Okay, what happened to the snake?"

Lauren made an obvious show of looking at her watch, then she glanced toward the road. "Hmm, I wonder where Archer is. He should have arrived with Evan by now. I hope everything's okay."

"You let it go, didn't you?" Brooke accused, though, to Lauren's surprise, a gentleness laced her voice this time. A hint of a smile hovered in her eyes as she caught and held Lauren's gaze.

"Yes. I don't like to take a life unnecessarily."

Brooke made a face. "Tell that to the poor worms you sacrificed to the hook god a while ago. So where did you put him? He probably crawled into the tackle box to hide, and then he'll slither out while we're cruising down the highway at a gazillion miles an hour, and you'll panic and lose control of that hillbilly machine you call transportation and—"

She caught herself, and her eyes widened. She shot her brother a quick apologetic look and immediately changed the subject. "Oh, well, whatever. Lauren, who's this Archie guy? Is he your boyfriend?" She reached down and cautiously opened the lid, and the subject was changed as quickly as that.

"Archer is my pastor." Lauren bent to help before Brooke managed to scatter her carefully organized gear onto the rocky bank.

"Is he married?"

"No."

"Is he elderly? I mean, more elderly than . . . well, you know what I mean. Is he too old for you?"

Lauren gave Grant a meaningful grimace, and found it mirrored on his face. "He's thirty-three."

"So if he hasn't taken a vow of celibacy or something, why aren't you dating him?"

"Brooke, what is the big push for me to date someone?" Lauren didn't attempt to conceal her confusion. "Have you decided to become my personal matchmaker?"

The teenager continued to select and then discard sinker after sinker. "Never hurts to look to the future."

"Brooke," Lauren said, and then paused until the girl looked up at her. "I'm not dating anyone, okay? Get used to it. Amazingly, life goes on, even for us *senior citizens.*"

Brooke's dark eyes sparkled with humor before she directed her attention once more to the contents of the tackle box. "Don't you have any bait in here that doesn't writhe in pain when you try to attach it to the hook?"

"Well, I did bring a little bag of Limburger cheese and some chicken livers, but I don't think you—"

"That's good. Where is it?"

"Brooke," Grant said, "Limburger cheese doesn't smell too—"

"I don't care about the smell, I just don't feel like killing any more innocent animals today." She reached into the box and pulled out a sinker that would anchor a small rowboat.

"Here, let me help you with that," Lauren said. "Bring your gear, and we'll hike upstream a bit. You've probably scared all the fish away from this spot, anyway."

To Lauren's surprise, Brooke followed her without protest. "So what's this youth group like at your church?" she asked when they were out of earshot of her family. "Are there any hot guys?"

Lauren shrugged. "I guess some of them aren't bad." She sank down on a boulder beside a quiet pool of water and scooted over so Brooke could join her.

"What about this Evan kid who's supposed to be here but isn't because your pastor can't find the way?" Brooke didn't sit down, but walked over to the water's edge and started tossing pebbles into the water. "I mean—I know he's a *fifteen-year-old,* but is he even anywhere close to having a birthday?"

Lauren sensed despair in the girl's voice and was dismayed that she felt a brief moment of identification. She knew what it felt like to be lonely for the company of members of the opposite sex. "I think you'll just have to meet him, Brooke. Give it some time."

"Yeah, sure." Brooke's tone made it clear that sixteen-year-old girls did not find fifteen-year-old boys appealing . . . or "hot," or whatever the term was this week.

"Were you active in your church in St. Louis?" Lauren asked.

Brooke nodded and then picked up a pebble and tossed it into the water. Her expression grew pensive. "Mom and Dad dragged us to church all the time."

"My parents did the same thing."

"I bet they didn't drag you away from all your friends and move you to the sticks two years before you graduated."

Lauren studied the girl's features for a moment. Physically, Brooke Sheldon was one of the most beautiful young women Lauren had ever seen. She had widely spaced eyes the same color as her father's, with thick lashes and perfectly arched eyebrows. Her chin came to a delicate yet very firm point that characterized her disposition perfectly. To Lauren's surprise, she felt another twinge of sympathy for Brooke, and it went far past compassion for this initial phase of homesickness.

Physical beauty could be a curse.

Lauren had known from a young age that people referred to her as the "pretty one" of the McCaffrey sisters, though she'd never been able to see it herself. She'd been the tomboy of the family, usually with dirt under her fingernails and on her face. She helped Dad on the farm along with her two younger brothers, while her sisters helped Mom in the house.

To Mom's disappointment, Lauren had never dated much in high school. She'd had lots of invitations, but for some reason, the guys she went out with couldn't seem to understand why she didn't want to make out like all the other girls, or why she had smacked their hands when they thought they had a right to explore parts of her anatomy that didn't belong to them.

That was when she had discovered that most men didn't want to look past her face or her body. They weren't interested in what lay in her heart. They weren't interested in her dreams, just their own.

Brooke tossed a final pebble and turned to slump onto the boulder beside Lauren.

"Do you miss your friends?" Lauren asked.

Brooke gave her an "I can't believe you're so stupid" look.

"Of course you do. I know I miss mine."

"So why did you move? At least you weren't forced to leave them. I was. Mom wouldn't have made me leave. Does Dad care? No." She picked up another pebble and tossed it.

"Good dads always care; they just don't always know how to communicate it. My dad's like that." Lauren rebaited her hook. "I don't remember him actually saying the words *I love you*, but he didn't have to. He showed his love by the way he talked to me—or, actually, by the way he listened while I talked, and talked, and talked."

Brooke sighed. Restlessly, she got up from the boulder and picked up her rod. "So are you going to teach me how to cast this thing?"

Lauren shook her head and stood up with her own rod. This kid could wear a person out in a hurry. After five minutes of instruction and awkward casting that actually landed the hook in the water less than half a dozen times, Brooke gave a frustrated groan and slumped once more against the boulder.

"You didn't answer my question. If you were going to leave home, why didn't you actually *go* someplace?"

Lauren continued to cast. "Dogwood Springs is a place."

"No it isn't. It's a nonplace. It's cut off from the whole world. These people practically speak a different language."

"It doesn't take too long to learn, though," Lauren said. "I like the country. I've never lived in the city except when I went to nursing school, and I was glad to get back home afterward." She reeled the line in and turned.

Brooke had her arms crossed over her chest, teeth biting into her lower lip, as she stared into the water. The child was hurting. Anyone could see that.

"Brooke, it'll probably take you a while to get used to the slower pace, but couldn't you at least wait until school starts before you pass judgment? You may surprise yourself and *like* it here, crazy as that may sound."

There was a long silence, and then Brooke sighed. "I don't have a choice, do I?"

"Maybe you could start by learning how to fish."

Archer reached the hospital in five minutes and parked in the spot marked for clergy. He leaped from the car without locking it and ran toward the emergency entrance. Maybe Gina had taken his advice and reported to the ER.

He raced through the nearly empty waiting room to the receptionist's desk. He recognized the young woman sitting there. "Hi, Gayle, I'm looking for Gina Drake. Did she come in here?"

Gayle looked up at him. "Gina? She was in this morning with an asthma patient. I guess she's either on the floor or in her own department."

Disappointed, he gave her a wave and ran down the wide, tiled hallway toward Radiology, dreading what he might find. She obviously hadn't taken his advice. She'd wanted to talk to Lauren, though. Maybe she was still trying to find her. He should take the time to call her as soon as he found Gina.

He should also call Evan. After all that poor kid had been through lately—now he was being stood up by a pastor.

Archer rounded a corner and nearly collided with Sarah Davis, the director of Respiratory. Her curly salt-and-pepper hair stuck out from her head at awkward angles, and her glasses rested halfway down her nose, as if she'd been too rushed to straighten them.

"Archer." She reached out and grabbed his arm. "What's wrong with Gina? I can't find her anywhere, and now you've got me scared half to death. What happened? Did she get sick?"

"I'm not sure. She called me from her desk, and she sounded confused. I'm afraid she might be having another bad episode."

"What do you mean?"

"Don't you remember when she hurt her feet three weeks ago?"

Sarah stared at him blankly. "What are you talking about? When did she hurt her feet?"

She didn't know. Obviously, Gina hadn't told her about the problem. "I'll explain later. Right now, would you please help me look for her? I think she's ill, and she sounded confused. You check the rest rooms. I'll go outside and see if she's on the hospital grounds."

Sarah's eyes widened in alarm. "*Confused?* You're talking as if she's lost her mind. What's wrong with her, Archer?"

"I'm not sure yet. Nobody is. Look, Sarah, can I explain this later? Right now we need to find Gina. Would you have someone call Rose Pascal? She needs to be aware of—"

"The social worker?" Sarah exclaimed. "Archer, what's going on here? Is Gina in trouble for—"

"Gina had some kind of seizure three weeks ago, and she was injured. We still haven't discovered what caused it, and so we don't know when it might affect her again. When she called me a few minutes ago she wasn't feeling well, and I'm afraid it has—"

"Seizures! You mean like epilepsy? And she didn't tell me about it? What could she be thinking?"

"No, I don't think epilepsy—"

"Didn't she give any thought to the patients she might be endangering?"

Archer laid a hand on her arm. "Sarah, please."

"Okay, I'll help you look for her," Sarah said. "But when we find her, she's going to have some explaining to do."

On his way out the door, Archer stopped by the emergency room and asked them to contact Grant on his beeper. Lauren didn't have a cell phone, so they couldn't explain the problem, but Grant would take the message seriously.

The smell of Limburger cheese wafted through the air and mingled with the scent of raw chicken liver as Lauren surreptitiously watched Brooke brave the cheese with her bare hands. Her reasoning was acceptable—she did not want to gore a living worm on the hook.

Lauren had to admit to herself that she was impressed by the girl's attempts to adapt to something that must seem completely foreign to her.

They had moved upstream about another hundred feet, to where the water was deep and clear just above a set of rapids that sparkled in the dappled sunlight. Grant and Beau had joined them after Lauren caught three trout within five minutes. Brooke had managed to frighten away the remainder of the fish—and probably the turtles, crayfish, birds, and any other living creature in the vicinity—by a loud screech of outrage after each successful catch.

The kid needed a gag.

"This stream feeds a reservoir that supplies drinking water for about a third of Dogwood Springs," Lauren explained to them. "The people complain a lot about the minerals in the water messing up their pipes, but I envy them. When I come fishing down here I usually bring some water jugs and fill them, then use that for drinking water at home. It's the best I've ever tasted."

"*Eeww.*" Brooke looked up from her intense concentration as she tried to fit cheese on a hook and get it to stick. "You drink this water? Animals poop in it, you know."

"The spring isn't too far from here." Lauren gestured toward the shallows that tumbled over rocks and pebbles with a series of whispered splashes. "That's where I collect it."

"But what about the people downstream? That is so disgusting."

Beau turned and gave his sister a long-suffering look. "It's water, Brooke. All water comes from somewhere. The city tests it, and if they find a problem they treat it. We're not *that* deep in the backwoods."

She made a face at him and returned to her baiting efforts.

Beau cleared his throat and stepped closer to Lauren. "Um, do you think you could get me the information about that health occupations course at school?"

"Yes, I'd love to." She looked over at Grant. "What do you say? You think he'll make a good ER doc someday?"

"The best," Grant said without hesitation. There was a pride in his eyes when he looked at his son that caught at Lauren's heart. "I just hope he decides to work in a small town like Dogwood Springs instead of a big city hospital. Sometimes it seems to me as if the ER docs in the bigger hospitals are expected to be health screeners for the entire population, especially with medical costs skyrocketing."

"It's going to be the same in the smaller hospitals before long, Dad," Beau said. "A lot of people without insurance won't go to a doctor unless it's an emergency, so they let their health problems slide. By the time they reach the emergency room, they're in terrible shape with multiple co-morbid illnesses, and those family practice docs who get called in the middle of the night don't appreciate it very much."

"Beau, English, please," Brooke protested. "*What* is a co-morbid illness?"

"Multiple system error," Beau explained. "Or, in your vernacular, one patient with several illnesses or diseases that—"

"Shut up. I know what a multiple system error is. Oh, did I tell you, Dad?" Brooke said. "Beau's been sneaking into your medical magazine stash when you're at work."

"I'm not sneaking," Beau protested. "Dad said I could read them."

Beau had a nice baritone voice with a gentle quality, much like his father's. Lauren decided he needed to use it more often—if Brooke would ever give him the opportunity.

"Beau, tell us more about the changes you think are going to take place in the future," Lauren said.

Brooke gave a long sigh and bent over her fishing pole.

"They'll do away with physician call and share the work with hospital specialists and twenty-four-hour clinics," Beau continued. "Anyway, that's what I read yesterday. They'll have to do that to handle the increasing volume."

"They won't be able to do that in small towns for a while," Grant said, "but definitely in the cities."

Brooke straightened and lifted the tackle box down from the boulder where she had placed it. "Okay, I've got the stupid bait stuck on the stupid hook. Now, would you show me how to do this again, Lauren?" She stepped over to the water's edge.

Lauren picked up her own rod and demonstrated once again how to cast by actually placing the baited hook in the water instead of around an overhanging branch or on the opposite bank. Lauren reeled the line in and Brooke got ready to execute her own cast.

Grant jerked his line and reeled it in. "Lost my bait again." He walked over to the boulder Brooke had just vacated. "I think I'm going to need some lessons next." He sat down and reached for the box.

Brooke drew her pole back. "Like this, Lauren?" She held the line with her thumb, then whipped the rod forward.

"Ow!" Grant jumped up from the boulder and swung around in

alarm, hands on his posterior. "Something bit me."

Brooke tried to reel in her line, but it snagged. She jerked hard.

"Ow!" Grant said again. "What's going—"

The deep sound of rich laughter reached them, and all three of them turned in surprise to find Beau with his hand over his mouth, pointing at his father. Lauren noticed that, although the laughter continued, there was no sign of humor in his expression. She remembered Grant's explanation about the damage to Beau's face from the accident that killed his mom.

"Don't look now, Dad, but you're the catch of the day."

The fishhook, complete with bait, was embedded in the lightweight khaki of Grant's pants, in a very delicate rear section of his anatomy.

Lauren could not resist a quick burst of laughter at his expression of outraged amazement.

"Oh, Dad, you sat on my hook," Brooke said. "No wonder I couldn't cast it. You ruined my bait. Do you know how much trouble I went to with that one?"

Grant reached back toward the seat of his pants.

Lauren rushed forward. "No, don't touch it or you'll—"

"Ow!"

"Grant, you'll just set the hook that way. Here, let me—"

"No, stay away from my pants." Grant turned and backed away from her. "I can fix this myself." The natural tan of his face deepened a shade. "I'll just take a little stroll into the woods and come back with my dignity intact, if you don't mind."

"Forget it, Dad," Brooke said. "You just helped Lauren perform surgery on a snake. What kind of dignity could you possibly have left?"

"Grant, really," Lauren said, taking the line in a firm grip to keep the hook from stabbing him. "I can get that out in just a few seconds if you'll just—"

He swung away too fast and too hard. The line drew taut and tangled in Lauren's fingers. There was a quick rip and a gasp, and a flap of khaki folded away from the slacks, revealing a flash of white underneath.

The four of them stared at each other for a moment of short, shocked silence.

"Oh, Grant, I'm sorry," Lauren said.

A small titter reached them over the sound of the creek, and Lauren turned to see Brooke, red-faced and giggling uncontrollably.

And then, above it all, came the sound of Grant's beeper.

He gave Lauren a look of horror, pulled the tiny beeper from the waistband of his damaged pants, and checked the number. He groaned.

"Who is it, Dad?" Beau asked.

"It's the hospital. Lauren, do you have a cell phone?"

"No, I'm sorry, I don't."

"Then do you mind driving me to the hospital?"

"Dad," Brooke protested. "You can't go to the hospital with the seat ripped out of your pants."

Grant shoved the pager into his pocket and reached for the tackle box. "I don't have a choice, honey. It could be an emergency."

CHAPTER 19

As soon as Lauren pulled into the employee parking lot, Grant saw Archer Pierce rushing around the outside of the hospital building to intercept them. There were no police cars, no ambulances, and no city warning alarms going off. Okay, so it wasn't a countywide emergency.

The young minister waved and motioned for them to stop. While Lauren parked he came toward them at a jog, and Grant could see long before he reached the lot that his expression was serious. Something was up.

Brooke scooted forward, her dark eyes widening with admiration that bordered on reverence. "*Who* is *that*?"

"That's my pastor." Lauren shoved the gearshift into park, turned off the engine and opened the door to get out. "The one who was supposed to go fishing with us." She shut the door behind her and hurried to meet Archer.

"Whoa, Dad, you've got some hefty competition," Brooke said in the sudden silence of the cab. "He's hot."

"I wouldn't know." Grant opened his door.

"Dad!" She scrambled across the seat and grabbed him by his shirt sleeve. "Your underwear. You can't go in there like that."

"Something's up, Brooke, can't you see that? I don't have time to worry about my fashion sense right now." He tried to pull free, but she held firm.

"This isn't fashion sense, it's social suicide!" she hissed, turning to her brother. "Beau, do something."

"Beau, stay out of this," Grant said.

Beau nodded. "Sure, Dad, but it wouldn't hurt you to untuck your shirttail. That'll cover everything unless you bend over or raise your arms. If you're going to commit social suicide, you might as well be cool about it."

"Okay, I'll untuck. Keep your sister occupied for a few minutes, okay?"

"I charge for baby-sitting."

"Hey!" Brooke released her dad and reached for Beau's head.

He ducked. "Come on, let's go check out the hospital. There'll be all kinds of guys doing summer work around here. We might even fill out a job application."

Brooke hesitated, obviously torn between the obligation she had to protect her father's social reputation and the opportunity to flirt with future dating material and take possible steps toward acquiring a car.

It didn't take long. "Fine, just don't tell them who our father is. I'll beat you to the building. Bye, Dad. Keep your heinie covered."

Before Grant reached Lauren and Archer the kids were racing across the parking lot toward the hospital building. Grant wondered, briefly, if Brooke remembered she still smelled like Limburger cheese.

"She said something about someone being after her, and that they wouldn't leave her alone." Archer's voice made Grant forget everything else. "She was terrified, and she was looking for you, Lauren."

Grant rushed forward, tugging the tail of his shirt from the waistband of his khakis. "Who are you talking about?"

"Gina's in trouble again, and they can't find her," Lauren explained hastily. "Has anyone checked the school grounds? That's where she went last time. In her confused state, she must be looking for her children."

"But the school is near her house," Archer said, "not the hospital."

"What direction is the school from her house?" Grant asked. "If she's disoriented, she might instinctively go that way again."

Archer pointed west.

"How long has she been gone?" Lauren asked. "Last time her

neighbor said she was gone about forty-five minutes, and that was about fifteen minutes before she arrived at the hospital."

"That wouldn't be a good predictor," Grant said. "Since we don't even know what's wrong with her."

"We can't rule out a psychological problem," Archer said, "especially after what she told me. She said 'they' were all around her, and that 'they' wouldn't shut up. If she's hearing voices that aren't—"

"Archer, have you called her IIS therapist?" Grant asked. "If I could talk to her—"

"I had Gina's director notify Rose Pascal. Apparently no one told Sarah Davis about Gina's problem, and she isn't exactly happy with Gina right now."

"I'll have a talk with Sarah," Grant said. "Gina has enough to worry about without an angry director breathing down her neck." He checked his watch. "I hate to call the police on her again, but I don't want to take any chances. Archer, you and Lauren check the streets west of here by foot. Separate and cover a block at a time, including the alleys and private yards. If you don't find her in fifteen minutes, take two more streets and come back this way. I'll go inside and see if I can round up any more help to search. I'll have Brooke and Beau paged to meet me in the ER. They can cover a lot of ground."

"Would you have one of them call Evan Webster?" Archer asked. "He's still waiting for me. The poor kid must think he's been stood up. Also, someone needs to contact the children's baby-sitter, in case their mother attempts to reach them."

Grant nodded. "I'll have them take care of it. Check your watches, and meet me in the ER in thirty minutes." He looked at his own watch, then shook his head and sighed. "I'm going to have to break down and buy a cell phone. We could sure use one right now."

They parted and began the search.

Fifteen minutes later, Lauren was just about to turn back in frustration when she caught sight of a young woman quickly rounding the corner up ahead, coming in her direction. She had short copper-colored hair and was wearing a hospital uniform. When she looked up, Lauren could see the anguish in her face.

"Gina!" she called, running toward her. "Are you okay? What happened? We've been looking for you." When they drew close, she instinctively reached her arms out. Gina walked into them and grabbed her in a tight, desperate, trembling grip. She buried her face against Lauren's shoulder.

"It's okay," Lauren soothed. "You're going to be—" But she couldn't promise Gina she would be fine. *Oh, Lord, please comfort her. Show her the peace she can find in you in spite of everything.*

"Help me, Lauren," Gina whispered. "I think I'm losing my mind. I'm messing up everything. I thought I could control this thing if I could just concentrate hard enough to keep it from happening again. I'm so sorry."

"You don't have to apologize for anything, honey. What happened?"

"I don't know. Maybe Rose was right. Maybe I'm having panic attacks. Or worse." For a few moments Lauren held Gina and let her cry, praying that Archer would look for her before he started back toward the hospital on another street, praying that God would show her how to comfort Gina, and praying that they would be able to find out what was wrong with her before something worse happened. Levi and Cody needed their mother, and Gina needed help, desperately.

When the younger woman's shoulders stopped shaking and she loosened her tight grip on Lauren's arms, Lauren gently eased back to look into her face. "Can you tell me what you remember before you ran away?"

"I don't know for sure." Gina's voice continued to wobble. "I panicked at my desk, and there were these . . ." She blinked and shook her head. "I was trying to call you, but I didn't get an answer, and . . . I found myself out here walking. I was terrified, and . . . How did you know where to look? What did I—Did I do something?" She gripped Lauren's arms, her unique eyes widened with growing horror. "Did I hurt—"

"No, it's okay, you didn't do anything wrong. You don't remember calling Archer?"

"No, I don't. . . ." She frowned, as if attempting to catch a thought that was just beyond the reach of her mind. "I don't know. It's so hazy."

"He located Dr. Sheldon and me, and Dr. Sheldon organized an informal search party. We were worried. Archer doesn't think anyone in your department even knew you were having a problem until he told them."

"Dr. Sheldon didn't call the police again, did he?"

"I don't know. He didn't want to, but he's worried about you. Gina, did you . . . hear something . . . some voices that bothered you?" Lauren hoped the younger woman didn't pick up on the uncertainty in her voice. "You told Archer they wouldn't shut up."

Gina's hands tightened on Lauren's arms. "Voices? What kind of . . . but that means—"

"We don't know what it means yet."

"Hearing voices is a symptom of psychosis. Oh, Lauren! Am I—"

"No. Don't start panicking again. Don't even go there right now. We can't jump to conclusions."

Gina closed her eyes and took a slow, deep breath. "I guess I'm in big trouble. Sarah didn't know anything about my injuries or the night when I left the kids at home. I couldn't bring myself to tell her. . . . I'm so new here, and—"

"Dr. Sheldon said he would talk to her. Are you feeling well enough to walk? I want to get you back to the ER. If we can run some tests on you right away, maybe there's a chance we can find the culprit."

"You're serious? You still think this could be something physical?"

"Right now I don't have any idea what it is. But no matter what it is, we need to track it down quickly, and—"

"But what if it *is* psychological? What if I truly am losing my mind? The fear I felt was so real, so . . . terrifying."

"But where is the fear coming from?"

"I'm not . . . sure." Gina looked away.

Lauren studied her closely. "But you have an idea, don't you?"

Gina hesitated a moment, then nodded.

"Come on," Lauren said. "We can talk about it on our way back to the hospital."

Gina didn't move. "I'm not sure I *can* talk about it."

"You need to try." Lauren tugged on Gina's arm and finally convinced her to move.

They walked about half a block in silence.

"If I tell you something, will you promise not to say anything to anyone?" Gina blurted.

"You're putting me on the spot. If it's something that could help us—"

Gina touched Lauren's arm. "Please, just listen. I've been doing a lot of research since I first started having these spells."

"Since you *first* started? When was that?"

Gina didn't look at her. "They've been worse since I moved here in February. I felt periods of confusion before that, but I never lost time, and I never left my kids alone at home. The fear wasn't . . . so bad before."

"The problem's escalating?" That was not a comforting thought. "You should tell Dr. Sheldon about this as soon as possible."

Gina didn't respond to the suggestion. "The escalation could mean that the stress of moving has aggravated a problem I already had." She slowed her steps and lowered her voice, and her gaze darted around them nervously, as if she were afraid someone might be eavesdropping. "I've been researching fugue states. That could be what's happening to me."

"What would make you think that?"

Again, that darting gaze around them. She moved closer to Lauren. "I haven't told this to anybody." She swallowed and searched Lauren's face.

"It's okay, Gina. You're not going to shock me."

"I had an aunt who was hospitalized with a mental disorder in Oregon." The words came in a rush, as if she'd suppressed them for a long time.

"What was the disorder?"

"Please promise you won't tell anyone."

"But why? If there truly is a mental disorder, we can find it and treat—"

"No, please, you don't understand. There's more to it than—"

"Hey! There you are!" They looked up to find Archer running toward them from a side street to their left. Lauren's nerves screamed with sudden frustration. Five minutes ago she'd been praying for him to find them. Now she wished she'd had just a few more moments alone with Gina. She could feel Gina closing in on herself as Archer drew near.

Who knew when she would open up again?

CHAPTER 20

G rant tried not to reveal his frustration when he completed a perfectly unremarkable neurological exam on Gina. He would normally be relieved that he could find no serious physical problem. But he saw his frustration mirrored in Gina's eyes, and in Lauren's, and in the face of the hospital social worker, Rose Pascal.

Rose was a pretty woman in her forties, with the sad gray gaze of someone who spent too many hours worrying about other people. She had short gray-blond hair that she constantly fingered away from her eyes in a subconscious gesture of excess nervous tension. At this moment her hair was tufted and her face was pale. If only Gina could see Rose's obvious concern as she stood quietly in the corner of the exam room with Lauren.

The physician on duty had been more than willing to allow Grant to treat this patient. Emma, the RN on duty, had drawn blood and taken vitals, and Gina was on a cardiac monitor. Nothing seemed irregular.

Grant stepped back from the bed, tugging at the sleeves of his borrowed lab coat, which stretched too tightly across his shoulders. "Everything looks normal, Gina. We can only wait and hope something turns up on the test reports."

She nodded and closed her eyes. "You've ordered another psychological exam?"

"You have an appointment for Monday morning in Springfield."

Rose stepped to the bed and laid a hand on Gina's arm. "Gina, I wish there was something we could do to help."

Gina tensed visibly. She gave Rose a look so filled with suspicion that Rose broke the physical connection and stepped back.

When Gina turned to Lauren, her expression suddenly metamorphosed to that of a frightened child looking to someone bigger and stronger for assurance. "What am I going to do?"

"We've talked about this, remember?" Lauren's voice was brisk and filled with confidence. "You're here and you're safe. That's what counts for now. Maybe the tests will show something and Dr. Sheldon will be able to figure this whole thing out."

Grant could only hope that would be the case, but so far it didn't look promising.

"And if he doesn't?" Gina rose up on her elbows. "What then? I feel like the vultures are waiting to pounce." She jerked her head toward Rose. "Tell her what Natalie said last week. It took me an hour to calm Levi down after he heard her talking about foster care."

Rose frowned. *"What?"*

Lauren turned to Rose to explain. "Natalie and Gina were discussing child care options in case Gina became incapable of caring for Levi and Cody. Levi overheard her mention foster care, and it frightened him."

The news obviously surprised Rose, and she shook her head and groaned softly. "Of course it would, but Gina, did she actually threaten to take your children from you?"

"No, but *you* did the night of the wraparound meeting. Remember? Ever since then it's been like a shadow looming over everything I do. The minute I make a move out of line, my kids are going to be snatched away from me." Her bitterness held a familiar edge. Lauren had heard it several times in the past three weeks.

Rose sighed and spread her hands in front of her. "Oh, Gina, no. I never meant that as a threat. I was simply voicing one of my own fears. Every day I do everything in my power to help keep families together— it's one of the main reasons I do this job."

Silence stole into the room as Gina studied the social worker's face.

"Please forgive me, Gina," Rose said softly.

Gina shifted on the bed and reached irritably for one of the monitor lines, as if the silence, and the subject matter, were making her uncomfortable. "Dr. Sheldon, my readings are normal, right?"

"That's right," Grant said. "Everything appears good so far." Which wasn't really good. There was nothing to fix.

"Then can we take this thing off?"

"Let's wait a few more minutes, then Lauren can remove the electrodes. I don't want to give up too soon. We're still waiting on test results."

Gina slumped back down onto the mattress and looked at Rose again. Her gaze slid away, as if she spoke with reluctance. "Natalie didn't really threaten me, okay? I'm not . . . I don't want to get her in trouble or anything. I just want some peace and quiet at home. I wish Archer hadn't called the whole city over a silly little phone call, because now she'll be all over me again."

"He thought you might be hurt," Grant said, compelled to defend the pastor. "All of us did. We were worried."

Rose raked her fingers through her hair until it stood out in short spikes. "Gina, I'll talk to Natalie. She's a young counselor—she's only been at the job for a year—and she's trying to do everything by the book. But she really wants to help. She's come to me about your case several times."

"I'll just bet she has," Gina grumbled. "She's come to me a few times, too."

"She's frustrated because the two of you can't seem to communicate."

"She doesn't realize how dangerous a little knowledge can be."

"What knowledge, Gina?" There was a thread of exasperation in Rose's voice. She turned and paced across the small exam room. "Is something else going on here? Is that why you won't cooperate?"

"I have my reasons."

"Natalie's on her way here now," Rose said. "Will you at least talk to her? Please?"

"I always talk to her."

Lines of frustration deepened around Rose's eyes. She took a step toward the bed, hesitant, as if afraid she might startle an already frightened child. "Gina," she said softly, "I know I didn't exactly get off on the right foot with you, and I'm sorry. I know it's hard to trust strangers, especially when your children are involved."

Something in Gina's face softened. She did not smile, and she did not relent, but the hard set of her jaw wasn't quite as defined as it had been a few moments ago. She nodded and closed her eyes.

Rose shook her head, shrugged at Grant and Lauren, and left the room.

As soon as the door closed, Gina's eyes opened. "Dr. Sheldon, do you mind if I talk to Lauren alone for a few minutes?"

Grant looked at Lauren, who nodded at him. "Of course not. I want to check you out one more time, then if you need me, I'll be in my office."

Archer found Evan Webster in the emergency waiting room, where the fifteen-year-old sat in a deserted corner, scribbling furiously in a notebook. He looked up when Archer sat down next to him, but the expression on his face was one of intense concentration, as if he was still focused on his writing. A small red and purple bruise smudged his left eye.

"Did you take a tumble?" Archer asked, indicating the bruise.

Evan ducked his head and flushed, and his eyes darkened. "Yeah, I fell against my *friend's* clenched fist."

"A friend did that?"

Evan looked down at his notebook. "He's the one who gave me the pills. He got mad because I told the police about him. When his parents found out they freaked. He's being shipped off to spend the summer with his uncle, who's a retired marine. Kent wanted me to have something to remember him by."

Good, the kid would be gone for three months. "I'm proud of you, Evan. You took a courageous stand, and I know that couldn't have been easy. Sometimes friends are hard to find."

"Yeah." Evan slumped back in his chair.

"Hey, I'm sorry I kept you waiting for so long this afternoon."

Evan grinned. "That's okay, Pastor Pierce. Unfortunately, I know how time flies when you are in the middle of an emergency."

Archer placed his hand on Evan's shoulder. "That's true. But I still wish I had called you right away. It wasn't right."

"Forget about it. I really understand." Evan ducked his head as if embarrassed by Archer's repeated apologies.

Relieved, Archer gestured to the notebook with a page full of scribbles. "Your father told me you're a fledgling reporter for the school paper."

"Not just the school paper." Evan straightened. "The editor at *The Dogwood* promised to read an article about my experience the night I came here with the overdose."

"Is he thinking about publishing it?"

"If it's good enough. I'm going to make sure it is."

"And you don't mind the fact that many people might read the story and judge you unkindly?"

Evan shook his head. "Writing is what I do. Most people know about what happened, anyway. Word gets around. Besides, it shouldn't have happened at all, and maybe my article will keep somebody else from swallowing pills just because some so-called *friend* tells him to."

"How do your parents feel about it?"

"Dad thinks I should do it." Evan shrugged. "I didn't ask Mom. She's planning a wedding, and she's not going to be around here much longer."

"She isn't? Are you moving?"

"*She's* moving."

"But you aren't?"

Evan shook his head. "She's getting married in a month, and they'll live in Springfield. I told her I wasn't living up there, and she said okay." He placed his pen in the center of the notebook on his lap and leaned back. "Just like that."

Archer grimaced. That had to hurt, even if the boy didn't want to live with his mother anymore. "You're moving in with your father?"

"Yep. She told Dad it's just for the summer, but Dad thinks we can convince her to let me stay with him for good if we don't make waves about it for a while, especially since her fiancé isn't too crazy about me right now."

"Your father must be happy that you're staying with him."

A slow grin spread across Evan's face. "Yeah, he is. He says we'll start attending your church on Sundays, and I can take those drug awareness classes you lead on Tuesdays."

Archer grinned. "Things are looking up."

Evan raised his hand. "If you'll let me take notes for my article in class."

"I'll do better than that. We tape those classes, and I'll give you a copy of the tape. We're going to have a special guest teacher next Tuesday. Do you remember reading about Sergeant Tony Dalton in *The Dogwood*?"

"The police guy who got blinded by that booby trap?" Evan looked impressed.

"That's the one. He's teaching the class."

"Yes!" Evan raised a fist of victory in the air, and the excitement transformed his face.

Archer couldn't help getting a little excited himself, as he realized some of his prayers for this boy were being answered. "We may still be able to go fishing for a couple of hours this afternoon. Are you interested?"

"Okay, that sounds like—" Evan's attention suddenly shifted, and Archer heard approaching voices.

The teenager swallowed, and his eyes widened. Archer turned and saw Grant's twins strolling side by side into the waiting room from the central hallway. There had been no time for introductions earlier, but Archer had noticed them in Lauren's truck when she pulled up in the parking lot.

"I don't care where they put me, as long as I get a paycheck," the girl, Brooke, chattered confidently to her brother. "If I can jam raw liver onto a fishhook, I can empty a bedpan. Maybe they'll let you work in the kitchen."

"Maybe they'll let me do data entry. I can—" Beau looked up and caught sight of Archer and Evan. He fell silent and seemed to close within himself.

Brooke saw Archer and stepped forward with a sudden smile. She was a beautiful girl, obviously without an ounce of shyness, and she held her hand out to Archer as he stood up. "Hi. You're Archer Pierce, the pastor of Lauren's church."

"And you're Brooke, Grant's daughter." Archer caught the smell as he released her hand. The scent of Limburger cheese and some other unmentionable foods wafted through the air. "Did you catch any fish?"

"I caught a snake." She rolled her eyes and shuddered dramatically. She had expressive, constantly moving features and eyes, like her father's, that seldom missed a single detail. She glanced at Evan and held her hand toward him. "Hi, I'm Brooke Sheldon. Are you the guy who got stood up this afternoon?"

Evan's ink pen fell to the floor as he took her hand. He didn't seem to notice. "Yes . . . um . . . I am. But Archer says we might be able to go back out."

Brooke's smile dazzled the recipient of her favor into forgetting the unfortunate fragrance accosting him, and her charm reflected her father's easy grace. Her brother, on the other hand, continued to hover a few feet away, hands in his pockets, eyes downcast.

Archer completed the introductions. It looked as if the kids would have some time to get acquainted after all.

After Grant stepped from the exam room and closed the door behind him, Gina held a hand of entreaty toward Lauren. "Will you take care of my kids if something happens to me?"

Lauren was reaching toward Gina when the impact of the question hit her. She froze in mid-movement. "What? *Me?* Gina, I'm not even a foster—"

"Please. You're the only person I know I can trust."

The sounds and smells of the busy ER faded into the background as Lauren pulled a chair close to Gina's bed. She didn't sit down immediately. This was serious. "In the first place, Natalie and Rose and a lot of other people are doing all they can to make sure your children don't have to leave you."

"But they're—"

"No, Gina, listen to me. Of course they're ready with foster care if something happens to you. Would you prefer they didn't care enough to make those preparations in advance?"

"No, but—"

"They've covered every possibility, because they want to do what's best for Levi and Cody, not because they want to snatch your children away from you. You need to understand the difference."

"Please, Lauren." Gina raised up on her elbows. "I need to know they'll be safe. I need to know they'll be with *you*. I can't . . . won't go back."

"Go back where? To Oregon?"

Gina's eyes remained dry, but a deep chasm of fear and frustration filled them, and the full lines of her face grew taut. "My children already adore you, especially Levi, and if Levi trusts you, so will Cody."

"But why are you talking about this now? All your safety nets are in place, and everything worked today. You called Archer, and he took action. It was what we hoped for. Why would—"

"I'm talking long term. Nobody knows what I'm going to do next. *I don't even know!* I can't take any chances with my children and their future."

"Just because your aunt was in a mental hospital for a while doesn't mean you're having the same problem. Usually we only check immediate family for related sympt—"

"Lauren, I can't trust myself!" Gina's voice swept through the room, and they both knew anyone standing outside the door would be able to hear it.

"Okay!" Lauren reached for her hand. "Shh, it's okay. Remember I told you that you're not alone. Lie back down." She waited until Gina's grip relaxed a little. "Tell me, what did you leave behind in Oregon? What are you so afraid of?"

Gina pressed her lips together and looked away.

"It's okay if you can't talk about it yet."

"M-my mother," she whispered.

Lauren sat down. She suddenly needed the support. "Gina?" She leaned close, until she could see the golden copper lights of the younger woman's eyes. "What about your mother?"

"She hates me." The words tumbled out. "She's a wicked, jealous shrew, and if she knew about all this, and if she had a chance, she'd try to get the kids from me. Not because she wants them, but because it would hurt me. And then she would hurt *them*."

"And she's in Oregon."

Gina nodded. "Please don't tell anyone."

"I won't. I promise. I just have trouble understanding how a mother could hate her own daughter."

"I never understood it, either, and I've always been afraid I'd turn out just like her."

"You shouldn't worry. It's obvious to everyone around you how much you love your children. Gina, you said your father died when you were ten—"

"When he died, I lost my only friend in the house. My mother said he played favorites between me and my sister."

"You have a sister? But you said you didn't have any family."

"I don't." Gina's voice and eyes hardened. "Levi and Cody are my only family now."

"Your sis—"

"She's five years older than me. *She's* the one who turned out like my mother. She hates me just as much, too. After my father died, I learned the meaning of pain. Few days went by that I didn't receive at least a slap in the face from my sister for some imagined slight. It made my mother laugh."

"Your mother allowed your sister to abuse you like that?"

"Allowed? She encouraged it. My mother didn't hit me that often. She just let her anger build. I could see it coming for days, and then when she went into a rage even my sister wasn't safe. I learned early to run away when Mother began to yell. It was like a shriek of warning."

Lauren listened with growing horror. "Oh, Gina."

"Two years after my father died, my mother remarried. I was excited, because I thought a stepfather would be a friend." She closed her eyes. "He wasn't."

"Did he hurt you, too?"

"He made . . . passes at me. He never forced it, but he kept trying. One day my mother was in the laundry room that connected to the kitchen pantry while I was cooking supper, and he didn't know it. She heard him say something lewd, and she came storming out of that laundry room like she was going to kill me."

"She blamed *you*?"

Gina nodded. "She punched me in the face and shoved me into the stove. My blouse caught fire and it burned my stomach. Three weeks ago, when I found out Levi had burned himself on the stove, I felt as if history was repeating itself—no matter how hard I've tried to keep it from happening. It's like some evil cosmic game is—"

"No, Gina. It doesn't work that way. You're a logical human being, and you know—"

"Just listen to me." Taking care not to dislodge the electrodes on her chest, Gina swung her feet over the side of the bed and leaned closer to Lauren. "Tell me if you don't think there's some kind of pattern. I was twelve when that happened. I went to school with a black eye from my mother's fists, and when I was undressing for gym some of the other girls saw my burned stomach. They reported it to a teacher, and Social Services stuck its nose into the mess."

Tears of sympathy stung Lauren's eyes. She swallowed them back. This did sound like a pattern, but it wasn't what Gina thought. There wasn't some cosmic inevitability working in her life.

"They took me out of my home and placed me in foster care," Gina said. "They seemed to think that would make everything better. It didn't."

"You must have been frightened."

"I was terrified. I didn't want to stay with my mother and sister, but I didn't want to live with strangers, either. When my father's Aunt Bridget found out about it and asked for custody, they didn't allow it because she had a history of mental illness. My mother got a real kick out of the fact that only a crazy lady would want me. Every time she saw me afterward, she reminded me of it. She told me I was going to turn out just like Aunt Bridget."

"What were the foster homes like?"

"Confusing. Frightening. Awkward for them—and horrible for me. Any time someone raised their voice in anger, I ran. I couldn't help it. I was too scared. I went through four foster homes in two years. They finally gave up on me and allowed me to stay with Aunt Bridget in spite of her history. They didn't have a choice."

"Then your aunt should be the one to care for—"

"She died two months before I graduated from high school," Gina said. Her voice caught, and she fought a visible battle with tears. "Those years with her were the best years I can remember in my life, and I owe her everything. When she left her estate to me, my mother and sister were livid. They protested in court, but Aunt Bridget's attorney was prepared for them. It wasn't a fortune, but it got me through college, and—"

"Okay, Gina, I'll do it."

"You will?"

"If something happens to you."

Some of the tight lines of strain disappeared from around Gina's eyes and mouth, and the relief in the room was palpable. If Lauren hadn't already known how much Gina loved her children, she would have no doubt now.

"You'll keep Levi and Cody?"

"I said *if* anything happens to you, I'll keep them." Lauren couldn't believe she was doing this, but what other choices did Gina have? "I don't believe it's going to come to that, and I don't believe there's some big cosmic pattern repeating itself, because you did not hit Levi and knock him into that stove—"

"But it's my fault he—"

"No, Gina, it is not your fault." Lauren didn't even attempt to hide her exasperation. "When will you stop blaming yourself for everything that's happening to you?"

"But you have to admit—"

"No. *You're* not doing all this. You're trying to take care of a problem you know nothing about. Gina, things happen in this world that none of us is strong enough to handle alone, and until you realize your own need and accept help, you're going to continue to struggle. If you could only allow yourself to trust—"

"I trust *you*, Lauren."

Those words, and the open look of friendship in Gina's eyes, struck deeply into Lauren's heart. "There's more to it than just trusting me," she said softly.

"You're talking about the God stuff again, aren't you?"

Lauren smiled. "In a way, what you and I do as professionals is a reflection of what God does. Our patients have to recognize their own weaknesses and trust someone else for the strength and abilities they don't have. When you treat your patients, isn't that what you're doing for them? You have what they need to help them breathe better, but they have to trust you to give the treatment."

"My problem isn't spiritual, Lauren, it's mental," Gina whispered. "I'm hearing voices. If I have schizophrenia, who's going to know how to treat that?"

"I don't think that's what it is. I think you're hearing your mother's voice, and maybe your sister's. What you're experiencing is leftover fear from your childhood."

"You mean repressed memories?"

"No, not repressed. You obviously remember them *too* well; you just haven't been able to deal with them. That was apparent to me immediately, because you've been so unwilling to talk about it before now. Whatever is triggering these episodes could be physical, and just because we haven't found it yet doesn't mean—"

There was a soft knock at the door, and Gina stiffened. "Yes?"

The door opened, and Grant stepped inside. He held a two-page printout, obviously the report on Gina's blood tests. Judging by his despondent expression, it was not good news.

"Lauren, you can disconnect Gina from the monitor now. She's in excellent physical condition."

CHAPTER 21

Grant sat at his desk, staring at the pages in front of him. He felt like tossing them into the trash.

Today had been wild, and it wasn't over yet. He hadn't experienced this many conflicting, powerful emotions in months—from frustration with Brooke's attitude to elation with Lauren's company, from humiliation when the fishhook ripped his pants to exhilaration when he thought they might finally discover what was wrong with Gina. That hadn't worked out. And now this.

He should have known what was coming when he saw the sheriff standing in the doorway to his office.

Grant shoved the pages to the side of the desk. The autopsy report on Mrs. Henson had cleared him of any blame. It had been determined that it was sudden cardiac death secondary to lethal arrhythmia. There was no stroke. There was no blockage of arteries. Case closed. It did not tell him why she had been so sick the night before she died, and therefore it couldn't give him any clues as to why so many more people were developing symptoms of the illness.

He glared at the other sheaf of stapled pages of interrogatories from a well-known St. Louis law firm. They were the kind of attorneys who advertised their services on billboards and television. They specialized in—

"Knock-knock," came a friendly male voice from the open doorway.

Grant turned and motioned for Archer to come in.

"Any luck?"

"None."

Archer sighed and slumped into a chair beside the desk. "Frustrating, isn't it? Where is she now?"

Grant pointed toward the flower garden outside the window, where Lauren and Gina strolled shoulder to shoulder between brightly colored rows of varied blooms. At least Gina seemed to be opening up to someone.

"If it's frustrating to us, imagine how much worse it must be for her," Archer said. "I'm glad Lauren's working her usual miracle."

Grant shrugged away his depression and concentrated on what Archer was saying. "Miracle?"

"Don't get me wrong—I know it's God who works the actual miracles, but sometimes it seems to me as if Lauren serves as a sort of vessel for them to flow through."

Grant knew exactly what he meant. Annette had been that way.

"She's got this kind of radar that picks up on hurting people," Archer continued. "Where most people might avoid someone like Gina and her problems, Lauren dives in up to her neck, the way she did the first time Gina came in here. I've seen her do it a lot of times over the years." There was no way to miss the note of admiration in his voice or the affectionate smile on Archer's face as he, too, watched Lauren through the window.

Grant turned his back to the depressing burden on his desk and studied Archer closely. "All that, and she's single."

"Maybe there's a reason she is."

"You mean because she's too busy for a relationship?"

Archer considered that for a moment. "No, I think maybe she's one of those people God has chosen to pour herself out for others. Someone who is married will naturally spend more time with a spouse."

"Unless she just happens to be married to a spouse who does the same thing. Is that why you're still single?" The words were out of Grant's mouth before he could stop them.

Archer's eyes flickered with a note of discomfort. "Good question."

"I'm sorry, that was a stupid thing to say. I know you had a broken engagement, I just didn't think—"

"It's okay. Actually, I've wondered about that a few times. When Jessica broke our engagement it seemed as if God was trying to tell me something about the necessity for singleness of purpose. Now I'm thinking maybe I just tried to move things along a little too quickly, going by my own timetable instead of God's."

"You mean you might consider marriage with the right person?"

"Oh, I already know the right person. My church seems to think that the pastorate needs a husband and a wife to do the job. I can't keep up with all the responsibilities by myself."

"Maybe your church expects too much from a pastor."

A hint of a smile touched Archer's eyes. "I've thought of that, too."

"I've noticed Lauren helps you a lot," Grant said.

"She does, and I need to stop taking advantage of her generous nature."

"But she seems to enjoy it. She was enjoying herself today. I know she was looking forward to your arrival." It had been obvious.

"Really?" A hint of a frown touched Archer's eyes. "I can't imagine why. I usually scare all the fish off."

"You couldn't possibly be as bad as Brooke."

The frown disappeared. "I wouldn't bet on that. Did you have a good time?"

"If snakes and torn pants and screaming teenagers are your idea of fun, I highly recommend it."

"I guess I'll have to teach Jessica to fish."

"Jessica?"

"That's my . . . ex-fiancée." A thoughtful smile touched his eyes. "Maybe she won't be an ex for long, though."

"Oh?" Grant was happy for Archer, but for Lauren's sake, he couldn't help feeling a twist of sympathy. She obviously felt more for the young pastor than simple friendship. Could Archer be so clueless? Maybe he chose to ignore an uncomfortable situation.

Or maybe Grant was being overly analytical because he was struggling with that invasive little attraction bug, himself, right now.

"A wife would probably keep the normal small-town gossip to a minimum," Archer said.

"That isn't a good reason to get married."

"Of course not." Archer grinned. "I'm beginning to learn how important it is to build a strong friendship as a foundation for marriage."

"Friendship is the most important thing, and I think you're wise enough to know it." Though Grant couldn't always close his eyes and picture Annette's face, he could still feel the overwhelming emptiness in his heart. "That's what I miss the most about my wife. She was my best friend on earth." He missed her now especially. If she were still alive, he would have immediately picked up the telephone and told her about the letter from the attorneys, and she would have reassured him, and she would have been on his side, and she would have contacted the best attorney she could find.

"I think your wife must have been a wonderful person," Archer said quietly.

"She was." Grant looked out across the broad hospital lawn again and watched as Lauren and Gina took a seat on a concrete bench in the center of the flower garden, beneath the shade of a weeping willow.

Far to the right of them, near the parking lot, Brooke's bright red T-shirt and shorts flashed in the sunshine, practically iridescent with the movements of her body. Brooke was never still. It was as if she had twice as much energy as her quiet brother, who sat in silence beside Evan Webster on another concrete bench. Both boys were watching Brooke, listening to whatever wild tale she was telling them.

Grant felt a familiar tug at his heart. He wanted so much for his children, but just as Archer felt he needed a wife to help with the responsibilities, Grant needed his wife to be the mother of his children, to guide them in ways he couldn't.

"I'll be free the rest of the afternoon to go fishing if you still want to try it," Archer said. "That is, if Gina's going to be okay."

Grant nodded. "She's eager to get back to work, but Lauren forestalled her for a while. I'm not sure we can stick another fishing pole in Brooke's hand, but I'm willing to give it a run." Once again Grant's eyes strayed to the offending papers. He couldn't work up any enthusiasm for the idea of fishing, but he knew the diversion would do him good, and it would be good for the kids, too.

Archer studied Grant's face more closely. "Okay, something else is going on here. What is it, Grant? What's wrong?"

Grant sighed and reached for the interrogatories. "I'm being sued for malpractice."

While Archer waited for Grant and Lauren to wrap up a meeting with Gina's supervisor and unruffle some feathers with the IIS therapist, who was trying so hard to convince Gina to trust her, he strolled down the familiar main hallway of Dogwood Springs Hospital, doing a prayer walk as he went.

First, he prayed for Grant, who might soon be up to his eyeballs in paper work for his lawsuit. At least his former employer had covered him with malpractice insurance. Grant needed to understand that he wasn't alone in this. They both knew that very few malpractice cases actually made it to court, and this one was obviously a big mistake.

Next, he prayed for Gina, for the physicians who treated her, and for her little boys.

Then he prayed that God would give him the wisdom to handle the nasty situation that was taking place within his own church.

He tried not to brood about the painful meeting with his personal referees earlier today. It was difficult, though, considering that this very hospital was reportedly the origin of the meanspirited gossip. Still, he didn't doubt that those three servants of the personnel committee meant well, as far as their understanding went.

But he didn't like the implications of their remarks. He resented their intrusion and their willingness to listen to outright lies about him. Though he tried to shake off that resentment, he wasn't having a lot of success. Apparently, he and Grant were struggling with the same kind of problem.

It disappointed him to realize that even though Mr. Netz and Mr. Hahnfeld had watched him grow up in "their" church since he was an infant, they were willing to believe he would father a child out of wedlock and then deny all responsibility for it.

What also hurt—possibly even worse—was that they would listen to gossip about Lauren. She was above reproach, and even if they hadn't known her as long as he had, couldn't they trust his judgment about her? What would make them even consider such a possibility?

A stray question occurred to him . . . and he quickly dashed it away.

They should be able to trust his word. They should know him well enough to give him the benefit of any doubt.

True, they might be listening not only to this one hospital rumor, but also to suggestions whispered by others in the congregation. . . .

No, he couldn't even think like that. Lauren had always behaved with the utmost propriety, and even though she did, at times, seem to seek his company a little more often than she had in the past, and even though he had caught hints from some of the elderly ladies in the church family . . . and even just now from Grant, that . . .

No. It wasn't possible. Archer and Lauren had always been close. She was like a big sister. If he had, in the past few weeks, misread her affection, it was only because of his own disappointment over his broken engagement. He was the one who'd had the crush when they were growing up, not Lauren. She was obviously homesick right now. And since he was the only old familiar face around, it was understandable that she would gravitate to him for friendship.

How could such influential members of his church be totally lacking in spiritual discernment? Did he really want to be the pastor of a church so worldly minded?

And yet weren't all churches like this? It was what this world was all about.

Still, Lauren McCaffrey did not deserve this kind of treatment.

Archer rounded a corner and strolled into the small gift shop that was run by volunteers from the community. He saw Mrs. Piedmont, in her pink smock, talking to a prospective customer about a bouquet of flowers. When she caught sight of him her smile broadened in warm welcome, and she waved at him. That smile soothed something inside him. At least *she* wasn't paying any attention to unfounded rumors. Mrs. Piedmont walked closer to heaven every day. Archer knew he was being selfish to hope she lived well past a hundred.

When he returned to the hallway and saw Fiona Perkins waddling toward him, Archer resisted the temptation to do an about-face and race away in the opposite direction.

"Hi, Archer." She said it in a sly, singsong voice that grated.

He braced himself. "Hello, Fiona."

Chunky and awkward, Fiona unfortunately had a personality to match. She had curly black hair and wide-set, pretty blue eyes, but as Archer and others had learned the hard way, her attitude could curdle coffee. He felt sorry for her and reminded himself that she needed to experience the love of Christ as much as the rest of the world.

She chugged up to stop at his side, peered into the gift shop as if to see what held his attention, then looked back at him as a knowing grin creased her face. "Looking for someone?"

"No, I just—"

"She doesn't work Fridays." The grin broadened. "It's her day off, same as you. But you already know that, don't you?"

Archer knew who she was talking about, but before he could think of a suitable reply she huffed away. He headed in the opposite direction. Typical of Fiona, she left her little barbs wherever she went. And she probably didn't even realize how much those barbs stung.

One of the benefits of being born and raised for thirty-three years in one small Missouri town was familiarity with all the other natives, particularly with wonderful souls like Mrs. Piedmont.

Ironically, with other souls who were not so benign, familiarity was one of the drawbacks. Many natives had a tendency to know too much about a person's business, and if they didn't know everything, they assumed that person was up to something he shouldn't be.

Fiona did not surprise him. She'd moved to Dogwood Springs with her family when Archer was a senior in high school and she was a freshman. She had not been overweight then, but she had quickly become unpopular because of her spiteful spirit. When Archer had gone out of his way to be kind to her she had developed a huge crush on him. Things had gone downhill from there.

"I give up!"

Archer stopped walking when the feminine voice filled with frustration reached him from behind a door that stood slightly ajar.

Natalie Frasier burst through that door and nearly tripped over his feet. "I don't know what more I can do for her!"

As Lauren followed the IIS therapist out the door she saw Archer and gave him an apologetic, slightly flushed smile.

"Problem with Gina?" he asked.

Natalie put her hands on her hips. "Lucky guess." Her voice dripped sarcasm. Her intense dark eyes shimmered with tears of frustration, and she folded her long arms into a protective, bony shield.

"Natalie, she has her reasons," Lauren said gently. "I understand that now."

"*I don't.* I'm tired of fighting this. I give up. I'll file my report, and it won't be a very good one, but—"

"No, Natalie, please don't do that," Archer said. "Not yet. Don't give up on her."

"What am I supposed to do? I can't get any cooperation from her."

"I'll talk to her again," Lauren assured her.

"I will, too," Archer said.

Natalie held her hands up to stop them. "It won't do any good. She won't listen, and you both know it. I'm finished. But just tell me one thing—why is it a nurse and a preacher and a doctor seem to know so much more about *my* client than *I* do? I've spent the past three weeks trying hard to get her to trust me."

"No, you've spent that time asking questions and making more demands on her than she feels she can handle." Lauren's voice was matter-of-fact, gentle—an observation, not a rebuke.

"But I'm just doing my job. Doesn't she see I'm trying to help her? What is it about me she doesn't like?"

Lauren laid a hand on Natalie's shoulder. "Her biggest fear is losing her children. Natalie, if you file your report and give up on her today, what's going to happen to her?"

"I don't know. The decision isn't up to me."

"But you must have some idea."

"I know I do," Archer said.

Both women looked at him.

"Gina *could* lose her children if you file a report on her now."

The young woman raised her hands in exasperation. She took several long-legged paces along the quiet hallway, arms falling at her sides in a curiously helpless gesture. When she turned back, the sheen of tears was still there but hadn't spilled over the dam.

"Is there another therapist in the area?" Archer asked. "Maybe another angle on this—"

"I don't think that's the problem," Lauren said. "It isn't a personality conflict."

"Oh, really?" Natalie said. "Tell that to Gina."

"She knows." Lauren's voice remained gentle. "Natalie, you're doing all you know to do, and you obviously care about your clients or you wouldn't be so frustrated. Gina recognizes that, whether she wants to admit it or not, and that's what will break down the barrier eventually."

"Eventually? Do you know how much longer I have to complete this assignment? Two weeks at best. Maybe three if I convince the right people I need more time, but I'm not making any headway with this woman. She's like an armored tank. I don't have enough evidence to convince anyone to even read my report!" She waved a hand in the air. "Report? That's a laugh."

Lauren caught the young woman's arm and eased it down. "Natalie, you already have Gina's safeguards in place, and they're working. She called Archer today when she realized she was in trouble. Her children know to go next door to Mrs. Walker's house if there's a problem at home. Why can't we just leave things as they are right now and see how this progresses?"

"But she isn't improving, and we can't find a problem. I don't know what good that psychological exam is going to do Monday. She won't trust the psychologist, either, and the last test didn't reveal any clues."

"Then let's wait," Archer said.

"If it will help you with the decision," Lauren said, "why don't I move in with Gina for the next week? That way you won't have to worry—"

"No." Natalie's angular face took on extra definition as her lower jaw grew firmer. "I can choose the hours I feel are necessary to work each case, and I have at least a couple of weeks left. If she needs someone to stay overnight with her, *I'll* do it."

Lauren blinked and doubt entered her eyes, but she said no more.

With tears still unspilled and arms jutting at an awkward angle from her straight, slender body, Natalie marched down the hallway and out the door.

Archer watched Lauren watch Natalie, and he knew from past experience what she was thinking. "Don't worry, you handled it well."

She turned back to him, still frowning. "I don't know, Archer." There was a moist sheen of sympathy in her green eyes. "She and Gina are both so headstrong."

"And they're both intelligent women. All you can do is pray about it and leave it in God's hands. You can't carry the load of the whole world on your back." Out of habit, he put a companionable arm across her shoulders, then realizing how the gesture might appear to onlookers, he abruptly withdrew it.

She looked up at him. "Archer? Is something wrong?"

Obviously, she knew him as well as he knew her. The words of warning were ready to spring from his lips, but he stopped them just in time. "I just realized that your meeting is over with Natalie, and if we wanted to we could round up the gang and go fishing."

The diversionary tactic worked just as he had known it would. Lauren smiled, and the light of eager anticipation entered her eyes. "Let me check on Gina one more time, then I'll find Grant. Oh, and Archer, would you see if you can round up a spare set of large scrub pants? I think Grant could use some extra coverage. I'll meet you in the parking lot."

He watched her rush away as relief and guilt battled for power over his conscience. How on earth could he tell her that people in this hospital, and even worse, in the church she served so faithfully, had accused her behind her back of carrying his child? The operative phrase was *behind her back*. Surely no one would be so crass as to confront her with the rumor. Not even Fiona. The only reason he had been confronted was because those three deluded men actually thought they were acting in the best interest of the church.

It was a distinct possibility that Lauren would never hear a whisper of it, because those people who loved to spread rumors so diligently wouldn't want to be caught in their lies. Dad had explained that to him years ago, and he'd been proven right so many times. So why cause Lauren unnecessary pain? What good would it do? She would only suffer humiliation for nothing.

No, he wasn't going to tell her.

Grant stepped out the back door at the east wing of the hospital, chafing at the sudden heat of the lush June day. He saw Brooke sitting on a bench by the smokers' area, still chattering to her brother and Evan Webster. The words *snake* and *stinks* drifted across the air to him.

Evan couldn't seem to close his mouth as he gazed at Brooke in youthful awe, laughing at every silly thing she said, automatically mimicking every nod of her head, every grimace, every smile. The poor kid was besotted already.

Grant smiled. In spite of his daughter's brazen audacity, she was not a snob in the traditional sense of the word. Brooke wouldn't encourage Evan's adoration, but she would be surprisingly gentle with it. Eventually, they would be friends. She was always kind to hurting things, whether they be furry little animals or unpopular people. In school she refused to play by the rules of the caste system that established the teenage pecking order, and consequently she had more friends than she could handle. She was very much like her mother in that way.

Today it looked as if she was being true to form. Maybe she would be okay in Dogwood Springs after all. If only Grant could convince her of that.

As he watched his kids interact with Evan, he heard the door open.

"You didn't warn me about her," came a sweet, teasing voice from behind him.

Grant turned to see Lauren smiling at him from the doorway. "I thought I'd let her catch you by surprise."

"It worked."

"You handled the shock well."

"I grew up on a farm." She crossed her arms and ambled out to stand beside him. "It takes a lot to shock me."

Grant chuckled. "Did I tell you she's already hitting me up for a car?"

"That's typical sixteen-year-old behavior," she said.

They watched the kids in silence for a moment. "She's trying to grow up too fast."

Lauren looked up at Grant. "What about Beau? Is he trying to grow up too fast?"

Grant shifted his attention to his son, to the serious face that held too much knowledge and pain for one so young. "Unfortunately, I think he already has, and it wasn't his idea."

"There's something special about him," Lauren said. "He has one of the sweetest spirits of any young man I've ever met."

If she was trying to win Grant's undying affection she was going about it the right way. "He has his mother's heart," Grant said.

"He'll be a good doctor someday."

Grant allowed the assurance of her words to warm him. "Yes, he will, if he can overcome his self-consciousness about his face when he is around strangers."

"Now that's something I can identify with," Lauren said.

Grant looked at her, raising an eyebrow to express his total disbelief. "Oh, sure."

"Really. I went through a time during high school when I felt so physically awkward and ugly I didn't want to go to church. Of course, being a deacon's daughter, I never got the chance to act on my feelings. Maybe Beau will outgrow his apprehension."

"I'm afraid his problem is a little more serious than *feeling* awkward and ugly."

"But he isn't ugly," Lauren said. "He's very attractive. Much like his father." She said it as a simple matter of observation.

The smile of pleasure slipped past Grant's defenses and spread across his face before he could do a thing about it. "Thank you, Lauren. I didn't mean to imply that I thought he was ugly."

"I know what you're talking about, but don't underestimate his ability to adjust. Look at him now. He and Brooke are obviously making a new friend."

"I think Evan needs some new friends."

"They'll be good for him." She paused a moment, and he saw an uncharacteristic frown mar her clear features. "You said something a while back that suggested you hovered over him too much." She spoke slowly and paused to glance up at him, as if afraid she might offend him. "Is it possible he picks up on your concern? I know my own parents are far too worried about my singleness at thirty-five, and that hurts me, because I know I'm disappointing them. I think families— especially loving ones—tend to be a little overprotective."

Grant was far from offended. "That's the word my kids use on me, especially Brooke."

Lauren's frown scattered with laughter, and she gestured toward his daughter. "Leave it to Brooke to point out exactly what she's thinking at any moment. I do wish you would bring them to church Sunday."

"I'll talk to them about it."

"They might be more willing to come if you joined them."

He paused. "I know. I'm not sure I'm ready for that."

"Have you been back to church since the accident?"

"A few times."

Lauren took a step closer to Grant. "My friend, it's no wonder you show such compassion for your patients. With everything that's happened in your life, you've experienced a taste of torture right here on earth."

"Are you talking about Brooke?" As soon as the words were out of Grant's mouth, he knew how inappropriate they sounded.

Lauren laughed, then grew serious again. "If you ever want to pray together about it, let me know. Maybe as a single woman without children I can't identify, but we can always talk to One who can."

Gratitude overwhelmed Grant. He swallowed. "Thank you."

CHAPTER 22

The next Wednesday morning Archer was sitting at his desk, doors closed, with the music on his CD turned up loud enough to drown out the clatter of computer keys and the quiet ring of the telephone at Mrs. Boucher's desk out in the church office. He was preparing a sermon, reveling in the heartfelt angst of Solomon in the book of Ecclesiastes, and half expecting the three wise men to come tromping through the door again to update him on the latest atrocities circulating about his steamy philanderings.

Archer had just begun to imagine what gracious words of compassionate wisdom might spring from his lips in such a situation when his telephone rang and crashed into his fantasy.

He picked up the receiver. "Dogwood Springs Bap—"

"Archer Pierce, I want to know what's going on at that church." The female voice was so filled with outrage that, for a moment, he didn't realize who it was.

When he did, he caught his breath. "Jessica?"

"I also want to know who gave grumpy old Mr. Netz my unlisted telephone number." The anger seemed to build with each word.

"He *called* you?"

"You'd better believe he called me, and get this: he thought he had a right to know why I broke our engagement. Of all the—"

"You're kidding."

"Do I sound like I'm kidding?"

Archer leaned back in his chair and braced himself. "No."

"So let's hear it."

He'd had every intention of telling her before this, but he hadn't spoken with her since last Saturday, and at the time they'd only had a chance for a quick meal in a busy restaurant between shows. The timing just hadn't seemed right. Of course, Archer had known he was only delaying the inevitable—and here it was. "There is apparently a rumor making the rounds about an illicit relationship I've been conducting."

There was a short silence. "How silly. Those people should know you better than that. Are you supposedly having an affair with a married woman or something?" The dry, tired tone of her voice gave him comfort. She had dismissed the possibility without even giving it a moment's serious consideration.

"Not with a married woman. It's bad enough, though. There is apparently a young woman carrying my child."

There was a gasp. "How could they even think such a thing? Archer, how *dare* they?"

Had he ever forgotten, for a moment, how much he loved Jessica, this moment would have served as an excellent reminder. "Thank you," he said quietly. "You can't know how much that means to me right now."

"Why? Anyone in his right mind—any logical, godly person without an ax to grind—would never listen to such garbage. Don't worry, it'll all blow over. I can't believe Mr. Netz had the audacity to bring up the subject. He should know better."

"It wasn't just Mr. Netz, and it hasn't blown over. Some people want me to resign."

This time the silence was long and screaming with increased outrage. And then the tone of it changed. Though Jessica didn't say a word, he could almost hear her mind working, could see her face growing still and her eyes darkening.

"Then resign," she said at last. "That church doesn't deserve you." She didn't wait for a reply. "In fact, maybe this is God's doing. You know what I heard yesterday? Your replacement at your old church in Branson didn't work out. They're looking for another youth minister, and all you would have to do—"

"Wait, Jessica. Hold it. You're saying I should resign? Just like that?"

"Isn't that what they want?"

"I'm not interested in what they want, I only care about what God wants."

"What if God does want this? Besides, are they going to give you a choice? If those people want you to resign, and you stay and fight, you could split that church right down the middle. Do you think that's what God wants?"

"If I resigned it would almost be like I was admitting to something I didn't do. How is that furthering the gospel? If I allow a group of petty gossips to control the future of the whole church, I'm playing right into the hands of evil. Are you saying that's what I should do?"

There was a soft sigh at the other end. "I don't know." It was almost a whisper. "Forgive me. I've been doing too much thinking and not enough praying. I'm jumping to too many conclusions. I just don't know how things could have deteriorated to this point."

"Which things are you talking about, Jess?" he asked gently.

There followed another one of those tightly strung silences as Jessica gathered her thoughts in logical order. He wished he could read those thoughts as well as he used to think he could. Would she be this upset if she didn't love him?

"What I think I'm saying is that I can't marry that church."

He closed his eyes and bowed his head. *No, Lord, please. Not this.* "I never asked you to marry the church, Jessica." He couldn't keep the sharpness from his voice. "And who said anything about marriage lately? We're not even engaged."

"I know, but I've been thinking about that a lot. Before Netz called me I had almost convinced myself to ask you for my ring back."

He felt the return of longing all the way to his feet. *Don't do this, Jessica. "Before* he called?"

"Yes, before. But this brought everything back to me in a rush. Archer, I asked myself, if you were still a youth minister, would I have married you? My answer was yes. I love you. That's the simple truth. If you weren't the pastor of Dogwood Springs Baptist we'd still be engaged. I know that's wrong. It's my natural instincts outshouting my spiritual maturity, but that's how I feel at this moment. It scares me to death to consider putting myself at the mercy of a bunch of people who don't even have the discernment to tell the difference between fact and fiction."

Archer bit his lower lip and controlled his breathing with difficulty. "And what if I were to take my old job back in Branson, then five years after our wedding, I once again became the pastor of Dogwood Springs Baptist? What would you do then? Would our marriage contract have carried the stipulation that I never answer God's call in my life to pastor a church?"

She groaned. "Oh, Archer, of course not. And you know I don't believe in divorce."

"Yes, I know. I'm sorry, Jess. Nobody but God tells me how I'm going to serve Him." Archer couldn't believe he was doing this. How could he allow the love of his life to slip from his grasp?

"But if we were married, it wouldn't be just you," she said quietly. "It would be us. Isn't that right?"

The truth of her words made his heart squeeze tight. He couldn't answer. He wasn't sure of the answer right now.

"I'm sorry," she said. "I know this must sound like I'm trying to manipulate you, but I'm not. I'm just being honest." There was a quiet sniff. "I'm sorry."

"So am I." Why couldn't he stop this? They belonged together. Hadn't God placed this special love in his heart for her? Or was that all just a part of his own fantasy?

"Do you mind if I ask you something?" Her voice came across the line with sudden, uncharacteristic timidity.

"No, Jessica. You know you can ask me anything."

"Who is the young woman?"

"Does it matter? It's a lie. You just told me you didn't want anything to do with people who listened to such—"

"It will matter if someone else calls me and tells me about it. I would feel a lot better if it came from you."

"But why should it matter if it isn't true?"

"Archer, who is it?"

"Lauren McCaffrey."

There was a long silence, and then she sucked in her breath. "Oh."

"But what difference does it—"

"Maybe you should consider something, Archer." Her voice grew stronger. "If you're spending enough time with Lauren that people are beginning to notice, it's because you *want* to spend that time with her. You haven't asked me to come down there and accompany you on visits or go on retreats with the youth lately."

"That isn't fair, Jess. How could I? You broke our engagement."

"You aren't engaged to Lauren."

"But she's an active member of this church, and she's an old friend—you know that. Be reasonable."

"I'm being as reasonable as I know how to be. I'm trying to be practical. Would you please do one thing for me?"

"What's that?"

"Would you please let me know what you decide about this church business?"

"Of course I will. We're still friends, aren't we?"

"Friends?" Her tone was sharp and edged with pain. "You mean like you and Lauren?"

"No, that isn't what I mean. We'll still talk to each other; we can keep—"

"I thought I was strong enough to do that, but I'm discovering some things about myself lately that I don't like. I'm confused right now, and being with you adds to the confusion."

Archer closed his eyes.

"I'm sorry," she said.

"About what?"

"About being so . . . I don't know . . . unpredictable. I guess I'm sorry about my own confusion."

"So am I, Jessica. I'm confused about this, too, but there are a few things I have no doubts about."

"What are those?"

"I don't doubt God is ultimately in control and knows our hearts better than we do. I don't doubt I was called to this church when I came. And I don't doubt that I love you. Whatever happens from here on out, those are absolutes."

"Oh, Archer," she whispered. "I love you, too." She fell silent for a moment, and then she sniffed. "How does life get so complicated?"

His heart echoed her pain and frustration. "We make it that way."

As soon as Grant opened his front door Wednesday night he was struck by such a wave of nostalgia that he nearly staggered across the threshold. The effect was so powerful that, for a moment, he couldn't pinpoint the source. When he closed the door behind him the mingling aromas of jalapeños and onions fried in abundant amounts of real butter made him ravenous. It also confused him. That recipe had been Annette's. She was the only one who had ever made the Sheldon family's special—white-hot chili.

Beau came out of Grant's home office at the far side of the living room with a notebook under his arm and an ink pen behind his ear. "Hi, Dad. Your malpractice insurance company called about the lawsuit today. The hospital faxed them the medical records they needed, and they want to set a date with you for a preliminary meeting. They're hoping to settle out of court."

"Settle? Just like that? I remember that case. I reviewed the records they faxed to me, too. There shouldn't be a case."

"Okay, works for me, but if you do have a case, I want to go to court with you. I need the practice so I'll be ready for the day I get sued. Brooke and I start our new jobs at the hospital next week. Did you find any more clues about the Dogwood Springs Virus?"

"A few." Grant sniffed the air again. "What are you cooking?"

"Nothing. What did you find?"

Grant took a list out of his pocket and handed it to Beau, who took it eagerly. "Where's that smell coming from if you're not cooking? I don't think I'm having olfactory hallucinations."

"Smell? Hey," Beau said, reading the list, "is this true? Out of sixty-five flu patients in the past three weeks, only five of them were Medicaid recipients? That's way off the percentages you usually get, isn't it?"

"Yes, and only three were cash patients. The rest were insurance or Medicare. I noticed that, too." Grant tried to step around his son to peer into the kitchen, but Beau was too busy studying the patient notes to realize the case studies didn't have his father's full attention.

Grant was beginning to feel particularly uneasy. By popular demand, he and Beau were the only ones in the household who cooked. Unless Beau and Brooke had gone behind his back and hired a housekeeper while he was at work—and they had threatened to do that a couple of times in the past year—the only other person who could possibly be cooking up those smells was his daughter. That was not something he wanted to contemplate after a busy day of treating fretful patients whom he could not diagnose satisfactorily.

"So this means we've got some kind of weird, middle- to upper-class virus at work, huh?" Beau asked. "Interesting. If you could get me a copy of the charts—"

"Are you sure you aren't cooking something in there? Did you order out?"

"No. What about those charts? I've got your copies of the hospital lab reports filed in your office. If you could get copies of any x-rays—"

"Beau, I can't give you confidential patient information. You know that."

"You could if you hired me as your home office administrator. Really, Dad. I have a lot more time than you do right now, and I could use one of your access codes for a medical Web search." He leaned closer and lowered his voice. "I need the experience, and Brooke's getting on my nerves."

Her voice reached them from the kitchen. "I heard that!"

If Grant's offspring-tracking radar was still working correctly, that voice came from somewhere in the vicinity of the stove. There was no way this could be a good thing.

Grant moved his mouth closer to Beau's ear. "She's cooking?"

Beau nodded, his face solemn.

"What is it?"

"She wants it to be a surprise."

Grant frowned. "She's still bothered by this Lauren thing, isn't she?"

Lauren barely made it to the break-room bathroom before her carefully chosen dinner of nonirritating foods abandoned her. She'd had to call in sick twice this month, so she'd been making up the time by working extra shifts for two other nurses who probably had the same nasty little bug. Her legs lost their strength, and she leaned against the side of the sink for several seconds to keep from sliding to the floor. Although she had only had minor bouts with this mystery illness during the first half of June, she hadn't been able to keep much food down the last few days. The sick taste in her mouth would require more than mouthwash or salt water to alleviate. And besides that, she had a pounding headache.

Frustrated and battling fear, she patted her face with cold water. From experience, she knew the weakness would probably go away. It had every time so far. For a moment, she thought about calling Grant at home, but what could she tell him that he didn't already know? The symptoms were the same as before, the same as most of the other patients.

She opened the door and stepped out of the bathroom, pausing to lean against the doorframe, wondering if she should try to call another nurse to take her place. If this illness was contagious, wouldn't she just make things worse for everyone if she stayed around here?

But she could wear a mask.

Fiona Perkins came waddling past her from the break room, and she stopped when she saw Lauren's face, crossed her arms, and gave Lauren a sly grin. "Morning sickness at night?"

Lauren didn't have the inclination or the energy to reply. She shook her head and waited for Fiona to leave. Maybe a soda would help ease the nausea. The ER was getting busier, and she didn't want to let the others down.

She would be okay.

The last time Brooke had attempted to prepare a meal for the family, the three of them had nearly starved before lunch. She'd used hot water to defrost a can of frozen orange juice, had oversalted the oatmeal, and had cooked the eggs until they were hard enough to break teeth. That had been sixteen months and two weeks ago. Grant remembered, because Brooke had vowed never to cook for the family again. Beau had promised to hold her to that vow. He'd let Grant down.

Grant and Beau stared at each other across the dining room table while Brooke carried in huge bowls of steaming white-hot chili. "I was looking through some of Mom's old recipes and I found this one." She placed cheddar and Monterey Jack cheese in the center of the table, along with some sour cream and a bowl of inexpertly torn lettuce. The drink of choice was milk. This family knew how to eat taste-bud-killing food with excellent natural tongue soothers.

Once again, for a moment, Grant was so steeped in bittersweet memories that he forgot to be afraid of the chili. He skeptically watched his daughter sit down and nudge her brother to put his research aside. She had her mother's gift of gab, but now she fell silent and waited for Beau to say grace. Prayer before meals was a family tradition Beau insisted on continuing, and with which Grant wholeheartedly agreed— particularly for this meal.

After the blessing—which sounded most passionate in its sincerity— Grant took a sip of his milk and watched as his children did the same. He picked up his spoon. Then he hesitated.

Brooke picked up a leaf of lettuce. "Dad, did Beau tell you we've got jobs? I get to help in the laundry, and Beau's in the kitchen. Evan's volunteering his time at *The Dogwood* for summer vacation." She rolled her eyes as if the very idea of working for no pay didn't register with her. "Oh, and he's going to interview that Sergeant Dalton who got blinded by the ammonia trap."

"For *The Dogwood*?"

"That's what he said. I told him if they print the interview he should at least get paid for that. And I bet they print it, because he's good. Have you read any of his writing?"

"Sure, Brooke," Beau said, "Dad has time to go rummaging through all those scribbles. The first thing Evan needs is a word processor. His handwriting's worse than Dad's."

Grant studied the chili more closely. It *looked* like Annette's. "So, Brooke, where did you say you found this recipe?"

"I was looking through some of those file drawers in the back bedroom. I thought I might dig out some of those scrapbooks Mom put together every year. I found some old love notes she used to put in your lunch bag. Remember them?"

Oops. He should have put those in a more private place. "Yes, I do." He had always looked forward to those notes, some of them homemade greeting cards with her creative stitching around the edges and her loving words of encouragement inside. They usually included a verse from the Bible that related in some way to the experiences they were facing at the time.

Brooke filled her spoon with chili and blew on it, then took a bite, apparently unaware that Grant and Beau watched her with sudden, deep interest. She didn't grimace. She didn't choke or stop breathing.

"Were you looking for something in particular in Mom's things?" Grant asked.

She took a swallow of milk. "Did you know you can smell Mom's perfume in those files? You know that honeysuckle stuff she wore? You can smell it. I just wanted to sit there and feel close to her. And I read some of the notes." Her somber expression lightened for a moment with a teasing glint. "Pretty intense stuff, Dad."

Grant willed away the flush of embarrassment that threatened to heat his face. Many of the love letters Annette had written to him were not intended for eyes other than his. Maybe he should have discarded them, but he just couldn't bring himself to do it.

"Did it help you feel closer to her?" he asked.

Brooke put her spoon into the bowl and looked down at the table for a moment. "At first it did. Then I just got depressed."

"I know. I've done the same thing late at night, when you two were in bed. Brooke, if it upsets you this much to think about my dating again, I won't—"

"But that's just it," Brooke said. "That's what I'm saying. I realized this afternoon that I couldn't bring Mom back. We've been saving all her stuff, even her favorite recipes, like they were some kind of a shrine to her memory. But she wouldn't want us to. She would want us to go forward with our lives, not sit around whining. I realized, reading her notes to you, that she wouldn't want you to be lonely."

Grant wanted to enfold Brooke in a big bear hug and tell her how much he loved her. But instead, he did something even more loving than that. He put a huge spoonful of the chili in his mouth. He was encouraged when Beau followed his example. The mingling of flavors and the feel of the heat—just the right amount of heat—on his tongue snapped him into the past with such force he could almost feel Annette's presence.

When they were first married and struggling to exist on school loans and Annette's small salary as a bank bookkeeper, she had developed this recipe, made with cheap ground turkey and white beans, which they had at least once a week. Until the twins were old enough to speak for themselves, Annette continued the tradition at least once every month, even when it was no longer necessary to stretch money so far.

When the kids were eleven, Brooke gave notice that the chili gave her gas, and if her parents really loved her they wouldn't make her suffer so horribly. The tradition was modified from then on to include spaghetti for the kids.

"Hey, this is good." Beau took another spoonful.

"Well, surprise, surprise," Brooke said dryly. "And you thought I couldn't cook."

"We all thought you couldn't cook," Grant said. "This is delicious. But I thought you didn't like this chili."

"I knew you loved it, though. And all I had to do was follow Mom's recipe. I started thinking about some things this afternoon while I was cooking."

"*You?*" Beau said. "Wow, Brooke, you really have been busy today."

"Shut up, Beau. Dad, you like Lauren, don't you?"

"She's a great nurse, and she's proving to be a good friend."

"Especially if she's willing to put up with Brooke for an afternoon of fishing," Beau said.

Brooke dipped another ladleful of chili into her brother's bowl. "Keep eating, Beau. I hope you blow up like a blimp. Dad, Lauren kind of grows on you, doesn't she?"

Grant remained noncommittal. Was this a setup? "You mean like a fungus?"

Brooke gave him a "get serious" look.

"She's easy to be around." What was he saying? She was a joy to be around.

"I was thinking I wouldn't mind seeing her again . . . I mean . . . if you wanted to take her out on a date or something. Every couple weeks or so."

Grant suppressed a smile. "You mean you *like* that female John Boy?"

Beau choked on his chili.

"Shut up, Beau. Dad, he's been making me feel guilty all week. He keeps telling me that I'm being selfish and hardhearted."

"You are," Beau said.

Grant placed his spoon back in the bowl. "No, she isn't. She's going through the grief process in her own way. We've all been doing that. The death of someone you love changes your whole outlook, your way of dealing with things. I know I've dealt with things poorly at times. I apologize. I'm trying to improve, but it just takes time."

"You mean you're going to try to stop nagging us so much?"

"Brooke, Dad isn't a nag."

Brooke rolled her eyes. "He's even worse with you than he is me, and he never lets up. 'Brooke, you're going to school to get an education, not to meet guys and form social relationships. Brooke, someday you're going to be sorry you didn't do your homework. Brooke, you're so much prettier without all that glop on your face. Brooke—' "

"Okay, okay, I hear you," Grant said with a chuckle. It was a good female rendition of his voice and accent. "I'm not that bad, am I?"

"You're even worse with Beau, except to him you say, 'Beau, you're getting a great education, but you need friends, too. Beau, there's more to life than reading. Beau—' "

"Stop it, Brooke." All the humor had left Beau's voice.

"No, it's okay," Grant said. "It's good for me to take a strong dose of Brooke's reality sometimes. I know I probably smother you both a little too much."

"At least you care," Beau said.

"I think subconsciously I'm trying to be a father *and* a mother to you guys."

"You're getting the job done," Brooke said. "Having you for a dad is like having a couple sets of parents." She took a sip of milk and dabbed at her lips with a napkin. "So, Dad, when are you going to ask Lauren out on a real date?"

"I'm not. It isn't that kind of a friendship. I already told you, there's someone else she cares about."

"Oh, yeah, Archer. But he isn't interested in Lauren. Doesn't she know that? I watched him the other day at the hospital, and then later when we went back to the fishing spot. He treated her the same way he did the rest of us. Dad, you need to learn how to read people better."

For a moment, Brooke's voice sounded so much like Annette's that it made Grant's eyes smart with tears. "Do you two know how much I love you?"

"Yes, Dad, we do," Beau said. "We love you, too."

Brooke put her spoon down. "If you're going to get mushy, I'm going to bed."

———

Lauren was beginning to feel better. She had completed the last of her charts and was just turning to grab another clipboard from the rack on the wall when she heard someone step up behind her. Two hands descended on her shoulders.

She stiffened and tried to turn, but the hands tightened their grip.

"Ready to join the team again, Lauren?" It was Dr. Mitchell Caine. He was standing too close, and she couldn't graciously step away from him because she was caught between him and the counter.

"Yes, Dr. Caine, I was just finishing a couple of charts."

The hands didn't release her, and she could feel the heat of his breath on her neck. She cringed.

"You're moving a little slowly tonight, aren't you?"

"Yes, Dr. Caine, it's possible."

"Feeling okay?"

I'll feel a lot better when you remove your grimy hands from me. "I'll be fine." The nausea had abated, but she wouldn't have admitted anything to him, anyway. The last time one of the nurses in the emergency department had left work due to illness, Dr. Caine had complained so loudly that she'd been suspended for a week.

This doctor had a lot of influence in this town. He had a busy practice, and he'd been in Dogwood Springs for twelve years. Popular homeboy.

Muriel came breezing through the workstation and plopped another chart in front of Lauren. "There you go, sweetie. I'll take care of two if you'll do the swab for me in five." She gave Dr. Caine a suspicious, bulldog gaze and looked pointedly at his hands.

To Lauren's relief, he removed them and stepped away.

Lauren grabbed the chart and fled to room five, thanking God for Muriel Stark.

CHAPTER 23

Thursday morning multiple birdsongs greeted Archer from the lush foliage of the Netzes' hedge-enclosed yard. He shut the car door behind him quietly. In case he decided to bolt at the last minute, he did not want to disturb the peace and alert Mr. Netz too quickly that he had company.

Archer wasn't sure he was ready for this yet. He'd called and made an appointment, though, and he seldom broke appointments. That was why he'd called—to keep himself from backing out at the last moment.

When Archer was five years old, just starting kindergarten, he'd had a *slight* disagreement with his mother when she took him to school for the first time. He'd kicked and screamed and hung on to Mom's thumb until he thought he might pull it off. After that publicly humiliating episode, Pastor and Mrs. Pierce decided their priority project from that day on was to teach Archer how to discipline his temper and his tongue. Twenty-eight years later, as he walked up the neatly trimmed sidewalk to Mr. Netz's house, Archer felt a distinct need to fall back on his early training and guard his tongue with utmost diligence.

There would be no "time out" if this conversation became too heated. Granted, he would get no spankings, but he could hurt his personal witness of the God of his life, and that would be so much more painful and lasting. He could recall his mother's gentle voice as he struggled through kindergarten and first grade: "Sweetheart, as soon as you have an angry thought, you give it to God. He's the only one big enough to handle it."

As he pressed the button for the doorbell, Archer picked up on the trail of prayer he had carried with him all the way from the church. He resisted the urge to demand from God an explanation of what good could possibly come of this situation. He simply asked God for guidance. Divine guidance. Gentle guidance.

Archer heard the sound of creaking-wood footsteps inside the house. When the knob turned, Archer begged a final few words of prayer for self-control, but he refused to fake a smile.

Mr. Netz pulled the door open and stepped into the doorway. He stepped back and held the door wide. "Come on in, Pastor."

Archer followed him into a cozy sitting room that Mrs. Netz kept decorated for company and sat in a straight-backed chair across from the old deacon. He wasn't in the mood to get tangled in the cushy folds of a comfortable sofa.

"Say your piece, Pastor, then I'll say mine."

Mr. Netz only called him Pastor when he was his most serious, but there always seemed to be something serious going on around this deacon. Some people said he stirred up trouble just for entertainment when he got bored. Dad had disagreed with them, but Dad tried to believe the best about people at all times. What would he say about this?

Archer leaned forward, elbows on knees, and waited until Netz met his gaze. "Why did you call Jessica?"

"I needed to know the truth."

"You're saying I didn't tell you the truth last Friday?"

Netz looked away. "It would've been hard to sit right there in front of three self-righteous troublemakers and admit you'd . . . done what they said."

Self-righteous troublemakers? At least the deacon had a good grasp of the situation. "In the years that you've known my family, have you ever known any of us to lie?"

"Nope."

"Then you could have come to me privately if you thought I was too much of a coward to say anything in front of the others." Archer could feel the sharpness biting at his words, and he had to remind himself again to be gentle. "My private life is not subject to public display, but if you were going to call someone, it should have been me."

The gray brows lowered. "When your private life affects my church, it is my business."

"But all you've heard is gossip. That isn't something to base a deci-sion—"

"Why do you think I called Jessica? I wanted to make sure that what I had heard wasn't true, that she hadn't broken the engagement because of . . . a . . . an affair." He looked away and cleared his throat. "I won't have my church—"

"*Your* church, Mr. Netz?" Archer asked quietly. "I thought we were God's church."

The older man leaned forward, his wrinkled gaze sober as he pinned Archer with a stern stare. "Dogwood Springs Baptist has been my church home for fifty years, and we've always had our problems. I saw a scandal back in sixty-five that like to have split us in two. I don't aim for anything like that to happen to us again, not if I have anything to say about it."

Archer had heard about that scandal. It had occurred a few years before Archer's father was called as pastor. Memories were long in Dog-wood Springs, and more than one of the natives had told him about the church music director—a single man—who had supposedly been caught in a somewhat compromising situation with a girl who was a senior in high school.

The compromise? He'd been holding her in his arms in the hallway after church one Sunday. When the girl's parents heard about it, they demanded, and got, his resignation. Half the congregation was furious about it, since the music director insisted he had only been comforting the girl, who had come to him in tears about a personal problem.

Archer should have heeded the warning as soon as he heard the story the first time. The people here were too quick to jump to unfounded, unfair conclusions, and it obviously didn't matter if the person they were hurting had been one of their own since birth. *Lord, forgive me for my bitterness. Give me your compassion. Direct my words.*

"Nowadays we make sure our staff leaders realize they are *ministers*, not just directors," Mr. Netz said.

"But aren't all believers called to be ministers of Christ? And as ministers, shouldn't we all avoid the specter of gossip in our midst? It hurts a lot of people."

"That's exactly right. True or not, those kinds of things cause trouble. Why do you think I wanted to get to the bottom of it? Lots of our old members have just quit coming over the years, and they didn't ever join anywhere else. It's like they got sick and tired of anything to do with church." He shook his head and sat back. "We can't take any chances."

Archer watched as the painful memories etched themselves across the old deacon's face, and he felt a pang of empathy. Hadn't he himself grieved over the ones who seemed unable to find a comfortable place of service within their membership? Even though church attendance was up, he felt the loss when he looked out over the sea of unfamiliar faces in the congregation and realized the changes that had taken place since his father was pastor. It was disheartening.

"Mr. Netz, I'm sure your telephone call to Jessica was made with the best of intentions, but it upset her a lot, and it may have destroyed any future relationship there might have been between us."

The lines of sadness deepened. "I'm sorry, Archer." The deacon twined his fingers together between his knees and studied them for a moment, then he looked back at Archer. "May not be worth much to you now, but I guess I've always had a hard time believing any kid of Pastor Aaron Pierce could do the thing they claimed you did."

"Thank you, Mr. Netz."

"You haven't forgotten my first name all of a sudden, have you?" Netz chided gently.

Archer hesitated. He wasn't ready to forgive. He studied the deacon's face and silently recited a prayer his mother had taught him as a child. *Dearest Lord Jesus, keep me from sin, protect me from Satan, and bring peace within.* It wasn't a mindless mantra, but a heartfelt plea. He knew he needed to forgive Mr. Netz and restore their fellowship. The man had been sincere in his actions, even though the basis for that action was a lie. But he'd gone about things the wrong way, and he'd hurt Jessica and Archer and no telling who else, and even though he'd been sincere, it was wrong, but—

Oh, no! What if, in his effort to "get to the bottom of things," he has said something about this mess to—

"Please tell me you haven't spoken to Lauren about the rumor."

Mr. Netz blinked at Archer in surprise. "That wouldn't have been proper."

"You called Jessica. That wasn't proper. What's the difference?"

"Tell you what I'll do, Pastor. I'll go pick up that telephone right now and call Jessica right back—"

"No!" Archer immediately leaned forward, hands upraised. "Please. No threats."

The man's surprise deepened. "I'm not threatening. She needs to know the truth, and I don't think I explained things too well when—"

"She knows the truth, Mr. Ne—John." Archer saw relief ease some of the creases on the deacon's face. And that showed, more than anything, how deeply he cared about their broken relationship. "The problem is, she doesn't want to be a part of a church that would carry that kind of gossip, or even listen to it. The problem is . . ." Archer had to admit it to himself, and the admission hurt. "She doesn't want to be a pastor's wife."

He could understand how she felt. In fact, right now he wasn't even sure he wanted to be a pastor. But it wasn't his decision. Ultimately, it was God's.

Archer stood up and offered his hand. "Thank you for seeing me, John. I trust you'll do what you can to explain to the others how I feel."

The deacon shook hands with him, his large, calloused fingers firm and strong. "I'll talk to them."

Maybe he should warn Lauren after all—just in case some other "well-meaning" busybody decided to get to the bottom of things.

"Tell me something," Archer said before he stepped out the door. "How did you get Jessica's unlisted telephone number?"

"Oh, that? I just asked Ruth Wecker. She's the choir secretary, and she has the addresses and telephone numbers of anyone who is active in the music ministry." He walked Archer out onto the sidewalk. "That Jessica sure can sing. I hope this thing works out between you two."

"So do I." But he could do no more to help it along. The rest was up to Jessica . . . and God.

Lauren pulled into the hospital employee parking lot Thursday evening, twenty minutes before she was due to start work. These night shifts were getting tedious and tiring. She would be glad when the hospital hired more nurses to work as needed, so the full-time staff wouldn't have so much overtime when someone got sick. At least Mitchell Caine wasn't on duty tonight. That made a big difference.

She was nearly to the ER entrance when she heard someone speak her name behind her. She turned to find Brooke Sheldon jogging from the far end of the parking lot. Her short, midnight brown hair formed a dark halo around her exotic woman-child features as she ran.

"I caught you! Dad told me you were scheduled to work tonight, and he let me drive the car alone. Can you believe he trusted me? Aren't you early?" She came to a breathless stop in front of Lauren.

"A little. Are you going to the movies or something?"

"No, I just wanted a chance to drive without Dad sitting three inches from my right shoulder, gripping the seat every time I put the brakes on too hard or hissing through his teeth when I take a curve too sharp. You know how dads are."

"Yes, but I had a lot of practice before I took the wheel of a car—driving tractors and trucks out on the farm. You learn quickly not to make a sharp turn or stop suddenly when you're pulling a wagon stacked high with hay bales and smart-mouthed guys."

Brooke's grin widened. "Can I walk you in? You have time to talk, don't you, since you're early?"

"Sure." Lauren turned and strolled beside Brooke. "What's on your mind?"

"Well, we *were* talking about dads. What's yours like?"

Lauren knew a fake pass when she saw one, but she decided to play along. Brooke was up to something. It showed in the tender dimples in her cheeks and her dark eyes filled with mischief. "He's an old farmer, and he makes a profit at it. He's the best daddy in the world."

"Does he ever get cranky?"

"Who doesn't? Supporting five kids on the wages of a farmer and a cake decorator might tend to make a guy cranky sometimes."

Brooke snorted. "No way! Your dad decorated cakes?"

Lauren rolled her eyes at the girl. "My mother did the cakes and helped with the farming, but my father did most of the worrying for the family. I had some interesting experiences on the farm. I remember one day an old farm rooster got after me and hit me in the leg with his spur."

"His *what*?"

"It's this hard appendage on the chicken's leg, shaped like a nail. They use them for fighting. It really hurts, too, when you're a little kid and you get flogged with one. When that old rooster hit me, I screamed so loud you could've heard me clear into town. When Daddy heard me crying, he went out and wrung that old rooster's neck. We had pressure-cooked chicken for dinner the next night."

"Eeeeww." Brooke glanced sideways at Lauren. "You still call him Daddy?"

"Sure. It takes a special man to earn the title. He isn't just a father, he's a daddy, someone who continues to love and support me in that special way only daddies have." She saw that Brooke was still watching her with curiosity. "So why are we talking about cranky fathers? *Yours* couldn't possibly be cranky, could he?" she teased.

"Nope." Brooke looked away.

"Not ever?"

"Well . . . sometimes, but not too much. He used to laugh a lot, but he doesn't do that so much lately. He's overprotective, but Beau says that's a good thing. Maybe he'll outgrow it when we get older."

"Don't count on it. Mine is still that way, just not as bad. I'm thirty-five. He's always checking the oil and tires on my truck when I go home for a visit, and he asks me if I lock my doors at night."

"Do you?"

"Usually."

Brooke grimaced, as if she couldn't imagine not locking the doors at night. "My dad wasn't so bad until after Mom died, but then he got carried away. I think he just needs more distraction in his life—you know, someone else to take some of his attention."

"He could volunteer to help out at the church."

"I don't recommend that. He's got enough stress in his life." Brooke looked at her watch, then indicated the concrete bench beneath a willow tree, where she had entertained Evan and Beau while Gina was being treated in the emergency room. "You don't have to go in yet, do you? Tell me more about yourself."

Lauren passed the bench and kept walking. "Brooke, you didn't hijack your father's car just to drive down here and get to know me better. What do you really have in mind?"

"I didn't hijack the car," Brooke protested. "I asked him if I could drive out for some Chinese."

"And he said yes, if you would drive straight there and back."

A sudden change of direction in Brooke's gaze worked like a lie detector. "I'm on my way there. One little stop doesn't mean—"

"The Chinese restaurant is on the other side of town."

"I took the scenic route. Dad should understand; he's always doing that. Do you know when we moved here, we took the scenic route instead of I–44? It took us nearly two days to get here."

"It sounds like a nice drive. Brooke, I should really get inside. The ER parking lot looks full, and we may be short a nurse tonight. Is everything okay? Is something bothering you? Because if there is, I'd be glad to get together with you later and talk about it. I know the move has been hard on—"

"No, no, it's nothing like that. I just thought . . . well . . . *I'm* not having as much trouble as Dad. I know he's lonely, and I think it would mean a lot to him to have someone to talk to."

"Of course. That's important for everyone. I know how it feels. He and Archer seem to get along well together, and—"

"Not *that* kind of lonely." Brooke's patience was stretching like an overextended bungee cord.

Lauren did not allow herself to smile. She knew Grant would never have put his daughter up to this, but what had given Brooke the idea that her father would be interested?

Brooke was silent for a moment, and Lauren couldn't help wondering what was going through the girl's mind.

"So you're really not after my dad's body," Brooke said at last.

Lauren barely managed to suppress a gasp. "His *what*? No!"

"Don't you even think he's hot? I mean, would it hurt to go out to dinner with him?"

"You actually want me to go out with your father? Brooke, the day we went fishing I got the distinct impression you were encouraging me to go out with anyone *but* him."

"I didn't know you. I do now. You're not the hillbilly I thought you were."

Lauren didn't want to insult Brooke or Grant. And she didn't want to hurt anyone's feelings. "Your father is a very attractive man. I enjoy working with him, and I've come to think of him as a friend." One of Grandma's favorite little idioms was "Never say never," but Lauren could not imagine herself ever involved in a relationship that would connect her to this mischievous, outspoken handful.

Brooke rolled her eyes. "Oh. I get it. You aren't attracted to Dad in *that* way."

"It wouldn't matter if I were. If I wanted to go out with someone he would have to share my spiritual beliefs and desire to actively serve God."

"We're Baptists, aren't we? What do you want from the guy?"

"I'm not talking denominations, I'm talking faith. There's a big difference."

"Dad knows God." Brooke's pretty eyes sparkled with the sudden gleam of righteous indignation. "He used to go to church with us when Mom was alive, but afterward he just kind of gave up. He made us keep going, but he didn't go very much." She stopped walking. "He really is a great guy, Lauren," she said softly, all the brashness suddenly gone from her voice.

"I can see that, and I understand that your father is a Christian." Even if he didn't believe it himself right now.

"He can cook."

"I know." And he was attractive, and Lauren liked him. Why ruin a good thing?

"And he even does dishes and vacuums the carpet and scrubs toilets."

"Does he do windows?"

Brooke frowned. "Huh?"

"Never mind."

"What would one little date hurt? Dinner. A trip to Branson. Fishing. Whatever."

"I know your father is a very special person, and I know I'll come to cherish his friendship. He's lonely right now, and it wouldn't be a good idea for me to encourage a kind of relationship that might be misleading."

"How do you know it would be misleading if you won't even go out with him one time?"

"Has anyone ever advised you to get into sales?"

"Does that mean you'll do it?"

"No." Lauren couldn't suppress a smile. This was the most single-minded kid she had ever met. "I've got to get to work, Brooke. You've got to get dinner for your family. Maybe you and I can go fishing again next week."

Brooke communicated her distaste for the idea without the slightest change of expression. "Can Dad go with us?"

"Sure. I'll call Archer. We can set up a date."

"It won't do you any good, you know."

"What?"

Brooke gave her a look of sympathy. "Dragging poor Archer along. Don't you think he would have asked you out already if he was going to?"

Lauren caught her breath. "Brooke—"

"Fine, don't take my advice." Brooke raised her hands in defeat. "At least I tried. You can't blame me when he dumps you."

"See you later, Brooke," Lauren said, a little more sharply than she'd intended.

CHAPTER 24

O n Friday afternoon Lauren walked down the central aisle of the circular auditorium of Dogwood Springs Baptist Church carrying a beautiful arrangement of peace roses and ferns in a cut-crystal vase. The roses would still be fresh for services Sunday morning, which was good because she was scheduled to work tomorrow and would have no time to check on them. When she wasn't working she planned to rest as much as possible.

The janitor was stirring up dust in the choir loft above the stage, vacuum cleaner wheezing loudly enough to drown out the chatter and laughter and occasional lyrics of a musical quartet practicing a new song for Sunday service over by the piano. Several of them waved at Lauren when they saw her. Five children between the ages of six and ten ran up and down the aisles of the church in a game of tag while their parents practiced.

Lauren loved the fact that this church family had put her to work right away, in several different positions, as soon as she joined, and she especially enjoyed the trust they placed in her with their children. In her old church back in Knolls they would have watched and waited for at least five years before allowing a new member to serve on any of their committees—just to make sure they hadn't accidentally voted a liberal ax murderer into their midst.

She arranged the blushing ivory roses on the Lord's Supper table, placed an old worn Bible on a stand beside them, draped a throw of ivory lace behind them, and stood back to see what else it needed. The table could use a good polishing. A pair of wire-framed reading glasses might help produce the effect she hoped for, and—

"Do you moonlight as an interior decorator?" came a friendly, familiar male voice from behind her, raised loudly enough to carry over all the other sounds.

She turned with a smile to see Archer coming to a stop beside the central front pew with a dustrag in his hand.

"No, do you moonlight as a janitor?"

"Not if I can get out of it. Our part-time custodian is out with knee surgery, so I told James I'd help out." He nodded toward the janitor in the choir loft, who smiled and waved with his free hand.

"You're well aware that I am definitely not artistic," Lauren assured him, "but I got drafted to take Mabel Long's place on the flower committee when she moved to live with her sister in Arkansas last month. I brought these flowers from Mom's garden."

"You went to Knolls today?"

"Yes, Mom was getting worried about me, and Dad wanted to check out the truck and make sure I'm keeping the oil changed. You know how they are."

"I sure do. So you're already on a committee? I thought they'd at least wait until the end of the summer to drag you onto their list."

"I didn't have to be dragged, I wanted to do it."

He held his hands up as if to shush her. "Don't let anyone hear you say that. You'll never have another moment's peace."

"Did you know our church has nineteen different committees? I found a booklet down in the library that listed the names, addresses, and telephone numbers of every person on every committee, and I couldn't believe it—I'm on three. I haven't figured out how I got so popular so fast."

"Three? Lauren, you and your big mouth."

"Shut up, Archer. You were probably the one who slipped them my name in the first place. Anyway, I'm happy to do it," she said. "I like to keep active, and the extra involvement is helping me get to know more of the people in a short period of time."

"It shows they're tired of all the work they've created for

themselves." There was a dry cynicism in his voice Lauren had never heard before. Now that she'd caught that strain of tension, she noticed that even his teasing held a somber note today.

He stepped over to admire the roses, then sniffed at them. "These smell good. Your mom has a way with flowers." He sounded a little depressed, and Lauren frowned at him.

"You've been making yourself scarce lately," she said. "*You're* not coming down with the flu, are you?"

"Nope, not sick yet." He looked tired, though, and his face lacked its expression of lighthearted optimism that was his trademark.

"Are you sure?"

"Positive."

Good. That made one of them. Even today, she continued to battle against fluctuating bouts of nausea and weakness and a nasty taste in her mouth, though she'd made sure her parents didn't pick up on it when she was home. Daddy worried about her too much.

Archer lifted the Bible from the stand to thumb through its yellowed pages. He paused from time to time, apparently to read different verses he found, then he sighed and replaced it on its stand.

"Working on a sermon?" Lauren asked. What was wrong with him?

"I'm always working on a sermon." He sank down onto the cushioned comfort of the first pew—where churchgoers seldom sat during worship service because they left it open for the folks who came forward during invitation time to pray. "I think the one I need to preach right now would be aimed mostly at myself." The janitor chose that moment to switch off the vacuum cleaner, and Archer lowered his voice. "I've allowed myself to get upset by an unfounded piece of malicious gossip." He gave Lauren a quick glance, then looked away.

"Malicious gossip is always upsetting." Lauren wondered briefly what it might be, but then dismissed it as none of her business. She didn't really want to be reminded just how mean some people were. Still, Archer was obviously concerned about it. "Especially if it attacks us personally, or someone we care about."

He looked at her, and if she didn't know better she would have thought that a blush was spreading across his face.

Two little girls came careening around from the side aisle and nearly toppled Lauren before she could catch them. Their mother stopped the music and called out to them to be careful, then the vacuum cleaner started up again.

"You know about the rumor?" Archer asked under cover of the noise.

"Me? No, I haven't heard anything."

Something in his expression disturbed her. He didn't quite meet her gaze. Lauren stepped over to him and reached for the dustrag. "Mind if I borrow this for a moment? The table needs polishing."

He didn't reply, just stared toward the flower arrangement as if he were deep in thought and let her take the rag from his hand without comment.

She hesitated. "Archer? This sounds serious. The rumor isn't about Gina, is it? Because if someone—"

"No, Lauren, it isn't Gina." He smiled at that, and it broke the tension. He reached up to massage his neck and shoulder muscles. "As I said, I shouldn't have allowed it to upset me."

Lauren watched him for a moment, then returned to the table and gave it a good polishing. Wire-framed glasses would, indeed, look good beside the Bible, but she didn't have a pair. She dusted the sides of the table, then went up the steps to the pulpit.

Before she could begin polishing around the microphone, Archer came up the steps and took the rag away from her. "I didn't come in here to give you my job. I think you have enough to do already."

She shrugged and went back down the steps to straighten the lace.

"Lauren," he said softly, under cover of the noise once again. "We've known each other forever. I feel as if I can talk to you openly. Do you mind if I ask you a question?"

"Of course not. What's on your mind?"

"You're an independent lady with your own career. Would someone like you ever consider the possibility of being a pastor's wife?"

All thoughts of glasses and Bibles and flowers scattered from her mind, and for a few seconds Lauren froze where she stood. She could not have heard what she thought—

"Lauren?"

"Uh . . . yeah?" She could barely hear his voice, and by now the pounding of her own heart had joined the din. He could not know how that question affected her. And he couldn't know how much she would love to give the idea more serious consideration. So why was he asking her? And right here in the middle of a busy church auditorium, of all places. Unless—

"Would you?"

She swallowed. "Honestly?" She braced herself and took the plunge, not allowing herself time to think. "Yes, I would consider it." She turned and looked at him. He was staring at the vase of flowers instead of her. "I think the office of a pastor's wife would be one of utmost honor and joy. To share in a partnership like that with someone you love and who loves God and wants to serve Him as much as . . . as you do . . . it would be close to my idea of heaven."

"But the people can be so hurtful at times." His focus still wasn't on her, and it seemed as if he were barely listening to her words.

"The people?" she asked.

"The church." He glanced toward the singers, who were busy collecting their music and purses and calling out to their children over the wheeze of the vacuum.

"I know a lot of pastors who have left the ministry because they've been hurt deeply and often by members of their congregations. Their wives suffer along with them. We're always conscious of the fact that we are employees and not really part of a church family. We can be fired at any time if the church votes on it. And sometimes it seems as if half the church members are constantly searching for some reason to do just that."

Lauren realized as Archer spoke that this conversation probably had nothing to do with her, and her automatic disappointment was first tempered, then replaced, by concern for his apparent struggle. "That doesn't happen in every church," she said gently. "It never happened at my home church in Knolls. Does this have anything to do with the rumor?"

He looked up at her at last, and she could see the anguish in his eyes. "I guess I'm pretty easy to read."

She leaned her elbows against the polished oak pulpit. "Do you want to talk about it?"

"I thought that's what I was doing."

"Well, then, carry on." Once again she dug deep and found the will-power to keep her mouth shut. Sometimes she amazed herself.

"You know, I never had an older sister, but I can't help envying your brothers. They didn't ever appreciate you enough when we were kids."

"They pick their moments." *Older sister*. She took that little unintentional slam in stride.

He laid the rag down and rubbed his face. "So, in spite of everything, you think it would be rewarding to be a pastor's wife?"

Again, that little skip of her heartbeat. "Yes, I do. I think the right person would feel it was an honor."

"Half of me wants to try to convince Jessica of that. The other half wants to warn her to keep running the other way."

This time the disappointment went all the way to Lauren's toes. Specters of Lukas Bower came back to haunt her. She had known better. This time she'd known, yet she had allowed herself a small piece of hope in spite of the fact that Archer had been in love with another woman when she came to Dogwood Springs. This friendship was merely an old friendship that had grown comfortable over the years of church camp and school games and Archer's visits to the farm. Had she betrayed her silly little crush in some way?

Suddenly overwhelmed by feelings of foolishness, Lauren stepped down to the roses, inhaled their delicate fragrance, and allowed the silence to wash over her. She shouldn't be surprised. Maybe she could blame Grant, because it was his encouragement, his suggestions a few weeks ago, that made her wonder if she really might be a good pastor's wife. Grant was the one who had told her she was such a source of encouragement, such a help to Archer and to others. He was the one who treated her as if she was someone special.

"You know," she said softly, "I've always loved the silence of a church auditorium when everyone was gone. I guess you have that experience every day, and it probably grows old to you, but somehow I feel a reverence here when I'm alone, kind of like I feel when I'm out on the creek talking to God. I know He doesn't actually live in this building. He's more likely to be out there on the creek, enjoying the beauty of His own creation rather than the stilted appearance of an auditorium wired for sound. But I believe wherever we are He will be there. Of course, you know all this, but I can remind you how much He cares." She was chattering again. "His will is going to take place no matter what we do here on earth. If it's His will for you and Jessica to be together, give it time. Is Jessica afraid of being married to a pastor, or is it this church that frightens her?"

"I'm not sure."

"Was it the rumor that caused her to break the engagement?"

Again, that slight flush, and then the shuttered look in his eyes as he avoided Lauren's gaze. It was something about that rumor. Did it involve. . . ? No, it couldn't.

"No," he said, "but it's messed things up since then. I think the aftermath of it is the reason we aren't back together."

"I'm sorry." Lauren tried not to judge Jessica for allowing something like a rumor to affect her commitment to Archer. "Please tell me it didn't originate here in our own church." She was fishing, and they both knew it. Even though she hated gossip, she wished she knew what this rumor was so she could help staunch it.

"No." He stood up and shoved his hands into his pockets. "It originated at the hospital."

"*Our* hospital?"

"Look, I shouldn't be talking about this to you. Enough people dump their burdens on you already. I'm your pastor. I should be—"

"You're my friend, and I'm yours. I've been a Christian long enough to see how often the pastor gets all the burdens but doesn't have a listening ear for his own struggles." Lauren wanted to tell him that a woman who wouldn't accept everything about him didn't deserve his love. She prayed for God to help her keep her mouth shut. In fact, she had no right to advise Archer about anything, even if he did think of her as the older sister he never had.

Older sister.

All she knew about romance was that it always happened for other people, never her.

"She doesn't believe the rumor," Archer said.

"Of course she doesn't. I've only met Jessica a couple of times, but she struck me as someone with a lot of common sense and a close walk with God." She was also beautiful and effervescent and larger than life, without an ounce of fat. She was almost as tall as Archer, with riotous brown hair and eyes filled with warmth. She had the voice of an angel, with an amazing range that held the listener breathless. Lauren had liked her immediately.

They heard the sound of a door opening and closing in the foyer, and they were alone in the auditorium.

Archer looked at his watch. "Time to get back to work. I have a meeting with a man about a computer. Ours is getting old and crotchety, and since I'm the only one on staff who knows anything about them, I get to choose the new system. Thanks for the counseling session, Lauren." He quick-stepped to the aisle and out of the auditorium. That salesman must be in a hurry.

Disappointment could be a debilitating emotion, but for Lauren it was an old acquaintance. She knew that the best way to deal with a slightly wounded heart was to divert her attention to other things. The first other thing she wanted to do was satisfy her curiosity. That shouldn't be too difficult.

She wasn't due to report to work tonight, but something about Archer's response to her questions made her uneasy—particularly the part about the rumor. She drove directly to the hospital and found Gina straightening her workstation, preparing to leave for the day.

Gina smiled when she saw Lauren. "Can't stay away from this place, can you?"

Lauren sat down at Gina's workstation and leaned close. "So, have you heard any good hospital gossip lately?"

"Good gossip? No. There isn't any such thing."

"Any gossip at all?"

Gina's smile faded. "Lauren, you don't listen to stuff like that." The heaviness of her voice betrayed her.

"What did you hear?"

Gina stood and pulled off her lab coat, then took great pains to fold it and drape it over her arm. She still didn't look at Lauren. "I'm always hearing things. You know what a—"

"Gina." Lauren felt a tightening of unease. "You might as well tell me, because I'll haunt you until you do. Does it have something to do with me? And . . . maybe Archer?"

Gina sat back down. "Well, if you already know, why are you asking me?"

"I was right." That's why he had been acting so uncomfortable. That's why he had been in such a hurry to get away from her today when everyone left the auditorium. Somehow, word had spread that she was attracted to him, and knowing human nature, a nice bit of fiction had been added. It made her sick to think about it.

"Let me guess: Fiona Perkins overheard me that day when you and I were eating lunch in the break room."

"Probably," Gina said. "It's just stupid stuff that'll blow over when everybody realizes it isn't true."

"How are they going to know?"

Gina blinked at Lauren, then looked pointedly at her stomach. "Because eventually it would start to show."

If Lauren hadn't been sitting down, she'd have crashed to the floor. She breathed deeply and sat back. The wash of shock and pain left her breathless. "People think I'm *pregnant!*"

"Oh, no. You really *haven't* heard."

"Fiona is telling people I'm pregnant?" Lauren suddenly wished she was a kid again and could get away with socking the big-mouthed class bully in the gut.

"It's stupid. I heard people talking about it upstairs today and told them to shut up. It didn't exactly endear me to my co-workers."

"It endears you to *me*. So that's what Fiona meant Wednesday night."

"What did she say?"

"She made a nasty remark about morning sickness, and I had no idea what she was talking about."

"So you ignored her, as you should have," Gina said. "Fiona Perkins is an interfering, mean, troublemaking—"

"Unhappy, hurting human being—"

"Who needs to lose about a hundred pounds. I could help. I'd be glad to kick her—"

"The problem is, her rumors haven't hurt me as badly as they have

Archer. People are listening to her," Lauren said.

Gina leaned forward, and the unusual paleness of her skin became obvious in the fluorescent glow of the overhead lights. "*I'm* not listening."

"I know. Thanks. Gina, are you feeling okay?"

"Other than starving to death, I'm fine. We had a busy day, and I didn't get lunch. Want to come to my house for some macaroni and cheese from a box?"

Feeling as if a sandbag had just been hoisted onto her shoulders, Lauren shook her head and stood. "Sounds tempting, but I've lost my appetite. I need to do some thinking." *And some praying.* A part of her still wanted to hunt Fiona down and punch her in the stomach. Lauren needed God's help, and she needed it now. "Is your car still in the shop? I could give you a lift home on my way out of town."

"You're going out of town? I thought you worked tomorrow."

"I'll be back. I just need some open air. It's oppressive around here. Need a ride?" Lauren felt like a crying jag might be sneaking up on her. She needed to leave soon.

"Thanks, but I'm going to walk home. I've got to do something to get some of this weight off. I don't want to end up fat and bitter and mean like Fiona."

"You won't." Lauren hesitated. She felt betrayed, deeply hurt, but it helped to think about someone besides herself. "How are things going with Natalie? Or should I ask?"

Gina paused, thoughtful. "She's checking into Aunt Bridget's hospital records for me."

"You told her?" Now *this* was good news.

"I took your advice. I just hope you know what you're talking about. She said if I have any more problems, she's going to start spending the nights with me. Just what I need, a constant slumber party."

The words were said with a grumble, but Lauren thought she picked up on a touch of warmth.

"Lauren, are you going to be okay?"

"I'll be fine. You?"

"Yeah. Me, too."

CHAPTER 25

The computer salesman spent an hour and seventeen minutes show-ing Archer computers in various price ranges with varying mega-bytes of RAM and processing systems. By the time the guy left, Archer was seeing the malignant negative of backlit screens on his lids when he closed his eyes. He realized he knew as much about com-puters as a Missouri mule knew about sermon notes, and the present church system started looking much more attractive.

The next church member who complained about the appearance of the bulletin would find himself—or herself—the first appointed chair-man of the computer search committee of Dogwood Springs Baptist Church. Archer would not feel the least bit guilty about it.

As the man carried his laptop out the door, he left it partially opened, and through that opening Archer saw John Netz sitting at quiet attention across from Mrs. Boucher's desk. Beside him sat Dwight Hahnfeld, and next to him, Gene Thomas. Computers suddenly became the least of Archer's concerns.

Why was he constantly agreeing to come to the church on his day off?

Mrs. Boucher said the dreaded words, "You can go in now," and they stood in unison, as if connected by manacles. Mr. Netz led the way to Archer's open door and paused at the threshold. The other two men nearly stumbled into him from behind.

In spite of sudden heart palpitations, Archer had to smile. Sometimes he had an ornery sense of humor. Here were three bumbling Christians, taking their positions in the church very seriously, wanting to do the right thing. The problem was, they sometimes tended to rely on their own judgment instead of taking their questions to God.

But at least they held positions of service. So few people were willing to do that these days. Some who did were power hungry, but most were sincerely trying to serve God and their church.

Maybe they knew something about computers.

"Pastor, do you mind if we talk to you for a minute?" John Netz asked.

"Of course not, John." Archer pushed back from his desk and stood, then gestured toward the chairs they had occupied the last time they visited. "Come on in, have a seat." He joined them, determined not to take an adversarial position behind his big desk, no matter what they might have in mind for this visit.

In tense silence punctuated by muffled footsteps and creaking knees, the men settled themselves. The youngest member, Gene, as usual, perched so close to the edge of his chair that Archer feared he would slide out of it. Dwight crossed his legs and cupped his hands around his knee, studying his knuckles. John cleared his throat. He was obviously the designated spokesman for this visit.

"Pastor, we—"

"John, have you forgotten my first name?" Archer asked gently.

The grooves deepened in Mr. Netz's wrinkled face, and his gaze filled with uncharacteristic amusement for a few seconds. "Archer, we're here to apologize."

Archer waited, allowing those precious words to flow over him while he struggled not to allow his emotions to get messy.

"You were right the other day," Gene Thomas said. His youthful face, lacking the lines traced by experience and hard years of service, looked eager. "We shouldn't have listened to the gossip about you, and it's my fault. I kept hearing things at work, and some of the people at church were . . . you know . . . grumbling about having a single pastor, and I got worried that . . . anyway, I shouldn't have said anything about you."

Archer swallowed. "Thank you." This was the way it should be—

imperfect Christians confessing their sins and struggles to one another. "I have to admit I was hurt, and I couldn't help wondering how many others felt the same way you did."

"I've talked to some of them," John said. "Most people see reason when you hit them in the head with it enough times. What counts is that they realize they're wrong."

"At least about *you*," Dwight Hahnfeld said quietly.

The other two men looked at him, then at the floor. It was the first time he'd spoken since they had arrived, and the implication of his words didn't sink in for a moment.

John and Gene remained silent.

Archer's relief seeped away. "Excuse me?"

"I'm sorry, Pastor," Dwight said. "I know how much you like the girl, but there's—"

"Lauren McCaffrey isn't a girl, she's a grown woman, an RN who works in the emergency room at our hospital saving lives. Lauren doesn't have time to spread rumors, and as far as I know, she hasn't heard this one, either. I would like to see it stay that way."

John Netz and Gene Thomas looked abashed. Dwight's jaw muscles worked overtime as he clenched and unclenched his teeth.

Archer continued. "Anyone in this church who has taken the time to get acquainted with Lauren will realize, without any doubt, that she is a dedicated Christian, above reproach."

Dwight waved that information away like a pesky gnat. "A source at the hospital overheard her admit she's having a child—"

"Which source is that?" Archer kept his voice as calm as humanly possible when seeing an innocent human being get slammed by a vicious tongue. He looked at Gene. "You work there."

"It wasn't me, Archer. I didn't hear her say it, but some of the techs were talking about it a couple of weeks ago. One of them heard her."

"Do you remember a name?"

"Um, I don't know all the hospital workers yet, but I know Lauren has been sick lately. She's missed work—"

"Of course she's been sick, just like half the people in our church— half the *town* has been sick."

"Pastor, we need you to see reason about this," Dwight said. "Look at it from my viewpoint. I have grandchildren in this church, and Lauren McCaffrey is popular with all the kids. If you had children, wouldn't you want to make sure their role models were above reproach?"

"We received a letter of recommendation from her church in Knolls when she joined us this year." Archer was suddenly overwhelmed with frustration and sadness. What did they want Lauren to do, submit to a pregnancy test? This was unconscionable.

"You know they never reveal anything bad in those letters," Dwight said.

"What do you propose to do about Lauren?" Archer asked. "You accepted her as a member. You can't go around dismissing her from her volunteer positions over a rumor any more than you can fire a pastor over that same rumor. It's a double standard."

Archer received no reply. He stood, feeling tired, as if he'd preached a long sermon to an empty auditorium. "Please, gentlemen, I want you to pray about this overnight. We can meet back here in the morning, but it looks as if we're going to have to do a lot of soul-searching before we can reach a mutual decision on this. And under no circumstances are you to say a word about this to Lauren. It would hurt her deeply."

At Archer's request, Dwight said a quick, awkward prayer, then the three men trooped out of his office, just as they had entered.

Grant swept past the ER central desk and placed a chart in the discharge slot, taking mental note of three more slots that had been filled since his last pass through. One down, sixteen to go—if he counted the patients in the waiting room still seeking attention.

Even as he paused to study the new charts, the bell rang for the triage nurse to report to her exam room. Make that seventeen to go.

A glance into the waiting room showed every chair filled with patients and their families and friends. Three children who looked to be under the age of five raced across the floor in a game of tag, stumbling into legs, stomping toes, creating chaos. A young woman pressed her fingers against her forehead and moaned, and a boy who looked like he was about thirteen held an emesis basin beneath his chin.

"What is this, a preschool?" an older man complained loudly to his friend. "Can't these people find baby-sitters? What's taking them so long back there?"

"Probably taking their coffee break," the friend said.

Grant shook his head and stepped away, hoping the rest of the staff didn't hear the complaints. They didn't deserve it. The triage nurse was getting things done. The secretary and tech were two of the most efficient workers in the hospital. The other two nurses on duty were new and inexperienced, and were nearly tripping over each other in their nervous awkwardness. They had forgotten orders three times in the past hour, and that slowed everything down, but they were trying.

Grant stifled his frustration. It wasn't the nurses' fault. It wasn't really anyone's fault. They were doing the best they could, and they hadn't been scheduled to work together in the first place—too many staff members were sick.

At this moment, someone occupied each of the ten exam rooms. Two of those patients were ready to be discharged as soon as a nurse could break free to do so.

Grant returned to the first cardiac room and did another assessment on the woman who had complained of chest pain. Her vitals looked good, and she was pain free after a GI cocktail. He didn't want to risk ruling out a heart problem too quickly, but this lady had experienced problems with acid reflux a year ago, and she had no history of cardiac problems. As he finished asking her a few more questions that satisfied him that she was out of danger, he heard an angry shout from across the hall. He reassured his patient, then stepped into Trauma One.

According to the report, the patient on the bed, strapped to a backboard, was a twenty-two-year-old male—the victim of a hit-and-run accident at the edge of town. Tina, one of the new nurses, was struggling to get his vitals as he growled curses and threats at her. Witnesses on the scene had called the ambulance immediately and had prevented the victim from moving until the attendants immobilized him. A sprinkling of glass from the impact remained in his hair, and his road-stained T-shirt held smudges of bloodstain. He jerked at the straps that restrained him and cursed at Tina again.

"That will be enough, Tina," Grant said softly.

When she turned there were tears in her eyes. "I'm sorry, Dr. Sheldon, I couldn't get—"

He reached for her chart. "I'll take care of it." He ignored the blast of renewed swearing that redirected its focus on him as he checked for tenderness in the man's neck. The man's appearance was all too familiar. His stringy hair obviously hadn't been washed in days. His eyes darted from Grant to the nurse to the ceiling. The knuckles of his right hand were abraded and blood encrusted.

If Grant were to make an informed guess, he'd say this guy had probably punched something in a fit of fury—perhaps even the car that hit him. That same informed guess said the young man was tweaking—coming down from a high of several days, maybe even weeks. Methamphetamine? Images of St. Louis flashed through Grant's mind.

"Mr. Smith, are you experiencing pain in a particular spot?" he asked as he palpated the man's pelvis and then slipped his hands along the backboard to palpate his back.

The patient—Smith was probably not his real name—glared at Grant, and his whole body seemed to radiate with pent-up fury. "Everywhere!" he growled. "Get these straps off me!" He spat another string of abusive swear words.

Grant turned to the nurse, who hovered near the doorway, and ordered a CBC and appropriate x-rays, then stepped closer to her and lowered his voice. "Are the police on their way?"

"Police!" shouted Smith. "What're you people up to?"

"Yes, Dr. Sheldon," Tina replied, ignoring the outburst. "They should be here any minute."

"Thank you. Let's give him twenty-five of Demerol, slow IV push."

She nodded and turned to leave, and he followed her out and caught her in the hallway. "Order a urine drug screen," he said quietly. "That can be done after he returns from Radiology."

"Yes, Dr. Sheldon."

Grant took the time to glance at his watch on his way to the next room with the sick child and discovered, to his surprise, that his shift ended in thirty minutes. Too bad the printed schedule rarely represented real life and the needs of real patients. At the rate patients were coming in—and at the rate charts were stacking up at his desk—he wouldn't be out of here until at least nine o'clock, and it was only six-thirty.

He checked the child and decided on a blood test. Ordinarily, the strong evidence of a simple flu wouldn't warrant a blood test, but things were different here lately. Now he just had to hunt down a nurse.

The good news was that since it was already six-thirty, fresh nurses must have arrived thirty minutes ago. Although he hadn't seen Lauren and she wasn't scheduled to work tonight, maybe she was one of them. He could always hope. An experienced emergency room nurse was always a treasure, worth double her pay. In fact, Lauren would make a good nurse practitioner or physician's assistant. She would make a great—

"Dr. Sheldon!" The secretary turned and waved at him before he could enter the second trauma room, where elderly Mr. Pope waited to be released from his neck brace. "There's an ambulance on its way here with a patient in full cardiac arrest."

"What's the ETA?"

"They're about five minutes out."

"Is Lauren here?"

"No, but Muriel and Eugene are, and Betsy and Tina are staying over to help out for a while."

"Call another nurse down from the floor, and send Betsy and Tina home. Assign Eugene to the Bob Smith case in Trauma One, and send the police there as soon as they arrive." If they had any trouble with Mr. Smith, Eugene could handle it. Tina had looked like she'd had enough for the day.

———

"Why, God?" Lauren drove along the potholed road a little faster than usual. She swerved and missed most of the deepest ruts, but right now she didn't care if she fell into one of those holes and never found her way out. "I don't understand. All these years I've served you, I've tried so hard to do what I knew you wanted me to do, and now I've been humiliated not only in my church, but also at work. It isn't as if I brought it on myself! Why is this happening?"

Besides all that, she was homesick. "Am I doomed to be alone the rest of my life? Will I never have a marriage, a family?" She knew she was working herself into a raging pity party, but she went with the mood.

When she had first told her parents that she was moving to Dogwood Springs they had been upset, to say the least. They had used every argument in the "Parent's Manual of Guilt Trips" to convince her to stay in Knolls and had enlisted the rest of the family for help—not just brothers and sisters, but nieces and nephews, aunts and uncles, cousins. If Grandma and Grandpa McCaffrey had still been alive the scales might have tipped in her family's favor. In fact, during one moment of weakness she had actually told Mom she would stay in Knolls with the condition that the whole family would stop trying so hard to marry her off to every man between the ages of twenty-six and sixty who walked into the church without a wedding ring on his finger.

She had won the challenge, as she had known she would. Within twenty-four hours of the time Lauren made her offer, Aunt Gertrude had actually set her up on a blind date with the son of one of the new farmers who had moved into their neck of the woods. Without even asking her! Lauren's humiliation had been complete.

"And without my family here to do it, I've taken on the task of humiliating myself," Lauren muttered, half to herself, half to God. "Haven't I learned enough humility already? Why is this happening?"

From childhood her parents and grandparents had taught her that she shouldn't waste her time asking God the whys and hows of life. Those problems were best left for Him to figure out. She was supposed to ask the "what" question. As in, "What do you want me to do for you, Lord?" And the "where" question, as in, "Where do you want me to serve?" And all this time, she'd believed she was doing the right thing. She served Him through the church, and she served Him at work when she ministered to the ill and prayed with them.

When it came to matters of the heart, Lauren knew she could get a little overeager—particularly when she was attracted to a kind, gentle Christian man. And there had been an embarrassing number of times that she'd wished she'd kept her mouth shut.

"I'm human," she grumbled, mostly to herself. "It's natural to want human companionship." It was also natural to smart from the pain of loss when she realized her attraction and affection were not returned.

Maybe she really was one of those people whom God chose to remain separate and single. But if she was, why did she have this strong longing to be a part of a family—with a husband and children? Did people see her as a poor, awkward hillbilly farm girl who scared men off the moment she opened her mouth?

Lauren slowed and turned onto the grassy trail where tires had worn dirt tracks deep into the ground. Oak and hickory and hedge trees loomed over those tracks to form a deep green tunnel. She parked in the shade of those trees, surprised that she didn't see the ancient brown pickup Mr. Rosewitz and Mr. Mourglia drove out here every Friday afternoon to catch their dinner. They would be here any time.

Taking advantage of the additional time alone, Lauren leaned her forehead against the steering wheel, praying silently, with communication too deep for words. The loneliness that had occasionally attacked her since moving from Knolls seemed to bite more deeply today, and she lacked the strength to tackle it the way she usually did. She felt overwhelmed.

She knew God was there and He was listening, but the insistent need for meaningful human contact continued to block the purging flow of words she often used when she sought comfort. Was this move to Dogwood Springs the wrong thing to do? Should she go back to Knolls, back to where she had so many friends and so much family she could scarcely take a breath, back to the fretful, loving attempts of her mother to see her happily married at any cost?

Lauren got out of the truck at last and ducked beneath the heavy overhang of branches, particularly avoiding the thorns of the hedge trees. As she stepped through the gloom of shade and listened to the rush of the waters ahead, she sought the familiar peace she always found when she was alone in the wilderness like this. Today, that peace eluded her.

Above the chatter of the racing creek, she caught the rumble of another sound and automatically glanced over her shoulder toward the parking area. No one was there, and no one drove up. The sound was almost a growl—low and guttural.

As Lauren frowned and halted in her steps, the growling stopped. She peered through the gloom of trees, past shadows and rotting tree trunks and piles of last year's leaves. Nothing moved.

After a final, slow study of the woods, she gave a shrug and ducked beneath another low-hanging limb and followed the overgrown trail toward the creek. She was stepping from the trees into a clearing when the growl reached her again, as if a stalker watched from some hidden spot above her. A pinprick of tension wormed its way across her shoulders and down her spine.

The growl roughened, stopped, deepened, then roared, and Lauren's stomach tightened into a knot of nausea. She gasped and turned back toward the truck. It was then that a mechanical grunt and cough metamorphosed in Lauren's mind from a furry flesh-eating creature of the forest to a gas-eating monster of steel. Of course. They were still excavating the site above Honey Spring.

Somehow it didn't give her any comfort to realize that the monster was not stalking her. It was stalking the future of Honey Creek and the hundreds of people who depended on its source for water, for recreation, even for an occasional fish dinner.

The vague unease in her stomach increased. "Oh no. Not now." She was getting sick again. The force of the nausea hit more swiftly and violently than ever before, and the future of Honey Creek fled from her thoughts. As she lost the contents of her stomach, the edges of her vision grew black. Lauren sank to her knees, unable to stand, and her prayers now deepened into silent desperation.

"Dad?" Beau's voice rang through the line, taut with excitement. "Sorry if I've caught you at a bad time, I've stumbled onto something I think you'll find interesting about the patient addresses, but I also noticed something strange about the bright white flecks on the x-ray films in some of these patient charts you gave me to look at."

"Beau, are you sure this can't wait? Things are really hopping right now, and—"

"I know, but this is really important."

Grant suppressed his frustration. "Those flecks on the films are artifacts from the ancient machine they need to replace in Radiology. They're just superficial scratches. Film processor defects. I hear the x-ray techs complaining about it all the time."

"Are you sure?"

"Listen, I don't have time to argue with you about—"

"Okay, okay, then listen to this. I checked the addresses of those patients, and almost all of them are located in the same area of town. The *same area,* Dad. Doesn't that seem weird?"

Grant frowned. "How did you find that out?"

"I used the map Brooke grabbed from City Hall the day we had to drag her out of there."

"Oh, yeah."

"Right. Remember the day we went fishing with Lauren, and she told us Honey Creek supplied about a third of the town's water, but only a certain section?"

"What are you getting at, Beau? Are you talking about some kind of water contamination?"

"Maybe. I need to make some calls and see if it fits, but I don't think the waterworks supervisor and the town mayor will listen to a sixteen-year-old kid."

"They will if you tell them you're calling on my behalf. While you're at it, find out what the mayor knows about a dump site cleanup above Honey Spring. We had a patient in here the other day who'd been working with a crew from Springfield."

"Does that mean you're giving me permission to make those calls?"

"Yes, Beau. Call whoever you need to call, and let me know what you find out." He glanced across the bustling ER. "And hurry, son."

rcher had just begun his heartfelt prayers in earnest when the church secretary—who always worked late when he worked late—knocked at the office door and stepped inside without waiting for an answer.

"Archer?"

He looked up in surprise. "What's wrong, Mrs. Boucher?"

"Do you know anything about a werewolf?"

"A werewolf?"

"There's a little child on the telephone, asking to speak to Mr. Archer. He says he's calling you about the werewolf."

Archer caught his breath. Werewolf . . . Gina! Of course! He'd heard the word just the other day, when Levi and Cody were talking to Lauren on the front-porch steps of their house.

He picked up his receiver and punched the button with the blinking light. "Hello? This is Mr. Archer. Levi? Is your mother acting funny?"

"Yes," came the tender, frightened voice. "She started shaking, and she won't talk to us. She doesn't have any claws or fur yet, but her eyes look all funny. They're white."

"Okay, Levi, remember what she told you to do when she started doing that?"

"She told me to call somebody."

"Yes, and she also told you to go to Mrs. Walker's house. You remember that, don't you?"

"But I don't want to leave my mom. What if she runs away again and we can't find her this time?"

"I'll be there as soon as I can, and I'll take care of her. You take your brother to Mrs. Walker's house. Do you understand?"

"You'll come now?"

"I'll be there in five minutes." He disconnected, grabbed his car keys from the corner of the desk, and ran out of the office. "Mrs. Boucher, I need you to call an ambulance," he said as he raced through the outer reception area. Over his shoulder, he gave her Gina's address. Maybe the ambulance would beat him there.

Lauren awakened to find herself face down in a tangle of vines and last year's moldy leaves. When she groaned and pushed herself up, a jangle of noise rang in her ears with the force of a train whistle, and the forest spun in a crazy pattern around her like a giant blender filled with leaves. The sound obviously came from inside her head. She blinked toward the sky but it looked as if clouds had drawn a blanket over the trees while she lay unconscious. Maybe her vision was dimming.

She was too weak and too sick to do battle with the twin forces of fear and confusion. She was alone in this place, and no one knew where she had gone. Someone had already died from the effects of an illness with the same symptons that were attacking her, and this time she couldn't push that memory from her mind.

Now she understood, more completely than ever before, why the patients who came into the emergency room were so often frightened. Although the energy it took to think made her more nauseated, she decided that if she lived through this, she would try harder to reassure her patients that they weren't alone.

Alone.

"Lord, am I alone?" Her voice was barely a croak of sound, and her arms threatened to give way and plunge her face down into the decomposing leaves once more.

No. He was there. He knew.

But did He want to rescue her from this? Maybe she had complained once too often about her loneliness. Maybe He was weary of her inability to accept Him as the sole focus of her life.

Or maybe this illness was affecting her mind and emotions with a strong dose of depression.

"Lord, help me." Lauren could barely whisper the words, but in her heart she shouted them. It didn't matter. God knew what she needed. "I'm sorry." He knew . . .

The nausea returned with a vengeance. As darkness once again rimmed her vision, she felt her body slump into the cushion of damp leaves. Her last coherent thought was one comforting memory—Mr. Mourglia and Mr. Rosewitz would be here any time. They always came fishing on Friday afternoon, the barber and his elderly buddy, the ones who had first told her about this place. They would be here before sunset, when the fish were hungry and the air was just right. . . .

Archer screeched his tires against the curb in front of Gina's house, parked the car, and raced past the overtrimmed hedges. The front door was unlocked, and he barely slowed his steps as he plunged inside, where the terrified moan of a child permeated the air.

"Levi!" Archer called.

A tiny form came racing through the doorway from the kitchen. "Help her! Help her! She's hurt, Mr. Archer!" He grabbed Archer's hand and tugged. "Hurry up!"

Archer swung the child up into his arms and ran with him to the threshold of the kitchen, where the horrifying sight of Gina in full, arching seizure held Cody wide-eyed and gasping in the far corner of the room. Gina's eyes were rolled back in their sockets, her face held a grimace, and her legs and arms flew in wild abandon.

"Levi, take Cody to your neighbor's house," Archer said, placing the child on his feet. "I'll take care of her now."

"How? Do you know what to do?"

"I've already called an ambulance, and they should be here any minute. Please, Levi, go now."

"But we can't go!" Levi cried. "Mama needs us!"

For a few precious moments, Gina's movements grew still. Her arms flopped to her sides and her head fell sideways. The only sound was the continued gasping sobs from Cody.

Archer knelt beside the boys' mother and placed a hand on her arm. She didn't react.

"Gina?"

She didn't move except to breathe. At least she was still breathing.

"Levi," Archer used his most authoritative voice, "your mother wants you and Cody to go to your neighbor's house now."

"But how do you know?" Levi's voice quivered.

"Because she loves you both very much. She's proud of you and knows you'll do what she told you to do. Remember? She wrote the rules down. You're supposed to go to Mrs. Walker's house when this happens. I'm going to take good care of her, and some people are going to help me take her to see Dr. Sheldon. You remember him, don't you?"

Levi nodded. "He made her better when she hurt her feet."

"He's going to make her better again. But if you aren't with Mrs. Walker when she wakes up, she'll be worried. Please go now." He wished he could take them himself, but he couldn't leave Gina.

"But what if she's not home?" Levi's lip quivered slightly as he wiped away a tear.

Archer refused to consider that possibility. "Then come back home. You need to go now, Levi."

With great reluctance, Levi walked over to his little brother, who continued to shake with spasms of soundless sobs. Levi took the younger child by the arm and led him from the room. They were stepping through the doorway when Archer felt Gina's arm tense. Her face tightened.

Levi turned and looked back at her.

"Go now," Archer said.

Levi reached up and grasped the doorknob, then pulled the door shut behind them just as Gina's arms jerked with a returning seizure. A hoarse moan spiraled from her throat.

Where was that ambulance? He'd given clear directions for Mrs. Boucher to relay to them. What if they'd misunderstood?

He pivoted in search of a telephone and saw one on the wall beside the kitchen entrance. He jerked up the receiver as Gina's convulsions intensified.

———

Grant answered an emergency telephone call from the front reception desk while an eager code team assembled in the newly evacuated cardiac room.

"Grant? This is Archer. I need your help."

A child screamed from one of the exam rooms, joining the chorus of children who continued to play in the waiting room, still bouncing off of legs and chairs and vending machines.

Grant covered his left ear so he could hear better. "What's wrong?"

"I think Gina has epilepsy."

"I've seen all her records. If she had epilepsy, I'd know about it."

After long experience working an always busy ER in St. Louis, Grant seldom felt overwhelmed here in Dogwood Springs. Right now he wished he could split into three or four different people.

Focus. "Where is she?"

"At home. I'm with her now. She's had more than one."

"Call an ambulance."

"I did. I tried twice, but no one's here yet. What can I—"

"For whatever reason, we have had a rash of emergencies. The ambulances are probably out on calls. We have one coming in now. How long have the seizures lasted?"

"I'm not sure—a few minutes, maybe. She was in the middle of one when I got here, then there was a break, but she didn't regain consciousness. That's happened twice, Grant. I've got to do something." Archer did not sound panicked, but the thread of concern intensified in his voice.

"Keep her from hurting herself." Until Grant was sure what was happening, he had to consider Gina's seizures to be life threatening.

"I put a pillow under her head."

Grant looked out the window. No ambulance yet. Any moment now—

"Don't I need to put something in her mouth to keep her from biting her tongue?" Archer asked.

"No. Don't worry about that during the seizure. It's afterward you need to watch her closely. If the seizure breaks and she's unconscious, turn her onto her side so her tongue won't block the air passage when she loses muscle tone. Is there any sugar nearby?"

"Sugar? I don't know. We're in the kitchen, though. Let me look—"

"Wait—Archer?" It was countdown time. The ambulance could arrive any second. "I may not be able to hold for you. When you find the sugar, try to place a little of it under her tongue. Don't use a spoon, because she could bite it suddenly and break some teeth. And don't put your fingers in her mouth."

"You don't think this is epilepsy?"

"I can't rule out a new onset, but I also can't rule out hypoglycemia, and even if it is epilepsy the sugar won't hurt her. It's an educated guess. Hurry, Archer."

He heard the slap of the receiver hitting the counter and then the rattle of dishes and the slam of cupboard doors. Chillingly, the familiar sound of a low moan punctuated the shuffle and combined with the sounds in the ER.

Grant turned to find the secretary pulling up a file on the computer at her desk. "Where are the first responders in this town?"

"Probably out on calls," she said. "Things are going nuts."

As she spoke, the siren call reached them, and the ambulance came racing around a corner and into the bay, lights flashing.

"Archer?" Grant called. "Hello?"

No answer.

He had no choice; he had to disconnect. As nurses ran out to meet the ambulance attendants, Grant hung up the phone and followed. Archer was on his own.

———

Archer found a canister of white stuff at the far end of the kitchen counter, and with the sound of Gina's moans seeming to bounce from the flat planes of counters and doors, he plunged his hand into the canister. It felt like sugar. He brought a handful out and touched his tongue to it. Not sugar, salt.

He shoved that container aside, dusted his hands, pulled the next container toward him, and was removing the lid when he realized the moaning had stopped. He pivoted toward Gina. Her head lolled to the side, and the spasms in her arms and legs had gentled and grown slower. The tight grimace released, and her mouth fell open.

Archer grabbed the receiver from the counter. "Grant, her seizure's break—"

The dial tone mocked him. His contact to help had disconnected. He was on his own.

Well . . . not quite.

No. Not at all.

"Lord, I don't know what's happening, but you do. Give me a double dose of your wisdom, and keep me calm." Archer dropped to his knees beside Gina as he prayed out loud. "Please give this lady your healing touch, and use me in any way you wish to keep her safe."

Her muscles gradually relaxed. He placed his hands on her left side and logrolled her toward him. Her whole body went limp, and her arms flopped uselessly against him. Her legs were heavier and less movable than he'd expected, and he had to hold her body on its side with one hand while he adjusted her legs with the other.

Once he had her securely on her side, he bent her legs to stabilize her in that position, then leaned forward until his ear was next to her mouth. He heard breath sounds. He rushed to the counter and jerked the lid from the next container, then plunged his hand inside and lifted his fingers to his tongue.

Sugar. This would work. He carried the container to the floor beside her and gently pried her mouth open, taking care not to put his fingers near her teeth. Her tongue presented another problem. Grant had instructed him to place the sugar under her tongue.

This could be done. "Lord, give her strength." He grabbed a generous three fingered pinch of sugar and reached for her slackened jaw. He needed three hands—one to hold the sugar, one to hold her chin, and one to move her tongue—but Grant had told him not to put his fingers near her teeth. Archer compromised by sprinkling the sugar along the side of her tongue.

That accomplished with no observable reaction, he reached for another pinch. However, before Archer could get it to her mouth, the moan began again. He tried to give her another dose before her face contracted and her mouth clamped shut, but all he managed to do was sprinkle sugar across her face and scatter it on the floor. Her body jerked and her elbow hit the container, knocking it over. Sugar streamed everywhere. She kicked him in the leg and rapped him on the arm with her fists. The grimace was back, the contortions returned. The invisible monster once more had her in its grasp.

Archer released her and reached an outspread hand to scrape up a fistful of the sweet medicine, praying under his breath that she wouldn't inhale what was already in her mouth and choke, praying that what he had already given her would work its way through her system, praying for divine intervention.

"Lord, please help us. Touch her. One breath from you, one thought, is all it would take to heal her, God. Show me what to do. Give me wisdom."

He waited, praying for Gina and her children, watching her movements, feeling inadequate and useless, wondering when someone would come.

Somewhere in the midst of his prayers the moaning stopped. Less than two minutes after it started, the seizure ended and her limbs relaxed. He scrambled to her side, prepared to reposition her, when she caught her breath suddenly, as if on a sigh. Her eyes fluttered but did not open.

"Gina?"

"Pulseless v-tach." Christy, the paramedic, pumped her patient's chest in the time-honored dance of desperation as she gave Grant a rushed report. "We shocked three times, we've given two doses of epi and one of lidocaine. We got him back for a few seconds, then he went down again."

The EMT handed over the bagging to the respiratory therapist on the code team. The elderly man had monitor leads across his bare chest, and his skin nearly matched the bed sheet. An IV had been established in his left forearm.

"How long since your last shock?"

"About two minutes."

"We need to shock again now."

Everyone cleared as the hum of the charge reached maximum. Grant pushed the defibrillator button and the old man's body arched and fell back.

"Nothing," Christy said.

"Continue CPR," Grant told the nurse. "Let's give lidocaine, 100 milligrams, IV push, and start a second line. We need a cardiac work-up and a blood gas."

In the room they switched from the paramedic's defibrillator unit to the hospital's Life Pak 11 when they transferred him from gurney to bed.

"What happened?" Grant asked.

"He went into respiratory arrest almost as soon as we arrived at his house," Christy said. "His friend, Mr. Rosewitz, drove by his house to see about him when he didn't show up at their usual rendezvous at City Hall for their fishing date."

At first glimpse of the unresponsive patient's face, Grant hadn't recognized him, but there had been something familiar about this elderly man with a full head of thick gray hair and heavy eyebrows that met in the center. "What was that about City Hall?"

"That's where we were supposed to meet." A man, probably in his sixties, had followed them inside, his pale face anxious, his hands wringing with nervous tension, as if a thin film of lotion covered his flesh and he was trying to rub it in. He must be Mr. Rosewitz. The man stepped to a corner, out of their way, keeping careful watch.

Grant looked again at the patient, and then he recognized his face. Ernest Mourglia, who loved to work the community puzzle at City Hall. He was the mayor's uncle.

"When did you find him like this?" Grant asked Mr. Rosewitz.

"Couldn't have been more than fifteen, maybe twenty, minutes ago."

"Has he complained about chest pain before this? Do you know if he's been feeling ill lately?"

"He was kind of sick when I talked with him yesterday." Mr. Rosewitz inched into the room, as if afraid to get too close. "He said he'd rather go fishing and be miserable than stay home and be miserable. He wanted to keep his mind off his stomach. If it helps, he told me he had a bad taste in his mouth. He said it tasted like he was sucking on a penny."

Some zephyr of awareness stirred Grant's memory. *A metallic taste in his mouth?*

They shocked Mr. Mourglia once again at 360 joules. The monitor's death march remained unchanged.

"The low dose epi isn't working," Grant said. "Give 5 milligrams of epinephrine now."

Less than a minute later they shocked again. The monitor beeped, then began a steady rhythm across the screen. There was a collective sigh of relief.

Grant pressed his fingers against the elderly gentleman's neck. There was a pulse. Yes!

"What's the bp?" he asked.

"It's 85 over 60 and climbing," Eugene replied.

Grant stepped closer to the patient's friend. "Mr. Rosewitz, do you go to City Hall very often?"

"Just to meet Ernest." The man gave his friend a frowning glance. "Is he going to be okay?"

"I don't know yet. We need to run some tests and find out how his heart is doing, see if there's a source of infection that could have caused this. Do you know if he's had heart problems in the past?"

"He's mentioned some trouble the last couple of years, but the stubborn cuss says he'd just as soon die as get all trussed up in a hospital. Couldn't ever get him into a doctor's office, and believe me, I've tried. If he dies of a heart attack in my barbershop, it'll be bad for business." Mr. Rosewitz's voice roughened, and he cleared his throat. "Wouldn't want the old fool to die on me."

"You're a barber?"

The man nodded, though he didn't make eye contact. "Been at it forty years." His voice was still wobbly.

On a hunch, Grant asked, "Mr. Rosewitz, where do you and Mr. Mourglia go fishing?"

Words could not have stated the man's confusion any more clearly than the tilt of his head and the meeting together of his eyebrows. The nurse, Muriel, turned from the patient's side with a frown on her bull-dog face.

Grant wasn't certain of where he was headed with his questions, but he had a hunch, and he needed to follow it further. He hoped Beau would call back with more information soon.

"Please humor me for a moment," Grant said. "It may be important."

"We fish at Honey Creek, up close to the source."

Grant's hunch, which had been foggy at best when he had talked to Beau, now began to take a more concrete form. "Do you, by chance, know a young woman by the name of Lauren McCaffrey?"

The man's features lightened a fraction. "Sure do. She's the one who sat down there in my barbershop and pestered me until I finally gave in and told her my fishing spot. I've seen her at the creek quite a few times since then." His brows lowered a fraction. "We try to beat her there. She gets all the good ones if she gets her line in the water first."

The possibilities frightened Grant. It looked like Beau might be onto something with those x-ray films. If those flecks weren't artifact—

Lauren had been sick, with a bad taste in her mouth.

"Mr. Rosewitz, have you felt ill in the past few weeks? Suffered any nausea, any of the symptoms your friend had?"

"Nope, can't say that I have."

"Do you eat the fish you catch?"

"Never. I don't like fish. I give 'em all to Ernest. He loves 'em, and he doesn't have much income. Besides, that keeps me from having to clean 'em."

Grant felt a strong welling of frustration with himself. Until today he'd been so sure the illness was some virus or bacteria, but heavy-metal poisoning could be the cause of those bright white flecks Beau had mentioned.

"He's pinking up nicely," Muriel said. "Looks like he'll make it."

Grant nodded. "Start a lidocaine drip at 2 milligrams a minute. We don't want him reverting to pulseless v-tach. I want dopamine on stand-by, and let me know immediately if his condition worsens. I'll be in Trauma One for a few minutes, then at my desk." He excused himself and rushed from the room.

He checked on an angry Mr. Smith and declined to release him from the backboard—not because of spinal damage, but because the man's continued combativeness not only endangered him, but others. Smith refused to give a urine sample and shouted his frustration at the straps that restrained him. After being assured by Eugene that the police were on their way, Grant rushed out of the room again.

He didn't go far before Dr. Mitchell Caine came striding through the side door to take over for his shift. The elegant doctor's steel gaze swept the central area of the Emergency Department, with its busy staff and crowded work areas, and a cloud of disgust darkened his features.

"This place is a zoo."

"We've been busy, Dr. Caine." And the patients and staff were human beings, not animals. Grant gave a quick report on the patients most in need of attention and then left Caine glaring after him as he rushed to his office.

As he reached for the phone Grant was reminded of Archer's frantic phone call. Gina was having seizures. Central nervous system . . . heavy-metal poisoning? How widespread was this problem? He dialed home and let the phone ring four times before Beau picked up.

"Son, what have you—"

"Dad, I need a little more time. I'm making calls now."

Grant's hand tightened on the receiver. "Find out what you can, and call me back as soon as possible. While you're at it, do a Web search for symptoms of mercury poisoning."

Beau caught his breath. "You think that's what these patients have?"

"I don't know, just check."

Grant hung up and jumped back into the patient race. He had a lot of faith in his son's deductive reasoning, but he was afraid they could already be too late to save a lot of people.

CHAPTER 27

After placing another generous pinch of sugar at the edge of Gina's tongue, Archer repositioned the pillow behind her head and gently straightened her arms and legs. His lips moved in a constant string of whispered prayers. "Please, Lord, send help soon. Protect her and heal her. Please don't leave those precious children without their mother."

While Archer watched Gina's face, her lids fluttered once again, but apparently she didn't have the strength to open her eyes.

"Gina? It's okay. You're not alone. I'm right here, and I'm not going to leave you until the ambulance comes."

She winced, and her shoulders moved slowly, as if she were struggling up from some deep subterranean pit in her mind.

"Lay still for a few minutes. I know the floor is hard, but we don't want to set off any more seizures."

Her lids fluttered again, and her pale, full lips parted. "What's . . . happening?" She winced again and lifted her arm a few inches from where Archer had positioned it across her stomach.

"You've been having some kind of seizures. How do you feel right now?"

Her soft breathing deepened. "Head hurts bad."

"I'm sorry. I wish—"

"My boys?" Her eyes came open then, slowly, with effort. "Levi? Cody?"

"They went to your neighbor's after I got here."

In slow motion she reached up and grasped Archer's arm. "What happened? Did I . . . did I hurt—"

"No, Gina, you didn't hurt them. Levi called me. When I got here, they were very frightened for you, but they were physically fine. As soon as the ambulance gets here I'll go to Mrs. Walker's house and reassure them before I follow you to the hospital."

At this promise, she released him, and a sheen of tears filmed her eyes. "I've messed up everything."

"No. How can you possibly blame yourself for an illness you did not create?"

"I thought I could . . . control . . . the attacks. If I just t-tried . . . hard enough. . . ." She closed her eyes again. But something about the tilt of her chin, the firm lines of her face, told him she would not easily give in to sleep.

"You haven't been having panic attacks, Gina. This is something else."

There was a slight nod of her head. "Lauren . . . she'll keep my children. If anything . . . happens . . ." A pause for breath. "Will you call her?"

"Yes, I would call her anyway. But you can't give up on yourself so easily. We don't even know—"

Her eyes opened again. The color in her face deepened to a healthier shade of pink. "I have to give it up. I can't keep . . . can't go on like this."

"No, Gina, you can't—"

"Shh. Listen." Her voice grew stronger, though it remained soft. "Lauren told me to . . . give it up."

Archer waited. Gina was certainly not talking about the obvious, because Lauren would never tell anyone to give up her children or her hope for a future.

"I tried to control my life . . . everything . . . too long." She stopped and swallowed, and her tongue worked across her lips in a grimace. "Sugar?"

"Doctor's orders. I called the hospital for advice, and Grant told me to try sugar under your tongue in case your seizures were a reaction to hypoglycemia."

Gina's eyelids drooped, her lips parted, and some of the firmness left her expression. Archer sat back and waited, resuming his prayers.

"Second opinion," she said a few seconds later.

He frowned at her. Was she hallucinating? "Gina?"

"I need a second opinion, like Lauren said." Her voice had an ethereal quality, half whisper, half rasp, but there was an assurance in it that hadn't been there before. "I asked for one. Do you think I'll get it?"

"Second opinion?"

"God . . . is the Great Physician. I give up on myself. I can't do it. He needs to take over for me. He'll help me."

"Yes, Gina, He will. He made you; He loves you. Turn it all over to Him."

"I need a new father."

Second opinion. Yes. That was the term Lauren used the day she tried to explain Christianity to Gina. "That's right. If you've asked Jesus for a second opinion, trust Him to take over for you. He always does."

"Why would He want to?"

"Because He loves you so much. You know how much you love your children? Multiply that by a billion, and He loves you that much more."

"Not . . . possible."

"It's true."

She was silent for a long moment, then she said, "You sound like Lauren."

"It runs in the family. You can join our family, Gina."

Another long thoughtful silence, then, "Yes." She said no more, but something changed in her face. Her expression went blank.

"Gina? How are you feeling? What's—"

With a sudden, violent thrust, the dreaded grimace returned to her face, and she jerked. At the same moment Archer heard the sweet, welcome sound of an ambulance siren.

"Please, Lord, don't take her now. Hold her just a little longer."

———

Grant ruled out heart damage on the lady in the cardiac room and advised her to see her family doc Monday. He was racing through the ER proper when Eugene intercepted him.

"Dr. Sheldon, Bob Smith is gone! I stepped out to help Muriel lift a patient, and when I went back into the room, I found the backboard empty. One of the straps was broken and the rest were dis—"

"What's going on here, Sheldon?" The mind-numbing chill of Dr. Mitchell Caine's voice grumbled behind Grant. "Does this nurse make a habit of releasing dangerous criminals before the police can reach them?"

Grant turned to find that not only was Caine bearing down on him, but he was trailed by two black-uniformed police officers, looking less than happy. "What do you mean, dangerous criminals?" Grant asked. "That man was the victim of a hit-and-run—"

One of the police officers stepped forward. "Dr. Sheldon, according to reports we received from the witnesses on the scene, that patient matched the description of a man we've been after for weeks. He uses the street name Peregrine."

Eugene groaned aloud. "The pusher? Dr. Sheldon, I'm sorry. I was only gone for a minute. Muriel needed me, and I couldn't—"

"It's okay, Eugene. You are not a security officer, and if that man was strong enough to break one of the straps on that spine board and escape, I don't want to think what he might have been willing to do to you if you'd tried to stop him."

"That's it?" Caine demanded. "You're blowing the whole thing off—"

"Dr. Caine, there are plenty of patients to be seen, and you're the physician on duty now," Grant said. "I suggest you get to work. I'll take care of this." He gestured for the police to follow him into his office.

Before he could reach the door, however, the night secretary turned and motioned to him. "Your son's on line two, Dr. Sheldon. He says it's—"

"Important. Thanks, Becky." Grant rushed into his office and grabbed the phone, with the officers behind him. "Beau? What have you found?"

"Dad, I made those calls." There was an edge of excitement in Beau's voice tonight that Grant hadn't heard in many months.

"Just a minute, son. It just so happens there are a couple of police officers right here. I'm putting the phone on the speaker so they can hear this. Okay, go ahead."

"I called the mayor. Honey Spring is the water source for the patients named in the charts you gave me. Honey Creek just happens to supply the water for a mostly middle-class neighborhood, and that's why this mystery flu appeared to limit itself to the middle class."

"Good job." Grant could kick himself for not thinking about this sooner. Why hadn't he picked up on it when Beau mentioned the middle-class thing the other day? He glanced at the police to see if they were listening. They were, with rapt attention.

"What about the excavation at the dump site above the spring?"

"That's when the mayor got really interested. She said she's going to check it all out, but she was preoccupied with a family emergency. She said you saw her uncle in the ER tonight."

Ernest Mourglia, who was now on his way to Springfield. "That's right. Jade Myers might be a little overwhelmed for a while."

"I offered to help. She gave me the number for the ditching service out of Springfield, and I called them. Get this, Dad, they started work on that project six weeks ago. They ran into all kinds of snags—had some complaints from the locals, and then they dug up a bunch of crushed plastic containers that weren't part of the bargain, and some of their guys got sick."

"Containers of what?"

"He said there were all kinds of them, but he was upset because he'd been told it was harmless construction material. He wouldn't admit his own earthmovers might have been the ones to crush the containers, but he did admit some of his guys got sick for no reason. Dad, I think you're right. That stuff's poison."

"Did he describe the sickness?"

"Like the flu."

That was probably good. The vomiting and diarrhea were the body's natural defense against a poison in the system, and as long as that poison was ejected from the body it would be less likely to cause lasting effects.

"I did that Web search you wanted," Beau said. "The symptoms in most of these patient charts do match the symptoms of mercury salt poisoning. What made you think about that?"

"Just a few hints here and there. That dump site above Honey Springs wasn't on private land. Anyone could have dumped waste there. Archer has warned me several times that methamphetamine production is a big problem in this part of the state. One of the by-products of meth production is mercury salt."

"Meth?" Beau said in a hushed whisper. "You think it could be that bad here in *Dogwood Springs*?"

"It's looking more and more likely. If I'm not mistaken, we just had a patient in who was tweaking—desperately in need of his next fix of meth." He didn't mention the fact that the man had escaped before the police arrived.

"So we're talking about a ground and water contamination of mercury," Beau said. "The x-rays, Dad, maybe those flecks on the film weren't artifact. If mercury was in the water these people drank—"

"I know." Grant tried not to think of the long-range implications right now. He just needed to concentrate on his next step. "I'm sorry I dismissed your question about it so easily. I don't want to jump to conclusions, but looking at all this evidence now, a heavy metal such as mercury would show up just that way on an x-ray."

"So far the symptoms haven't been so bad," Beau said. "The only thing that worries me is that things can get worse. When mercury gets into the groundwater it can undergo a chemical reaction and convert to methyl mercury, which can affect the central nervous system. But it doesn't look like that's happened . . . yet."

Yet. Grant knew the facts, but he let his son talk, and looked up to make sure the officers were paying attention. They were.

"Methyl mercury can cause all kinds of nasty permanent damage," Beau continued. "Especially if it's been in someone's system for a few weeks. Do you know that it only takes a small amount of mercury to poison a whole lake?"

"Yes, I know. Have you called anyone besides the mayor and the excavators?"

"No. Jade Myers was going to try to get a hazmat team down here from Springfield. She said she'll need to talk to you."

"Sounds like I'm in for a busy night." Grant was becoming more and more overwhelmed by the potential impact of this situation. He couldn't stifle the fear that the mercury salt could be converting to methyl mercury.

"What are you going to do now?" Beau asked.

"I'll call our administrator, and he can call County Health." Grant glanced again at the officers, who hovered beside the desk, their expressions grim, on full alert.

Peregrine's evil had spread.

"This is dangerous stuff, Dad," Beau said. "Do you really think it could be from a meth lab?"

"From what I hear, it's the most likely cause." Grant remembered his most recent visit from Brisco and Scroggs. "We had a farmer in here the other day who had been attacked in his own barn in the middle of the afternoon. Want to take a guess what the intruder was stealing?"

"Farm supplies?"

"Liquid fertilizer."

"Oh. That's used to make meth."

"And they're getting bold enough to try to steal it in the middle of the day." He saw one of the officers nod at his partner.

"I thought we moved here to get away from that kind of stuff, Dad."

"I don't think we can move far enough to totally escape evil. I think we're going to have to stay and fight."

"Then you'd better start praying."

"I already have been. I just hope He's listening."

There was a silence filled with surprise, then, "You really are, Dad? You're back on speaking terms with God?" In spite of the situation, there was a trace of joy in Beau's voice that filled Grant with bittersweet awareness.

"As I said, He may not listen to me."

"He will. He's answering my prayers right now. Keep praying, Dad." He hung up.

Something stirred deep inside Grant—a pain he had pushed back for so long that he'd learned to ignore it. But mixed with the pain was a sense of relief and quiet hope engendered by his son's excitement—his joy at his father's simple return to prayer. The pain was uppermost.

How much had he hurt his children by his damaged relationship with God over Annette's death?

Those thoughts remained with Grant as he spoke with the police, gave them all the information he could, and explained his fears about the mercury poisoning.

They used his telephone to call the station.

"Dr. Sheldon?"

He looked up to find the secretary standing at the doorway to his office. "You wanted me to let you know when the ambulance made a call with the next patient. They'll be here in about five minutes."

"Thanks, Becky, I'll be there." He wanted to take care of Gina himself, and Mitchell Caine had better not give him any grief about it. "Becky, I need a copy of Gina Drake's medical records, complete with any previous x-rays."

"How soon?"

"Now."

She picked up her phone and dialed while Grant used the telephone in the back to dial Mr. Butler's home number. A recorder intercepted his call after the second ring, so Grant left a message. No help there. He had the authority and the information, and he definitely had a state of emergency, so there was no need to wait on the administrator to take action. The police were already on it.

He dialed Lauren's number and spoke to yet another machine. "Lauren, this is Grant. Please call me when you get in, no matter what time. I'll be at the hospital for at least another hour or so, maybe longer." Maybe a lot longer. "Whatever you do, don't drink any more of your springwater and don't eat any more fish. It could be poisoned. Lauren, *please call me.*"

He hung up, dissatisfied with the results of his efforts so far. As he walked toward the front of the ER, he remembered eight-year-old Stacie Kimble, who had suffered the effects of diabetic coma after an apparent flu virus that had affected other family members. Hindsight was so much more accurate than medical instinct. Her family lived in that same section of town, and the onset of diabetes would have caused a lot of thirst. The increased water intake would have exacerbated Stacie's condition as the poison entered her system, just as the severity of the gastrointestinal illness could have affected Mr. Mourglia's heart if it was already weak.

How many other mystery cases would this discovery reveal to him? And how many might have been helped if he'd known sooner?

He could hear the ambulance approaching, and he needed to stop wallowing in what-ifs. Logic told him there was no way he could have foreseen this problem. Right now he had a patient who needed help, and he needed to contact Poison Control. The situation was out of hand, and he wasn't going to stop it alone. No human could do that.

Lord, I know you haven't heard from me in a long time. That's going to change. Right now we need your help desperately here. Would you please take control of the situation? Please don't let it be too late for Gina.

Grant picked up the telephone at the reception desk as the ambulance pulled into the bay. Methyl mercury poisoning was rare, but it could very likely cause the symptoms Gina had been experiencing. Would Poison Control even know how to treat it?

"Mr. Archer, Mr. Archer!" Levi came running toward him at full speed from across the Walkers' large family room.

At the sound of his older brother's voice, Cody turned from his television cartoons. His face brightened. He leaped from the sofa and raced after Levi.

Both children ran past Archer and Mrs. Walker and rushed to the door. They stopped and looked back at Archer. "Where's Mama?" Cody asked.

Levi didn't wait for an answer, but pulled open the door and stepped to the screen to peer outside. Cody stepped up beside him. They stared at the empty porch and the empty sidewalk, then looked back at Archer.

"Mr. Archer, where's Mama?" Levi asked. "Did the doctor come and get her?"

"Mr. Archer, is Mama a werewolf?"

"Why was she kicking the kitchen floor?"

Their voices competed with each other, getting louder with each word, until Mr. Walker came rushing into the room from the kitchen, dish towel in one hand and spatula in the other, to join his wife. He placed a hand on Archer's shoulder to get his attention. "Pastor, is she going to be okay? I was just baking some cookies with the children to keep them occupied, but they can't stop worrying about their mother."

Archer shook his head to silently signal that he had no answers yet, then knelt and reached out to the children. They hesitated, as if sensing by his actions and his silence that the news about their mother was not good. Levi stepped into the invitation of his arms, and Cody imitated his brother. Both fell silent, eyes wide, obviously haunted by the things they had seen and the fear that had attacked them far too often these past few weeks.

"Did you see the ambulance when it came a few minutes ago?" he asked them.

Mr. Walker gestured to Archer and shook his head. "We had the television turned up. We were afraid the sirens would scare them."

"Well, your mama's on her way to the hospital to see Dr. Sheldon. You remember him from last time, don't you?"

Levi nodded.

"He's going to take good care of her, but he may want her to spend the night at the hospital—just to make sure she doesn't get sick."

"But can't we go see her?" Levi asked.

"We want to see Mama." Cody's voice was hushed, still fearful.

Archer swallowed. "Your mama wants you to do something for her tonight. She wants you to stay here and help Mr. Walker bake cookies, and then when she starts to feel better, you can visit her." He could promise no more than that. He wanted to tell them their mother would be home first thing in the morning, as good as new, but he would not lie to them.

He hugged the children and kissed their soft cheeks and said another prayer for their mother and for them. When he released them, Levi took his little brother by the arm.

"Mom wants us to be good, Cody. We have to sit down and eat cookies and do what Mr. and Mrs. Walker tell us to."

"You know what?" Mr. Walker said, laying a hand on the top of Levi's head, "I think our first batch is almost ready to come out of the oven. Why don't you join me in the kitchen and help me do the taste test." He led the way, and the children followed while he explained that the cookies couldn't pass the taste test unless they'd been washed down with milk, so they had a lot of work to do.

Archer silently thanked God for answering one of his prayers. The children were in good hands with loving people. One down, several to go.

He made arrangements with Mrs. Walker to take care of the children overnight. She had a key to Gina's house and would go over later to collect some of the children's clothing and toys.

"Mrs. Walker, is it okay if I use your telephone?"

"Of course, but you'll have to start calling me Agnes. Gina has taught Levi and Cody to call me Miss Agnes." Her tender smile radiated across her face. "They are special children. Levi wouldn't let us go over to the house to check on Gina. He insisted that the preacher was taking care of her, and nobody else should be there. Cody was in tears, so we obeyed orders and stayed with the boys. The telephone is this way." She led him down a hallway and into a small office.

After she left, Archer dialed Lauren's number. He knew he should call Natalie, but he decided he could do that from the hospital. Gina would want to see Lauren first. As he listened to the telephone ring he prayed that Gina would be alive to see Lauren when she arrived—and to see her children again.

The answering machine picked up, and he heard Lauren's voice, light and clear and filled with her typical vitality as she left precise instructions for the caller.

"Lauren, this is Archer. Call me as soon as you get home. I'll probably be at the hospital until midnight. Have me paged."

CHAPTER 28

S harp pain streaked across Lauren's forehead. She slowly opened her eyes but could not lift her head from the forest floor. The pain grew worse. She recognized the familiar thrust of a sinus headache and almost welcomed the reminder that she was still alive. She vaguely recalled the continuous nausea—broken by vomiting and then blackness—that had attacked her for what seemed like endless hours.

How long had she lain unconscious this time? The haze in her mind cleared enough for her to think coherently, but she couldn't focus on a time frame. Had she been here for an hour? Longer? All night? Twilight hovered around her, confusing her as she opened her eyes once more. Could she possibly have slept all night?

If so, what had happened to Mr. Mourglia and Mr. Rosewitz? Was it possible they had come and gone without her knowing—and without them seeing her?

Lauren braced herself for the possibility of another sharp stab of pain and managed to raise her head from the pillow of leaves. She looked up into the sky, where the vivid pink of a Missouri sunset shone past the grasping fingers of two leafless sycamore branches, ghostly white in their deadness.

Slowly, tentatively, she attempted to raise her torso from the bed of old leaves infused with mold and . . . worse. After her last bout with nausea, she'd been too weak to move, too weak, for a while, to even think.

Finally some strength returned to her arms, and she managed to sit up. The forest spun around her as she breathed deeply to keep herself from falling. More of the fuzz cleared from her mind, and she gradually grew aware of the sounds around her, the peep of frogs, the rustle of some nearby nocturnal rodent and—most important—the muted splash of water in Honey Creek.

Water.

Though she was not thirsty and didn't know if she could keep the fluid down even if she was able to swallow it, she had to try. She was alone. Her fishing buddies apparently had not come, and there was no one to help her.

Alone.

Lord, have I been abandoned? Are you even there?

Still taking controlled breaths in through her nose and out through her mouth, Lauren pushed herself to her knees. A little more strength permeated her body, almost as if in answer to her one-line prayer. Perhaps God was answering prayers she didn't even have the strength, or the mental acuity, to voice.

After a moment of rest, she tried to rise to her feet but stumbled back to her knees. Her hand came into contact with a fallen branch covered with leafy limbs.

"Please, Lord, help me," she whispered and was alarmed by the faint rattle of her voice. She squeezed the limb with all the strength she could muster. There wasn't much.

Her body needed fluids. She couldn't get stronger without water, and there was no one to help her to the creek. She had to do this herself.

Alone.

But she was never completely alone.

She wasn't, was she?

Using the branch for support, Lauren pushed herself to her feet, stumbled, and stood, breathing quickly, shallowly this time, so as not to set off further spasms of nausea.

Twilight hovered ever nearer, hiding the trail from view, yet somehow Lauren avoided tripping over brush or stumbling into briars. The untrimmed branch gave her enough support to keep her on her feet, yet it was light enough to be carried without weighing her down. She followed the wet chatter of the creek until she saw the glimmer of dancing water as it reflected the bare glow from the sky.

"Thank you, Lord." Lauren sank to her knees in the rough gravel of the creek bed and laid the branch beside her as she reached toward the water. The icy sharpness cleared her head and slapped away the clinging remnants of nausea. She would drink, slowly, cautiously, and replenish some of the fluids she had lost. She would use the water to wash away some of the filth that clung to her. Then she would try to get home.

Gina's chart had not arrived from Medical Records by the time Grant got off the telephone with Poison Control, but there was no time to wait. With a quick order for Becky to bring it to him as soon as possible, he turned to meet the attendants wheeling Gina from the ambulance.

Gina wasn't seizing, but her face was pale. Her eyes were slightly open but glazed, and it looked as if it was only the sheer force of her will that kept them open at all. Her paper-white skin strobed red and blue from the lights across the roof of the ambulance. The paramedic had established an IV and attached a monitor.

"She was seizing when we reached her, Dr. Sheldon," Christy said. "The seizures began at least twenty minutes ago, probably longer."

"Yes, Archer called me from her house."

"Status epilepticus," Christy said. "Dangerous."

"Thank you, Christy. We've already called for an airlift. Muriel, start her on Cerebyx." He gave her the correct dosage amounts for the anticonvulsant drug. There was a high incidence of mortality related to seizures of the magnitude Gina had experienced, and they could have been brought on by a number of things.

"Her blood sugar was 31 when we were finally able to get a finger stick," Christy said.

"Thirty-one?" Grant felt a swift surge of elation at the low number, but he controlled it just as swiftly.

"That's what it read."

Hypoglycemia often did a sneak attack, then disappeared before tests could pinpoint the source of the problem. But the low sugar count could also be a symptom of a more malevolent opponent. He couldn't pin his hopes to a simple answer this quickly, especially in light of the blood sugar tests that had been run on her already, the results of which had always been normal.

"Blood pressure is 100 over 65," Christy said, continuing with her report. "Respirations 15. She's been sliding in and out of consciousness. I gave her an amp of D–50 on scene, and we saw marked improvement."

Grant turned to Eugene, who hovered nearby. "I want a stat CT of the abdomen and a c-peptide level." He turned to the secretary. "Becky, did you alert St. John's to my concern about Mr. Mourglia's mercury poisoning?"

"Yes, Dr. Sheldon. They have BAL on hand as an antidote."

"Good. Call them back and tell them we may be sending them another patient with the same thing."

Muriel paused only long enough to give him a quick glance. "You think Gina's been poisoned, too?"

"I'm taking no chances."

"Good for you, Dr. Sheldon."

Grant thanked God for the seasoned nurse's presence tonight, and then was surprised by the automatic prayer. It was as if the old habit had returned to him the instant he initiated the communication with God again.

Mercury had shown up on x-rays of other patients, so he guessed if Gina had any mercury in her system, they would find it. Even if it didn't prove conclusive, he wanted treatment available immediately, just in case. He could only pray that if there was poisoning involved, the mercury had not yet undergone an ionic conversion to methyl mercury. There was no effective treatment for much of the damage that could be caused by that kind of poisoning, but there was a good chance they could eventually control the outcome for all the patients involved—as long as it hadn't converted.

Grant prayed that Gina's blood sugar problem was simply hypoglycemia, maybe even a tumor of the pancreas that could be cured by surgery. This was the first time in Grant's life he had actually hoped to find a tumor in a patient, but the alternative could be much more destructive.

Christy followed Grant and Muriel into the room they'd cleared and helped transfer Gina onto the bed. "The pastor, Archer Pierce, told us he tried to put some sugar under her tongue. I don't know how much he gave her, but he sure did scatter it across the floor. I slipped on it and nearly fell when we were loading her."

"Did he say if it helped?"

"He thought it did."

Gina gasped and her facial muscles tightened.

"Muriel, we need that drug on board now," Grant said. "And get a repeat fingerstick glucose. She'll seize again if her sugar is still low."

The older nurse nodded, using spare, quick movements to complete her task.

Gina's face relaxed again, and her breath came like a sigh of relief. She moistened her lips with her tongue, swallowed, opened her eyes, then winced and closed them again.

"No seizure," she whispered. "Not this time."

"Thank goodness for that," Muriel said.

"Where . . . my boys?"

"The pastor has them, Gina," Christy said as she disconnected the ambulance monitor from the leads on Gina's chest and replaced it with the hospital monitor.

Gina frowned. "Did I hear you say mercury?" Her eyes came open again, and she studied the faces around her until she found Grant. "You said something about mercury poisoning. I heard you."

"There may be some contamination in the area," he admitted.

"What area?"

Grant didn't want to alarm her and take a chance on another seizure. "Part of the town's water supply. Gina, I want to run some tests on you." He checked to make sure Muriel added the anticonvulsant through the IV tubing. "Just try to relax until I can get some tests taken."

"But my children."

"We'll test them as soon as possible." He took her hand and checked for a pulse. Good and strong. A little fast. He needed to reassure her. "Tell me, Gina, didn't I hear someone say you live near the school?"

"Yes."

"That's good. The schools are nowhere near the affected area." He pulled a penlight out of his pocket and shined it into her eyes. Her pupils were equal and briskly reactive. And wide open with concern.

"Do you ever eat fish that has been caught locally?" he asked her. "Maybe Lauren has given you some of hers in the past few weeks."

"My boys don't like fish, and I don't take the time to fix it just for myself."

"Where does your baby-sitter live?"

"A block from the school."

This was getting better. "I'll have our secretary or a nurse call your sitter, but it sounds less and less likely that your children have been affected. Have you or either of your boys felt any nausea recently?"

"No."

"Do you ever get bad headaches?"

"Some," she said, getting drowsy again. "Not as bad now."

Grant relaxed a little more. "Gina, just a few more questions, and then I'll let you rest for a few minutes, okay?"

She nodded.

As Grant continued his neurological assessment he prayed silently, and the comfort of that fresh connection with his Lord gave him a peace he had been missing since the wreck. Two years of grief and spiritual starvation had done their damage, but God had the power to restore everything. All Grant prayed for now was Gina's life.

Darkness had begun its attack on the sky, and the air turned chilly, biting into Lauren's skin. She'd made the mistake of trying to wash some of the evidence of sickness from her shirt and arms, and now the cold combined with a heavy lethargy to seep past her wet clothes and skin and set up camp around her bones. She should have known better.

Would she make it back to the truck? She had to get up and move or she could quickly develop hypothermia, especially in her weakened condition. Her old fishing jacket and a blanket were in the truck. She just had to get back to the truck.

Using the branch once again for support, Lauren pulled herself to her feet and stumbled, slowly, in the direction of the parking area. "Lord, help me, please," she murmured. "I don't even know if I can find my way." But she had to try.

She took a step, and her toe caught a stray stem from the branch she carried. She lost her grip and pitched forward into the gravel. She fell hard on her shoulder and cried out with pain.

"Oh, Lord, please!"

The sound of the water overwhelmed her, pressing her down as the gravel dug into her exposed flesh. She couldn't ignore the specter of death as it loomed in the deepening gray around her, and there was no way to fight it. Not alone. Depression and fear attacked her without mercy, and for countless moments she lay in the gravel, overwhelmed by her weakness.

But somehow she retained her connection with consciousness this time. Perhaps it was the pain. Perhaps it had something to do with the shivering that began in the bottom of her spine and worked its way upward and outward, preying on her body like a living, writhing creature.

She concentrated on her breathing and then on making small movements with her fingers. She couldn't do this by herself. The truck was so far away, and she felt as if she had no strength left.

Never had she felt so far from human contact and yet in so much need of it. She often came out here alone. But that was because with her schedule, all her friends were working when she had a day off. She could hop into her truck and drive back to town when she got lonely.

Even living alone, she had never been far from the sound of a human voice—all she needed to do was pick up the telephone and dial. She had enough friends and family that there was always someone willing to talk.

Until now she had never been truly alone. Shame followed this realization. So many times, especially in the past couple of years, she had complained to God—and to anyone else who would listen—that she was lonely. She wanted a life mate—someone with whom she could connect, someone with whom she could share everything.

How must her complaints have sounded to God? As if He weren't enough?

The pain cut deeply.

"Lord, forgive me. I'm so sorry," she whispered. Earlier, she'd been praying for God to send someone to help her. Mourglia and Rosewitz would have been nice . . . but where was her faith?

"If I truly believe in you, then all I really need is you. And if I don't believe, then I'm doomed for sure. Save me, Lord."

Alone.

"If you want me to live alone for the rest of my life . . . or if this is the end of my life . . . it's yours to take. It's yours to direct. Please help me never to complain about loneliness again."

She waited for another moment, then tested her strength. She would move forward until she could no longer move at all. And she would trust God with every step.

"Lord, one step at a time." That was all she could ask. "Keep me moving forward."

Lauren reached out beside her until her fingers came into contact once again with the branch. As she shivered, she felt along the sides of the limb and used all her strength to tug the excess leaves and stems from the base of the stick. She wouldn't trip again.

———————

Activity in the emergency room had dwindled from frantic to merely hectic, and Grant stepped back into Gina's room to find her smiling weakly at her children, whom Archer and the Walkers had brought in moments ago. The boys chattered excitedly about experiences as sons of a werewolf.

"Mama, that means Cody and I are werepups, doesn't it?" Levi said, his young voice bright and filled with life now that his mother was awake and apparently out of danger. "But you didn't ever grow any hair. Let me see your teeth. Do you have fangs now? Why did you have to come to see the doctor? The doctor never . . ."

Gina looked up and saw Grant, and she gave him a weak smile. "I think those cartoons have created a monster," she said softly. Some pink had returned to her cheeks, and though she was still weak from the seizures, she was obviously putting forth all her energy to spend these few minutes with her children while she had them.

"No, Mama, you *are* a monster. You're a good monster. You fight crime and drag bad guys to jail, and—"

"I am *not* a werewolf. I think we're going to stop watching so much television on Saturday mornings."

"No, Mama!" Cody and Levi cried in unison.

"I'll start reading to you."

"No! We want cartoons!" Levi cried. "We want to see you fighting the forces of evil with your—"

"I help people breathe better, Levi. That's all."

"Yes, and at night you turn into Supermonstermom and bash bad guys, and . . ."

As the boys continued to entertain their mother, Grant checked Gina's most recent vitals on the chart and noted that her sugar level was up to normal. It was looking more and more likely that blood sugar was the only culprit in this case, but after the harrowing seizures and the mercury scare that was now swarming across the town, he wasn't taking any chances with the mother of these little boys. She was on her way to St. John's in Springfield as soon as her flight arrived.

While Levi and Cody kept their mother occupied, Grant stepped out of the room and found Archer talking to the Walkers in the waiting room.

Archer saw him gesture and went over immediately. "How's she doing, Grant?"

"Good. I don't want to raise any false hopes for her, but I'm waiting on the results of the CT. Her c-peptide level is high, which is good, but I don't want to rule out anything that might raise its ugly head when we're not prepared. She's been through too much. I still want to have the chelating agent available—"

"Hold it, Doc." Archer made his typical time-out gesture. "Remember who you're talking to. English, please."

Grant smiled. "I think she's out of danger, but I'm not taking chances. You did the right thing with the sugar. I was concerned about mercury poisoning, but that's looking less and less likely."

"Mercury poisoning?"

"I'm checking on that right now. I don't know for sure. I want to talk to Gina alone before her ride arrives. Do you think you can lure her werepups out of the exam room and back home with the Walkers so it won't be so traumatic for them when the flight crew straps her in for takeoff?"

"I'll get right on it," Archer said.

———

Prayer supported Lauren more solidly than her newly trimmed branch as she moved forward one step at a time. She trusted God to keep her from falling, and she trusted Him to hear her prayers even when she ran out of breath and could no longer speak.

And so she felt her way through the shadowy woods, slowly, prayerfully, knowing that she could not do this alone—that she *wasn't* doing it alone. At one point during her struggle she realized she had stopped shivering and a peaceful warmth permeated her body. Though the nausea hovered and threatened to descend once again, it did not attack.

Somewhere in the midst of her prayers Lauren understood, with fresh joy, the word picture God had given her when she first picked up the branch that helped support her. She had pruned it so it wouldn't trip her again, just as God was pruning her—perhaps so she wouldn't get in the way of His perfect will for her life.

Tonight she was releasing some of her own expectations for her life and leaving everything open for Christ's control. She would allow Him to prune away her desire for a husband and children. That passion had driven her to humiliation more than once in the past year, and now she released it. She prayed for the willingness to remain single the rest of her life if God so desired. And she prayed that God would help her find joy in that condition.

And if her life lasted for only a few more hours, or even a few more minutes, that too, was in God's hands.

She wasn't alone.

With each step she took, the truth became more apparent. No matter what happened from this point forward, she would have the support of her Savior, who walked beside her. The reality wouldn't have been more clear to her if a sudden light had come down from the sky and illuminated the figure of Jesus walking between the trees, snapping twigs and clearing a path through the brush.

Another step and Lauren felt the soft crush of leaves beneath her feet. She peered ahead of her and thought she saw the outline of the truck in the shadow of the trees. Was her mind playing tricks?

She drew closer. It was no trick. She reached out and felt the cool metal of the front fender, then leaned on it for support as she stumbled alongside the precious cab, opened the back door, leaned against the long bench seat, and used the freshly pruned branch to heft herself inside. The relief overwhelmed her more than the fear had earlier. She grabbed the blanket from the floorboard and wrapped herself in it.

Closing the door, Lauren lay across the seat. No way could she drive home tonight. She would spend the night here and leave the future in God's hands. She hadn't felt this much loving peace in a long time.

"Thank you, dear Lord," she whispered as she drifted off to sleep.

CHAPTER 29

To Grant's surprise, after his first tentative venture into prayer, he found himself welcomed into God's presence, and the floodgates opened. Old habits returned like beloved friends, and his conversations with God—which had ended abruptly with the crash of metal two years ago—resumed with all the force of love he remembered.

But there was no time to pause and relish the joy right now—he looked forward to doing that later, in generous measure. Dogwood Springs needed God's healing touch tonight, and now, for the first time, Grant realized God might have him in mind to help administer that touch.

For the second time in five minutes Grant returned to exam room three, where Gina continued to await an airlift to Springfield. In the interim she was being closely monitored by Muriel, who hovered at the side of her bed, ever vigilant to changes reflected on the monitor screen.

"Dr. Sheldon, you're in here again?" Muriel greeted him with a chuckle. "I'm beginning to think you don't trust me."

"I trust you completely, Muriel," he assured her. "I just feel the need to pamper Gina. She's been through a lot."

Gina gave Grant a sleepy smile. "Muriel's barely left this room since I got here."

Grant pulled the backless exam stool beside Gina's bed and sat down. "Getting groggy again?"

"Very."

"You've had a harrowing experience, and—"

"—and my body will take some time to recover," she said weakly. "I know the drill. I'll be okay."

"Yes, I think you will. We checked Levi and Cody, and everything looks good. I've asked the Walkers to keep a close watch for any unusual signs that might alert us to mercury poisoning, but that's purely precautionary."

"Thank you, Dr. Sheldon. And thank you for letting me see them." Her voice was still weak, but it radiated continued joy from the reunion. "My blood sugar really was low this time, wasn't it?"

"Yes, and even more revealing, your insulin level was high."

"Why did you do the abdominal CT?"

"I was looking for a tumor. I didn't find anything obvious, but I haven't heard back from the radiologist. I saw no scatter artifact on the film—which would have shown up if you had mercury in your abdomen."

There was no change in her expression. Her eyes focused on his with perfect trust. "You think I have a tumor?"

"An insulinoma is a possibility. I don't want to alarm you, but you know enough about medicine to understand—"

"I'm not alarmed, Dr. Sheldon. An insulinoma is usually benign, right?"

"Ninety percent of the time."

"So it isn't very dangerous, just a tumor of the pancreas."

He had never had a patient receive this kind of news with such equanimity. "I don't want to dismiss this lightly, Gina. The low blood sugar that results from an insulinoma is a serious concern. It could be the cause of what you've been thinking were panic attacks."

She raised her head from the pillow, her expression growing more animated. "But don't you see? A tumor would explain the unpredictable onset of my symptoms. A tumor would explain everything; I wouldn't have to worry any longer about losing my kids." She fumbled with her blanket and tried to sit up, as if she couldn't express her emotions as succinctly as she needed to without getting her whole body involved.

Muriel put a hand on her shoulder. "You lie right there, young lady. You need to take it easy until your flight arrives."

Gina obeyed with obvious reluctance, but the excitement continued to radiate from her face. "Dr. Sheldon, there were times I could be on the go for a whole shift—miss two or even three meals—and feel fine, even if I was always hungry. Then the next day if I missed one meal I would crash. If I have a tumor, that could explain the inconsistency."

"Depending on the amount of insulin a tumor wanted to release into your body at any given time, you would have been at its mercy," Grant agreed. "But there are still risks involved, and we don't know for sure about it yet. I don't want to trust my own judgment for something this serious, so I'm sending you to someone who knows more about it than I do. We'll definitely need a second opinion."

She blinked up at him, and her smile widened. "A second opinion?"

"Yes. Have you heard of Dr. Manfred in Springfield? He's an endocrinologist, and he's handled many insulinoma cases. I'd like him to have a look at—"

"A second opinion." She repeated the common term as if she'd just made a new and exciting discovery. "Someone wiser and more knowledgeable, who can take control," she said. "Yes. Exactly."

Grant looked at Muriel, then at the monitor. Nothing had changed. "Gina? Are you feeling okay?"

"I'm feeling better every minute. God doesn't waste any time, does He?"

"God?"

"Yes, God. The Great Physician. You've just told me what you think my problem is, and it doesn't sound like schizophrenia to me."

"No, it doesn't to me, either."

"Lauren tried to tell me all along that I needed to turn it all over to Him—not just this illness, but my whole life. She said it's like getting a second opinion from the Great Physician, and then letting Him take over the case."

Grant had never heard salvation put that way before. Trust Lauren to word things in her own unique way. "She was right, Gina."

"He *does* know what He's doing."

"Yes." Grant had no doubt about that now. He'd never had any doubt about God's ability, only about His love and patience. Doubts brought on by shock and grief.

Some of the excitement faded from Gina's expression. "Dr. Sheldon, you asked me earlier if I ate any of the fish Lauren caught. Is Lauren going to be okay? She eats that fish all the time, and she's been sick. She also carries the water home to drink."

"I know. I tried calling her earlier, and I left a message on her recorder."

"She's probably not home."

"How do you know?"

"She tried to hide it, but she was pretty upset when she left here. She said she needed some time to think."

"When was she here?"

"Just before I got off work tonight."

"She wasn't sick then?"

"Nope, just upset."

There was a knock at the door, and Becky stepped in. "Dr. Sheldon, I've got an urgent call for you from the mayor. Can you take it?"

Grant looked at his watch. "Yes, I'll be right there. What's Lifeline's ETA?"

"They notified us about two minutes ago that they were about eight minutes out."

"Thank you." He turned back to his patient. "Gina, I'll try to be back before they load you in the chopper."

Though Lauren somehow knew she was only dreaming, she couldn't control the sensation that she was falling headlong into an abyss. She awoke with a gasp and bumped her head against something hard and unyielding. This wasn't her bedroom.

"Where am I?" she cried hoarsely, blinking through the dark. Her head pounded with pain, and her stomach burned as if it were being eaten with acid.

She reached out blindly, and her hand smacked against something soft.

Upholstered cushion.

Her memory returned, and she could not prevent the fear that accompanied it, the horror that burst past the wall of courage she had built around her through prayer earlier tonight . . . or last night . . . or whenever she had last been conscious.

"Lord, are you still there?" Her throat was raw, and movement sliced pain through her head. She continued in silent prayer until the darkness once more overtook her.

"Dr. Sheldon, I need your help." Jade Myers sounded tired. "I've spoken with Mr. Butler, and he's making arrangements for us to use the hospital's outpatient clinic for the weekend. Now we need to staff it."

"Staff it? For what?"

"I want to offer screening, testing, and treatment for victims of mercury poisoning."

"This weekend? Mayor, we don't even have the agents to treat it."

"I know. I've called our local pharmacists and they're going to see what they can do. Meanwhile we can at least get the screening started, and that's where our local docs get involved. Since the test results will take too long to get back from the lab, we need people with professional clinical skills to help us sort out the symptoms and begin treatment even before the results get back. This thing with Uncle Ernest has made a believer out of me."

A steamroller had nothing on this lady. "Have you heard from County Health?"

"They called the state. Someone is on his way down to test the water, but do you know it could take three weeks to get the results back? I know the state wants to be sure of their results before they make any announcements and have a panic on their hands, but we can't wait that long. I've already arranged for a public service announcement to be made over the Springfield TV stations as well as the local radio stations. I'm not waiting around for more people to get sick."

"How did you manage to get so much done in such a short time?"

"Delegation. I practice it daily."

"What about the water supply?" Grant asked.

"We shut off the reservoir fed by Honey Creek," she said. "We have nearly a thousand residences without running water, and you should hear the complaints. I've spoken with some of them myself. Do you know that some of the people are demanding that we prove there's a problem before we shut off their supply? *Proof?* Uncle Ernest is proof enough for me. Have you heard how he's doing?"

"He arrived safely in Springfield, and we're waiting to hear the blood test results, but it will be several hours. Mercury is not something routinely tested."

"And that's another thing. Do you know a urine test for mercury takes twenty-four hours? I wanted blood tests, but those have to go to a lab at the Mayo Clinic, then they fax the reports."

Grant shook his head in amazement. "You found all this out already?"

"You just need to be connected to the right people. Our city employees are moving fast, and more help is on the way."

Obviously, when Jade Myers decided to do something, it got done.

"So, will you help me?" she asked. "I need a medical advisor."

"I'm not an expert on mercury poisoning," he warned her.

"I've come to the conclusion that nobody in Dogwood Springs is. Do you know how many people I've called, trying to find someone who could help me? Your son is on the Internet as we speak, printing as much information as he can find on the subject. He's a smart kid. You've got a regular father-son medical team going there. He'll make a great doc someday."

"Thank you."

"I wish I'd listened to you the day you tried to convince me our community puzzle might be spreading the contamination. I wish I'd paid more attention."

She had a strong voice, well modulated, persuasive, and she was being very complimentary. No wonder she was a popular mayor.

"But the puzzle wasn't spreading disease," Grant said.

"No, but if I'd listened then we might have put our heads together and come up with the solution before so many people got sick. I've called an emergency meeting, and I'm going to suggest the city pick up the initial tab for the public testing and treatment. I don't think I'll have any trouble getting that approved, but to prevent any controversy, will you attend the meeting? You can explain the situation so much better than I could."

"When will you meet?"

"In about forty-five minutes, in conference room B, there at the hospital."

"Tonight?"

"I told you, it's an emergency."

Grant thought of all the things he needed to get done before that, but how could he refuse? This was an emergency. "You don't waste time, Mayor."

"I'll call you Grant if you'll call me Jade."

"What about state assistance, Jade?"

"The state might help us pay for some of it later, but I'm not waiting around on the big boys to come storming in here and take charge. Who knows when they'll get here? We're making some money with our community projects, and we have plenty on hand. Everyone in this town is going to be affected in some way, and I don't want any more deaths on our conscience."

Grant heard the first growl of warning that the airlift helicopter was approaching. He didn't have a lot of time, and he wanted to check on Gina again.

"So will you come to our meeting, Grant?"

He hesitated. He wished he knew where Lauren was and how she was feeling. But Gina had said she wasn't sick earlier. . . . "I'll be there."

"Good. I'll see you then."

He hung up and tried to call Lauren again. No answer. The recorder did its spiel. "Lauren, this is Grant again. I need you to call me as soon as you get home, no matter what time." He knew she was scheduled for a shift in the morning. "If you can't get me at home, call me at the hospital. At least leave a message and let me know you're okay."

He returned to Gina's room to find Muriel preparing her for the flight team's arrival. Gina was awake, functioning normally, and though she admitted to being groggy, she looked good. In fact, she was doing so well the flight team might question his decision to call them. But status epilepticus, or a long-lasting seizure, was not something to mess with.

"Gina, we have the results from the CT, and the radiologist didn't see any obvious tumor, but a CT isn't nearly as definitive as an MRI.

You'll have one done in Springfield," Grant said.

The growl from the air reverberated and changed to a high-speed *thump-thump-thump* and then to a roar that seemed to shake the walls.

"Thanks. Dr. Sheldon, I'm worried about Lauren. She might be in trouble. This mercury poisoning must be why she's been so sick."

"I've been worried about the same thing." He didn't tell her about Mr. Mourglia, another avid fisherman who frequented Honey Creek. The elderly man's near-death experience would not bring Gina any comfort right now. It certainly wasn't helping Grant's peace of mind. "But you told me she wasn't sick when you saw her tonight, right?"

"That's right, just upset."

"How upset?" Grant asked. "How was she behaving? Did she act confused?"

"No. I know what you're thinking, and it wasn't as if her central nervous system had been affected by poisoning."

"Did she say anything specific about her plans tonight?" Grant asked.

"Maybe she went to visit her family in Knolls," Gina suggested with a shrug. "She's close to them. It's something Lauren would do."

Yes, Lauren would do that, especially if she were upset.

The swish of doors and the rumble of voices indicated the flight crew's entrance into the ER.

"Dr. Sheldon, would you do something for me?" Gina asked. "Would you have somebody call Natalie and let her know where they're taking me? She'll be worried."

Grant smiled down at her. Things were definitely changing for this young lady. "I'll have Becky call her, but you realize, don't you, that if she knows, she'll probably be at the landing pad to greet you at St. John's?"

"She means well."

"Yes, I think she does."

The team entered the room in a burst of energy, and in moments they had Gina ready for transport.

Archer made one more attempt to call Lauren when he got home.

Gina would definitely need her now, and he didn't intend to leave Lauren out of the loop just because some bored busybodies had decided to think the worst about her. She would want to be notified about the town emergency.

Still no answer. He left another message and hung up.

Barely five seconds later the phone rang and startled him. Lauren? He grabbed the receiver. "Hello?"

"Archer, we've got ourselves a problem." It was not Lauren. It was the gravelly bass tones of John Netz.

Archer deflated like a punctured air cushion. "What kind of a problem, John?"

"Where've you been? I tried calling you three or four times."

"Did you leave a message on my answering machine?"

"Nope. Hate those things," John grumbled. "Anyway, I've got you now. Some guy from the city got in touch with Dwight about an hour ago. They're contacting all the churches in town for help. We've got some kind of crisis on our hands. You hear anything about Honey Creek getting poisoned?"

Word got out in a hurry. "I've been out of the loop for a few hours, John, but Dr. Sheldon mentioned it to me at the hospital this evening. I didn't get much of a chance—"

"Well, the mayor's having a fit. She says we've got a problem, and she's not waiting around for the state guys to come down. I think that new ER doctor has her all upset. These newcomers like to stir up trouble."

"Dr. Sheldon doesn't stir up trouble, John. If he thinks there's a problem, there is. What's the mayor doing about it?"

"She and Mr. Butler from the hospital have gotten their heads together, and they want to set up relief areas at the churches. Since our church is the biggest of the bunch and it's centrally located, we'll probably get the brunt of the incoming."

"Incoming?"

"Refugees. And they need some volunteers to gather up cots and such and to spread the word about the poisoning."

"Refugees?"

"Or evacuees, or something like that," John sounded as if he was getting a little irritated with the questions. "The wife and I are heading out right now. You might want to meet us down at the church."

Archer knew he was lacking a hefty chunk of information, but it didn't sound as if he was going to get all he needed from John.

"You know," John's voice took on that familiar tone of gentle chiding that he'd used when Archer was a teenager, "you could stand to get a little more involved in things. All chaos is breaking loose in this town. Where's your father when we need him? He could've taken—"

"I'll be at the church in ten minutes, John," Archer said, then hung up. No, he did not intend to allow the bossy old deacon to run his life, but he did want to know more about what was going on in town, and he *was* the pastor of Dogwood Springs Baptist Church. It was his responsibility. He welcomed that burden on his shoulders. It had nothing to do with John Netz.

Practically nothing.

The phone line at home was busy when Grant tried to call, and he realized Beau was probably still on the Internet, hunting information. Why hadn't they called the telephone company to install that additional line? He needed to talk to Beau. He also needed to touch base with Mr. Butler before the meeting. And he intended to find Lauren.

Grant looked at his watch. There was time to drive to her house and back before the meeting. He pulled his car keys out of his desk and headed out. He would leave a note of warning on her door. Then if for some reason she didn't listen to her messages tonight, she would still see the note and call him.

Was he blowing all this out of proportion?

Probably. He preferred that possibility to the alternative.

This was going to be a long night.

CHAPTER 30

Every branch that does bear fruit he prunes so that it will be even more fruitful . . . every branch . . . more fruitful . . .

Lauren heard her mother's voice quoting the familiar Bible passage through the darkness, past the pain, and she awakened for a moment. She opened her eyes, but all remained black, as it had been when she had last closed them.

"Mom?" She couldn't speak past a whisper.

Lauren listened for the voice again, but all she heard was the continual chatter of the creek.

How long had she been out this time? Mom's voice had felt so real, her presence so familiar. So comforting.

That passage of Scripture . . . Mom had helped her memorize that verse from the book of John years ago. Maybe that was why it had come to Lauren's mind so easily.

When she had driven out here tonight—it *had* been tonight, hadn't it?—she'd been very unhappy with God, and she'd let Him know it.

But now that the energies of her anger and frustration were weakened, spent, and finally transformed, Lauren felt her heart drawing closer to Christ. In the midst of her fear she felt God was being especially tender with her, especially personal.

Every branch that does bear fruit he prunes so that it will be even more fruitful. It was a passage Mom quoted a lot when Lauren or one of her brothers or sisters was hurt or struggling through their teen years and early adulthood. Until now, it had always felt oppressive to Lauren. Nobody wanted to be pruned. Nobody wanted to suffer loss and heartache in order to mature spiritually.

But this time the abiding comfort of the words found root in her heart. They reminded her that God had not forgotten about her, and even better than that, He considered her worthy to bear more fruit. That might even mean she was going to live through this—otherwise, how would she be able to bear fruit?

Maybe someday that fruit could actually be children of her own . . . but if it never happened, God was drawing her closer to the place where she could accept that.

Right now, she would just be glad to see another sunrise.

————

In the wee hours of Saturday morning, Archer awakened on his cot in the church basement to the fragrance of freshly perking coffee. He heard soft voices echoing from the far side of the cavernous room and the crack of sizzling bacon—or was that sausage? It smelled like heaven. The cooks had promised to start breakfast early for the volunteers who took shifts during the night.

Archer held his watch close to his eyes and peered at the lighted numbers. One o'clock. He'd had a good thirty minutes of sleep. Now to get to work. The good folks of Dogwood Springs would just have to endure his wrinkled jeans and T-shirt.

The door at the top of the basement steps opened and allowed light from the upstairs hallway to glow down onto the sleeping evacuees scattered across the far end of the room on borrowed cots. The door closed again, and a newcomer made a dark, cautious descent, obviously keeping as silent as possible in order not to disturb anyone.

Archer couldn't help wondering about the fresh arrival. Ordinarily, everyone knew to enter the basement through the side of the building, where the double doors opened onto a level, paved playground and additional parking area. Right now, there was a huge, hastily painted sign in the middle of that playground offering water, food, and even a place to sleep for those people who were panicked by the possibility of mercury in their homes.

The experts said that the homes were safe, as was the food that had been purchased from local grocery stores. Still, some families had come for the night after hearing the first of the public service announcements. If the mercury had crept into their water supply, how could they be sure it hadn't contaminated other areas?

People were frightened. Archer couldn't blame them. This whole thing was a frightening experience.

With one Dogwood Springs reservoir disconnected due to possible contamination, the city was hard-pressed to supply enough water for the whole town, and Jade Myers had vowed not to rest until she had been assured alternate sources would be available.

That had apparently been taken care of late last night. The town would weather this storm as it had many others over the years. Dr. Grant Sheldon and his son were already local heroes because Jade had "leaked" to the television and radio personnel that the Sheldon family had tracked the deadly poison to its source.

Now there would be an interesting situation. If Archer knew Jade—and he did, because she'd only been a year ahead of him in school and she'd been a member of Dogwood Springs Baptist for the past seven years—she was definitely attracted to heroes. And Jade was single again, after a quiet divorce a year ago from a man who had decided to become someone else's hero. But there wasn't time to think about that now.

The newcomer, still in the shadows, reached the bottom of the stairs and quietly stepped past cots and sleeping bags toward the designated kitchen area. There was something familiar about those movements, so Archer folded his blanket and laid it on his cot, then made his way toward the smell of coffee.

He was halfway there when he heard the melodious sound of a warm voice joining the soft chatter of the others.

"You're still singing for our Fourth of July celebration, aren't you?" Mrs. Netz asked.

"I wouldn't miss it."

It was Jess. Archer rushed to greet her.

"Jessica?" he said quietly.

She turned, and the smile broadened across her face. "Hi, Archer. I thought you might want some help."

He entered the circle of light as he beheld the vision so breathtaking that all the cobwebs and dreams of the night deserted him. "How did you know?"

"Dogwood Springs has made the news. I heard it just before I went to bed, and I couldn't sleep for thinking about you, so here I am." She wore a pair of old sweat pants and a T-shirt that said, in faded letters "Two From Galilee," the scruffy hem of which hung to the middle of her thighs. Her tangle of glorious wavy brown hair was held away from her face, somewhat, with one of those clawlike clips that could be used as weapons if wielded with the proper aim.

Archer accepted two cups of extremely weak coffee from Mrs. Netz, who manned the huge percolator at the end of the long kitchen counter. He thanked her, then gave one of the cups to Jessica and took her arm.

"How about a short stroll?" he whispered.

"Good," she whispered back. "You can walk me to my car. I brought some supplies for breakfast."

He smiled. Spoken like a true pastor's wife. And that was what he wanted to talk to her about—he needed to talk to her before they were caught up in the night's chaos and separated for however long it took to clear things up and set everything right in the town—which, according to the guys he'd talked to a couple of hours ago, could be days or even weeks.

He held the door for her, and she stepped out. As soon as it closed behind them, he asked her, "Don't you have to sing tomorrow—I mean tonight?"

"Yes, but I'm free till then."

"But the last time we spoke I got the distinct impression that you didn't want anything to do with this church."

Jessica stopped walking and turned to him. "Archer Pierce, after all this time, I would expect you to know me better than that."

"Better than what?"

"Than for you to listen to me when I'm mad and blowing off steam."

He couldn't let her get away with that. "Excuse me, but you were not just blowing off steam when you told me you could not marry Dogwood Springs Baptist Church."

"I told you I was confused. You reminded me, in so many words, that the subject was moot, because you hadn't asked me to marry you lately." He could see her face in the dim light. She didn't look angry. She looked like she was enjoying herself.

"Do you remember what you said?" he asked.

"Not as well as what *you* said." There were definite signs of a smile in her eyes as she continued to remind him of his words, as if she wanted to relish them for a second time. "There are three things about which you have no doubts."

He returned the smile. "I don't doubt that God is in control. I don't doubt that I was called to this church, and—"

"And you said you didn't doubt that you loved me. Has any of that changed?"

"No."

"Good."

"But, Jessica, that also means I'm staying here, at this church, as their pastor—if they don't take a vote and throw me out."

"Yes."

"I've prayed about it, and thought about it, and prayed some more. I'm not finished here."

Her expression didn't change. "No."

It occurred to him that the exhilaration of being in love with Jessica could be compared to a wild roller-coaster ride. Or maybe surfing the highest waves in the world. Or skiing down Mount Everest. What would marriage to her be like?

He cleared his throat. "You understand that, then?"

"Yes."

He took a deep breath. He'd taken the ring out of its case several times recently, just to look at it and wonder about its future. It was a beautiful ring, and it had looked beautiful on Jessica's left hand. He wished he had it now.

Ask her.

"Jessica—"

The church door opened. "Archer?" It was Mrs. Netz.

Archer groaned softly. "I'll be there in a few moments," he called over his shoulder, then returned his attention to the most beautiful woman in his life. "Jessica, would you—"

"Archer, I hate to interrupt," Mrs. Netz said. "This is important."

This was not a good time. "I'm sorry, Jessica, it looks as if things are going to get crazy, but before it does, I need to—"

The door squeaked open further. "Archer?" This time the voice didn't belong to Mrs. Netz. It was Grant Sheldon.

Archer sighed and turned. "Grant? What's wrong?"

"Do you know where Lauren is?"

There was a feminine groan of frustration behind him. "Lauren," Jessica muttered.

"Grant, can it wait a few minutes?" Archer asked.

"I'm sorry, I don't think so. I'm worried about her."

"Why?"

"I've tried several times to call her tonight, but she hasn't answered. I left a note on her door instructing her to call me, but she hasn't."

"Maybe she heard about Gina and drove to Springfield."

"I tried St. John's. Natalie was with Gina, and she hasn't seen or heard from Lauren." The concern was evident in Grant's voice. "She has a shift in the morning, and she obviously isn't home yet—or she's too sick to answer her calls. I thought she might be at her parents' house, but Beau called them for me earlier and she wasn't there."

Okay, maybe there was reason to worry. "No, she wouldn't be in Knolls, because she just came back from there. She brought flowers back from her mother's garden to decorate the church for Sunday service."

"Then where is she?" Grant asked with increased emphasis.

With a sigh of resignation, Jessica laid a hand on Archer's shoulder. "I think you need to go find Lauren. I'll be here when you get back." She reached into her pocket and pulled out a cell phone. "Take this with you, just in case."

———

Grant retraced the route to Lauren's house with Archer riding silently in the passenger seat. When they arrived, they saw Grant's note fluttering from the door where he had left it.

"She could still be inside," Grant insisted.

"It's possible." Archer got out of the car and disappeared into the darkness at the back of the house. When he returned he held up a key. "Old McCaffrey family habit. Hide a spare behind a drainpipe. I don't know why Lauren even bothers to lock her doors." He led the way to her front porch and unlocked it, then charged inside, turning on lights and calling her name.

While Archer disappeared into the kitchen, Grant checked the bathroom and bedrooms. The place was deserted. They met back at the front door.

"What now?" Grant asked.

"There's one other place I can think of that she might have gone—her fishing spot."

"In the middle of the night?"

Archer held his hands out from his sides. "I know, it's unlikely. It's a Friday night party spot, so she avoids it after dark on the weekends."

"Where else can we look?"

"I don't know. Grant, there's probably a reasonable explanation for all this. She's undoubtedly heard about the mercury and is going door to door to warn all the people she's given fish to in the past month. That could take her all night. She gives away a lot."

Grant wasn't satisfied with that answer. She was probably fine, but what if she wasn't? "Can you help me get to her fishing spot? I've never been there at night—I might miss the turn. Please, Archer."

"Of course. Let's go."

CHAPTER | 31

A muffled thump in the darkness and the echo of a man's voice helped Lauren fight her way back to consciousness, but she couldn't tell if they were products of her dream state or of reality.

She opened her eyes to the same darkness that had held her in its murky prison for countless hours. A brief reflection of light flashed through the truck, barely there before it was gone again. She blinked and tried to raise her head.

Was she hallucinating?

She closed her eyes and stumbled back into silent prayer, still too weak to say a word.

Another voice, another thump, like the closing of a door—a car door? She had to see. If there was someone out there . . . had to get their attention.

With heroic effort she raised her right arm and placed her hand against the side window. She rested for a moment and listened, then doubted her sanity once again. Auditory hallucinations. She thought about Gina.

Voices again . . . a male voice and the rustle of brush, the rattle of footsteps on gravel.

"Help me," she whispered. "Please help me."

More footsteps. Another thump. She concentrated all her strength into her right arm and raised it from the window, then slapped it back down as hard as she could.

She took a deep breath and forced the air from her lungs. "H-h-help me." Her voice was only a rasp of sound that couldn't have made it past the door.

Had to get out of the truck.

She willed her hand to slide down to the handle, and she pulled. Hard. It unlatched and opened with the weight of her shoulders against it. The interior light came on and blinded her.

"Help me," she called again.

She heard the voice more clearly, and then the sound of a door slamming, and the start of a motor.

"No, please!" She reached for the armrest, and the door swung out, taking her with it. Her body plunged headlong from the truck, and she landed hard in the dirt.

Blackness once again wrapped its blanket around her in a smothering embrace as she heard tires spin in gravel, followed by the fading sound of a car engine, leaving her alone again.

No . . . never alone. He had promised she would never be alone. But she was so cold.

Grant's grip on the steering wheel was so tight the tips of his fingers felt numb. He loosened them slightly and tried to see past the perimeter of road revealed by his headlights while he struggled to keep his imagination from taking his fear to unknown regions. Prayers whipped fast and furious through his mind, almost as fast as his car was speeding down the road.

"Uh, Grant, there's a curve up ahead that you can't take at eighty-five miles an hour." Archer's voice sounded forcibly relaxed, as if he were trying to calm a frightened, dangerous animal.

Grant looked at the speedometer and pulled his foot back from the accelerator. "Sorry. How much farther to the turnoff?"

"Not far. About a mile and a half. At this rate we'll make it in about sixty seconds."

Grant took the heavy hint and pressed the brake. "You say she wasn't sick this afternoon when you saw her?"

"That's right. I don't think she'd have bothered with altar flowers if she weren't feeling well. She's probably out with the other volunteers. That's where she would be if she knew what was going on."

"But she would have called someone."

"Grant, she's single and lives alone. Who would she call? How was she supposed to know you'd go tearing off after her like some half-crazed maniac?"

Grant took his eyes from the road for a half second to frown at Archer. "I notice you came out, too."

"Somebody had to slow you down."

They reached the curve just as a flash of headlights glared around it like horizontal lightning, zagging out of control. Grant swung the wheel sharply toward the shoulder of the road and slammed the brakes as the oncoming car squealed its tires and roared on down the road and out of sight.

After a moment of shocked silence, Archer said "Good job" and released his death hold on the armrest.

Grant steered back onto the blacktop at a more cautious speed.

"I guess I didn't mention that this is a party road, did I?"

"I should have listened to your cautions. Lauren said something about it the day we came fishing out here."

"Look, Grant, I know she's special to you, that's obvious. Just admit it and get it over with."

"You think I'm overreacting."

"If it were Jessica I'd be reacting the same way. You obviously care a lot for Lauren."

"It's pretty apparent, huh?"

"I would say so. You might try prayer."

"I'm relying on it," Grant said, then felt Archer's surprised attention focusing on him.

"Really?"

"Yes, Archer, I am. In fact, I can't help wondering if my revitalized spiritual connection has served as an alarm system. Ordinarily, I don't think I would be so concerned about a grown woman who knows how to take care of herself. But the poison could have taken her by surprise. All she had to do was drink some water after you saw her this afternoon. In fact, she wouldn't even have had to do that. It could hit her at any time. That's the effect this stuff has on people."

Archer pointed to a sign that reflected in the glow from their head-lights. "Turn up there. On Friday and Saturday nights teenagers come out here to drink. The sheriff has tried to put a stop to it, but they can't always catch them."

Grant turned onto the rough dirt road.

"See the cloud they raised?" Archer pointed to the dust that hovered around them. "They obviously just came from here."

Grant's hands tightened once more on the steering wheel, and his thoughts returned to his most immediate fear. "If they did, wouldn't they have seen Lauren's truck?"

Archer didn't reply, and Grant gave the shocks of his car an interest-ing workout. From the corner of his eye he saw Archer lean forward in his seat and plant his hands on the dashboard.

Grant's prayers seemed to hit the windshield and bounce back at him. Archer didn't have to tell him when the road turned again. He remembered this drive now, even in the darkness. He remembered the potholes and the broken-down fence and the tree branches that reached down and threatened to slap him in the face but brushed over the top of the car at the last minute. He'd never been here in the dark, but he remembered the gravel. It meant they were close. . . . and then he saw the familiar reflection of a bumper and red reflector and the glow of an interior light, and he caught his breath.

"It's hers!" Archer shouted in horrified surprise. "It's Lauren's!"

Grant was out of the car before the motor died, with Archer on his heels. He ran to the open door and nearly stumbled over Lauren's still form, which was lying face down in the dirt beside her truck.

"No, God, please!" He fell to her side and reached for her shoulders as Archer knelt beside him. She was warm.

He felt for a pulse at her throat. "Her heart's still beating." Her clothes were damp, and a familiar smell lingered in the still night air. "She's been sick." He leaned close. "A lot." She was still breathing reg-ularly.

"Lauren!" he shouted, rubbing her face with his fingers. "Lauren, can you hear me?"

In the glow from the interior light, he could see her lips move, but no sound came out.

"Archer, didn't Jessica give you her cell phone?"

"Yes." Archer was on his feet before Grant said another word. "I'll call an ambulance."

Grant lifted Lauren into his arms. "Tell them to make it an ALS ambulance. Tell them to drive in this direction and watch for our flashing lights. We'll meet them on the road."

She wasn't alone. In the distant darkness she heard voices again, but this time they sounded vaguely familiar. She would be okay.

Her prayers . . . they were being answered. She felt herself being lifted by strong arms. She heard the kind voice, the words of assurance. If God was taking her home now, that would be okay, but this didn't feel like the arms of an angel ushering her into heaven.

Would an angel hold her this tightly? Would an angel sound frightened? Wouldn't angels be singing songs of joy instead of shouting in urgent, clipped voices?

And heaven didn't have blaring sirens and uncomfortably bright lights that flashed against her eyelids and threatened to drag her from her slumber.

The murmuring of a deep voice punctured her consciousness more forcefully. "Lauren! Can you hear me?" Gentle but insistent hands nudged her, and she tried to reach up and push them away.

"I can . . . hear you." The words were a whisper, but she heard a shout of triumph in response.

Her thoughts continued to sharpen.

"She's dehydrated. I want an IV . . ."

She felt the puncture in her arm but didn't have the strength to protest.

No, she wasn't on her way to heaven. There was no pain like this in heaven. Still, everything was going to be all right. God was in control.

CHAPTER | 32

By noon on Saturday the flurry of activity had settled into a comfortable routine at Dogwood Springs Baptist Church. Frightened families had been reassured that their homes were safe as long as they didn't drink water from the contaminated reservoir, and they had returned home. The cots had been folded and put away—except for one.

At seven in the morning, while the noise had been at its peak, Archer had allowed himself a few minutes of rest in the far corner of the room. Sleep had immediately reached up and jerked him down like a helpless victim for five hours of unconsciousness.

Now, as he shook his head and tried to revive, a few volunteer workers were trickling in for lunch. The aroma of grilling hamburgers brought him upright in the cot just in time to see Jessica walking toward him with a tray that held two plates with hamburgers and fries and two cups of coffee. She wore the same clothes she'd been wearing last night, only they were a little more wrinkled. Her face had been scrubbed free of makeup, and her eyes were puffy. Somehow her familiar beauty took him by surprise again. Would she always have this effect on him?

"Did you get any sleep?" He stood and took the tray from her.

"Eight hours, exactly. I just conked out in one of the pews upstairs, and nobody bothered me." She sat down on one end of the cot and patted the space beside her for him to join her. "As soon as I eat I have to drive to Branson and get ready for a show." She cradled her cup of coffee so the steam would rise into her face, and she inhaled with obvious appreciation.

"Speaking of show, you handled the reporters beautifully," Archer told her.

"Thank you."

At three o'clock that morning a news team from Springfield's channel 33 had arrived to assess the damage, and Jessica had unwittingly become the spokesperson for Dogwood Springs when someone recognized her as a Branson celebrity. The footage would be aired on the evening news.

Jessica leaned over and placed her cup on the floor, then straightened and looked at Archer. "Before I leave I need to ask you for something."

"Name it, Jess. After all you did last night, I don't know how I'll ever repay you. How many different ways are there to say thank you?" Not only had she charmed the people from channel 33, but she had helped with the cooking and spent nearly thirty minutes making her peace with John Netz and his two buddies on the personnel committee. By the time she finished with them, they had apologized to Archer for the recent problems and promised that Lauren McCaffrey would hear nothing about their questions and accusations. Jessica Lane definitely had a way of getting what she wanted.

"Archer, will you marry me?"

He nearly dropped his coffee cup. "What?"

"I said, will you—"

"Yes!"

Jessica chuckled. "Whew. For a minute there I thought you were going to turn me down."

"Never. You just took me by surprise. I was planning to drive up to Branson tonight between shows. I wanted to at least have my teeth brushed and my hair combed, and I'd thought about buying you some flowers, and—"

She took his coffee from him and set it next to hers, then drew him to her and kissed him. "Can we swing by your house and pick up my ring? I don't want to wait until this afternoon. There's no telling what other calamity might befall this church before you can drive to Branson."

He cupped his hands around her face and returned her kiss. "I love you, Jessica. I always will."

———————

Lauren was in no mood for company, but did that mean anything to her family? No. They were having a McCaffrey reunion in the waiting area just down the hall from her private room. At this moment the word *private* was a joke. Two nurses had already warned the guys to keep their laughter to a minimum and not to bother the patient, but her brothers and two of her cousins had managed to use the McCaffrey charm to keep from being evicted.

If she'd been the nurse on duty, they'd have been out of there.

She continued to remind herself that it was wonderful to be a part of such a big loving family, and that this gathering was a precious opportunity—not to be avoided. It was also an easy way to spread the word that they needed to dispose of the fish she'd been sharing with everyone within a fifty mile radius of Dogwood Springs.

And then Lauren reminded herself about how much better she felt today compared to last night. Last night, she'd expected to be dead by morning. Amazing what a little rehydration could do, along with her first dose of the chelating agent that would clear her system of the mercury—eventually.

Grant had told her that she shouldn't have any lasting damage. Judging by the type of complaints from other victims of the poisoning, the heavy metal had not converted to methyl mercury in the water. By God's grace the town had avoided a major catastrophe that would have produced deadly effects for years to come. Lauren and the other patients would recover. Mr. Mourglia was doing well this morning, and Gina would undergo surgery Monday for the insulinoma they had discovered with the MRI.

As for Mrs. Henson, who died last week, the poison had just been too much for her system to handle. According to the experts with whom Grant had consulted, she might have had a reaction to the poison that triggered the lethal cardiac arrhythmia.

"Guess what?" came a familiar female voice from the doorway, and Lauren looked to see Brooke and Beau Sheldon entering her room. They had been in her room off and on since early this morning, mingling with Lauren's family, trading jokes, and soaking up old stories about Lauren's childhood. Brooke now had enough ammunition to use against Lauren for the next three years.

To Lauren's dismay, the twins had charmed Mom and Dad within the first thirty minutes of meeting.

"What?" Lauren could not infuse much excitement into her voice.

Brooke held up a shopping bag from Bass Pro. "We got you a present."

"It's a fishing game," Beau announced as he grabbed the bag from Brooke and removed the contents.

"Oh, stop it, Mr. Popularity," Brooke complained, reaching for the bag. Beau held it away from her. "Hey, it was my idea in the first place!"

Beau gave his sister the empty bag and handed Lauren the game before Brooke could stop him. "It's a little computer, see? It simulates fishing, and it even vibrates when you catch something."

"Yes," Brooke added, "and it has a little screen to show you what kind of fish you caught, and you can choose your bait and everything. That way you don't have to gore innocent little worms to death just for a little excitement."

"She doesn't fish for excitement, Brooke," Beau informed her, "she fishes for food, and to relax, and to get away from . . ."

Lauren smiled and closed her eyes as the brother and sister continued to chatter. What ever made her think she was lonely?

"Okay, you two, it's time to give her a break." It was the voice of the "angel" from last night.

Lauren opened her eyes and watched Grant enter the room.

"Oh, Dad, we just got back," Brooke complained. "I haven't even had a chance to tease her about the time she got sick chewing tobacco out in the barn with—"

"There'll be time for that later. Out. Lauren needs her rest."

"Okay, fine, but Dad, you could at least take advantage of her weakened condition and ask her out on another date. After all, you did save her life last night, and—"

"Out!"

Brooke gave Lauren a smile full of mischief and preceded her brother out the door. Beau turned and looked back at Lauren, as if to assess her for himself, then he waved and left.

Lauren laughed. "You're a strong man, Grant Sheldon."

He had a beautiful smile, full of kindness. And, yes, a little hint of Brooke's mischief. "Not as strong as I'd like to be sometimes."

Gina was right, he did look a little like Antonio Banderas. "Did you ever have a ponytail?"

Grant's smile broadened. "Twenty years ago. What made you ask that?"

"Just a guess."

"I'm sorry about Brooke's big mouth. Don't let her coerce you into anything. But if you ever want a fishing buddy or even somebody to help with those teenagers at your church, you might give me a call."

"Really? You mean it? You'd help with the kids at church?"

"Do you know anyone more qualified to help with rowdy teenagers than the father of Brooke Sheldon? Besides, she and Beau will be part of that church. And so will I."

She caught her breath. "You will?"

He straightened the blanket around her shoulders. He looked into her eyes and held her gaze. He was serious. "Yes. I will."

"Why the change of heart?"

He checked her IV, glanced at the chart at the end of her bed, then nodded and returned to her side, as if deciding how best to put his thoughts into words. "Because I realized last night that God hadn't given up on me. I'd just given up on myself."

Thank you, Lord! "I'm glad."

"That doesn't mean I won't still have some questions."

"I had plenty of questions last night."

"Did any of them get answered?"

"Yes, they did," she said.

"How?"

Lauren reached up and touched his arm. "You found me. It wasn't my night to die. God is in control of me and my future. Whatever happens is up to Him. It takes the pressure off."

Grant took Lauren's hand in both of his and smiled down at her. "I know exactly what you mean."